LONGSHOT
&
RISK

Dick Francis has written over forty-one international best-sellers and is widely acclaimed as one of the world's finest thriller writers. His awards include the Crime Writers' Association's Cartier Diamond Dagger for his outstanding contribution to the crime genre, and an honorary Doctorate of Humane Letters from Tufts University of Boston. In 1996 Dick Francis was made a Mystery Writers of America Grand Master for a lifetime's achievement and in 2000 he received a CBE in the Queen's Birthday Honours list.

Dick Francis

LONGSHOT
&
RISK

PAN BOOKS

Longshot first published 1990 by Michael Joseph.
First published in paperback 1991 by Pan Books.
Risk first published 1977 by Michael Joseph.
First published in paperback 1979 by Pan Books.

This omnibus first published 2005 by Pan Books
an imprint of Pan Macmillan Ltd
Pan Macmillan, 20 New Wharf Road, London N1 9RR
Basingstoke and Oxford
Associated companies throughout the world
www.panmacmillan.com

ISBN 0 330 44372 0

Copyright © Dick Francis 1977, 1990

1 3 5 7 9 8 6 4 2

A CIP catalogue record for this book is available from
the British Library.

Printed and bound in Great Britain by
Mackays of Chatham plc, Chatham, Kent

LONGSHOT

With love to

JOCELYN
MATTHEW
BIANCA
TIMOTHY
WILLIAM

Our grandchildren

and acknowledgements to

The SAS Survival Handbook
by John Wiseman

and

No Need To Die
by Eddie McGee

CHAPTER ONE

I accepted a commission that had been turned down by four other writers, but I was hungry at the time.

Although starving in a garret had seemed a feasible enough plan a year earlier, the present realities of existence under the frozen eaves of a friend's aunt's house in a snowy January were such that without enough income to keep well fed and warm I was a knockover for a risky decision.

My state, of course, was my own fault. I could easily have gone out looking for paid muscular employment. I didn't have to sit shivering in a ski-suit biting the end of a pencil, hunched over a notebook, unsure of myself, of my ability and of the illuminations crashing about my head.

The spartan discomfort was not, either, a self-pitying morass of abject failure, but more the arctic doldrums between the high elation of the recent acceptance of my first novel for publication and the distant date of its launch into literary orbit. This was the downside after the heady receipt of the first advance payment and its division into past debts, present expenses and six months' future rent.

Give it two years, I'd thought, kissing farewell to the security of a salary: if I can't get published in two years I'll admit that the compulsion to write fiction is fools' gold and settle for common sense. Tossing away the pay-cheques had been a fairly desperate step, but I'd tried writing before work and after, in trains and at weekends, and had produced only dust. A stretch of no-excuse solitude, I'd thought, would settle things one way or another. Incipient hypothermia wasn't in any way diminishing the intense happiness of having put my toe into the first crack of the rock face.

I did as it happened know quite a lot about survival in adverse circumstances and the prospect of lean times hadn't worried me. I'd rather looked forward to them as a test of ingenuity. I just hadn't realised that sitting and thinking in itself made one cold. I hadn't known that a busy brain sneakily stole warmth from inactive hands and feet. In every freezing configuration I'd lived through before, I'd been moving.

The letter from Ronnie Curzon came on a particularly cold morning when there was ice like a half-descended curtain over the inside of my friend's aunt's attic window. The window, with its high view over the Thames at Chiswick, over the ebb-tide mud and the wind-sailing seagulls, that window, my delight, had done most, I reckoned, to release invention into words. I'd rigged a chair onto a platform so that I could sit there to write with a long view to the tree-chopped horizon over Kew Gardens. I'd never yet managed an even passable sentence when faced with a blank wall.

'Dear John,' the letter said.
'Care to drop into the office? There's been a suggestion about American rights in your book. You might be interested. I think we might discuss it, anyway.

Yours ever, Ronnie.
Why can't you have a telephone like everyone else?'

American rights! Incredible words.

The day warmed up miraculously. American rights were things that happened to successful authors, not to people struggling in an unfamiliar landscape, afflicted by self-doubts and insecurities, with a need to be told over and over that the book is OK, it's OK, don't worry so much.

'Don't worry,' Ronnie had said heartily, summoning me to his presence after reading the manuscript I'd dumped unheralded on his desk a couple of weeks earlier. 'Don't worry, I'm sure we can find you a publisher. Leave it to me. Let me see what I can do.'

Ronnie Curzon, authors' agent, with his salesman's subtle tongue, had indeed found me a publisher, a house more prestigious than I would have aimed for.

'They have a large list,' Ronnie explained kindly. 'They can afford to take a risk on a few first-timers, though it's all much harder than it used to be.' He sighed. 'The tyrannical bottom line and so on. Still,' he beamed, 'they've asked you to lunch to get acquainted. Look to the bright side.'

I'd grown used to Ronnie's fast swings to pessimism and back. He'd told me in the same breath that I'd sell two thousand copies if I was very lucky indeed, and that a certain lady novelist counted her paperbacks in millions.

'Everything's possible,' he said, encouragingly.

'Including falling flat on one's face?' I asked.

'Don't worry so much.'

On the day of the American rights letter I walked as usual from the friend's aunt's house to Ronnie's office four miles away in Kensington High Street and, as I'd learned a thing or two by that time, I went not precipitously as soon as possible but later in the morning, so as to arrive at noon. Shortly after that hour, I'd discovered, Ronnie tended to offer wine to his visitors and to send out for sandwiches. I hadn't told him much about my reduced domestic arrangements; he was naturally and spontaneously generous.

I misjudged things to the extent that the door of his own room was firmly shut, where normally it stood open.

'He's with another client,' Daisy said.

Daisy smiled easily, an unusual virtue in a receptionist. Big white teeth in a black face. Wild hair. A neat Oxford accent. Going to night school for Italian classes.

10

'I'll let him know you're here,' she said, lifting her telephone, pressing a button and consulting with her boss.

'He wants you to wait,' she reported, and I nodded and passed some time with patience on one of the two semi-comfortable chairs arranged for the purpose.

Ronnie's suite of offices consisted of a large outer room, partly furnished by the desks of Daisy and her sister Alice, who kept the firm's complicated accounts, and partly by a wall of box-files on shelves and a large central table scattered with published books. Down a passage from the big room lay on one side the doors to three private offices (two housing Ronnie's associates) and on the other the entrance into a windowless store like a library, where from floor to ceiling were ranked copies of all the books that Ronnie and his father before him had nursed to birth.

I spent the time in the outer room looking at a framed corkboard on which were pinned the dust jackets of the crop still in the shops, wondering yet again what my own baby would looked like. First-time authors, it seemed, were allowed little input in the design department.

'Trust the professionals,' Ronnie had said comfortingly. 'After all, they know what will sell books.'

I'd thought cynically that sometimes you'd never guess. All I could do, though, was hope.

Ronnie's door opened and out came his head, his neck and a section of shoulder.

11

'John? Come along in.'

I went down to his room which contained his desk, his swivelling armchair, two guest chairs, a cupboard and roughly a thousand books.

'Sorry to keep you,' he said.

He was as expansively apologetic as if I'd had a definite appointment and waved me into his office with every appearance of being delighted by my presence. He showed the same manner to everyone. A very successful agent, Ronnie.

He was rounded and enthusiastic. Cuddly was almost the word. Short, with smooth dark hair and soft dry hands, wearing always a business suit over a white shirt and a striped tie. Authors, his presentation seemed to say, could turn up if they pleased in pale blue and red ski-suits and snow-defeating moon-boots, but serious business took place in sober worsted.

'A cold day,' he said, eyeing my clothes forgivingly.

'The slush in the gutters has frozen solid.'

He nodded, only half listening, his eyes on his other client who had remained settled in his chair as if there for the day. It seemed to me that Ronnie was stifling exasperation under a façade of aplomb, a surprising configuration when what he usually showed was unflagging, effortless bonhomie.

'Tremayne,' he was saying jovially to his guest, 'this is John Kendall, a brilliant young author.'

As Ronnie regularly described all his authors as brilliant, even with plentiful evidence to the contrary, I remained unembarrassed.

Tremayne was equally unimpressed. Tremayne, sixty-ish, grey-haired, big and self-assured was clearly not pleased at the interruption.

'We haven't finished our business,' he said ungraciously.

'Time for a glass of wine,' Ronnie suggested, ignoring the complaint. 'For you, Tremayne?'

'Gin and tonic.'

'Ah . . . I meant, white wine or red?'

After a pause, Tremayne said with a show of annoyed resignation, 'Red, then.'

'Tremayne Vickers,' Ronnie said to me non-committally, completing the introduction. 'Red do you, John?'

'Great.'

Ronnie bustled about, moving heaps of books and papers, clearing spaces, producing glasses, bottle and corkscrew and presently pouring with concentration.

'To trade,' he said with a smile, handing me a glass. 'To success,' he said to Vickers.

'Success! What success? All these writers are too big for their boots.'

Ronnie glanced involuntarily at my own boots, which were big enough for anyone.

'It's no use you telling me I'm not offering a decent fee,' Tremayne told him. 'They ought to be glad of the work.' He eyed me briefly and asked me without tact, 'What do you earn in a year?'

I smiled as blandly as Ronnie and didn't answer.

'How much do you know about racing?' he demanded.

'Horse racing?' I asked.

'Of course horse racing.'

'Well,' I said. 'Not a lot.'

'Tremayne,' Ronnie protested, 'John isn't your sort of writer.'

'A writer's a writer. Anyone can do it. You tell me I've been wrong looking for a big name. Very well then, find me a smaller name. You said your friend here is brilliant. So how about *him*?'

'Ah,' Ronnie said cautiously. 'Brilliant is just . . . ah . . . a figure of speech. He's inquisitive, capable and impulsive.'

I smiled at my agent with amusement.

'So he's *not* brilliant?' Tremayne asked ironically, and to me he said, 'What have you written, then?'

I answered obligingly, 'Six travel guides and a novel.'

'Travel guides? What sort of travel guides?'

'How to live in the jungle. Or in the Arctic. Or in deserts. That sort of thing.'

'For people who like difficult holidays,' Ronnie said, with all the indulgent irony of those devoted to comfort. 'John used to work for a travel agency which specialises in sending the intrepid out to be stretched.'

'Oh.' Tremayne looked at his wine without enthusiasm and after a while said testily, 'There must be someone who'd leap at the job.'

I said, more to make conversation than out of urgent curiosity, 'What is it that you want written?'

Ronnie made a gesture that seemed to say 'Don't ask', but Tremayne answered straightforwardly.

'An account of my life.'

I blinked. Ronnie's eyebrows rose and fell.

Tremayne said, 'You'd think those race-writing johnnies would be falling over themselves for the honour, but they've all turned me down.' He sounded aggrieved. 'Four of them.'

He recited their names, and such was their eminence that even I, who seldom paid much attention to racing, had heard of them all. I glanced at Ronnie, who showed resignation.

'There must be others,' I said mildly.

'There's some I wouldn't let set foot through my door.' The truculence in Tremayne's voice was one of the reasons, I reflected, why he was having trouble. I lost interest in him, and Ronnie, seeing it, cheered up several notches and suggested sandwiches for lunch.

'I hoped you'd be lunching me at your club,' Tremayne said grouchily, and Ronnie said vaguely 'Work' with a flap of the hand to indicate the papers on his desk. 'I mostly have lunch on the run, these days.'

He went over to the door and put the same section of himself through it as before.

'Daisy?' He called to her along the passage. 'Phone down to the shop for sandwiches, would you? Usual

15

selection. Everyone welcome. Count heads, would you? Three of us here.'

He brought himself in again without more discussion. Tremayne went on looking disgruntled and I drank my wine with gratitude.

It was warm in Ronnie's office. That, too, was a bonus. I took off the jacket of the ski-suit, hung it over a chair back and sat down contentedly in the scarlet sweater I wore underneath. Ronnie winced as usual over the brightness of my clothes but in fact I felt warmer in red, and I never discounted the psychology of colours. Those of my travel-agency friends who dressed in army olive-browns were colonels at heart.

Tremayne went on niggling away at his frustration, not seeming to mind if I learned his business.

'I offered to have them stay,' he complained. 'Can't do fairer than that. They all said the sales wouldn't be worth the work, not at the rate I was offering. Arrogant lot of bastards.' He gloomily drank and made a face over the taste. 'My name alone would sell the book, I told them, and they had the gall to disagree. Ronnie says it's a small market.' He glowered at my agent. 'Ronnie says that he can't get the book commissioned by a publisher without a top-rank writer, and maybe not even then, and that no top-rank writer will touch it without a commission. See where that gets me?'

He seemed to expect an answer, so I shook my head.

'It gets me into what they call vanity publishing. Vanity! Bloody insult. Ronnie says there are companies that will print and bind any book you give them, but *you* have to pay *them*. Then I'd also have to pay someone to write the book. Then I'd also have to sell the book myself, as I would be my own publisher, and Ronnie says there's no way I'd sell enough to cover the costs, let alone make a profit. He says that's why no regular publisher will take the book. Not enough sales. And I ask you, why not? Why not, eh?'

I shook my head again. He seemed to think I should know who he was, that everyone should. I hardly liked to say I'd never heard of him.

He partially enlightened me. 'After all,' he said, 'I've trained getting on for a thousand winners. The Grand National, two Champion Hurdles, a Gold Cup, the Whitbread, you name it. I've seen half a century of racing. There's stories in all of it. Childhood . . . growing up . . . success . . . My life has been *interesting*, dammit.'

Words temporarily failed him, and I thought that everyone's life was interesting to themselves, tragedies and all. Everyone had a story to tell: the trouble lay in the few who wanted to read it, the fewer still who were ready to pay for the privilege.

Ronnie soothingly refilled the glasses and gave us a regretful summary of the state of the book trade, which was in one of its periodical downswings on account of current high interest rates and their adverse effects on mortgage payments.

'It's the people with mortgages who usually buy books,' he said. 'Don't ask me why. For every mortgage there are five people saving into the building societies, and when interest rates are high *their* incomes go up. They've more money to spend, but they just don't seem to buy books with it.'

Tremayne and I looked blank over this piece of sociology, and Ronnie further told us, without noticeably cheering us up, that for a publisher in the modern world turnover was all very well but losses weren't, and that it was getting more and more difficult to get a marginal book accepted.

I felt more grateful than ever that he'd got one particular marginal book accepted, and remembered what the lady from the publisher's had said when she'd taken me for the getting-acquainted lunch.

'Ronnie could sweet-talk the devil. He says we need to catch new authors like you in their early thirties, otherwise we won't have any big names ten years from now. No one knows yet how you'll turn out in ten years. Ronnie says that all salmon are small fry to begin with. So we're not promising you the world, but an opportunity, yes.'

An opportunity was all one could ask, I thought.

Daisy at length appeared in the doorway to say the food had arrived, and we all went along to the big room where the central table had been cleared of books and relaid with plates, knives, napkins and two large platters of healthy-looking sandwiches decorated with a drizzle of cress.

Ronnie's associates emerged from their rooms to join

us, which made seven altogether, including Daisy and her sister, and I managed to eat a lot without, I hoped, it being noticeable. Fillings of beef, ham, cheese, bacon: once-ordinary things that had become luxuries lately. Free lunch, breakfast and dinner. I wished Ronnie would write summoning notes more often.

Tremayne harangued me again over the generic shortcomings of racing writers, holding his glass in one hand and waving a sandwich in the other as he made his indignant points, while I nodded in sympathetic silence and munched away as if listening carefully.

Tremayne made a great outward show of forceful self-confidence, but there was something in his insistence which curiously belied it. It was almost as if he needed the book to be written to prove he had lived; as if photographs and records weren't enough.

'How old are you?' he said abruptly, breaking off in mid flow.

I said with my mouth full, 'Thirty-two.'

'You look younger.'

I didn't know whether 'good' or 'sorry' was appropriate, so I merely smiled and went on eating.

'Could you write a biography?' Again the abruptness.

'I don't know. Never tried.'

'I'd do it myself,' he said belligerently, 'but I haven't got time.'

I nodded understandingly. If there was one biography I didn't want to cut my teeth on, I thought, it was his. Much too difficult.

Ronnie fetched up beside him and wheeled him away, and in between finishing the beef-and-chutney and listening to Daisy's problems with scrambled software I watched Ronnie across the room nodding his head placatingly under Tremayne's barrage of complaints. Eventually, when all that was left on the plates were a few pallidly wilting threads of cress, Ronnie said a firm farewell to Tremayne, who still didn't want to go.

'There's nothing I can usefully offer at the moment,' Ronnie was saying, shaking an unresponsive hand and practically pushing Tremayne doorwards with a friendly clasp on his shoulder. 'But leave it to me. I'll see what I can do. Keep in touch.'

With ill grace Tremayne finally left, and without any hint of relief Ronnie said to me, 'Come along then, John. Sorry to have kept you all this time,' and led the way back to his room.

'Tremayne asked if I'd ever written a biography,' I said, taking my former place on the visitors' side of the desk.

Ronnie gave me a swift glance, settling himself into his own padded dark green leather chair and swivelling gently from side to side as if in indecision. Finally he came to a stop and asked, 'Did he offer you the job?'

'Not exactly.'

'My advice to you would be not to think of it.' He gave me no time to assure him that I wouldn't, and went straight on, 'It's fair to say he's a good racehorse trainer, well known in his own field. It's fair to say he's a better man than you would have guessed today. It's even fair to agree he's had an interesting life. But that isn't enough. It all depends on the writing.' He paused and sighed. 'Tremayne doesn't really believe that. He wants a big name because of the prestige, but you heard him, he thinks anyone can write. He doesn't really know the difference.'

'Will you find him someone?' I asked.

'Not on the terms he's looking for.' Ronnie considered things. 'I suppose I can tell you,' he said, 'as he made an approach to you. He's asking for a writer to stay in his house for at least a month, to go through all his cuttings and records and interview him in depth. None of the top names will do that, they've all got other lives to lead. Then he wants seventy per cent of royalty income which isn't going to amount to much in any case. No top writer is going to work for thirty per cent.'

'Thirty per cent . . . including the advance?'

'Right. An advance no bigger than yours, if I could get one at all.'

'That's starvation.'

Ronnie smiled. 'Comparatively few people live by writing alone. I thought you knew that. Anyway,' he leaned forward, dismissing Tremayne and saying more briskly, 'about these American rights . . .'

It seemed that a New York literary agent, an occasional associate of Ronnie's, had asked my publishers routinely whether they had anything of interest in the pipeline. They had steered him back to Ronnie. Would I, Ronnie asked, care to have him send a copy of my manuscript to the American agent, who would then, if he thought the book saleable in the American market, try to find it an American publisher.

I managed to keep my mouth shut but was gaping and gasping inside.

'Well?' Ronnie said.

'I . . . er . . . I'd be delighted,' I said.

'Thought you would. Not promising anything, you realise. He's just taking a look.'

'Yes.'

'If you remember, we gave your publisher here only British and Commonwealth rights. That leaves us elbowroom to manoeuvre.' He went on for a while discussing technicalities and possibilities his pendulum way. I was left with a feeling that things might be going to happen but on the other hand probably not. The market was down, everything was difficult, but the publishing machine needed constant fodder and my book might be regarded as a bundle of hay. He would let me know, he said, as soon as he got an opinion back from the New York agent.

'How's the new book coming along?' he asked.

'Slowly.'

He nodded. 'The second one's always difficult. But just keep going.'

'Yes.'

He rose to his feet, looking apologetically at his waiting paperwork, shaking my hand warmly in farewell. I thanked him for the lunch. Any time, he said automatically, his mind already on his next task, and I left him and walked along the passage, stopping at Daisy's desk on the way out.

'You're sending my manuscript to America,' I said, zipping up my jacket and bursting to tell someone, anyone, the good news.

'Yes,' she beamed. 'I posted it last Friday.'

'Did you indeed!'

I went on out to the lift not sure whether to laugh or be vaguely annoyed at Ronnie's asking permission for something he had already done. I wouldn't have minded at all if he'd simply told me he'd sent the book off. It was his job to do the best for me that he could; I would have thought it well within his rights.

I went down two floors and out into the bitter afternoon air thinking of the steps that had led to his door.

Finishing the book had been one thing, finding a publisher another. The six small books I'd previously written, though published and on sale to the public, had all been part of my work for the travel firm who had paid me pretty well for writing them besides sending me to far-flung places to gather the knowledge. The travel firm owned the guides and published them themselves, and they weren't in the market for novels.

I'd taken my precious typescript personally to a small but well-known publisher (looking up the address in

the phone book) and had handed it to a pretty girl
there who said she would put it in the slush pile and
get round to it in due course.

The slush pile, she explained, showing dimples, was
what they called the heap of unsolicited manuscripts
that dropped through their letter-box day by day. She
would read my book while she commuted. I could
return for her opinion in three weeks.

Three weeks later, the dimples still in place, she told
me my book wasn't really 'their sort of thing', which
was mainly 'serious literature', it seemed. She suggested
I should take it to an agent, who would know where
to place it. She gave me a list of names and addresses.

'Try one of those,' she said. 'I enjoyed the book very
much. Good luck with it.'

I tried Ronnie Curzon for no better reason than I'd
known where to find his office, as Kensington High
Street lay on my direct walk home. Impulse had led to
good and bad all my life, but when I felt it strongly, I
usually followed it. Ronnie had been good. Opting for
poverty had been so-so. Accepting Tremayne's offer
was the pits.

CHAPTER TWO

As I walked back to Chiswick from Ronnie's office, I hadn't the slightest intention of ever meeting Tremayne Vickers again. I forgot him. I thought of the present book I was writing: especially of how to get one character down from a runaway, experimental helium-filled balloon with its air pumps out of order. I had doubts about the balloon. Maybe I'd rethink the whole thing. Maybe I'd scrap what I'd done and start again. The character in the balloon was shitting himself with fear. I thought I knew how he felt. The chief unexpected thing I'd learned from writing fiction was fear of getting it wrong.

The book that had been accepted, which was called *Long Way Home*, was about survival in general and in particular about the survival, physical and mental, of a bunch of people isolated by a disaster. Hardly an original theme, but I'd followed the basic advice to write about something I knew, and survival was what I knew best.

In the interest of continuing to survive for another

week or ten days, I stopped at the supermarket nearest to the friend's aunt's house and spent my food allotment on enough provisions for the purpose: bunch of packet soups, loaf of bread, box of spaghetti, box of porridge oats, pint of milk, a cauliflower and some carrots. I would eat the vegetables raw whenever I felt like it, and otherwise enjoy soup with bread in it, soup on spaghetti and porridge with milk. Items like tea, Marmite and salt cropped up occasionally. Crumpets and butter came at scarce intervals when I could no longer resist them. Apart from all that I bought once a month a bottle of vitamin pills to stuff me full of any oddments I might be missing and, dull though it might seem and in spite of frequent hunger, I had stayed in resounding good health all along.

I opened the front door with my latchkey and met the friend's aunt in the hall.

'Hello, dear,' she said. 'Everything all right?'

I told her about Ronnie sending my book to America and her thin face filled with genuine pleasure. She was roughly fifty, divorced, a grandmother, sweet, fair-haired, undemanding and boring. I understood that she regarded the rent I paid her (a fifth of what I had had to fork out for my former flat) as more a bribe to get her to let a stranger into her house than as an essential part of her income. In addition, though, she had agreed I could put milk in her fridge, wash my dishes in her sink, shower in her bathroom and use her washer-drier once a week. I wasn't to make a noise or ask anyone in. We had settled these details amicably. She had installed a coin-in-the-slot electric meter for me, and approved a toaster, a kettle, a tiny table-top cooker and new plugs for a television and a razor.

I'd been introduced to her as 'Aunty' and that's what I called her, and she seemed to regard me as a sort of extension nephew. We had lived for ten months in harmony, our lives adjacent but uninvolved.

'It's very cold . . . are you warm enough up there?' she asked kindly.

'Yes, thank you,' I said. The electric heater ate money. I almost never switched it on.

'These old houses . . . very cold under the roofs.'

'I'm fine,' I said.

She said, 'Good, dear,' amiably, and we nodded to each other, and I went upstairs thinking that I'd lived in the Artic Circle and if I hadn't been able to deal with a cold London attic I would have been ashamed of myself. I wore silk jersey long-sleeved vests and long johns under sweaters and jeans under the ski-suit, and I slept warmly in a sleeping bag designed for the North Pole. It was writing that made me cold.

Up in my eyrie I struggled for a couple of hours to resolve the plight of the helium balloon but ended with only a speculation on nerve pathways. Why didn't terror make one *deaf*, for instance? How did it always beeline to the bowel? My man in the balloon didn't know and was too miserable to care. I thought I'd have to invent a range of mountains dead ahead for him to come to grief on. Then he would merely have the problem of descending from an Everest-approximation with only fingers, toes and resolution. Much easier. I knew a tip or two about that, the first being to look for the longest way down because it would be the least steep. Sharp-faced mountains often had sloping backs.

My attic, once the retreat of the youngest of Aunty's daughters, had a worn pink carpet and cream wallpaper sprigged with pink roses. The resident furniture of bed, chest of drawers, tiny wardrobe, two chairs and a table was overwhelmed by a veritable army of crates, boxes and suitcases containing my collected worldly possessions: clothes, books, household goods and sports equipment, all top quality and in good shape, acquired in carefree bygone affluence. Two pairs of expensive skis stood in their covers in a corner. Wildly extravagant cameras and lenses rested in dark foam beds. I kept in working order a windproof, sandproof, bugproof tent which self-erected in seconds and weighed only three pounds. I checked also climbing gear and a camcorder from time to time. A word processor with a laser printer, which I still used, was wrapped most of the time in sheeting. My helicopter pilot's licence lay in a drawer, automatically expired now since I hadn't flown for a year. A life on hold, I thought. A life suspended.

I thought occasionally that I could eat better if I sold something, but I'd never get back what I'd paid for the skis, for instance, and it seemed stupid to cannibalise things that had given me pleasure. They were mostly the tools of my past trade, anyway, and I might need them again. They were my safety net. The travel firm had said they would take me back once I'd got this foolishness out of my system.

If I'd known I was going to do what I was doing I would have planned and saved a lot more in advance, perhaps: but between the final irresistible impulse and its execution there had been only about six weeks. The vague intention had been around a lot longer; for most of my life.

Helium balloon . . .

The second half of the advance on *Long Way Home* wasn't due until publication day, a whole long year ahead. My small weekly allotted parcels of money wouldn't last that long, and I didn't see how I could live on much less. My rent-in-advance would run out at the end of June. If, I thought, if I could finish this balloon lark by then and if it were accepted and if they paid the same advance as before, then maybe I'd just manage the full two years. Then if the books fell with a dull thud, I'd give up and go back to the easier rigours of the wild.

That night the air temperature over London plummeted still further, and in the morning Aunty's house was frozen solid.

'There's no water,' she said in distress when I went

downstairs. 'The central heating stopped and all the pipes have frozen. I've called the plumber. He says everyone's in the same boat and just to switch everything off. He can't do anything until it thaws, then he'll come to fix any leaks.' She looked at me helplessly. 'I'm very sorry, dear, but I'm going to stay in a hotel until this is over. I'm going to close the house. Can you find somewhere else for a week or two? Of course I'll add the time on to your six months, you won't lose by it, dear.'

Dismay was a small word for what I felt. I helped her close all the stopcocks I could find and made sure she had switched off her water heaters, and in return she let me use her telephone to look for another roof.

I got through to her nephew, who still worked for the travel firm.

'Do you have any more aunts?' I enquired.

'Good God, what have you done with that one?'

I explained. 'Could you lend me six feet of floor to unroll my bedding on?'

'Why don't you gladden the life of your parents on that Caribbean island?'

'Small matter of the fare.'

'You can come for a night or two if you're desperate,' he said. 'But Wanda's moved in with me, and you know how tiny the flat is.'

I also didn't much like Wanda. I thanked him and said I would let him know, and racked my brains for somewhere else.

It was inevitable I should think of Tremayne Vickers.

I phoned Ronnie Curzon and put it to him straight. 'Can you sell me to that racehorse trainer?'

'What?'

'He was offering free board and lodging.'

'Take me through it one step at a time.'

I took him through it and he was all against it.

'Much better to get on with your new book.'

'Mm,' I said. 'The higher a helium balloon rises the thinner the air is and the lower the pressure, so the helium balloon expands, and goes on rising and expanding until it bursts.'

'*What?*'

'It's too cold to invent stories. Do you think I could do what Tremayne wants?'

'You could probably do a workmanlike job.'

'How long would it take?'

'Don't do it,' he said.

'Tell him I'm brilliant after all and can start at once.'

'You're mad.'

'I might as well learn about racing. Why not? I might use it in a book. And I can ride. Tell him that.'

'Impulse will kill you one of these days.'

I should have listened to him, but I didn't.

I was never sure exactly what Ronnie said to Tremayne, but when I phoned again at noon he was mournfully triumphant.

'Tremayne agreed you can write his book. He quite took to you yesterday, it seems.' Pessimism vibrated down the wire. 'He's agreed to guarantee you a writing fee.' Ronnie mentioned a sum which would keep me eating through the summer. 'It's payable in three instalments – a quarter after a month's work, a quarter when he approves the full manuscript, and half on publication. If I can get a regular publisher to take it on, the publisher will pay you, otherwise Tremayne will. He's agreed you should have forty per cent of any royalties after, not thirty. He's agreed to pay your expenses while you research his life. That means if you want to go to interview people who know him he'll pay for your transport. That's quite a good concession, actually. He thinks it's odd that you haven't a car, but I reminded him that people who live in London often don't. He says you can drive one of his. He was pleased you can ride. He says you should take riding clothes with you and also a dinner jacket, as he's to be guest of honour at some dinner or other and he wants you to witness it. I told him you were an expert photographer so he wants you to take your camera.'

Ronnie's absolute and audible lack of enthusiasm for the project might have made me withdraw even then had Aunty not earlier given me a three o'clock deadline for leaving the house.

'When does Tremayne expect me?' I asked Ronnie.

'He seems pathetically pleased that anyone wants to take him on, after the top men turned him down. He says he'd be happy for you to go as soon as you can. Today, even, he said. Will you go today?'

'Yes,' I said.

'He lives in a village called Shellerton, in Berkshire. He says if you can phone to say what train you're catching, someone will meet you at Reading station. Here's the number.' He read it out to me.

'Fine,' I said. 'And Ronnie, thanks very much.'

'Don't thank me. Just . . . well, just write a brilliant chapter or two and I'll try to get the book commissioned on the strength of them. But go on writing fiction. That's where your future is.'

'Do you mean it?'

'Of course, I mean it.' He sounded surprised I should ask. 'For someone who's not afraid of jungles you exhibit the strangest self-confidence deficiency.'

'I know where I am in jungles.'

'Go and catch your train,' he said, and wished me luck.

I caught, instead, a bus, as it was much cheaper, and was met outside the Reading bus station by a shivering young woman in a padded coat and woollen hat who visually checked me over from boots six feet up via ski-suit to dark hair and came to the conclusion that I was, as she put it, the writer.

'You're the writer?' She was positive, used to authority, not unfriendly.

'John Kendall,' I said, nodding.

33

'I'm Mackie Vickers. That's m, a, c, k, i, e,' she spelled. 'Not Maggie. Your bus is late.'

'The roads are bad,' I said apologetically.

'They're worse in the country.' It was dark and extremely cold. She led the way to a chunky jeep-like vehicle parked not far away and opened the rear door. 'Put your bags in here. You can meet everyone as we go along.'

There were already four people in the vehicle, it seemed, all cold and relieved I had finally turned up. I stowed my belongings and climbed in, sharing the back seat with two dimly seen figures who moved up to give me room. Mackie Vickers positioned herself behind the wheel, started the engine, released the brake and drove out into a stream of cars. A welcome trickle of hot air came out of the heater.

'The writer says his name is John Kendall,' Mackie said to the world in general.

There wasn't much reaction to the introduction.

'You're sitting next to Tremayne's head lad,' she went on, 'and his wife is beside him.'

The shadowy man next to me said, 'Bob Watson.' His wife said nothing.

'In front,' Mackie said, 'next to me, are Fiona and Harry Goodhaven.'

Neither Fiona nor Harry said anything. There was an intense quality in the collective atmosphere that dried up any conversational remark I might have thought of making, and it had little to do with temperature. It was as if the very air were scowling.

Mackie drove for several minutes in continuing silence, concentrating on the slush-lined surface under the yellowish lights of the main road west out of Reading. The traffic was heavy and slow moving, the ill-named rush hour crawling along with flashing scarlet brake lights, a procession of curses.

Eventually Mackie said to me, turning her head over her shoulder as I was sitting directly behind her, 'We're not good company. We've spent all day in court. Tempers are frayed. You'll just have to put up with it.'

'No trouble,' I said.

Trouble was the wrong word to use, it seemed.

As if releasing tension Fiona said loudly, 'I can't *believe* you were so stupid.'

'Give it a rest,' Harry said. He'd already heard it before.

'But you know damned well that Lewis was drunk.'

'That doesn't excuse anything.'

'It *explains* things. You know damned well he was drunk.'

'Everyone *says* he was drunk,' Harry said, sounding heavily reasonable, 'but I don't *know* it, do I? I didn't *see* him drinking too much.'

Bob Watson beside me said 'Liar' on a whispered breath, and Harry didn't hear.

'Nolan is going to *prison*,' Fiona said bitterly. 'Do you realise? *Prison*. All because of you.'

35

'You don't *know* he is,' Harry complained. 'The jury haven't found him guilty yet.'

'But they *will*, won't they? And it will be *your fault*. Dammit, you were under *oath*. All you had to do was say Lewis was drunk. Now the jury thinks he wasn't drunk, so he must be able to remember everything. They think he's lying when he says he can't remember. Christ Almighty, Nolan's whole *defence* was that Lewis can't remember. How could you be so *stupid*?'

Harry didn't answer. The atmosphere if possible worsened, and I felt as if I'd gone into a movie halfway through and couldn't grasp the plot.

Mackie, without contributing any opinions, turned from the Great West Road onto the M4 motorway and made better time westwards along an unlit and uninhabited stretch between snow-covered wooded hills, ice crystals glittering in the headlights.

'*Bob* says Lewis was drunk,' Fiona persisted, 'and he should know, he was serving the drinks.'

'Then maybe the jury will believe Bob.'

'They believed him until you stood there and blew it.'

'They should have had *you* in the witness box,' Harry said defensively, 'then you could have sworn he was paralytic and had to be scraped off the carpet, even if you weren't there.'

Bob Watson said, 'He wasn't paralytic.'

'You keep out of it, Bob,' Harry snapped.

'Sorr-ee,' Bob Watson said, again under his breath.

'All you had to do was swear that Lewis was drunk.'

Fiona's voice rose with fury. 'That's *all* the defence called you for. Then you didn't say it. Nolan's lawyer could have killed you.'

Harry said wearily, '*You* didn't have to stand there answering that prosecutor's questions. You heard what he said, how did I know Lewis was drunk? Had I given him a breath test, a blood test, a urine test? On what did I base my judgment? Did I have any clinical experience? You heard him. On and on. How many drinks did I see Lewis take? How did I know what was in the drinks? Had I ever heard of Lewis having black-outs any other time after drinking?'

'That was disallowed,' Mackie said.

'You let that prosecutor tie you in *knots*. You looked absolutely *stupid* . . .' Fiona ran on and on, the rage in her mind unabating.

I began to feel mildly sorry for Harry.

We reached the Chieveley interchange and left the motorway to turn north on the big A34 to Oxford. Mackie had sensibly taken the cleared major roads rather than go over the hills, even though it was further that way, according to the map. I'd looked up the whereabouts of Tremayne's village on the theory that it was a wise man who knew his destination, especially when it was on the Berkshire Downs a mile from nowhere.

Silence had mercifully struck Fiona's tongue by the time Shellerton showed up on a signpost. Mackie slowed, signalled, and cautiously turned off the main road into a very narrow secondary road that was little more than a lane, where snow had been roughly pushed to the sides but still lay in shallow frozen brown ruts over much of the surface. The tyres scrunched on them, cracking the ice. Mist formed quickly on the inside of the windscreen and Mackie rubbed it away impatiently with her glove.

There were no houses beside the lane: it was well over a mile across bare downland, I found later, from the main road to the village. There were also no cars: no one was out driving if they could help it. For all Mackie's care one could sometimes feel the wheels sliding, losing traction for perilous seconds. The engine, engaged in low gear, whined laboriously up a shallow incline.

'It's worse than this morning,' Mackie said, sounding worried. 'This road's a skating rink.'

No one answered her. I was hoping, as I expect they all were, that we would reach the top of the slope without sliding backwards; and we did, only to see that the downside looked just as hazardous, if not more so. Mackie wiped the windscreen again and with extra care took a curve to the right.

Caught by the headlights, stock-still in the middle of the lane, stood a horse. A dark horse buckled into a dark rug, its head raised in alarm. There was the glimmer of sheen on its skin and luminescence in its wide eyes. The moment froze like the landscape.

'*Hell!*' Mackie exclaimed, and slammed her foot on the brake.

The vehicle slid inexorably on the ice and although Mackie released the brakes a moment later it did as much harm as good.

The horse, terrified, tried to plunge out of the lane into the field alongside. Intent on missing him, and at the same time fighting the skid, Mackie miscalculated the curve, the camber and the speed, though to be fair to her it would have taken a stunt driver to come out of there safely.

The jeep slid to the side of the lane, spun its wheels on the snow-covered grass verge, mounted it, ran along and across as if making for the open fields under its own volition and tipped over sideways into an unseen drainage ditch, cracking with noises like pistol shots through a covering sheet of ice.

We'd been going slowly enough for it not to be an instantly lethal crunch, though it was a bang hard enough to rattle one's teeth. The nearside wheels, both front and back, finished four feet lower than road level, the far side of the ditch supporting the length of the roof of the vehicle so that it lay not absolutely flat on its side. I was opening my door, which was half sloping skywards, and hauling myself out more or less before the engine had time to stall.

The downland wind, always on the move, stung my face sharply with a freezing warning. Wind-chill was an unforgiving enemy, deadly to the unwary.

Bob Watson had fallen on top of his wife. I reached
down into the car and grasped him, and began to pull
him out.

He tried to free himself from my hands, crying
'Ingrid' urgently, and then in horror, 'It's wet . . . she's
in water.'

'Come out,' I said peremptorily. 'Then we can both
pull her. Come out, you're heavy on her. You'll never
get her out like that.'

Some vestige of sense got through to him and he let
me yank him out far enough so that he could stretch
back in for his wife. I held him and he held her, and
between the two of us we brought her out onto the
roadway.

The ditch was almost full of muddy freezing water
under its coating of ice. Even as we lifted Ingrid out
the water deepened fast in the vehicle, and in the front
seat Fiona was yelling to Harry to get her out. Harry,
I saw in horror, was underneath her and in danger of
drowning.

The one headlight which had still been shining suddenly went out.

Mackie hadn't moved to save herself. I pulled open
her door and found her dazed and semi-conscious, held
in her place by her seat belt.

'Get us out,' Fiona yelled.

Harry, below her, was struggling in water and heaving, whether to save her or himself was impossible to
tell. I felt round Mackie until I found the seat-belt

clasp, released it, hauled her out bodily and shoved her into Bob Watson's arms.

'Sit her on the verge,' I said. 'Clear the snow off the grass. Hold her. Shield her from the wind.'

'Bob,' Ingrid said piteously, standing helplessly on the road and seeming to think her husband should attend to her alone, 'Bob, I need you. I feel awful.'

Bob glanced at his wife but took Mackie's weight and helped her to sit down. She began moving and moaning and asking what had happened, showing welcome signs of life.

No blood, I thought. Not a drop. Bloody lucky. My eyes became accustomed to the dark.

Fiona, halfway panic-stricken, put her arms up to mine and came out easily into the air, lithe and athletic. I let go of her and leaned in for Harry, who now had his seat belt unfastened and his head above water and had got past the stage of abject fright. He helped himself to climb out and went dripping over to Mackie, showing most concern for her, taking her support from Bob Watson.

Ingrid stood in the road, soaked, thin, frightened, helpless and crying. The wind was piercing, relentless . . . infinitely dangerous. It was easy to underestimate how fast cold could kill.

I said to Bob Watson, 'Take all your wife's clothes off.'

'*What*?'

'Take her wet clothes off or she'll freeze into a block of ice.'

He opened his mouth.

'Start at the top,' I said. 'Take everything off and put my ski jacket on her, quickly. It's warm.' I unzipped it and took it off, folding it together so as to keep the warmth of my body in it as much as possible. The cold bit through my sweater and undershirt as if they were invisible. I was infinitely grateful to be dry.

'I'll help Ingrid,' Fiona said, as Bob still hesitated. 'You don't mean her bra as well?'

'Yes, everything.'

While the two women unbuttoned and tugged I went to the rear of the overturned vehicle and found to my relief that the luggage door would still open. I pushed up my sleeves and literally fished out my two bags and Harry, close behind me, watched the water drip off them with gloom.

'Everything will be wet,' he said defeatedly.

'No.' Waterproof, sandproof, bugproof were the rules I travelled by, even in rural England. I found the aluminium camera case under the water and set it on the road beside the bags.

'Which would you prefer,' I asked Harry, 'bathrobe or dinner jacket?'

He actually laughed.

'Strip off,' I said, 'in case the ice-man cometh. Top half first.'

They had all been dressed for a day in court, not for

42

trudging about in the open. Even Mackie and Bob Watson, who were dry, hadn't enough on for the circumstances.

Bob Watson took over again with Mackie, and Harry began to struggle out of his sodden overcoat, business suit, shirt and tie, wincing with pain as the cold hit his wet flesh. His singlet was sticking to him. I gave him a hand.

'What did you say your name was?' he said, teeth clenched, shuddering.

'John.'

I handed him a navy blue silk undershirt and long johns, two sweaters, grey trousers and the bathrobe. No one ever dived into clothes faster. My shoes were a size too big, he ironically complained, hopping around and pulling them on over dry socks.

Fiona had changed Ingrid to the waist and was waiting to do the second half. I took off my boots and then my ski-pants, which Fiona put on Ingrid after trying to shield her brief lower nakedness from my eyes, which amazed me. It was hardly the time for fussing. The boots looked enormous, once they were on, and Ingrid was nine inches shorter than my ski-suit.

For myself I brought out a navy blazer and jodphur boots, feeling the ice strike up through wool to my toes.

'My feet are squelching,' Fiona said, eyeing the boots with strong shivers, 'and I'm wet to the neck. Is there anything left?'

'You'd better have these.'

'Well ... I ...' She looked at my bare socks, hesitating.

I thrust the boots and blazer into her hands. My black evening shoes, which were all that remained in the way of footwear, would have fallen off her at every step.

I dug into the bag again for jodphurs, black socks and a sweatshirt. 'These any good to you?' I asked.

She took all the clothes gratefully and hid behind Ingrid to change. I put on my black shoes and the dinner jacket: a lot better than nothing.

When Fiona reappeared, her shivers had grown to shakes. She still had too few layers, even if now dry. The only useful thing still unused in my belongings was the plastic bag which had contained my dinner jacket. I put it over Fiona's head, widening the hole where the hanger usually went, and, if she didn't care to be labelled 'Ace Cleaners' at intervals front and back, at least it stopped the wind a bit and kept some body heat in.

'Well,' Harry said with remarkable cheerfulness, eyeing the dimly seen final results of the motley redistribution, 'thanks to John we should live to see Shellerton. All you lot had better start walking. I'll stay with Mackie and we'll follow when we can.'

'No,' I said. 'How far is it to the village?'

'A mile or so.'

'Then we all start now. We'll carry Mackie. It's too cold, believe me, for hanging about. How about a chair lift?'

So Harry and I sat the semi-conscious Mackie on our linked wrists and draped her arms round our necks, and we set off towards the village with Bob Watson carrying all the wet clothes in one of my bags, Fiona carrying dry things in the other and Ingrid shuffling along in front in the moon-boots with my camera case, lighting the way with the dynamo torch from my basic travel kit.

'Squeeze it.' I showed her how. 'It doesn't have batteries. Shine it on the road, so we can all see.'

'Thank God it isn't snowing,' Harry said: but there were ominous clouds hiding the stars. What little natural light there was was amplified by the whiteness of the snow, the only good thing about it. I was glad it wasn't too far to the village. Mackie wasn't draggingly heavy, but we were walking on ice.

'Doesn't any traffic ever come along this road?' I asked in frustration when we'd gone half a mile and still seen no one.

'There are two other ways into Shellerton,' Harry said. 'God, this wind's the devil. My ears are dropping off.'

My own head also was achingly cold. Mackie and Fiona had woollen hats, Ingrid was warmest in the hood of my ski-suit, Bob Watson wore a cap. Ingrid had my gloves. Harry's hands and mine were going numb under Mackie's bottom. If I'd brought any more socks we could have used them as mitts.

45

'It's not far now,' Bob said. 'Once we're round the bend you'll see the village.'

He was right. Electricity twinkled not far below us, offering shelter and warmth. Let's not have a power cut, I prayed.

Mackie suddenly awoke to full consciousness on the last stretch and began demanding to know what was happening.

'We skidded into a ditch,' Harry said succinctly.

'The horse! Is the horse all right? Why are you carrying me? Put me down.'

We stopped and set her on her feet, where she swayed and put a hand to the side of her head.

'Did we hit the horse?' she said.

'No,' Harry answered. 'Better let us carry you.'

'What happened to the horse?'

'It buggered off across the Downs. Come on, Mackie, we're literally freezing to death standing here.' Harry swung his arms in my bathrobe, then hugged his body and tried to warm his hands in his armpits. 'Let's get on, for God's sake.'

Mackie refused to let us lift her up again so we began to struggle on towards the village, a shadowy band slipping and sliding downhill, holding on to each other and trying not to fall, cold to the bone. I should have brought the skis, I thought, and it seemed an extraordinarily long time since that morning.

One reason for the dearth of traffic became clear as we reached the first houses; two cars lay impacted across the width of the lane, and certainly nothing was leaving the village that way.

'You'd better all come to our house,' Fiona said in a shaking voice as we edged round the wreck. 'It's nearest.'

No one argued.

We turned into a long village street with no lighting, and passed a garage, darkly shut, and a pub, open.

'How about a quick one?' Harry suggested, half serious.

Fiona said with some of her former asperity, 'I should think you've heard enough about drink for one day. And you're not going anywhere dressed like that except straight home.'

It was too dark to see Harry's expression. No one cared to comment, and presently Ingrid with the torch turned into a driveway which wound round behind some cottages and opened into a snowy expanse in front of a big Georgian-looking house.

Ingrid stopped. Fiona said, 'This way,' and led a still silent procession round to a side door, which she unlocked with a key retrieved from under a stone.

The relief of being out of the wind was like a rebirth. The warmth of the extensive kitchen we filed into was a positive life-giving luxury; and there in the lights I saw my companions clearly for the first time.

CHAPTER THREE

Everyone except Ingrid was visibly trembling, John Kendall included. All the faces were bluish-white, suffering.

'God,' Fiona said, 'that was hell.'

She was older than I'd thought. Forties, not thirties. The Ace Cleaners bag reached nearly to her knees, covering her arms, bordering on the farcical.

'Take this damned thing off me,' she said. 'And don't bloody laugh.'

Harry obligingly pulled the cleaner's plastic bag up and over her head, taking her knitted hat with it, freeing heavy silver-blond hair and transforming her like a *coup de théâtre* from a refugee to an assured, charismatic woman in jodphurs and blue blazer with the turtle-neck sweatshirt showing white at throat and cuffs.

Although she was tall the sleeves were all too long for her; which had been a blessing, it seemed, as she had been able to tuck her hands inside them, using them as gloves. She stared at me across her kitchen, looking with curiosity at the man whose clothes she wore, seeing I supposed a tallish, thinnish, youngish brown-eyed person in jeans, scarlet sweater and incongruous dinner jacket.

I smiled at her and she, aware of the admiration in my expression, swept a reviving glance round her other unexpected guests and went over to the huge red Aga which warmed the whole place, lifting the lid, letting volumes of heat flow out. The bad temper of the journey had disappeared, revealing a sensible, competent woman.

'Hot drinks,' she said decisively. 'Harry, fill the kettle and get some mugs.'

Harry, my height but fair and blue-eyed, complied with the instructions as though thoroughly accustomed to being bidden, and began rootling round also for spoons, instant coffee and sugar. Swaddled in my blue bathrobe he looked ready for bed; and he too was older than I'd thought. He and Fiona were revealed as well off and perhaps rich. The kitchen was large, individual, a combination of technology and sitting-room, and the manner and voices of its owners had the unselfconscious assurance of comfortable social status.

Mackie sat down uncertainly at the big central table, her fingers gingerly feeling her temple.

'I was looking at the horse,' she said. 'Must have hit my head on the window. Is the jeep all right?'

'Shouldn't think so,' Harry said without emotion. 'It's lying in water which will be frozen over again by morning. The door on my side buckled when we hit. Filthy ditch-water just rushed in.'

'Damn,' Mackie said wearily. 'That on top of everything else.'

She huddled into her fawn-coloured padded coat, still deeply shivering, and it was hard to tell what she would look like warm and laughing. All I could see were reddish curls over her forehead followed by closed eyes, pale lips and the rigid muscles of distress.

'Is Perkin home?' Fiona asked her.

'He should be. God, I hope so.'

Fiona, recovering faster than anyone else, perhaps because she was in her own house, went across to a wall telephone and pressed buttons. Perkin, whoever he was, apparently answered and was given a variety of bad news.

'Yes,' Fiona said repeating thing, 'I did say the jeep's in a ditch . . . it's in that hollow just over the top of the hill after you leave the A34 . . . I don't know whose horse, damn it . . . No, we had an *abysmal* day in court. Look, can you get down here and collect everyone? Mackie's all right but she hit her head . . . Bob Watson and his wife are with us . . . Yes, we did pick up the writer, he's here too. Just *come*, Perkin, for God's sake. Stop dithering.' She hung up the receiver with a crash.

Harry poured steaming water onto instant coffee in a row of mugs and then picked up a milk carton in one hand and a bottle of brandy in the other, offering a choice of additives. Everyone except Ingrid chose brandy, and Harry's idea of a decent slug cooled the liquid to drinking point.

Although if we had still been outside the alcohol wouldn't have been such a good idea, the deep trembles in all our bodies abated and faded away. Bob Watson took off his cap and looked suddenly younger, a short stocky man with wiry brown hair and a returning glint of independence. One could still see what he must have looked like as a schoolboy, with rounded cheeks and a natural insolence not far from the surface but controlled enough to keep him out of trouble. He had called Harry a liar, but too quietly for him to hear. That rather summed up Bob Watson, I thought.

Ingrid, swamped in the ski-suit, looked out at the world from a thinly pretty face and sniffed at regular intervals. She sat beside her husband at the table, unspeaking and forever in his shadow.

Standing with his backside propped against the Aga, Harry warmed both hands round his mug and looked at me with the glimmering amusement that, when not under stress from giving evidence, seemed to be his habitual cast of mind.

'Welcome to Berkshire,' he said.

'Thanks a lot.'

'I would have stayed by the jeep and waited for someone to come,' he said.

'I thought someone would,' I agreed.

Mackie said, 'I hope the horse is all right,' as if her mind were stuck in that groove. No one else, it seemed to me, cared an icicle for the survival of the cause of our woes; and I suspected, perhaps unfairly, that Mackie kept on about the horse so as to reinforce in our consciousness that the crash hadn't been her fault.

Warmth gradually returned internally also and everyone looked as if they had come up to room temperature, like wine. Ingrid pushed back the hood of my ski-suit jacket revealing soft mouse-brown hair in need of a brush.

No one had a great wish to talk, and there was something of a return to the pre-crash gloom, so it was a relief when wheels, slammed doors and approaching footsteps announced the arrival of Perkin.

He hadn't come alone. It was Tremayne Vickers who advanced first into the kitchen, his loud voice and large personality galvanising the subdued group drinking coffee.

'Got yourself into a load of shit, have you?' he boomed with a touch of not wholly unfriendly scorn. 'Roads too much for you, eh?'

Mackie went defensively into the horse routine as if she'd merely been rehearsing earlier.

The man who followed Tremayne through the door looked like a smudged carbon copy: same height, same build, same basic features, but none of Tremayne's bullishness. If that was Perkin, I thought, he must be Tremayne's son.

The carbon copy said to Mackie crossly, 'Why didn't

you go round the long way? You ought to have more sense than to take that short cut.'

'It was all right this morning,' Mackie said, 'and I always go that way. It was the horse . . .'

Tremayne's gaze fastened on me. 'So you got here. Good. You've met everyone? My son, Perkin. His wife, Mackie.'

I'd assumed, I realised, that Mackie had been either Tremayne's own wife or perhaps his daughter; hadn't thought of daughter-in-law.

'Why on earth are you wearing a dinner jacket?' Tremayne asked, staring.

'We got wet in the ditch,' Harry said briefly. 'Your friend the writer lent us dry clothes. He issued his dinner jacket to himself. Didn't trust me with it, smart fellow. What I've got on is his bathrobe. Ingrid has his ski-suit. Fiona is his from head to foot.'

Tremayne looked briefly bewildered but decided not to sort things out. Instead he asked Fiona if she'd been hurt in the crash. 'Fiona, my dear . . .'

Fiona, his dear, assured him otherwise. He behaved to her with a hint of roguishness, she to him with easy response. She aroused in all men, I supposed, the desire to flirt.

Perkin belatedly asked Mackie about her head, awkwardly producing anxiety after his ungracious criticism. Mackie gave him a tired understanding smile, and I had a swift impression that she was the one in that marriage who made allowances, who did the looking after, who was the adult to her good-looking husband-child.

'But,' he said, 'I do think you were silly to go down that road.' His reaction to her injury was still to blame her for it, but I wondered if it weren't really a reaction to fright, like a parent clouting a much-loved lost-but-found infant. 'And there was supposed to be a police notice at the turn-off saying it was closed. It's been closed since those cars slid into each other at lunchtime.'

'There wasn't any police notice,' Mackie said.

'Well, there must have been. You just didn't see it.'

'There was no police notice in sight,' Harry said, and we all agreed, we hadn't seen one.

'All the same . . .' Perkin wouldn't leave it.

'Look,' Mackie said, 'if I could go back and do it again then I wouldn't go along there, but it looked all right and I'd come up in the morning, so I just *did*, and that's that.'

'We all saw the *horse*,' Harry said, drawling, and from the dry humour lurking in his voice one could read his private opinion of Perkin's behaviour.

Perkin gave him a confused glance and stopped picking on Mackie.

Tremayne said, 'What's done's done,' as if announcing his life's philosophy, and added that he would 'give the police a ring' when he got home, which would be very soon now.

'About your clothes,' Fiona said to me, 'shall I send them to the cleaners with all our wet things?'

'No, don't bother,' I said. 'I'll come and collect them tomorrow.'

'All right.' She smiled slightly. 'I do realise we have to thank you. Don't think we don't know.'

'Don't know what?' Perkin demanded.

Harry said in his way, 'Fellow saved us from ice-cubery.'

'From *what*?'

Ingrid giggled. Everyone looked at her. 'Sorry,' she whispered, subsiding.

'Quite likely from death,' Mackie said plainly. 'Let's go home.' She stood up, clearly much better for the warmth and the stiffly laced coffee and also, it seemed to me, relieved that her father-in-law hadn't added his weight to her husband's bawling-out. 'Tomorrow,' she added slowly, 'which of us is going back to Reading?'

'Oh, God,' Fiona said. 'For a minute I'd forgotten.'

'Some of us will have to go,' Mackie said, and it was clear that no one wanted to.

After a pause Harry stirred. 'I'll go. I'll take Bob. Fiona doesn't have to go, nor does Ingrid. Mackie . . .' he stopped.

'I'll come with you,' she said. 'I owe him that.'

Fiona said, 'So will I. He's my cousin, after all. He deserves us to support him. Though after what Harry did today I don't know if I can look him in the face.'

'What did Harry do?' Perkin asked.

55

Fiona shrugged and retreated. 'Mackie can tell you.'
Fiona, it seemed, could attack Harry all she liked herself, but she wasn't throwing him to other wolves. Harry
was no doubt due for further tongue-lashing after we'd
gone, and in fact was glancing at his wife in a mixture
of apprehension and resignation.

'Let's be off,' Tremayne said. 'Come along, Bob.'

'Yes, sir.'

Bob Watson, I remembered, was Tremayne's head
lad. He and Ingrid went over to the door, followed by
Mackie and Perkin. I put down my mug, thanking
Harry for the reviver.

'Come down this time tomorrow to fetch your
clothes,' he said. 'Come for a drink. An ordinary drink,
not an emergency.'

'Thank you. I'd like that.'

He nodded amiably, and Fiona also, and I picked up
my dry clothes-bag and the camera case and followed
Tremayne and the others out again into the snow. The
six of us squeezed into a large Volvo, Tremayne driving,
Perkin sitting beside him, Ingrid sitting on Bob's lap in
the back with Mackie and me. At the end of the village
Tremayne stopped to let Bob and Ingrid get out, Ingrid
giving me a sketchy smile and saying Bob would bring
my suit and boots along in the morning, if that would
be all right. Of course, I said.

They turned away to walk through a garden gate
towards a small shadowy house, and Tremayne started
off again towards open country, grousing that the trial

56

would take his head lad away for yet another day. Neither Mackie nor Perkin said anything, and I still had no idea what the trial was all about. I didn't know them well enough to ask, I felt.

'Not much of a welcome for you, John, eh?' Tremayne said over his shoulder. 'Did you bring a typewriter?'

'No. A pencil, actually. And a tape recorder.'

'I expect you know what you're doing.' He sounded cheerfully more sure of that than I was. 'We can start in the morning.'

After about a mile of cautious crawling along a surface much like the one we'd come to grief on, he turned in through a pair of imposing gateposts and stopped outside a very large house where many lights showed dimly through curtains. As inhabitants of large houses seldom used their front doors we went into this one also at the side, not directly into the kitchen this time but into a warm carpeted hall leading to doorways in all directions.

Tremayne, saying, 'Bloody cold night,' walked through a doorway to the left, looking back for me to follow. 'Come on in. Make yourself at home. This is the family room, where you'll find newspapers, telephone, drinks, things like that. Help yourself to whatever you want while you're here.'

The big room looked comfortable in a sprawling way, not tidy, not planned. There was a mixture of patterns and colours, a great many photographs, a few poinsettias left over from Christmas and a glowing log fire in a wide stone fireplace.

Tremayne picked up a telephone and briefly told the local force that his jeep was in the ditch in the lane, not to worry, no one had been hurt, he would get it picked up in the morning. Duty done, he went across to the fire and held out his hands to warm them.

'Perkin and Mackie have their own part of the house, but this room is where we all meet,' he said. 'If you want to leave a message for anybody, pin it to that board over there.' He pointed to a chair on which was propped a corkboard much like the one in Ronnie's office. Red drawing pins were stuck into it at random, one of them anchoring a note which in large letters announced briefly, 'BACK FOR GRUB'.

'That's my other son,' Tremayne said, reading the message from a distance. 'He's fifteen. Unmanageable.' He spoke, however, with indulgence. 'I expect you'll soon get the hang of the household.'

'Er . . . *Mrs* Vickers?' I said tentatively.

'Mackie?' He sounded puzzled.

'No . . . Your wife?'

'Oh. Oh, I see. No, my wife took a hike. Can't say I minded. There's just me and Gareth, the boy. I've a daughter, married a Frog, lives outside Paris, has three children, they come here sometimes, turn the place upside down. She's the eldest, then Perkin. Gareth came later.'

He was feeding me the facts without feelings, I

thought. I'd have to change that, if I were to do any good: but maybe it was too soon for feelings. He was glad I was there, but jerky, almost nervous, almost – now we were alone – shy. Now that he had got what he wanted, now that he had secured his writer, a lot of the agitation and anxiety he'd displayed in Ronnie's office seemed to have abated. The Tremayne of today was running on only half-stress.

Mackie, coming into the room, restored him to his confident self. Carrying an ice-bucket, she glanced quickly at her father-in-law as if to assess his mood, to find out if his tolerance in Fiona and Harry's kitchen was still in operation. Reassured in some way she took the ice over to a table bearing a tray of bottles and glasses and began mixing a drink.

She had taken off her padded coat and woolly hat, and was wearing a blue jersey dress over knee-high narrow black boots. Her red-brown hair, cut short, curled neatly on a well-shaped head and she was still pale, without lipstick or vivacity.

The drink she mixed was gin and tonic, which she gave to Tremayne. He nodded his thanks, as for something done often.

'For you?' Mackie said to me. 'John?'

'The coffee was fine,' I said.

She smiled faintly. 'Yes.'

Truth to tell I was hungry, not thirsty. Thanks to no water in the friend's aunt's house, all I had had that day apart from the coffee was some bread and Marmite and two glasses of milk, and even that had been half frozen in its carton. I began to hope that Gareth's return, 'back for grub', was imminent.

Perkin appeared carrying an already full glass of brown liquid that looked like Coca-Cola. He sank into one of the armchairs and began complaining again about the loss of the jeep, not seeing that he was lucky not to have lost his wife.

'The damned thing's insured,' Tremayne said robustly. 'The garage can tow it out of the ditch in the morning and tell us if it can be salvaged. Either way, it's not the end of the world.'

'How will we manage without it?' Perkin grumbled.

'Buy another,' Tremayne said.

This simple solution silenced Perkin and Mackie looked grateful. She sat on a sofa and took her boots off, saying they were damp from snow and her feet were freezing. She massaged her toes and looked across at my black shoes.

'Those shoes of yours are meant for dancing,' she said, 'and not for carrying females across ice. I'm sorry, I really am.'

'*Carrying?*' Tremayne said, eyebrows rising.

'Yes, didn't I tell you? John and Harry carried me for about a mile, I think. I can remember the crash, then I sort of passed out and I woke up just outside the village. I do vaguely remember them carrying me ... it's a bit of a blur ... I was sitting on their wrists ... I knew I mustn't fall off ... it was like dreaming.'

Perkin stared, first at her, then at me. Not pleased, I thought.

'I'll be damned,' Tremayne said.

I smiled at Mackie and she smiled back, and Perkin very obviously didn't like that. I'd have to be careful, I thought. I was not there to stir family waters but simply to do a job, to stay uninvolved and leave everything as I'd found it.

Thankful for the heat of the fire I shed the dinner jacket, laying it on a chair and feeling less like the decadent remains of an orgy. I wondered how soon I could decently mention food. If it hadn't been for the bus fare I might have bought something sustaining like chocolate. I wondered if I could ask Tremayne to reimburse the bus fare. Frivolous thoughts, mental rubbish.

'Sit down, John,' Tremayne said, waving to an armchair. I sat as instructed. 'What happened in court?' he asked Mackie. 'How did it go?'

'It was awful.' She shuddered. 'Nolan looked so ... so *vulnerable*. The jury think he's guilty, I'm sure they do. And Harry wouldn't swear after all that Lewis was drunk ...' She closed her eyes and sighed deeply. 'I wish to God we'd never had that damned party.'

'What's done is done,' Tremayne said heavily, and I wondered how many times they'd each repeated those regrets.

Tremayne glanced at me and asked Mackie, 'Have

you told John what's going on?' She shook her head and he enlightened me a little. 'We gave a party here last year, in April, to celebrate winning the Grand National with Top Spin Lob. Celebrate! There were a lot of people here, well over a hundred, including of course Fiona and Harry who you met. I train horses for them. And Fiona's cousins were here, Nolan and Lewis. They're brothers. No one knows for sure what happened, but at the end of the party, when most people had gone home, a girl died. Nolan swears it was an accident. Lewis was there . . . he should have been able to settle it one way or the other, but he says he was drunk and can't remember.'

'He *was* drunk,' Mackie protested. 'Bob testified he was drunk. Bob said he served him getting on for a dozen drinks during the evening.'

'Bob Watson acted as barman,' Tremayne told me. 'He always does, at our parties.'

'We'll never have another,' Mackie said.

'Is Nolan being tried for murder?' I asked, into a pause.

'For assault resulting in death,' Tremayne said. 'The prosecution are trying to prove intent, which would make it murder. Nolan's lawyers say the charge means manslaughter but they are pressing hard for involuntary manslaughter, which could be called negligence or plain accident. The case has been dragging on for months. At least tomorrow it will end.'

'He'll appeal,' Perkin said.

'They haven't found him guilty yet,' Mackie protested.

Tremayne told me, 'Mackie and Harry walked together into Mackie and Perkin's sitting-room and found Nolan standing over the girl who was lying on the floor. Lewis was sitting in an armchair. Nolan said he'd put his hands round the girl's neck to give her a shaking, and she just went limp and fell down; and when Mackie and Harry tried to revive her, they found she was dead.'

'The pathologist said in court today that she died from strangulation,' Mackie said, 'but that sometimes it takes very little pressure to kill someone. He said she died of vagal inhibition, which means the vagus nerve stops working, which it apparently can do fairly easily. The vagus nerve keeps the heart beating. The pathologist said it's always dangerous to clasp people suddenly round the neck, even in fun. But there's no doubt Nolan was furious with Olympia – that's the girl – and he had been furious all the evening, and the prosecution produced someone who'd heard him say, "I'll strangle the bitch," so that he had it in his mind to put his hands round her neck . . .' She broke off and sighed again. 'There wouldn't have been a trial at all except for Olympia's father. The pathologist's original report said it could so easily have been an accident that there wasn't going to be a prosecution, but Olympia's father insisted on bringing a private case against Nolan.

He won't let up. He's obsessed. He was sitting there in court glaring at us.'

'If he'd had his way,' Tremayne confirmed, 'Nolan would have been behind bars all this time, not out on bail.'

Mackie nodded. 'The prosecution – and that's Olympia's father talking through his lawyers – wanted Nolan to be remanded in jail tonight, but the judge said no. So Nolan and Lewis have gone back to Lewis's house, and God knows what state they're in after the mauling they got in court. It's Olympia's father who deserves to be strangled for all the trouble he's caused.'

It seemed to me that on the whole it was Nolan who had caused the trouble, but I didn't say so.

'Well,' Tremayne said, shrugging, 'it happened in this house but it doesn't directly concern my family, thank God.'

Mackie looked as if she weren't so sure. 'They are our friends,' she said.

'Hardly even that,' Perkin said, looking my way. 'Fiona and Mackie are friends. That's where it starts. Mackie came to stay with Fiona, and I met her in Fiona's house . . .' he smiled briefly, 'and so, as they say, we were married.'

'And lived happily ever after,' Mackie finished loyally, though I reckoned if she were happy she worked at it. 'We've been married two years now. Two and a half, almost.'

'You won't put all this Nolan business in my book, will you?' Tremayne asked.

'I shouldn't think so,' I said, 'not if you don't want me to.'

'No, I don't. I was saying goodbye to some guests when that girl died. Perkin came to tell me, and I had to deal with it, but I didn't know her, she'd come with Nolan and I'd never met her before. She isn't part of my life.'

'All right,' I said.

Tremayne showed no particular relief, but just nodded. Seen in his own home, standing by his own fire, he was a big-bodied man of substantial presence, long accustomed to taking charge and ruling his kingdom. This was the persona, no doubt, that the book was to be about: the face of control, of worldly wisdom and success.

So be it, I thought. If I were to sing for my supper I'd sing the songs he chose. But meanwhile, *where* was the supper?

'In the morning,' Tremayne said to me, changing the subject and apparently tired of the trial and its tribulations, 'I thought you might come out with me to see my string at morning exercise.'

'I'd like to,' I said.

'Good. I'll wake you at seven. The first lot pulls out at seven-thirty, just before dawn. Of course at present, with this freeze, we can't do any schooling but we've got an all-weather gallop. You'll see it in the morning. If it should be snowing hard, we won't go.'

'Right.'

He turned his head to Mackie, 'I suppose you won't be out for first lot?'

'No, sorry. We'll have to leave early again to get to Reading.'

He nodded, and to me he said, 'Mackie's my assistant.'

I glanced at Mackie and then at Perkin.

'That's right,' Tremayne said, reading my thought. 'Perkin doesn't work for me. Mackie does. Perkin never wanted to be a trainer and he has his own life. Gareth ... well ... Gareth might take over from me one day, but he's too young to know what he'll want. But when Perkin married Mackie he brought me a damned smart assistant, and it's worked out very well.'

Mackie looked pleased at his audible sincerity and it seemed the arrangement was to Perkin's liking also.

'This house is huge,' Tremayne said, 'and as Perkin and Mackie couldn't afford much of a place of their own yet we divided it, and they have their private half. You'll soon get the hang of it.' He finished his drink and went to pour himself another. 'You can have the dining-room to work in,' he said to me over his shoulder. 'Tomorrow I'll show you where to find the cuttings, video tapes and form books, and you can take

what you like into the dining-room. We'll fix up the
video player there.'

'Fine,' I said. Food in the dining-room would be
better, I thought.

Tremayne said, 'As soon as it thaws I'll take you
racing. You'll soon pick it up.'

'Pick it up?' Perkin repeated, surprised. 'Doesn't he
know about racing?'

'Not a lot,' I said.

Perkin raised ironic eyebrows. 'It's going to be some
book.'

'He's a writer,' Tremayne said, a touch defensively.
'He can learn.'

I nodded to back him up. It was true that I had
learned the habits and ways of life of dwellers in far
places, and didn't doubt I could do the same to the
racing fraternity at home in England. To listen, to see,
to ask, to understand, to check; I would use the same
method that I'd used six times before, and this time
without needing an interpreter. Whether I could
present Tremayne's life and times in a shape others
would enjoy, that was the real, nagging, doubtful
question.

Gareth at long last blew in with a gust of cold air
and, stripping off an eye-dazzling psychedelic padded
jacket, asked his father, 'What's for supper?'

'Anything you like,' Tremayne said, not minding.

'Pizza, then.' His gaze stopped on me. 'Hello, I'm
Gareth.'

Tremayne told him my name and that I would be writing the biography and staying in the house.

'Straight up?' the boy said, his eyes widening. 'Do you want some pizza?'

'Yes, please.'

'Ten minutes,' he said. He turned to Mackie. 'Do you two want some?'

Mackie and Perkin simultaneously shook their heads and murmured that they'd be off to their own quarters, which appeared to be what Gareth and Tremayne expected.

Gareth was perhaps five foot six with a strong echo of his father's self-confidence and a voice still half broken, coming out hoarse and uneven. He gave me an all-over glance as if assessing what he'd got to put up with for the length of my visit and seemed neither depressed nor elated.

'I heard the weather news at Coconut's,' he told his father. 'Today's been the coldest for twenty-five years. Coconut's father's horses have their duvet rugs on under the jute.'

'So have ours,' Tremayne said. 'Did they forecast more snow?'

'No, just cold for a few more days. East winds from Siberia. Have you remembered to send my school fees?'

Tremayne clearly hadn't.

'If you'll just sign the cheque,' his son said, 'I'll give it to them myself. They're getting a bit fussed.'

'The cheque book's in the office,' Tremayne said.

'Right.' Gareth took his Joseph's coat with him out of the door and almost immediately returned. 'I suppose there isn't the faintest chance,' he said to me, 'that you can cook?'

CHAPTER FOUR

In the morning I went downstairs to find the family room dark but lights on in the kitchen.

It wasn't a palatial kitchen like Fiona's but did contain a big table with chairs all round it as well as a solid fuel cooker whose warmth easily defeated the pre-dawn refrigeration. I had been hoping to borrow a coat from Tremayne to go out to watch the horses, but on a chair I found my boots, gloves and ski-suit with a note attached by a safety pin, 'Thanks ever so much.'

Smiling, I unpinned the note and put on the suit and boots and Tremayne, in a padded jacket, cloth cap and yellow scarf came in blowing on his bare hands and generally bringing the arctic indoors.

'Ah, there you are,' he said, puffing. 'Good. Bob Watson brought up your clothes when he came to feed. Ready?'

I nodded.

'I'll just get my gloves.' He checked also that I had gloves. 'It's as cold as I've ever known it. We won't stay out long, the wind's terrible. Come along.'

As we went through the hall I asked him about the feeding.

'Bob Watson comes at six,' he said briefly. 'All horses in training get an early-morning feed. High protein. Keeps them warm. Gives them energy. A thoroughbred on a high-protein diet generates a lot of heat. Just as well in weather like this. You rarely find a bucket of water frozen over in a horse's box, however cold it is outside. Mind you,' he said, 'we do our best to stop draughts round the doors, but you have to give them fresh air. If you don't, if you molly-coddle them too much, you get viruses flourishing.'

As we stepped out into the open, the wind pulled his last words away and sucked the breath out of our lungs and I reckoned we were still dealing with perhaps ten degrees of frost, plus chill factor, the same as the evening before. It wouldn't go on freezing for as long as in 1963, I thought: that had been the coldest winter since 1740.

A short walk took us straight into the stable-yard, dark the night before and dimly seen, now lit comprehensively and bustling with activity.

'Bob Watson,' Tremayne said, 'is no ordinary head lad. He has all sorts of skills, and takes pride in them. Any odd job, carpentering, plumbing, laying concrete, anything to improve the yard and working conditions, he suggests it and mostly does it himself.'

The object of this eulogy came to meet us, noticing I wore the ski-suit, acknowledging my thanks.

'All ready, guv'nor,' he said to Tremayne.

'Good. Bring them out, Bob. Then you'd better be off, if you're going to Reading.'

Bob nodded and gave some sort of signal and from many open doors came figures leading horses; riders in hard helmets, horses in rugs. In the lights and the dark, with plumes of steam swirling as they breathed, with the circling movements and the scrunching of icy gravel underfoot, the great elemental creatures raised in me such a sense of enjoyment and excitement that I felt for the first time truly enthusiastic about what I'd set my hand to. I wished I could paint, but no canvas, and not even film, could catch the feeling of primitive life or the tingle and smell of the frosty yard.

Bob moved through the scene giving a leg-up to each lad and they resolved themselves into a line, perhaps twenty of them, and processed away through a far exit, horses stalking on long strong legs, riders hunched on top, heads bobbing.

'Splendid,' I said to Tremayne, almost sighing.

He glanced at me. 'Horses get to you, don't they?'

'To you too? Still?'

He nodded and said, 'I love them,' as if such a statement were no more than normal, and in the same tone of voice went on, 'As the jeep's in the ditch we'll have to go up to the gallops on the tractor. All right with you?'

'Sure,' I said, and got my introduction to the training of steeplechasers perched high in the cab over chain-wrapped wheels which Tremayne told me had been up to the Downs with his groundsman once already that morning to harrow the tracks and make them safe for the horses to walk on. He drove the tractor himself with the facility of long custom, spending most of his time not looking where he was going but at anything else visible around him.

His house and stables, I discovered, were right on the edge of the grassy uplands so that the horses had merely to cross one public road to be already on a downland track, and the road surface itself had been thinly covered with unidentified muck to make the icy crossing easier.

Tremayne waited until his whole string was safely over before following them at enough distance not to alarm them, then they peeled off to the right while we lumbered onwards and upwards over frozen rutted mud, making for a horizon that slowly defined itself out of shadows as the firmament grew lighter.

Through the wind Tremayne remarked that perfectly still mornings on the long east-west sweep of downland across Berkshire and Wiltshire were as rare as honest beggars. Apart from that the day broke clear and high with a pale grey washed sky that slowly turned blue over the rolling snow-dusted hills. When Tremayne stopped the tractor and the silence and isolation crept into the senses, it was easy to see that this was what it had looked like up here for thousands of years, that this primordial scene before our present eyes had also been there before man.

Tremayne prosaically told me that if we had continued up over the next brow we would have been close to the fences and hurdles of his schooling ground where his horses learned to jump. Today, he said, they would be doing only half-speed gallops on the all-weather track, and he led the way on foot from the tractor across a stretch of powdery snow to a low mound from where we could see a long dark ribbon of ground winding away down the hill and curving out of sight at the bottom.

'They'll come up here towards us,' he said. 'The all-weather surface is wood chips. Am I telling you what you already know?'

'No,' I said. 'Tell me everything.'

He grunted noncommittally and raised a pair of binoculars powerful enough to see into the riders' minds. I looked where he was looking, but it took me much longer to spot the three dark shapes moving over the dark track. They seemed to be taking a long time to come up head-on towards us but the slowness was an illusion merely. Once they drew near and passed us their speed was vivid, stirring, a matter of muscles stretching and hooves thudding urgently on the quiet surface.

Two or three times they all came up in their turn. 'Both of those are Fiona's,' Tremayne said from behind the binoculars, giving me a commentary as a pair of chestnuts scurried past, and, 'The one on the left of this next three is my Grand National winner, Top Spin Lob.'

With interest I watched the pride of the stable go past us and begin to pull up as he reached the prow of the rise, but beside me Tremayne was stiffening in dismay and saying, 'What the hell—?'

I looked back down the hill in the direction of his binoculars but could see only three more horses coming up the track, two in front, one behind. It wasn't until they were almost upon us that I realised that the one at the rear had no rider.

The three horses passed us and began to slow down and Tremayne said 'Shit' with fervour.

'Did the lad fall off?' I asked inanely.

'No doubt he did,' Tremayne said forcefully, watching through his glasses, 'but he's not one of mine.'

'How do you mean?'

'I mean,' Tremayne said, 'that's not my horse. Just look at him. That's not my rug. That horse isn't saddled and has no bridle. Can't you see?'

When I looked, when he'd told me what to look for, then I could see. Tremayne's horses had fawn rugs with horizontal red and blue stripes; rugs which covered the ribs and hindquarters but left the legs free for full movement. The rug of the riderless horse was brownish grey, much thicker, and fastened by straps running under the belly and round in front of the shoulders.

'I suppose you'll think me crazy,' I said to Tremayne, 'but maybe that's the horse that was loose in the lane last night when we crashed. I mean, I saw it for only a split second, really, but it looked like that. Dark, with that sort of rug.'

'Almost every racehorse wears that sort of rug at night in the winter,' Tremayne said. 'I'm not saying you're wrong, though. In a minute, I'll find out.'

He swung his binoculars back to where another couple of his string were putting on their show and calmly watched them before referring again to the stranger.

'They're the last,' he said as they sped past us. 'Now let's see what's what.'

He began to walk up beside the gallop in the direction of the horses and I followed, and we soon came over the brow to where his whole string was circling on snowy grass, steam swelling in clouds from their breath after their exertions. They were silhouetted against the eastern sun, their shapes now black, now gleaming. Brilliant, freezing, moving; unforgettable morning.

Away to the left, apart from the string, the riderless horse made his own white sun-splashed plume, his nervousness apparent, his herding instincts propelling him towards his kin, his wild nature urging flight.

Tremayne reached his horses and spoke to his lads.

'Anyone know whose horse that is?'

They shook their heads.

'Walk on back to the yard then. Go back down the

all-weather track. No one else is using it this morning. Take care crossing the road.'

They nodded and began to form into a line as they had in the stables, walking off in self-generated mist towards the end of the gallop.

Tremayne said to me, 'Go back to the tractor, will you? Don't make any sudden moves. Don't alarm this fellow.' His eyes slid in the direction of the loose horse. 'In the tractor's cab you'll find a rope. Bring it back here. Move slowly when you're coming into sight.'

'Right,' I said.

He nodded briefly and as I turned to go on the errand he reached into a pocket and produced a few horse-feed cubes which he held out to the runaway, speaking to him directly.

'Come on, now, fella. Nice and easy. Come along now, you must be hungry . . .' His voice was calm and cajoling, absolutely without threat.

I walked away without haste and retrieved the rope from the cab, and by the time I cautiously returned over the brow into Tremayne's sight he was standing close to the horse feeding him cubes with his left hand and holding a bunch of mane with his right.

I stopped, then went forward again slowly. The horse quivered, his head turning my way, his alarm transmitting like electricity. With small movements I made a big loop in one end of the supple old rope and tied a running bowline, then went slowly forward holding the rope open, not in a small circle that might

77

frighten the horse more but in a big loop drooping almost to my knees.

Tremayne watched and continued to talk soothingly, feeding horse cubes one by one. I walked cautiously forward suppressing anything that could seem like doubt or anxiety and paused again a step or two away from the horse.

'There's a good fella,' Tremayne said to him, and to me in the same tone, 'If you can put the rope over his head, do it.'

I took the last two paces and without stopping walked alongside the horse on the far side from Tremayne so that the horse's head came as if naturally into and through the dangling loop. Tremayne moved his hand with the horse cubes away from the black muzzle just long enough for the rope to pass, and then still without abruptness I pulled the slack through the bowline until the noose was snug but not tight round the horse's neck.

'Good,' Tremayne said. 'Give me the rope. I'll walk him down to my yard. Can you drive the tractor?'

'Yes.'

'Wait until I'm out of sight at the bottom. We don't want him bolting from fright. I couldn't hold him if he did.'

'Right.'

Tremayne fished a few more cubes out of his pocket and offered them as before but tugged gently on the rope at the same time. Almost as if making up his mind, as if settling for food and captivity, the great creature moved off with him peacefully, and the two of them trailed down to the dark strip of wood chips and plodded towards home.

Food and warmth, I thought. Maybe I had a lot in common with that horse. What had I settled for, but a form of captivity?

I shrugged. What was done was done, as Tremayne would say. I went down to the tractor and in due course drove it back and parked it where it had been before we started out.

In the now sunlit kitchen Tremayne was standing by the table talking crossly into a telephone.

'You'd have thought someone would have noticed by now that they're missing a horse?' He listened a bit, then said, 'Well, I've one here that's surplus to requirements, so let me know.' He put the receiver down with destructive force. 'No one's told the police, would you believe it?'

He took off his coat, scarf and cap and hung them on a single peg, revealing a big diamond-patterned golfing sweater over a boldly checked open-necked shirt. The same eye-clutter as in the family room; same taste.

'Coffee?' he said, going towards the Aga. 'You won't mind getting your own breakfast, will you? Look around, take anything you want.' He slid the heavy kettle on to the hotplate and went along to a refrigerator which disgorged sliced bread, a tub of yellowish spread and a pot of marmalade. 'Toast?' he said, putting two slices in a wire mesh holder which he slid under the second hotplate lid of the cooker. 'There's cornflakes, if you'd rather. Or cook an egg.'

Toast would be fine, I said, and found myself delegated to making sure it didn't burn while he put through two more phone calls, both fairly incomprehensible to my ears.

'Plates,' he said, pointing to a cupboard, and I found those and mugs also and, in a drawer, knives, forks and spoons. 'Hang your jacket in the cloakroom, next door.'

He went on talking; positive, decisive. I hung my jacket, made the coffee and more toast. He put the receiver down with another crash and went out into the hall.

'Dee-Dee,' he shouted. 'Coffee.'

He came back and sat down to eat, waving to me to join him, which I did, and presently in the doorway appeared a slight brown-haired woman who wore jeans and a huge grey sweater reaching to her knees.

'Dee-Dee,' Tremayne said round a mouthful of toast, 'this is John Kendall, my writer.' To me he added, 'Dee-Dee's my secretary.'

I stood up politely and she told me unsmilingly to sit down. My first impression of her as she went across to the Aga to make her own coffee was that she was like a cat, ultra soft-footed, fluid in movement and totally self-contained.

Tremayne watched me watching her and smiled with

amusement. 'You'll get used to Dee-Dee,' he said. 'I couldn't manage without her.'

She took the compliment without acknowledgement and sat half on a chair as if temporarily, as if about to retreat.

'Phone up a few people to see if they've lost a horse,' Tremayne told her. 'If anyone's panicking, he's here. Unhurt. We've given him water and feed. He was out all night on the Downs, it seems. Someone's in for a bollocking.'

Dee-Dee nodded.

'The jeep's in a ditch on the south road to the A34. Skidded last evening with Mackie. No one hurt. Get the garage to fish it out.'

Dee-Dee nodded.

'John, here, will be working in the dining-room. Anything he wants, give it to him. Anything he wants to know, tell him.'

Dee-Dee nodded.

'Get the blacksmith over for two of the string who lost shoes on the gallop this morning. The lads found the shoes, we don't need new ones.'

Dee-Dee nodded.

'If I'm not here when the vet comes, ask him to take a look at Waterbourne after he's cut the colt. She's got some heat in her near-fore fetlock.'

Dee-Dee nodded.

'Check that the haulage people will be on time

delivering the hay. We're running low. Don't take snow for an answer.'

Dee-Dee smiled, which in a triangular way looked feline also, although far from kittenish. I wondered fleetingly about claws.

Tremayne ate his toast and went on giving sporadic instructions which Dee-Dee seemed to have no trouble remembering. When the spate slowed she stood, picked up her mug and said she would finish her coffee in the office while she got on with things.

'Utterly reliable,' Tremayne remarked to her departing back. 'There's always ten damned trainers trying to poach her.' He lowered his voice. 'A shit of an amateur jockey treated her like muck. She's not over it yet. I make allowances. If you find her crying, that's it.'

I was amazed by his compassion and felt I should have recognised earlier how many unexpected layers there were to Tremayne below the loud executive exterior: not just his love of horses, not just his need to be recorded, not even just his disguised delight in Gareth, but other, secret, unrevealed privacies which maybe I would come to in time, and maybe not.

He spent the next half-hour on the telephone both making and receiving calls: it was the time of day, I later discovered, when trainers could most reliably be found at home. Toast eaten, coffee drunk, he reached for a cigarette from a packet on the table and brought a throwaway lighter out of his pocket.

'Do you smoke?' he asked, pushing the pack my way.

'Never started,' I said.

'Good for the nerves,' he commented, inhaling deeply. 'I hope you're not an anti fanatic.'

'I quite like the smell.'

'Good.' He seemed pleased enough. 'We'll get on well.'

He told me that at ten o'clock, by which time the first lot would have been given hay and water and the lads would have had their own breakfasts, he would drive the tractor back to the gallops to watch his second lot work. He said I needn't bother with that: I could set things up in the dining-room, arrange things however I liked working. As all racing was off from frost he could, if I agreed, spend the afternoon telling me about his childhood. When racing began again, he wouldn't have so much time.

'Good idea,' I said.

He nodded. 'Come along, then, and I'll show you where things are.'

We went out into the carpeted hall and he pointed to the doorway opposite.

'That's the family room, as you know. Next to the kitchen . . .' he walked along and opened a closed door, '. . . is my dining-room. We don't use it much. You'll have to turn the heating up, I dare say.'

I looked into the room I was to get to know well; a spacious room with mahogany furniture, swagged crimson curtains, formal cream-and-gold striped walls and a plain dark green carpet. Not Tremayne's own choice, I thought. Much too coordinated.

'That'll be great,' I said obligingly.

'Good.' He closed the door again and looked up the stairs we had climbed to bed the night before. 'We put those stairs in when we divided the house. This passage beside them, this leads to Perkin and Mackie's half. Come along, I'll show you.' He walked along a wide pale-green-carpeted corridor with pictures of horses on both walls and opened double white-painted doors at the end.

'Through here,' he said, 'is the main entrance hall of the house. The oldest part.'

We passed on to a big wood-blocked expanse of polished floor from which two graceful wings of staircase rose to an upper gallery. Under the gallery, between the staircases, was another pair of doors which Tremayne, crossing, opened without flourish, revealing a vista of gold and pale blue furnishings in the same formal style as the dining-room.

'This is the main drawing room,' he said. 'We share it. We hardly use it. We used it last for that damned party...' He paused. 'Well, as Mackie said, I don't know when we'll have another.'

A pity, I thought. It looked a house made for parties. Tremayne closed the drawing-room door, and pointed straight across the hall.

'That's the front entrance, and those double doors on the right open into Perkin and Mackie's half. We built a new kitchen for them and another new staircase. We planned it as two separate houses, you see, with this big common section between us.'

'It's great,' I said to please him, but also meaning it.

He nodded. 'It divided quite well. No one needs houses this size these days. Take too much heating.' Indeed, it was cold in the hall. 'Most of this was built about nineteen six. Edwardian. Country house of the Windberry family, don't suppose you've ever heard of them.'

'No,' I agreed.

'My father bought the place for peanuts during the Depression. I've lived here all my life.'

'Was your father a trainer also?' I asked.

Tremayne laughed. 'God, no. He inherited a fortune. Never did a day's work. He liked going racing, so he bought a few jumpers, put them in the stables that hadn't been used since cars replaced the carriages and engaged a trainer for them. When I grew up, I just took over the horses. Built another yard, eventually. I've fifty boxes at present, all full.'

He led the way back through the doors to his own domain and closed them behind us.

'That's more or less all,' he said, 'except for the office.'

Once back in his own hall he veered through the last of the doorways there and I followed him into yet another big room in which Dee-Dee looked lost behind a vast desk.

'This used to be the Windberry's billiards room,' Tremayne said. 'When I was a child, it was our playroom.'

'You had brothers and sisters?'

'One sister,' he said briefly, looking at his watch. 'I'll leave you to Dee-Dee. See you later.'

He went away purposefully, and, after the time it would have taken him to replace coat, cap and scarf, the door out to the yard slammed behind him. He was a natural slammer, I thought; there seemed to be no ingredient of ire.

Dee-Dee said, 'How can I help you?' without any great enthusiasm.

'Don't you approve of the biography project?' I asked.

She blinked. 'I didn't say that.'

'You looked it.'

She fiddled lengthily with some papers, eyes down.

'He's been on about it for months,' she said finally. 'It's important to him. I think . . . if you must know . . . that he should have held out for someone better . . .' She hesitated. 'Better *known*, anyway. He met you one day and the next day you're here, and I think it's too *fast*. I suggested that we should at least run a check on you but he said Ronnie Curzon's word was good enough. So you're here.' She looked up, suddenly fierce. 'He deserves the best,' she said.

'Ah.'

'What do you mean by Ah?'

I didn't answer at once but looked round the jumbo

office, seeing the remains of the classical decorative style overlaid by a host of modern bookshelves, filing cabinets, cupboards, copier, fax, computer, telephones, floor safe, television, tapes by the dozen, cardboard boxes, knee-high stacks of newspapers and another corkboard with red drawing-pinned memos. There was an antique kneehole desk with an outsize leather chair, clearly Tremayne's own territory, and on the floor a splatter of overlapping Persian rugs in haphazard patterns and colours covering most of an old grey carpet. Pictures of horses passing winning posts inhabited the walls alongside a bright row of racing silks hanging on pegs.

I ended the visual tour where I'd begun, on Dee-Dee's face.

'The more you help,' I said, 'the more chance he has.'

She compressed her mouth obstinately. 'That doesn't follow.'

'Then the more you obstruct, the less chance he has.'

She stared at me, her antagonism still clear, while logic made hardly a dent in emotion.

She was about forty, I supposed. Thin but not emaciated, from what one could see via the sweater. Good skin, bobbed straight hair, unremarkable features, pink lipstick, no jewellery, small, strong-looking hands. General air of reserve, of holding back. Perhaps that was habitual; perhaps the work of the shit of an amateur jockey who had treated her like muck.

'How long have you worked here?' I asked, voice neutral, merely enquiring.

'Eight years, about.' Straightforward answer.

'What I chiefly need,' I said, 'are cuttings books.'

She almost smiled. 'There aren't any.'

With dismay I protested, 'There must be. He mentioned cuttings.'

'They're not in books, they're in boxes.' She turned her head, nodding directions. 'In that cupboard over there. Help yourself.'

I went across and opened a white-painted door and inside found stacked on shelves from floor to head height a whole array of uniform white cardboard boxes, all like shirt-boxes but about eight inches deep, all with dates written on their ends in black marker ink.

'I re-boxed all the cuttings three or four years ago,' Dee-Dee said. 'Some of the old boxes were falling to bits. The newspaper is yellow and brittle. You'll see.'

'Can I take them all into the dining-room?'

'Be my guest.'

I loaded up four of the boxes and set off with them, and in a minute found her following me.

'Wait,' she said inside the dining-room door, 'mahogany gets scratched easily.'

She went over to a large sideboard and from a drawer drew out a vast green baize cloth which she draped over the whole expanse of the large oval table.

'You can work on that,' she said.

'Thank you.'

I put down the boxes and went to fetch another load, ferrying them until the whole lot was transferred. Dee-Dee meanwhile went back to her desk and her work, which largely consisted of the telephone. I could hear her still talking on and off while I arranged the boxes of cuttings chronologically and took the lid off the first, realising from the date on its end that it had to go back beyond Tremayne; that he hadn't started training when he was a baby. Tattered yellow pieces of newsprint informed me that Mr Loxley Vickers, of Shellerton House, Berkshire, had bought Triple Subject, a six-year-old gelding, for the record sum for a steeplechaser of twelve hundred guineas. A house, an astonished reporter wrote, could be bought for less.

I looked up, smiling, and found Dee-Dee standing in the doorway, hesitantly hovering.

'I've been talking to Fiona Goodhaven,' she said abruptly.

'How is she?'

'All right. Thanks to you, it seems. Why didn't you tell me about your rescue job?'

'It didn't seem important.'

'Are you mad?'

'Well, it didn't seem important in the context of whether I could or couldn't do justice to Tremayne's biography.'

'God Almighty.' She went away but shortly came back. 'If you turn that thermostat,' she said, pointing, 'it will get warmer in here.'

She whisked away again before I could thank her, but I understood that peace had been declared, or, at the very least, hostilities temporarily suspended.

Tremayne returned in time. I heard him talking forcefully into an office telephone and presently he strode into the dining-room to tell me that someone had finally found they had a horse missing.

'It came over the hill from the next village. They're sending a box to pick it up. How are you doing?'

'Reading about your father.'

'A lunatic. Had an obsession about how things would look in his stomach after he'd eaten them. He used to make his butler put an extra serving of everything he was going to eat into a bucket and stir it round. If my father didn't like the look of it, he wouldn't eat his dinner. Drove the cook mad.'

I laughed. 'What about your mother?'

'She'd fallen off the perch by then. He wasn't so bad when she was alive. He went screwy after.'

'How old were you when she ... er ... fell off the perch?'

'Ten. Same age as Gareth when *his* mother finally hopped it. You might say I know what it's like to be Gareth. Except *his* mother's still alive and he sees her sometimes. I can't remember mine very clearly, to be honest.'

After a moment I said, 'How much can I ask you?'

'Ask anything. If I don't want to answer, I'll say so.'

90

'Well ... you said your father inherited a fortune. Did he ... er ... leave it to you?'

Tremayne laughed in his throat. 'A fortune seventy or eighty years ago is not a fortune now. But yes, in a way he did. Left me this house. Taught me the principles of landowning which he'd learnt from *his* father but hardly practised. My father spent; my grandfather accumulated. I'm more like my grandfather, though I never knew him. I tell Gareth sometimes that we can't afford things even if we can. I don't want him to turn out a spender.'

'What about Perkin?'

'Perkin?' For a second Tremayne looked blank. 'Perkin has no money sense at all. Lives in a world of his own. It's no use talking to Perkin about money.'

'What does he do,' I asked, 'in his world?'

Tremayne looked as if his elder son's motivations were a mystery, but somewhere also I sensed a sort of exasperated pride.

'He makes furniture,' he said. 'Designs it. Makes it himself, piece by piece. Chests, tables, screens, anything. Two hundred years from now they will be valuable antiques. That's Perkin's money sense for you.' He sighed. 'Best thing he ever did was marry a smart girl like Mackie. She sells his pieces, makes sure he makes a profit. He used to sell things sometimes for less than they cost to make. Absolutely hopeless.'

'As long as he's happy.'

Tremayne made no comment on his son's state of happiness but asked about my tape recorder.

'Didn't it get wet last night? Won't it be ruined?'

'No. I keep everything in waterproof bags. Sort of habit.'

'Jungles and deserts?' he asked, remembering.

'Mm.'

'Then you go and fetch it, and we'll start. And I'll move the office television in here with the video player so you can watch the races I've won. And if you want any lunch,' he added as an afterthought, 'I nearly always have beef sandwiches; buy them by the fifty, ready-made from the supermarket, and put them in the freezer.'

We both ate mostly-thawed uninteresting beef sandwiches in due course and I thought that even if Tremayne's housekeeping were slightly eccentric, at least he hadn't stirred his food up first in a bucket.

CHAPTER FIVE

At about six-thirty that day I walked down to Shellerton to collect my clothes from the Goodhavens, Fiona
and Harry. Darkness had fallen but it seemed to me
that the air temperature hadn't, and there was less
energy in the wind than in the morning.

I had by that time taped three hours' worth of Tremayne's extraordinary childhood and walked round
with him to inspect his horses at evening stables. At
every one of the fifty doors he had stopped to check
on the inmate's welfare, discussing it briefly with the
lad and dispensing carrots to enquiring muzzles with
little pats and murmurs of affection.

In between times as we moved along the rows he
explained that the horses would now be rugged up
against the frost in wool blankets and duvets, then
covered with jute rugs (like sacking) securely buckled
on. They would be given their main feed of the day
and be shut up for the night to remain undisturbed
until morning.

'One of us walks round last thing at night,' he said,

93

'Bob or Mackie or I, to make sure they're all right. Not kicking their boxes and so on. If they're quiet they're all right, and I don't disturb them.'

Like fifty children, I thought, tucked up in bed.

I'd asked him how many lads he had. Twenty-one, he said, plus Bob Watson, who was worth six, and the travelling head lad and a box driver and a groundsman. With Mackie and Dee-Dee, twenty-seven full-time employees. The economics of training racehorses, he remarked, put the book trade's problems in the shade.

When I reminded him that I was going down to Fiona and Harry's to fetch my belongings he offered me his car.

'I quite like walking,' I said.

'Good God.'

'I'll cook when I get back.'

'You don't have to,' he protested. 'Don't let Gareth talk you into it.'

'I said I would, though.'

'I don't care much what I eat.'

I grinned. 'Maybe that will be just as well. I'll be back soon after Gareth, I expect.'

I'd discovered that the younger son rode his bicycle each morning to the house of his friend Coconut, from where both of them were driven to and from a town ten miles away, as day boys in a mainly boarding school. The hours were long, as always with that type of school: Gareth was never home much before seven, often later. His notice 'BACK FOR GRUB' seemed to be a fixture. He removed it, Tremayne said, only when he knew in the morning that he would be out until bedtime. Then he would leave another message instead, to say where he was going.

'Organised,' I commented.

'Always has been.'

I reached the main street of Shellerton and tramped along to the Goodhavens' house, passing three or four cars in their driveway and walking round to the kitchen door to ring the bell.

After an interval the door was opened by Harry whose expression changed from inhospitable to welcoming by visible degrees.

'Oh, hello, come in. Forgot about you. Fact is, we've had another lousy day in Reading. But home without crashing, best you can say.'

I stepped into the house and he closed the door behind us, at the same time putting a restraining hand on my arm.

'Let me tell you first,' he said. 'Nolan and Lewis are both here. Nolan got convicted of manslaughter. Six months' jail suspended for two years. He won't go behind bars but no one's happy.'

'I don't need to stay,' I said. 'Don't want to intrude.'

'Do me a favour, dilute the atmosphere.'

'If it's like that . . .'

He nodded, removed his hand and walked me through the kitchen into a warm red hallway and on into a pink-and-green chintzy sitting-room beyond.

DICK FRANCIS

Fiona, turning her silver-blond head said, 'Who was it?' and saw me following Harry. 'Oh, good heavens, I'd forgotten.' She came over, holding out a hand, which I shook, an odd formality after our previous meeting.

'These are my cousins,' she said. 'Nolan and Lewis Everard.' She gave me a wide don't-say-anything stare, so I didn't. 'A friend of Tremayne's,' she said to them briefly. 'John Kendall.'

Mackie, sitting exhaustedly in an armchair, waggled acknowledging fingers. Everyone else was standing and holding a glass. Harry pressed a pale gold drink into my hand and left me to discover for myself what lay under the floating ice. Whisky, I found, tasting it.

I had had no mental picture of either Nolan or Lewis but their appearance all the same was a surprise. They were both short, Nolan handsome and hard, Lewis swollen and soft. Late thirties, both of them. Dark hair, dark eyes, dark jaws. I supposed I had perhaps expected them to be like Harry in character if not in appearance, but it was immediately clear that they weren't. In place of Harry's amused urbanity, Nolan's aristocratic-sounding speech was essentially violent and consisted of fifty per cent obscenity. The gist of his first sentence was that he wasn't in the mood for guests.

Neither Fiona nor Harry showed embarrassment, only weary tolerance. If Nolan had spoken like that in court, I thought, it was no wonder he'd been found guilty. One could quite easily imagine him throttling a nymph.

96

Harry said calmly, 'John is writing Tremayne's biography. He knows about the trial and the Top Spin Lob party. He's a friend of ours, and he stays.'

Nolan gave Harry a combative stare which Harry returned with blandness.

'Anyone can know about the trial,' Mackie said. 'It was in all the papers this morning, after all.'

Harry nodded. 'To be continued in reel two.'

'It's not an expletive joke,' Lewis said. 'They took photos of us when we were leaving.' His peevish voice was like his brother's though a shade higher in pitch and, as I progressively discovered, instead of truly offensive obscene words he had a habit of using euphemisms like 'expletive', 'bleep' and 'deleted'. In Harry's mouth it might have been funny; in Lewis's it seemed a form of cowardice.

'Gird up such loins as you have,' Harry told him peaceably. 'The public won't remember by next week.'

Nolan said between four-letter words that everyone that mattered would remember, including the Jockey Club.

'I doubt if they'll actually warn you off,' Harry said. 'It wasn't as if you hadn't paid your bookmaker.'

'Harry!' Fiona said sharply.

'Sorry, m'dear,' murmured her husband, though his lids half veiled his eyes like blinds drawn over his true feelings.

Tremayne and I had each read two accounts of the previous day's proceedings while dealing with the

sandwiches, one in a racing paper, another in a tabloid.
Tremayne's comments had been grunts of disapproval,
while I had learned a few facts left out by the Vickers
family the evening before.

Fiona's cousin Nolan, for starters, was an amateur
jockey ('well-known', in both papers) who often raced
on Fiona's horses, trained by Tremayne Vickers. Nolan
Everard had once briefly been engaged to Magdalene
Mackenzie (Mackie) who had subsequently married
Perkin Vickers, Tremayne's son. 'Sources' had insisted
that the three families, Vickers, Goodhavens and Everards were on friendly terms. The prosecution, not dis-
puting this, had suggested that indeed they had all
closed ranks to shield Nolan from his just deserts.

A demure photograph of Olympia (provided by her
father) showed a fair-haired schoolgirl, immature, an
innocent victim. No one seemed to have explained why
Nolan had said he would strangle the bitch, and now
that I'd heard him talk I was certain those had not
been his only words.

'The question really is,' Fiona said, 'not whether the
Jockey Club will warn him off racecourses altogether,
because I'm sure they won't – they let real villains
go racing – but whether they'll stop him riding as an
amateur.'

Harry said, as if sympathetically, to Nolan, 'It's rather
put paid to your ambitions to be made a *member* of
the Jockey Club, though, hasn't it, old lad?'

Nolan looked blackly furious and remarked with

venom that Harry hadn't helped the case by not swearing to hell and back that Lewis had been comprehensively pissed.

Harry didn't reply except to shrug gently and refill Lewis's glass, which was unquestionably comprehensively empty.

If one made every possible allowance for Nolan, I thought; if one counted the long character-withering ordeal of waiting to know if he were going to prison; if one threw in the stress of having undoubtedly killed a young woman, even by accident; if one added the humiliations he would forever face because of his conviction; if one granted all that, he was still unattractively, viciously ungrateful.

His family and friends had done their best for him. I thought it highly likely that Lewis had in fact perjured himself and that Harry had also, very nearly, in the matter of the alcoholic blackout. Harry had at the last minute shrunk from either a positive opinion or from an outright lie, and I'd have put my money on the second. They had all gone again to court to support Nolan when they would much rather have stayed away.

'I still think you ought to appeal,' Lewis said.

Nolan's pornographic reply was to the effect that his lawyer had advised him not to push his luck, as Lewis very well knew.

'Bleep the lawyer,' Lewis said.

'Appeal courts can *increase* sentences, I believe,'

Fiona said warningly. 'They might cancel the suspension. Doesn't bear thinking about.'

'Olympia's father was incandescent afterwards,' Mackie said gloomily, nodding. 'He wanted Nolan put away for life. Life for a life, that's what he was shouting.'

'You can't just appeal against a sentence because you don't happen to like it,' Harry pointed out. 'There has to be some point of law that was conducted wrongly at the trial.'

Lewis said obstinately, 'If Nolan doesn't appeal it's as good as admitting he's expletive guilty as charged.'

There was a sharp silence all round. They all did think him guilty, though maybe to different degrees. Don't push your luck seemed good pragmatic advice.

I looked speculatively at Mackie, wondering about her sometime engagement to Nolan. She showed nothing for him now but concerned friendship: no lingering love and no hard feelings. Nolan showed nothing but concern for himself.

Fiona said to me, 'Stay to dinner?' and Harry said, 'Do,' but I shook my head.

'I promised to cook for Gareth and Tremayne.'

'Good God,' Harry said.

Fiona said, 'That'll make a change from pizza! They have pizza nine nights out of ten. Gareth just puts one in the microwave, regular as clockwork.'

Mackie put down her glass and stood up tiredly. 'I

think I'll go too. Perkin will be waiting to hear the news.'

Nolan remarked tartly between 'f's that if Perkin had bothered to put in an appearance at Reading he would know the news already.

'He wasn't needed,' Harry said mildly.

'Olympia died in his half of the house,' Lewis said. 'You'd have thought he'd have taken an interest.'

Nolan remembered with below-the-waist indelicacies that Tremayne hadn't supported him either.

'They were both busy,' Mackie said gamely. 'They both work, you know.'

'Meaning we don't?' Lewis asked waspishly.

Mackie sighed. 'Meaning whatever you like.' To me she said, 'Did you come in Tremayne's car?'

'No, walked.'

'Oh! Then . . . do you want a lift home?'

I thanked her and accepted and Harry came with us to see us off.

'Here are your clothes in your bag,' he said, handing it to me. 'Can't thank you enough, you know.'

'Any time.'

'God forbid.'

Harry and I looked at each other briefly in the sort of appreciation that's the beginning of friendship, and I wondered whether he, of all of them, would have been least sorry to see Nolan in the cells.

'He's not always like that,' Mackie said as she steered

101

out of the drive. 'Nolan, I mean. He can be enormously good fun. Or rather, he used to be, before all this.'

'I read in today's paper that you were once engaged to him.'

She half laughed. 'Yes, I was. For about three months, five years ago.'

'What happened?'

'We met in February at a Hunt Ball. I knew who he was. Fiona's cousin, the amateur jockey. I'd been brought up in eventing. Had ponies before I could walk. I told him I sometimes went to stay with Fiona. Small world, he said. We spent the whole evening together and . . . well . . . the whole night. It was sudden, like lightning. Don't tell Perkin. Why does one tell total strangers things one never tells anyone else? Sorry, forget it.'

'Mm,' I said. 'What happened when you woke up?'

'It was like a roller-coaster. We spent all our time together. After two weeks he asked me to marry him and I said yes. Blissful. My feet never touched the ground. I went to the races to watch him . . . he was spell-binding. Kept winning, saying I'd brought him luck.' She stopped, but she was smiling.

'Then what?'

'Then the jumping season finished. We began planning the wedding . . . I don't know. Maybe we just got to know each other. I can't say which day I realised it was a mistake. He was getting irritable. Flashes of rage, really. I just said one day, "It won't work, will it?" and he said, "No," so we fell into each other's arms and had a few tears and I gave him his ring back.'

'You were lucky,' I commented.

'Yes. How do you mean?'

'To come out of it without a fighting marriage and a spiteful divorce.'

'You're so right.' She turned into Tremayne's drive and came to a halt. 'We've been friends ever since, but Perkin has always been uncomfortable with him. See, Nolan is brilliant and brave on horses and Perkin doesn't ride all that well. We don't talk about horses much, when we're alone. It's restful, actually. I tell Perkin he ought to be grateful to Nolan that I was free for *him*, but I suppose he can't help how he feels.'

She sighed, unbuckled her seat belt and stood up out of the car.

'Look,' she said, 'I like you, but Perkin does tend to be jealous.'

'I'll ignore you,' I promised.

She smiled vividly. 'A touch of old-fashioned formality should do the trick.' She began to turn away, and then stopped. 'I'm going in through our own entrance, Perkin's and mine. I'll see how he's doing. See if he's stopped work. We'll probably be along for a drink. We often do, at this time of day.'

'OK.'

She nodded and walked off, and I went round and into Tremayne's side of the house as if I'd lived there

DICK FRANCIS

for ever. Yesterday morning, I thought incredulously, I awoke to Aunty's freeze.

Tremayne in the family room had lit the log fire and poured his gin and tonic and, standing within heating range of the flames, he listened with disillusion to the outcome of Nolan's trial.

'Guilty but unpunished,' he observed. 'New-fangled escape clause.'

'Should the guilty always be punished?'

He looked at me broodingly. 'Is that a character assessment question?'

'I guess so.'

'It's unanswerable, anyway. The answer is, I don't know.' He turned and with a foot pushed a log further into the fire. 'Help yourself to a drink.'

'Thanks. Mackie said they might be along.'

Tremayne nodded, taking it for granted, and in fact she and Perkin came through from the central hall while I was dithering between the available choices of whisky or gin, neither of which I much liked. Perkin solved the liquid question for himself by detouring into the kitchen and reappearing with a glass of Coke.

'What do you actually *like*?' Mackie asked, seeing my hesitation as she poured tonic into gin for herself.

'Wine, I suppose. Red for preference.'

'There will be some in the office. Tremayne keeps it for owners, when they come to see their horses. I'll get it.'

She went without haste and returned with a Bordeaux-shaped bottle and a sensible corkscrew, both of which she handed over.

Tremayne said, as I liberated the Château Kirwan, 'Is that stuff any good?'

'Very,' I said, smelling the healthy cork.

'It's all grape-juice as far as I'm concerned. If you like the stuff, put it on the shopping list.'

'The shopping list,' Mackie explained, 'is a running affair pinned to the kitchen corkboard. Whoever does the shopping takes the list with him. Or her.'

Perkin, slouching in an armchair, said I might as well get used to the idea of doing the shopping myself, particularly if I liked eating.

'Tremayne takes Gareth to the supermarket sometimes,' he said, 'and that's about it. Or Dee-Dee goes, if there's no milk for the coffee three days running.' He looked from me to Mackie. 'I used to think it quite normal until I married a sensible housekeeper.'

Perkin, I thought, as he reaped a smile from his wife, was a great deal more relaxed than on the evening before, though the faint hostility he'd shown towards me was still there. Tremayne asked him his opinion of the verdict on Nolan and Perkin consulted his glass lengthily as if seeking illumination.

'I suppose,' he said finally, 'that I'm glad he isn't in jail.'

It was a pretty ambiguous statement after so much thought, but Mackie looked pleasantly relieved. Only she of the three, it was clear, cared much for Nolan the man. To father and son, having Nolan in jail would have been an inconvenience and an embarrassment which they were happy to avoid.

Looking at the two of them, the differences were as powerful as the likenesses. If one discounted Tremayne's hair, which was grey where Perkin's was brown, and the thickness in Tremayne's neck and body that had come with age, then physically they were of one cloth; but where Tremayne radiated strength, Perkin was soggy; where Tremayne was a leader, Perkin retreated. Tremayne's love was for living horses, Perkin's was for passive wood.

It came as a shock to me to wonder if Tremayne wanted his own achievements written in an inheritable book because Perkin's work would be valuable in two hundred years. Wondered if the strong father felt he had to equal his weaker son. I dismissed the idea as altogether too subtle and as anyway tactless in an employed biographer.

Gareth came home with his usual air of a life lived on the run and eyed me with disapproval as I sat in an armchair drinking wine.

'I thought you said—' he began, and stopped, shrugging, an onset of good manners vying with disappointment.

'I will,' I said.

'Oh, really? Now?'

I nodded.

'Good. Come on, then, I'll show you the freezers.'

'Let him alone,' Mackie said mildly. 'Let him finish his drink.'

Perkin reacted to this harmless remark with irritation. 'As he said he'd cook, let him do it.'

'Of course,' I said cheerfully, getting up. I glanced at Tremayne. 'All right with you?'

'You're all right with me until further notice,' he said, and Perkin didn't like that testimony of approval either, but Gareth did.

'You're home and dry with Dad,' he told me happily, steering me through the kitchen. 'What did you do to him?'

'Nothing.'

'What did you do to me?' he asked himself comically, and answered himself, 'Nothing. I guess that's it. You don't have to do anything, it's just the way you are. The freezers are through here, in the utility room. If you go straight on through the utility room you get to the garage. Through that door there.' He pointed ahead to a heavy-looking door furnished with business-like bolts. 'I keep my bike through there.'

There were two freezers, both upright, both with incredible contents.

'This one,' Gareth said, opening the door, 'is what Dad calls the peezer freezer.'

'Or the pizza frizza?' I suggested.

'Yes, that too.'

It was stacked with pizzas and nothing else, though only half full.

'We eat our way down to the bottom,' Gareth said reasonably, 'then fill up again every two or three months.'

'Sensible,' I commented.

'Most people think we're mad.'

He shut the freezer and opened the other, which proved to contain four packs of beef sandwiches, fifty to a pack. There were also about ten sliced loaves (for toast, Gareth explained), one large turkey (someone gave it to Tremayne for Christmas), pints galore of chocolate ripple ice-cream (Gareth liked it) and a whole lot of bags of ice-cubes for gins and tonic.

Was it for this, I surmised wildly, that I'd sold my soul?

'Well,' I said in amusement, 'what do we have in the larder?'

'What larder?'

'Cupboards, then.'

'You'd better look,' Gareth said, closing the second freezer's door. 'What are you going to make?'

I hadn't the faintest idea; but what Tremayne, Gareth and I ate not very much later was a hot pie made of beef extracted from twenty defrosted sandwiches and chopped small, then mixed with undiluted condensed mushroom soup (a find) and topped with an inch-thick layer of sandwich breadcrumbs fried crisp.

Gareth watched the simple cooking with fascination and I found myself telling him about the techniques I'd been taught of how to live off the countryside without benefit of shops.

'Fried worms aren't bad,' I said.

'You're kidding me.'

'They're packed with protein. Birds thrive on them. And what's so different from eating snails?'

'Could you really live off the land? You yourself?'

'Yes, sure,' I said. 'But you can die of malnutrition eating just rabbits.'

'How do you *know* these things?'

'It's my business, really. My trade.' I told him about the six travel guides. 'The company used to send me to all those places to set up holiday expeditions for real rugged types. I had to learn how to get them out of all sorts of local trouble, especially if they struck disasters like losing all their equipment in raging torrents. I wrote the books and the customers weren't allowed to set off without them. Mind you, I always thought the book on how to survive would have been lost in the raging torrent with everything else, but maybe they would remember some of it, you never know.'

Gareth, helping make breadcrumbs in a blender, said a shade wistfully, 'How did you ever start on something like that?'

'My father was a camping nut. A naturalist. He worked in a bank, really, and still does, but every spare second he would head for the wilds, dragging me and my mother along. Actually I took it for granted, as just a fact of life. Then after college I found it was all pretty useful in the travel trade. So bingo.'

'Does he still go camping? Your father, I mean?'

'No. My mother got arthritis and refused to go any more, and he didn't have much fun without her. He's worked in a bank in the Cayman Islands for three or four years now. It's good for my mother's health.'

Gareth asked simply, 'Where are the Cayman Islands?'

'In the Caribbean, south of Cuba, west of Jamaica.'

'What do you want me to do with these bread-crumbs?'

'Put them in the frying pan.'

'Have *you* ever been to the Cayman Islands?'

'Yes,' I said, 'I went for Christmas. They sent me the fare as a present.'

'You are *lucky*,' Gareth said.

I paused from cutting up the beef. 'Yes,' I agreed, thinking about it. 'Yes, I am. And grateful. And you've got a good father, too.'

He seemed extraordinarily pleased that I should say so, but it seemed to me, unconventional housekeeping or not, that Tremayne was making a good job of his younger son.

Notwithstanding Tremayne's professed lack of interest in food he clearly enjoyed the pie, which three healthy appetites polished off to the last fried crumb. I got promoted instantly to resident chef, which suited me fine. Tomorrow I could do the shopping, Tremayne said, and without ado pulled out his wallet and gave me enough to feed the three of us for a month, though he said it was for a week. I protested it was too much and he kindly told me I had no idea how much things cost. I thought wryly that I knew how much things cost to the last anxious penny, but there was no point in arguing. I stowed the money away and asked them what they didn't like.

'Broccoli,' Gareth said instantly. 'Yuk.'

'Lettuce,' said Tremayne.

Gareth told his father about fried worms and asked me if I had any of the travel guides with me.

'No, sorry, I didn't think of bringing them.'

'Couldn't we possibly get some? I mean, I'd buy them with my pocket money. I'd like to keep them. Are they in the shops?'

'Sometimes, but I could ask the travel company to send a set,' I suggested.

'Yes, do that,' Tremayne said, 'and I'll pay for them. We'd all like to look at them, I expect.'

'But Dad . . .' Gareth protested.

'All right,' Tremayne said, 'get two sets.'

I began to appreciate Tremayne's simple way of solving problems and in the morning, after I'd driven him on the tractor up to the Downs to see the horses exercise, and after orange juice, coffee and toast, I phoned my friend in the travel agency and asked him to organise the books.

'Today?' he said, and I said, 'Yes, please,' and he said

111

he would Red-Star-parcel them by train, if I liked. I
consulted Tremayne who thought it a good idea and
told me to get them sent to Didcot station where I
could go to pick them up when I went in to do the
shopping.

'Fair enough,' the friend said. 'You'll get them this
afternoon.'

'My love to your aunt,' I said, 'and thanks.'

'She'll swoon.' He laughed. 'See you.'

Tremayne began reading the day's papers, both of
which carried the results of the trial. Neither paper
took any particular stance either for or against Nolan,
though both quoted Olympia's father at length. He
came over as a sad, obsessed man whose natural grief
had turned to self-destructive anger and one could feel
sorry for him on many counts. Tremayne read and
grunted and passed no opinion.

The day slowly drifted into a repetition of the one
before. Dee-Dee came into the kitchen for coffee and
instructions and when Tremayne had gone out again
with his second lot of horses I returned to the boxes
of clippings in the dining-room.

I decided to reverse yesterday's order; to start at the
most recent clippings and work backwards.

It was Dee-Dee, I had discovered, who cut the sections out of the newspapers and magazines, and certainly she had been more zealous than whoever had
done it before her, as the boxes for the last eight years
were much fuller.

I laid aside the current box as it was still almost empty and worked through from January to December of the previous year, which had been a good one for Tremayne, embracing not only his Grand National win with Top Spin Lob but many other successes important enough to get the racing hacks excited. Tremayne's face smiled steadily from clipping after clipping including, inappropriately, those dealing with the death of the girl, Olympia.

Drawn irresistibly, I read a whole batch of accounts of that death from a good many different papers, the number of them suggesting that someone had gone out and bought an armful of everything available. In total, they told me not much more than I already knew, except that Olympia was twice described as a 'jockette', a word I somehow found repulsive. It appeared that she had ridden in several ladies' races at point-to-point meetings which one paper, to help the ignorant, described as 'the days the hunting classes stop chasing the fox and chase each other instead'. Olympia the jockette had been twenty-three, had come from a 'secure suburban background' and had worked as an instructor in a riding-school in Surrey. Her parents, not surprisingly, were said to be 'distraught'.

Dee-Dee came into the dining-room offering more coffee and saw what I was reading.

'That Olympia was a sex-pot bimbo,' she remarked flatly. 'I was there at the party and you could practically

DICK FRANCIS

smell it. Secure little suburban riding instructor, my foot.'

'Really?'

'Her father made her out to be a sweet innocent little saint. Perhaps he even believes it. Nolan never said any different because it wouldn't have helped him, so no one told the truth.'

'What was the truth?'

'She had no underclothes on,' Dee-Dee said calmly. 'She wore only a long scarlet strapless dress slit halfway up her thigh. You ask Mackie. She knows, she tried to revive her.'

'Er . . . quite a lot of women don't wear underclothes,' I said.

'Is that a fact?' She gave me an ironic look.

'My blushing days are over.'

'Well, do you or don't you want any coffee?'

'Yes, please.'

She went out to the kitchen and I continued reading clippings, progressing from 'no action on the death at Shellerton House' to 'Olympia's father brings private prosecution' and 'Magistrates refer Nolan Everard case to Crown Court'. A *sub judice* silence then descended and the clippings stopped.

It was after a bunch of end-of-jumping-season statistics that I came across an oddity from a Reading paper published on a Friday in June.

'Girl groom missing', read the headline, and there

was an accompanying photo of Tremayne, still looking cheerful.

> Angela Brickell, 17, employed as a 'lad' by prominent racehorse trainer Tremayne Vickers, failed to turn up for work on Tuesday afternoon and hasn't been seen in the stables since. Vickers says lads leave without notice all too often, but he is puzzled that she didn't ask for pay due to her. Anyone knowing Angela Brickell's whereabouts is asked to get in touch with the police.

Angela Brickell's parents, like Olympia's, were reported to be 'distraught'.

CHAPTER SIX

By the following week, Angela Brickell's disappearance had been taken up by the national dailies who all mentioned the death of Olympia at Shellerton two months earlier but drew no significant conclusions.

Angela, I learned, lived in a stable hostel with five other girls who described her as 'moody'. An indistinct photograph of her showed the face of a child, not a young woman, and pleas to 'Find This Girl' could realistically never have been successful if they depended on recognising her from her likeness in newsprint.

There was no account, in fact, of her having been found, and after a week or so the clippings about her stopped.

There were no cuttings at all for July, when it seemed the jump racing fraternity took a holiday, but they began again with various accounts of the opening of the new season in Devon in August. 'Vickers' Victories Continue!'

Nolan had ridden a winner on one of Fiona's horses:

116

'the well-known amateur now out on bail facing charges of assault resulting in death . . .'

In early September Nolan had hit the news again, this time in giving evidence at a Jockey Club enquiry in defence of Tremayne, who stood accused of doping one of his horses.

With popping eyes, since Tremayne to me even on such short acquaintance seemed the last person to put his whole way of life in jeopardy for so trivial a reason, I read that one of his horses had tested positive to traces of the stimulants theobromine and caffeine, prohibited substances.

The horse in question had won an amateurs' race back in May. Belonging to Fiona, it had been ridden by Nolan, who said he had no idea how the drugs had been administered. He had himself been in charge of the horse that day since Tremayne hadn't attended the meeting. Tremayne had sent the animal in the care of his head travelling lad and a groom, and neither the head lad nor Tremayne knew how the drugs had been administered. Mrs Fiona Goodhaven could offer no explanation either, though she and her husband had attended and watched the race.

The Jockey Club's verdict at the end of the day had been that there was no way of determining who had given the drugs or how, since they couldn't any longer question the groom who had been in charge of the horse as she, Angela Brickell, could not be found.

Angela Brickell. Good grief, I thought.

Tremayne had nevertheless been adjudged guilty as charged and had been fined fifteen hundred pounds. A slapped wrist, it seemed.

Upon leaving the enquiry Tremayne had shrugged and said, 'These things happen.'

The drug theobromine, along with caffeine, commented the reporter, could commonly be found in chocolate. Well, well, I thought. Never a dull moment in the racing industry.

The rest of the year seemed an anti-climax after that, though there had been a whole procession of notable wins. 'The Stable in Form' and 'More Vim to Vickers' and 'Loadsa Vicktories', according to which paper or magazine one read.

I finished the year and was simply sitting and thinking when Tremayne breezed in with downland air still cool on his coat.

'How are you doing?' he said.

I pointed to the pile of clippings out of their box. 'I was reading about last year. All those winners.'

He beamed. 'Couldn't put a foot wrong. Amazing. Sometimes things just go right. Other years, you get the virus, horses break down, owners die, you have a ghastly time. All the luck of the game.'

'Did Angela Brickell ever turn up?' I asked.

'Who? Oh, her. No, silly little bitch, God knows where she made off to. Every last person in the racing world knows you mustn't give chocolate to horses in training. Pity really, most of them love it. Everybody also knows a Mars Bar here or there isn't going to make a horse win a race, but there you are, by the rules chocolate's a stimulant, so bad luck.'

'Would the girl have got into trouble if she'd stayed?'

He laughed. 'From me, yes. I'd have sacked her, but she'd gone before I heard the horse had tested positive. It was a routine test; they test most winners.' He paused and sat down on a chair across the table from me, staring thoughtfully at a heap of clippings. 'It could have been anyone, you know. Anyone here in the yard. Or Nolan himself, though God knows why he should. Anyway,' he shrugged, 'it often happens because the testing techniques are now so highly developed. They don't automatically warn off trainers any more, thank God, when odd things turn up in the analysis. It has to be gross, has to be beyond interpretation as an accident. But it's still a risk every trainer runs. Risk of crooks. Risk of plain malice. You take what precautions you can and pray.'

'I'll put that in the book, if you like.'

He looked at me assessingly. 'I got me a good writer after all, didn't I?'

I shook my head. 'You got one who'll do his best.'

He smiled with what looked like satisfaction and after lunch (beef sandwiches) we got down to work again on taping his early life with his eccentric father. Tremayne seemed to have soared unharmed over such psychological trifles as being rented out in Leicestershire as a harness and tack cleaner to a fox-hunting

119

family and a year later as stable boy to a polo player in Argentina.

'But that was child abuse,' I protested.

Tremayne chuckled unconcernedly. 'I didn't get buggered, if that's what you mean. My father hired me out, picked up all I earned and gave me a crack or two with his cane when I said it wasn't fair. Well, it wasn't fair. He told me that that was a valuable lesson, to learn that things weren't fair. Never expect fairness. I'm telling you what he told me, but you're lucky, I won't beat it into you.'

'Will you pay me?'

He laughed deeply. 'You've got Ronnie Curzon looking after that.' His amusement continued. 'Did your father ever beat you?'

'No, he didn't believe in it.'

'Nor do I, by God. I've never beaten Perkin, nor Gareth. Couldn't. I remember what it felt like. But then, see, he did take me with him to Argentina and all round the world. I saw a lot of things most English boys don't. I missed a lot of school. He was mad, no doubt, but he gave me a priceless education and I wouldn't change anything.'

'You had a pretty tough mind,' I said.

'Sure.' He nodded. 'You need it in this life.'

You might need it, I reflected, but tough minds weren't regulation issue. Many children would have disintegrated where Tremayne had learned and thrived.

I tended to feel at home with stoicism and, increasingly, with Tremayne.

About mid-afternoon, when we stopped taping, he lent me his Volvo to go to Didcot to fetch the parcel of books from the station and to do the household shopping, advising me not to slide into any ditches if I could help it. The roads, however, were marginally better and the air not so brutally cold, though the forecasters still spoke of more days' frost. I shopped with luxurious abandon for food and picked up the books, getting back to Shellerton while Tremayne was still out in his yard at evening stables.

He came into the house with Mackie, both of them stamping their feet and blowing onto their fingers as they discussed the state of the horses.

'You'd better ride Selkirk in the morning,' Tremayne said to her. 'He's a bit too fresh these days for his lad.'

'Right.'

'And I forgot to tell Bob to get the lads to put two rugs on their mounts if they're doing only trotting exercise.'

'I'll remind him.'

'Good.'

He saw me in the kitchen as I was finishing stowing the stores and asked if the books had arrived. They had, I said.

'Great. Bring them into the family room. Come on, Mackie, gin and tonic.'

The big logs in the family room fireplace never

entirely went cold; Tremayne kicked the embers smartly together, adding a few small sticks and a fresh chunk of beech to renew the blaze. The evening developed as twice before, Perkin arriving as if on cue and collecting his Coke.

With flattering eagerness Tremayne opened the package of books and handed some of them to Mackie and Perkin. So familiar to me, they seemed to surprise the others, though I wasn't sure why.

Slightly larger than paperbacks, they were more the size of video tapes and had white shiny hard covers with the title in various bright black-edged colours: *Return Safe from the Jungle* in green, *Return Safe from the Desert* in orange, *Return Safe from the Sea* in blue, *Return Safe from the Ice* in purple, *Return Safe from Safari* in red, *Return Safe from the Wilderness* in a hot rusty brown.

'I'll be damned,' Tremayne said. 'Real books.'

'What did you expect?' I asked.

'Well . . . pamphlets, I suppose. Thin paperbacks, perhaps.'

'The travel agency wanted them glossy,' I explained, 'and also useful.'

'They must have taken a lot of work,' Mackie observed, turning the pages of *Ice* and looking at illustrations.

'There's a good deal of repetition in them, to be honest,' I said. 'I mean, quite a lot of survival techniques are the same wherever you find yourself.'

'Such as what?' Perkin asked, faintly belligerent as usual.

'Lighting fires, finding water, making a shelter. Things like that.'

'The books are fascinating,' Mackie said, now looking at *Sea*, 'but how often do people get marooned on desert islands these days?'

I smiled. 'Not often. It's just the *idea* of survival that people like. There are schools where people on holiday go for survival courses. Actually the most lethal place to be is up a British mountainside in the wrong clothes in a cold mist. A fair number of people each year don't survive *that*.'

'Could you?' Perkin asked.

'Yes, but I wouldn't be up there in the wrong clothes in the first place.'

'Survival begins before you set out,' Tremayne said, reading the first page of *Jungle*: he looked up, amused, quoting, ' "Survival is a frame of mind." '

'Yes.'

'I have it,' he said.

'Indeed you do.'

All three of them went on reading the books with obvious interest, dipping into the various sections at random, flicking over pages and stopping to read more: vindicating, I thought, the travel agency's contention that the back-to-nature essentials of staying alive held irresistible attractions for ultra-cosseted sophisticates, just as long as they never had to put them into practice in bitter earnest.

Gareth erupted into the peaceful scene like a rehearsing poltergeist.

'What are you all so busy with?' he demanded, and then spotted the books, 'Boy, oh *boy*. They've come!'

He grabbed up *Return from the Wilderness* and plunged in, and I sat drinking wine and wondering if I would ever see four people reading *Long Way Home*.

'This is pretty earthy stuff,' Mackie said after a while, laying her book down. 'Skinning and de-gutting animals, ugh.'

'You'd do it if you were starving,' Tremayne told her.

'I'd do it *for* you,' Gareth said.

'So would I,' said Perkin.

'Then I'll arrange not to get stranded anywhere without you both.' She was teasing, affectionate. 'And I'll stay in camp and grind the corn.' She put a hand to her mouth in mock dismay. 'Dear heaven, may feminists forgive me.'

'It's pretty boring about all these jabs,' Gareth complained, not being interested in gender typing.

' "Better the jabs than the diseases", it says here,' Tremayne said.

'Oh well, then.'

'And you've had tetanus jabs already.'

'I guess so,' Gareth agreed. He looked at me. 'Have you had all these jabs?'

'Afraid so.'

'Tetanus?'

'Especially.'

'There's an awful lot about first aid,' he said, turning pages. ' "How to stop wounds bleeding ... pressure points," A whole map of arteries. "How to deal with poisons ... swallow *charcoal*"!' He looked up. 'Do you mean it?'

'Sure,' I said. 'Scrape it into water and drink it. The carbon helps take some sorts of poison harmlessly through the gut, if you're lucky.'

'Good God,' Tremayne said.

His younger son went on reading. 'It says here you can drink urine if you distil it.'

'Gareth!' Mackie said, disgusted.

'Well, that's what it says. "Urine is sterile and cannot cause diseases. Boil it and condense the steam which will then be pure distilled water, perfectly safe to drink." '

'John, really!' Mackie protested.

'It's true,' I said, smiling. 'Lack of water is a terrible killer. If you've a fire but no water, you now know what to do.'

'I couldn't.'

'Survival is a frame of mind,' Tremayne repeated. 'You never know what you can do until you have to.'

Perkin asked me, 'Have you ever drunk it?'

'Distilled water?'

'You know what I mean.'

I nodded. 'Yes, I have. To test it for the books. And

125

I've distilled all sorts of other things too. Filthy jungle water. Wet mud. Sea water, particularly. If the starter liquid is watery and not fermenting, the steam is pure H_2O. And when sea water boils dry you have salt left, which is useful.'

'What if the starter liquid *is* fermenting?' Gareth asked.

'The steam is alcohol.'

'Oh yes, I'm supposed to have learned that in school.'

'Gin and tonic in the wilderness?' Tremayne suggested.

I said with enjoyment, 'I could certainly get you *drunk* in the wilderness, but actual gin would depend on juniper bushes, and tonic on chinchona trees for quinine, and I don't think they'd both grow in the same place, but you never know.' I paused. 'Ice cubes might be a problem in the rain forest.'

Tremayne laughed deep in his chest. 'Did you ever rely on all this stuff to save your life?'

'Not entirely,' I said. 'I lived by these techniques for weeks at a time, but someone always knew roughly where I was. I had escape routes. I was basically testing what was practicable and possible and sensible in each area where the agency wanted to set up adventure holidays. I've never had to survive after a plane crash in the mountains, for instance.'

There had been a plane crash in the Andes in 1972 when people had eaten other people in order to stay alive. I didn't think I would tell Mackie, though.

'But,' she said, 'did things ever go wrong?'

'Sometimes.'

'Like what? Do say.'

'Well . . . like insect bites and eating things that disagreed with me.'

They all looked as if these were everyday affairs, but I'd been too ill a couple of times to care to remember.

I said with equal truth but more drama, 'A bear smashed up my camp in Canada once and hung around it for days. I couldn't reach anything I needed. It was a shade fraught there for a bit.'

'Do you mean it?' Gareth was open-mouthed.

'Nothing happened,' I said. 'The bear went away.'

'Weren't you afraid he would come back?'

'I packed up and moved somewhere else.'

'Wow,' Gareth said.

'Bears eat people,' his brother told him repressively. 'Don't get any ideas about copying John.'

Tremayne looked at his sons mildly. 'Have either of you ever heard of vicarious enjoyment?'

'No,' Gareth said. 'What is it?'

'Dreaming,' Mackie suggested.

Perkin said, 'Someone else does the suffering for you.'

'Let Gareth dream,' Tremayne said, nodding. 'It's natural. I don't suppose for one moment he'll go chasing bears.'

'Boys do stupid things, Gareth included.'

127

DICK FRANCIS

'Hey,' his brother protested. 'Who's talking? Who climbed on to the roof and couldn't get down?'

'Shut your face,' Perkin said.

'Do give it a rest, you two,' Mackie said wearily. 'Why do you always quarrel?'

'We're nothing compared with Lewis and Nolan,' Perkin said. 'They can get really vicious.'

Mackie said reflectively, 'They haven't quarrelled since Olympia died.'

'Not in front of us,' her husband agreed, 'but you don't know what they've said in private.'

Diffidently, because it wasn't really my business, I asked, 'Why do they quarrel?'

'Why does anyone?' Tremayne said. 'But those two envy each other. You met them last night, didn't you? Nolan has the looks and the dash, Lewis is a drunk with brains. Nolan has courage and is thick, Lewis is a physical disaster but when he's sober he's a whiz at making money. Nolan is a crack shot, Lewis misses every pheasant he aims at. Lewis would like to be the glamorous amateur jockey and Nolan would like to be upwardly disgustingly rich. Neither will ever manage it, but that doesn't stop the envy.'

'You're too hard on them,' Mackie murmured.

'But you know I'm right.'

She didn't deny it, but said, 'Perhaps the Olympia business has drawn them together.'

'You're a sweet young woman,' Tremayne told her. 'You see good in everyone.'

128

Perkin said, 'Hands off my wife,' in what might or might not have been a joke. Tremayne chose to take it lightly, and I thought he must be well used to his son's acute possessiveness.

He turned from Perkin to me and with a swift change of subject said, 'How well do you ride?'

'Er . . .' I said, 'I haven't ridden a racehorse.'

'What then?'

'Hacks, dude ranch horses, pony trekking, arab horses in the desert.'

'Hm.' He pondered. 'Care to ride my hack with the string in the morning? Let's see what you can do.'

'OK.' I must have sounded half-hearted, because he pounced on it.

'Don't you want to?' he demanded.

'Yes, please.'

'Right, then,' he nodded. 'Mackie, tell Bob to have Touchy saddled up for John, if you're out in the yard before me.'

'Right.'

'Touchy won the Cheltenham Gold Cup,' Gareth told me.

'Oh, did he?' Some hack.

'Don't worry,' Mackie said, smiling, 'he's fifteen now and almost a gentleman.'

'Dumps people regularly on Fridays,' Gareth said.

*

129

With apprehension, I went out into the yard on the following morning, Friday, in jodhpurs, boots, ski-jacket and gloves. I hadn't sat on a horse of any sort for almost two years and, whatever Mackie might say, my idea of a nice quiet return to the saddle wasn't a star steeplechaser, pensioned or not.

Touchy was big with bulging muscles; he would have to be, I supposed, to carry Tremayne's weight. Bob Watson gave me a grin, a helmet and a leg-up, and it seemed a fair way down to the ground.

Oh well, I thought. Enjoy it. I'd said I could ride: time to try and prove it. Tremayne, watching me appraisingly with his head on one side, told me to take my place behind Mackie who would be leading the string. He himself would be driving the tractor. I could take Touchy up the all-weather gallop at a fast canter when everyone else had worked.

'All right,' I said.

He smiled faintly and walked away and I collected the reins and a few thoughts and tried not to make a fool of myself.

Bob Watson appeared again at my elbow.

'Get him anchored when you set off up the gallop,' he said, 'or he'll pull your arms out.'

'Thanks,' I said, but he had already moved on.

'All out,' he was saying, and out they all came from the boxes, circling in the lights, breathing plumes, moving in circles as Bob threw the lads up, all as before, only now I was part of it, now on the canvas in the picture, as if alive in a Munnings painting, extra-ordinary.

I followed Mackie out of the yard and across the road and on to the downland track, and found that Touchy knew what to do from long experience but would respond better to pressure with the calf rather than to strong pulls on his tough old mouth.

Mackie looked back a few times as if to make sure I hadn't evaporated and watched while I circled with the others as it grew light and we waited for Tremayne to reach the top of the hill.

Drifting alongside, she asked, 'Where did you learn to ride?'

'Mexico,' I said.

'You were taught by a Spaniard!'

'Yes, I was.'

'And he had you riding with your arms folded?'

'Yes, how do you know?'

'I thought so. Well, tuck your elbows in on old Touchy.'

'Thanks.'

She smiled and went off to arrange the order in which the string should exercise up the gallop.

Snow still lay thinly over everything and it was another clear morning, stingingly, beautifully cold. January dawn on the Downs; once felt, never forgotten.

Bit by bit the string set off up the wood-chippings track until only Mackie and I were left.

'I'll go with you on your right,' she said, coming up behind me. 'Then Tremayne can see how you ride.'

'Thanks very much,' I said ironically.

'You'll do fine.'

She swayed suddenly in the saddle and I put out a hand to steady her.

'Are you OK?' I asked anxiously. 'You should have rested more after that bang on the head.' She was pale. Huge-eyed. Alarming.

'No . . . I . . .' She took an unsteady breath. 'I just felt . . . oh . . . oh . . .'

She swayed again and looked near to fainting. I leaned across and put my right arm round her waist, holding her tight to prevent her falling. Her weight sagged against me limply until I was supporting her entirely, and since she had an arm through her reins her horse was held close to mine, their heads almost touching.

I took hold of her reins in my left hand and simply held her tight with my right, and her horse moved his rump sideways away from me until she slid off out of her saddle altogether and finished half lying across my knee and Touchy's withers, held only by my grasp.

I couldn't let her fall and I couldn't dismount without dropping her, so with both hands I pulled and heaved her up onto Touchy until she was half sitting and half lying across the front of my saddle, held in my arms. Touchy didn't much like it and Mackie's horse had backed away sharply to the length of his reins and was on the edge of bolting, and I began to wonder if I should just let him go free in spite of the icy dangers everywhere lurking. I might then manage to walk Touchy back to the stable with his double cargo and we might yet not have a worse disaster than Mackie's unconsciousness. The urgency of getting help for her made more things possible than I could have thought.

Touchy got an unmistakable signal from my leg and obediently turned towards home. I decided I would hold on to Mackie's horse as long as it would come too, and as if by magic he got the going-home message and decided not to object any further.

We had gone perhaps three paces in this fashion when Mackie woke up and came to full consciousness as if a light had been switched on.

'What happened . . .?'

'You fainted. Fell this way.'

'I can't have done.' But she could see that she must have. 'Let me down,' she said. 'I feel awfully sick.'

'Can you stand?' I asked worriedly. 'Let me take you home like this.'

'No.' She rolled against me onto her stomach and slid down slowly until her feet were on the ground. 'What a stupid thing to do,' she said. 'I'm all right now, I am really. Give me my reins.'

'Mackie . . .'

She turned away from me suddenly and vomited convulsively onto the snow.

133

I hopped down off Touchy with the reins of both horses held fast and tried to help her.

'God,' she said weakly, searching for a tissue, 'must have eaten something.'

'Not my cooking.'

'No.' She found the tissue and smiled a fraction. She and Perkin hadn't stayed for the previous evening's grilled chicken. 'I haven't felt well for days.'

'Concussion,' I said.

'No, even before that. Tension over the trial, I suppose.' She took a few deep breaths and blew her nose. 'I feel perfectly all right now. I don't understand it.'

She was looking at me in puzzlement and I quite clearly saw the thought float into her head and transfigure her face into wonderment and hope ... and joy.

'Oh!' she said ecstatically. 'Do you think ... I mean, I've been feeling sick every morning this week ... and after two years of trying I'd stopped expecting anything to happen, and anyway, I didn't know it could make you feel so ill right at the beginning ... I mean, I didn't even *suspect* ... I'm always wildly irregular.' She stopped and laughed. 'Don't tell Tremayne. Don't tell Perkin. I'll wait a bit first, to make sure. But I *am* sure. It explains all sorts of odd things that have happened this last week. Like my nipples itching. My hormones must be rioting. I can't believe it. I think I'll burst.'

I thought that I had never before seen such pure uncomplicated happiness in anyone, and was tremendously glad for her.

'What a revelation!' she said. 'Like an angel announcing it . . . if that's not blasphemous.'

'Don't hope too much,' I said cautiously.

'Don't be silly. I *know*.' She seemed to wake suddenly to our whereabouts. 'Tremayne will be going mad because we haven't appeared.'

'I'll ride up and tell him you're not well and have gone home.'

'No, definitely not. I *am* well. I've never felt better in my whole life. I am gloriously and immensely well. Give me a leg-up.'

I told her she needed to rest but she obstinately refused, and in the end I bowed to her judgment and lifted her lightly into the saddle, scrambling up myself onto Touchy's broad back. She shook up her reins as if nothing had happened and set off up the wood chippings at a medium canter, glancing back for me to follow. I joined her expecting to go the whole way at that conservative pace but she quickened immediately I reached her and I could hardly hang back and say hold on a minute, I haven't done this in a while and could easily fall off. Instead, I tucked in my elbows as instructed and relied on luck.

Towards the end Mackie kicked her horse into a frank gallop and it was at that speed that we both passed Tremayne. I was peripherally aware of him standing four-square on the small observation mound, though all my direct attention was acutely focused on balance, grip and what lay ahead between Touchy's ears.

Touchy, I thanked heaven, slowed when Mackie slowed and brought himself to a good-natured halt without dumping his rider, Friday or not. I was breathless and also exhilarated and thought I could easily get hooked on Touchy after a fix or two more like that.

'Where the hell did you get to?' Tremayne enquired of me, joining us and the rest of the string. 'I thought you'd chickened out,'

'We were just talking,' Mackie said.

Tremayne looked at her now glowing face and probably drew the wrong conclusion but made no further comment. He told everyone to walk back down the gallop and dismount and lead them the last part of the way, as usual.

Mackie, taking her place at the head, asked me to ride at the back, to make sure everyone returned safely, which I did. Tremayne's tractor followed slowly, at a distance.

He came stamping into the kitchen where I was fishing out orange juice and without preamble demanded, 'What were you and Mackie talking about?'

'She'll tell you,' I said, smiling.

He said belligerently, 'Mackie's off limits.'

I put down the orange juice and straightened, not knowing quite what to say.

'If you mean do I fancy Mackie,' I said, 'then yes, she's a great girl. But off limits is right. We were not flirting, chatting up, or whatever else you care to call it. *Not*.'

After a grudging minute he said, 'All right then,' and I thought that in his way he was as possessive of Mackie as Perkin was.

A short while later, munching the toast I'd made for him, he seemed to have forgotten it.

'You can ride out every morning,' he said, 'if you'd like.'

He could see I was pleased. I said, 'I'd like it very much.'

'Settled, then.'

The day passed in the way that had become routine: clippings, beef sandwiches, taping, evening drinks, Gareth home, cook the dinner. Dee-Dee's distrust of me had vanished; Perkin's hadn't. Tremayne seemed to have accepted my assurance of the morning, and Mackie smiled into her plain tonic and carefully avoided my eyes for fear of revealing that a secret lay between us.

On Saturday morning I rode Touchy again but Mackie didn't materialise, having phoned Tremayne to say she wasn't well. She and Perkin appeared in the kitchen during breakfast, he with an arm round her shoulders in a supremely proprietary way.

'We've something to tell you,' Perkin said to Tremayne.

'Oh, yes?' Tremayne was busy with some papers.

'Yes. Do pay attention. We're having a baby.'

'We think so,' Mackie said.

Tremayne paid attention abruptly and was clearly profoundly delighted. Not an over-demonstrative man he didn't leap up to embrace them but literally purred in his throat like a cat and beat the table with his fist. Son and daughter-in-law had no difficulty in reading the signals and looked smugly pleased with themselves, sitting down, drinking coffee and working out that the birth would occur in September, but they weren't quite sure of the date.

Mackie gave me a shy smile which Perkin forgave. Each of them looked more in love with the other, more relaxed, as if the earlier failure to conceive had caused tension between them, now relieved.

After that excitement I laboured all morning again on the clippings, unsustained by cups from Dee-Dee, who didn't work on Saturdays. Gareth went to Saturday morning school and pinned a second message on the corkboard – 'FOOTBALL MATCH PM' – leaving 'BACK FOR GRUB' in place.

Tremayne, cursing the persistent absence of racing even on television, taped the saga of his younger life up to the time he accompanied his father to a brothel.

'My father wouldn't have anybody but the madam and she said she'd retired long ago but she accommodated him in the end. Couldn't resist him, the mad old charmer.'

In the evening I fed the three of us on lamb chops, peas and potatoes in their skins and on Sunday morning Fiona and Harry came to the stables to see her horses and drink with Tremayne afterwards in the family room. Nolan came with them, but not Lewis. An aunt of Harry's, another Mrs Goodhaven, tagged quietly along. Mackie, Perkin and Gareth congregated as if for a normal ritual.

Mackie couldn't keep her good news to herself and Fiona and Harry hugged her while Perkin looked important and Nolan gave half-hearted congratulations. Tremayne opened champagne.

At about that time, ten miles away in lonely woodland, a gamekeeper came across what was left of Angela Brickell.

CHAPTER SEVEN

The discovery made no impact on Shellerton on that Sunday because at first no one knew whose bones lay among the dead brambles and the dormant oaks.

The gamekeeper went home to his Sunday lunch and telephoned the local police after he'd eaten, feeling that as the bones were old it wouldn't matter if they waited one hour longer.

In Tremayne's house, when the toasts to the future Vickers had been drunk, Gareth showed Fiona a couple of the travel guides and Fiona in astonishment showed Harry. Nolan picked up *Safari* as if absent-mindedly and said that no one but a bloody fool would go hunting tigers in Africa.

'There aren't any tigers in Africa,' Gareth said.

'That's right. He'd be a bloody fool.'

'Oh ... it's a joke,' Gareth said, obviously feeling that it was he who'd been made a fool of. 'Very funny.'

Nolan, though the shortest man there, physically

dominated the room, eclipsing even Tremayne. His strong animal vigour and powerful saturnine features seemed to charge the very air with static, as if his presence alone could generate sparks. One could see how Mackie had been struck by lightning. One could see how Olympia might have died by violent accident. One's reactions to Nolan had little to do with reason, all with instinct.

Harry's aunt was looking into *Ice* in a faintly superior way as if confronted with a manifestation of the lower orders.

'How frightfully *rugged*,' she said, her voice as languid as Harry's but without the God-given amusement.

'Er,' Harry said to me. 'I didn't introduce you properly. I must present you to my aunt, Erica Goodhaven. She's a writer.'

There was a subterranean flood of mischief in his eyes. Fiona glanced at me with a hint of a smile and I thought both of them looked as though I were about to be thrown to the lions for their entertainment. Anticipation of enjoyment, loud and clear.

'Erica,' Harry said, 'John wrote these books.'

'And a novel,' Tremayne said defensively, coming to an aid I didn't realise I needed. 'It's going to be published. And he's writing my biography.'

'A *novel*,' Harry's aunt said, in the same way as before.

'Going to be published. How *interesting*. I, also, write novels. Under my unmarried name, Erica Upton.'

141

Thrown to a literary lion, I perceived. A real one, a lioness. Erica Upton's five-star prize-winning reputation was for erudition, elegant syntax, esoteric backgrounds, elegiac characters and a profound understanding of incest.

'Your aunt?' I said to Harry.

'By marriage.'

Tremayne refilled my glass with champagne as if I would need it and muttered under his breath, 'She'll eat you.'

From across the room she did look faintly predatory at that moment, though was otherwise a slender, intense-looking, grey-haired woman in a grey wool dress with flat shoes and no jewellery. A quintessential aunt, I thought; except that most people's aunts weren't Erica Upton.

'What is your novel *about?*' she enquired of me. Her voice was patronising but I didn't mind that: she was entitled to it.

The others all waited with her to hear my answer. Incredible, I thought, that nine people in one room weren't carrying on noisy separate conversations, as usually happened.

'It's about survival,' I said politely.

Everyone listened. Everyone always listened to Erica Upton.

'What sort of survival?' she asked. 'Medical? Economic? Creative?'

'It's about some travellers cut off by an earthquake. About how they coped. It's called *Long Way Home*.'

'How *quaint*,' she said.

She wasn't intending to be outright offensive, I thought. She seemed merely to know that her own work was on a summit I would never reach, and in that she was right. All the same I felt again the mild recklessness that I had on Touchy: even if I lacked confidence, relax and have a go.

'My agent says,' I said neutrally, 'that *Long Way Home* is really about the spiritual consequences of deprivation and fear.'

She knew a gauntlet when she heard one. I saw the stiffening in her body and suspected it in her mind.

She said, 'You are too young to write with authority of spiritual consequences. Too young for your soul to have been tempered. Too young to have learned the intensity of understanding that comes only through deep adversity.'

Was that true, I wondered? How old was old enough?

I said, 'Shouldn't contentment be allowed its insights?'

'It has none. Insight grows best on stony ground. Unless you have suffered or are poor or can tap into melancholy, you have defective perception.'

I rolled with that one. Sought for a response.

'I *am* poor,' I said. 'Well, fairly. Poor enough to perceive that poverty is the enemy of moral strength.'

143

She peered at me as if measuring a prey for the pounce.

'You are a lightweight person,' she said, 'if you have no conception of the moral strength of redemption and atonement in penury.'

I swallowed. 'I don't seek sainthood. I seek insight through a combination of imagination and common sense.'

'You are not a serious writer.' A dire accusation; her worst.

'I write to entertain,' I said.

'I,' she said simply, 'write to enlighten.'

I could find no possible answer. I said wryly, with a bow, 'I am defeated.'

She laughed with pleasure, her muscles loosening. The lion had devoured the sacrifice and all was well. She turned away to begin talking to Fiona, and Harry made his way to my side, watching me dispatch my champagne with a gulp.

'You didn't do too badly,' he said. 'Nice brisk duel.'

'She ran me through.'

'Oh yes. Never mind. Good sport, though.'

'You set it up.'

He grinned. 'She phoned this morning. She comes occasionally for lunch, so I told her to beetle over. Couldn't resist it.'

'What a pal.'

'Be honest. You enjoyed it.'

I sighed. 'She outguns me by far.'

'She's more than twice your age.'

'That makes it worse.'

'Seriously,' he said, as if he thought my ego needed patching, 'these survival guides are pretty good. Do you mind if we take a few of them home?'

'They're Tremayne's and Gareth's, really.'

'I'll ask them then.' He looked at me shrewdly. 'Nothing wrong with your courage, is there?'

'How do you mean?'

'You took her on. You didn't have to.'

I half laughed. 'My agent calls it impulsive behaviour. He says it will kill me, one day.'

'You're older than you look,' he said cryptically, and went off to talk to Tremayne.

Mackie, her drink all but untouched, took his place as kind blotter of bleeding feelings.

'It's not fair of her to call you lightweight,' she said. 'Harry shouldn't have brought her. I know she's highly revered but she can make people cry. I've seen her do it.'

'My eyes are dry,' I said. 'Are you drinking that champagne?'

'I'd better not, I suppose.'

'Care to give it to the walking wounded?'

She smiled her brilliant smile and we exchanged glasses.

'Actually,' she said, 'I didn't understand all Erica was saying.'

'She was saying she's cleverer than me.'

DICK FRANCIS

'I.'

'I,' I agreed.

'I'll bet she can't catch people who're fainting off horses.'

Mackie was, as Tremayne had said, a sweet young woman.

Angela Brickell's remains lay on the Quillersedge Estate at the western edge of the Chilterns.

The Quillersedge gamekeeper arranged on the telephone for the local police to collect him from his cottage on the estate and drive as near to the bones as possible on the estate's private roads. From there, everyone would have to go through the woods on foot.

The few policemen on duty on Sunday afternoon thought of cold wet undergrowth and shivered.

In Tremayne's house, the informal party lingered cheerfully. Fiona and Mackie sat on a sofa, silver-blond head beside dark red-brown, talking about Mackie's baby. Nolan discussed with Tremayne the horses Nolan hoped still to be riding when racing resumed. Gareth handed round potato crisps while eating most of them himself and Perkin read aloud how to return safely from getting lost.

' "Go downhill, not up," ' he read. ' "People live in valleys. Follow streams in their flow direction. People live beside rivers." I can't imagine I'll ever need this advice. I steer clear of jungles.'

'You could need it in the Lake District,' I said mildly.

'I don't like walking, period.'

Harry said, 'John, Erica wants to know why you've ignored mountain climbing in your guides.'

'Never got round to it,' I said, 'and there are dozens of mountain climbing books already.'

Erica, the sparkle of victory still in her eyes, asked who was publishing my novel. When I told her she raised her eyebrows thoughtfully and made no disparaging remarks.

'Good publishers, aren't they?' Harry asked, his lips twitching.

'Reputable,' she allowed.

Fiona, getting to her feet, began to say goodbyes, chiefly with kisses. Gareth ducked his but she stopped beside me and put her cheek on mine.

'How long are you staying?' she asked.

Tremayne answered for me forthrightly. 'Three more weeks. Then we'll see.'

'We'll fix a dinner,' Fiona said. 'Come along, Nolan. Ready, Erica? Love you, Mackie, take care of yourself.'

When they'd gone Mackie and Perkin floated off home on cloud nine, and Tremayne and I went round collecting glasses and stacking them in the dishwasher.

Gareth said, 'If we can have beef sandwich pie again, I'll make it for lunch.'

*

147

At about the time we finally ate the pie, two policemen and the gamekeeper reached the pathetic collection of bones and set nemesis in motion. They tied ropes to trees to ring and isolate the area and radioed for more instructions. Slowly the information percolated upwards until it reached Detective Chief Inspector Doone, Thames Valley Police, who was sleeping off his Yorkshire pudding.

He decided, as daylight would die within the hour, that first thing in the morning he would assemble and take a pathologist for an on-site examination and a photographer for the record. He believed the bones would prove to belong to one of the hundreds of teen-agers who had infested his patch with all-night parties the summer before. Three others had died on him from drugs.

In Tremayne's house Gareth and I went up to my bedroom because he wanted to see the survival kit that he knew I'd brought with me.

'Is it just like the ones in the books?' he asked as I brought out a black waterproof pouch that one could wear round one's waist.

'No, not entirely.' I paused. 'I have three survival kits at present. One small one for taking with me all the time. This one here for longer walks and difficult areas. And one that I didn't bring, which is full camping

148

survival gear for going out into the wilds. That's a back-pack on a frame.'

'I wish I could see it,' Gareth said wistfully.

'Well, one day, you never know.'

'I'll hold you to it.'

'I'll show you the smallest kit first,' I said, 'but you'll have to run down and get it. It's in my ski-suit jacket pocket in the cloakroom.'

He went willingly but presently returned doubtfully with a flat tin, smaller than a paperback book, held shut with black insulating tape.

'Is that it?' he said.

I nodded. 'Open it carefully.'

He did as I said, laying out the contents on the white counterpane on the bed and reciting them aloud.

'Two matchbooks, a bit of candle, a little coil of thin wire, a piece of jagged wire, some fishhooks, a small pencil and piece of paper, needles and thread, two sticking plasters and a plastic bag folded up small and held by a paperclip.' He looked disappointed. 'You couldn't do much with those.'

'Just light a fire, cut wood, catch food, collect water, make a map and sew up wounds. That jagged wire is a flexible saw.'

His mouth opened.

'Then I always carry two things on my belt.' I unstrapped it and showed it to him. 'The belt itself has a zipped pocket all along the inside where you can keep money. What's in there at the moment is your father's. I don't often carry a wallet. Those other things on the belt, one is a knife, one is a multi-purpose survival tool.'

'Can I look?'

'Yes, sure.'

The knife, in a black canvas sheath with a flap fastened by Velcro, was a strong folding knife with a cunningly serrated blade, very sharp indeed, nine inches overall when open, only five when closed. Gareth opened it until it locked with a snap and stood looking at it in surprise.

'That's some knife,' he said. 'Were you wearing it while we were having drinks?'

'All the time. It weighs only four and a half ounces, about one eighth of a kilo. Weight's important too, don't forget. Always travel as light as you can if you have to carry everything.'

He opened the other object slotted onto the belt, a small leather case about three inches by two and a half, which contained a flat metal rectangular object a shade smaller in dimension: total weight altogether, three and a half ounces.

'What's this?' he asked, taking it out onto his hand. 'I've never seen anything like this.'

'I carry that instead of an ordinary penknife. It has a blade slotted in one side and scissors in the other. That little round thing is a magnifying glass for starting fires if there's any sun. With those other odd-shaped edges you can make holes in a tin of food, open crown cork bottles, screw in screws, file your nails and sharpen knives. The sides have inches and centimetres marked like a ruler, and the back of it all is polished like a mirror for signalling.'

'Wow.' He turned it over and looked at his own face. 'It's really brill.'

He began to pack all the small things back into the flat tin and remarked that fishhooks wouldn't be much good away from rivers.

'You can catch birds on fishhooks. They take bait like fish.'

He stared at me. 'Have you eaten birds?'

'Chickens are birds.'

'Well, ordinary birds?'

'Pigeons? Four and twenty blackbirds? You eat anything if you're hungry enough. All our ancestors lived on whatever they could get hold of. It was normal, once.'

Normal for him was a freezer full of pizzas. He had no idea what it was like to be primevally alone with nature, and it was unlikely he would ever find out, for all his present interest.

I'd spent a month once on an island without any kit or anything modern at all, knowing only that there was water and that I would be collected at the end, and even with those certainties and all the craft I'd ever learned, I'd had a hard job lasting out; and it was then that I'd discovered for myself that survival was a matter of mind rather than body.

The travel agency, on my urgent advice, had decided against offering holidays of that sort.

'What about a group?' they said. 'Not one alone.'

'A group eats more,' I pointed out. 'The tensions are terrible. You'd have a murder.'

'All right. Full camping kit then, with essential stores and radios.'

'And choose the leader before they set out.'

Even so, few of the 'marooned' holidays had passed off without trouble, and in the end the agency had abandoned them.

Gareth replaced the coil of fine wire in the tin and said, 'I suppose this wire is for all the traps in the books?'

'Only the simplest ones.'

'Some of the traps are really sneaky.'

'I'm afraid so.'

'There you are, a harmless rabbit, hopping along about your business and you don't see the wire hidden in dead leaves and you trip over it and suddenly pow! you're all tied up in a net or squashed under logs. Have you done all that?'

'Yes, lots of times.'

'I like the idea of the bow and arrows better,' he said.

'Yes, well, I put in the instructions of how to make them effectively because our ancestors had them, but it's not easy to hit anything if it's moving. Impossible, if it's small. It's not the same as using a custom-made bow shooting metal arrows at a nice round stationary target, like in archery competitions. I've always preferred traps.'

'Didn't you ever hit *anything* with a bow and arrow?'

I smiled. 'I shot an apple off a tree in our garden once when I was small because I was only allowed to eat windfalls, and there weren't any. Bad luck that my mother was looking out of the window.'

'Mothers!'

'Tremayne says you see yours sometimes.'

'Yes, I do.' He glanced up at me quickly and down again. 'Did Dad tell you my mother isn't Perkin's mother?'

'No,' I said slowly. 'I guess we haven't come to that bit yet.'

'Perkin and Jane's mother died yonks ago. Jane's my sister – well, half-sister really. She's married to a French trainer and they live in Chantilly, which is a sort of French Newmarket. It's good fun, staying with Jane. I go summers. Couple of weeks.'

'Do you speak French?'

He grinned. 'Some. I always seem to come home just when I'm getting the hang of it. What about you?'

'French a bit, but Spanish more, only I'm rusty in both now too.'

He nodded and fiddled for a bit putting the insulating tape back on the tin.

I watched him, and in the end he said, 'My mother's

on television quite a lot. That's where Dad means I see.'

'Television? Is she an actress?'

'No. She cooks. She does one of those afternoon programmes sometimes.'

'A *cook*?' I could hardly believe it. 'But your father doesn't care about food.'

'Yeah, that's what he says, but he's been eating what you've made, hasn't he? But I think she used to drive him barmy always inventing weird fancy things he didn't like. I didn't care that much except that I never got what I liked either, so when she left us we sort of relapsed into what we *did* like, and we stayed like that. Only recently I've been wishing I could make custard and I tried but I burned the milk and it tasted awful. Did you know you could burn milk? So, anyway, she's married to someone else now. I don't like him though. I don't bother with them much.'

He sounded as if he'd said all he wanted to on the subject and seemed relieved to go back to simple things like staying alive, asking to see inside kit number two, the black pouch.

'You're not bored?' I said.

'Can't wait.'

I handed it to him and let him open its three zipped and Velcroed pockets, to lay the contents again on the bed. Although the pouch itself was waterproof, almost every item inside it was further wrapped separately in a small plastic bag, fastened with a twist tie; safe from sand and insects. Gareth undid and emptied some of the bags and frowned over the contents.

'Explain what they are,' he said. 'I mean, twenty matchbooks are for lighting fires, right, so what are the cotton wool balls doing with them?'

'They burn well. They set fire to dry leaves.'

'Oh. The candle is for light, right?'

'And to help light fires. And wax is useful for a lot of things.'

'What's this?' He pointed to a short fat spool of thin yellow thread.

'That's kevlar fibre. It's a sort of plastic, strong as steel. Six hundred yards of it. You can make nets of it, tie anything, fish with it, twist it into fine unbreakable rope. I didn't come across it in time to put in the books.'

'And this? This little jar of whitish liquid packed with the sawn-off paintbrush?'

I smiled. 'That's in the *Wilderness* book. It's luminous paint.'

He stared.

'Well,' I said reasonably, 'if you have a camp and you want to leave it to go and look for food or firewood, you want to be able to find your way back again, don't you? Essential. So as you go, you paint a slash of this on a tree trunk or a rock, always making sure you can see one slash from another, and then you can find your way back even in the dark.'

'Cool,' he said.

'That little oblong metal thing with the handle,' I

said, 'that's a powerful magnet. Useful but not essential. Good for retrieving fishhooks if you lose them in the water. You tie the magnet on a string and dangle it. Fishhooks are precious.'

He held up a small, cylindrical transparent plastic container, one of about six in the pouch. 'More fish-hooks in here,' he said. 'Isn't that what films come in? I thought they were black.'

'Fuji films come in these clear cases. As you can see what's inside, I use them all the time. They weigh nothing. They shut tight. They're everything-proof. Per-fect. These other cases contain more fishhooks, needles and thread, safety-pins, aspirins, water purifying tables, things like that.'

'What's this knobbly-looking object? Oh, it's a tele-scope!' He laughed and weighed it in his hand.

'Two ounces,' I said, 'but eight by twenty magnifi-cation.'

He passed over as mundane a torch that was also a ball-point pen, the light in the tip for writing, and wasn't enthralled by a whistle, a Post-it pad, or a thick folded wad of aluminium foil. ('For wrapping food to cook in the embers,' I said.) What really fascinated him was a tiny blow-torch which shot out a fierce blue flame hot enough to melt solder.

'Cool,' he said again. 'That's really *ace*.'

'Infallible for lighting fires,' I said, 'as long as the butane lasts.'

'You said in the books that fire comes first.'

I nodded. 'A fire makes you feel better. Less alone. And you need fire for boiling river water to make it OK to drink, and for cooking, of course. And signalling where you are, if people are looking for you.'

'And to keep warm.'

'That too.'

Gareth, had come to the last thing, a pair of leather gloves, which he thought were sissy.

'They give your hands almost double grip,' I said. 'They save you from cuts and scratches. And apart from that they're invaluable for collecting stinging nettles.'

'I'd hate to collect stinging nettles.'

'No, you wouldn't. If you boil the leaves they're not bad to eat, but the best things are the stalks. Incredibly stringy. You can thrash them until they're supple enough for lashing branches together, for making shelters and also racks to keep things off the ground away from damp and animals.'

'You know so much,' he said.

'I went camping in my cradle. Literally.'

He methodically packed everything back as he'd found it and asked what it weighed altogether.

'About two pounds. Less than a kilo.'

A thought struck him. 'You haven't got a compass!'

'It's not in there,' I agreed. I opened a drawer in the chest of drawers and found it for him: a slim liquid-filled compass set in a clear oblong of plastic which had inch and centimetre measures along the sides. I showed him how it aligned with maps and made setting a course relatively easy, and told him I always carried it in my shirt pocket to have it handy.

'But it was in the drawer,' he objected.

'I'm not likely to get lost in Shellerton.'

'You could up on the Downs,' he said seriously.

I doubted it, but said I would carry it to please him, which earned the sideways look it deserved.

Putting everything on top of the chest of drawers I reflected how little time I'd spent in that room amid the mismatched furniture and faded fabrics. I hadn't once felt like retreating to be alone there, though for one pretty accustomed to solitude it was odd to find myself living in the lives of all these people, as if I'd stepped into a play that was already in progress and been given a walk-on part in the action. I would spend another three weeks there and exit, and the play would go on without me as if I hadn't been onstage at all. Meanwhile, I felt drawn in and interested and unwilling to miss any scene.

'This room used to be Perkin's,' Gareth observed, as if catching a swirl of my thought. 'He took all his own stuff with him when they divided the house. It used to be terrif in here.' He shrugged. 'You want to see my room?'

'I'd love to.'

He nodded and led the way. He and I shared the bathroom which lay between us, and along the hallway lay Tremayne's suite into which he was liable to vanish with a brisk slam of the door.

Gareth's room was all pre-adolescent. He slept on a platform with a pull-out desk below and there were a good many white space-age fitments liberally plastered with posters of pop stars and sportsmen. Prized objects filled shelves. Clothes adorned the floor.

I murmured something encouraging but he swept his lair with a disparaging scrutiny and said he was going to do the whole thing over, Dad willing, in the summer.

'Dad got this room done for me after Mum left, and it was top ace at the time. Guess I'm getting too old for it now.'

'Life's like that,' I said.

'Always?'

'It looks like it.'

He nodded as if he'd already discovered that changes were inevitable and not always bad, and in undemanding accord we shut the door on his passing phase and went down to the family room, where we found Tremayne asleep.

Gareth retreated without disturbing him and beckoned me to follow him through to the central hall. There he walked across and knocked briefly on Mackie and Perkin's door, which after an interval was opened slowly by Perkin.

'Can we come in for five mins?' Gareth said. 'Dad's asleep in his chair. You know what he's like if I wake him.'

Perkin yawned and opened his door wide though without excessive willingness, particularly on my account. He led the way into his sitting-room where it was clear he and Mackie had been spending a lazy afternoon reading the Sunday newspapers.

Mackie started to get up when she saw me and then relaxed again as if to say I was now family, not a visitor, and could fend for myself. Perkin told Gareth there was Coke in the fridge if he wanted some. Gareth didn't.

I remembered with a small jerk that it was in this room, Perkin and Mackie's sitting-room, that Olympia had died. I couldn't help but glance around wondering just where it had happened; where Mackie and Harry had found Nolan standing over the girl without underclothes in a scarlet dress, with Lewis – drunk or not – in a chair.

There was nothing left of that violent scene now in the pleasant big room, no residual shudder in the comfortable atmosphere, no regrets or grief. The trial was over, Nolan was free, Olympia was ashes.

Gareth, unconcerned, asked Perkin, 'Can I show John your workroom?'

'Don't touch anything. I mean *anything*.'

'Cross my heart.'

With me still obediently in tow he crossed Perkin and Mackie's inner hall and opened a door which led into a completely different world, one incredibly fragrant with the scent of untreated wood.

The room where Perkin created his future antiques was of generous size, like all the rooms in the entire big house, but also no larger than the others. It was extremely tidy, which in a way I wouldn't have expected, with a polished wood-block floor swept spot-less, not a shaving or speck of sawdust in sight.

When I commented on it Gareth said it was always like that. Perkin would use one tool at a time and put it away before he used another. Chisels, spokeshaves, things like that.

'Dead methodical,' Gareth said. 'Very fussy.'

There was surprisingly a gas cooker standing against one wall. 'He heats glue on that,' Gareth said, seeing me looking, 'and other sorts of muck like linseed oil.' He pointed across the room. 'That's his lathe, that's his saw-bench, that's his sanding machine. I haven't seen him working much. He doesn't like people watching him, says it interferes with the feeling for what he's doing.'

Gareth's voice held disbelief, but I thought if I had to write with people watching I'd get nothing worth-while done either.

'What's he making at the moment?' I asked.

'Don't know.'

He swanned round the room looking at sheets of veneer stacked against a wall and at little orderly piles of square-cut lengths from exotic black to golden walnut. 'He makes legs with those,' Gareth said, pointing.

He stopped by a long solid worktop like a butcher's

block and said to me over his shoulder, 'I should think he's just started on this.'

I went across to look and saw a pencil drawing of a display cabinet of sharply spare and unusual lines, a piece designed to draw the eye to its contents, not itself.

The drawing was held down by two blocks of wood, one, I thought, cherry, the other bleached oak, though I was better at living trees than dead.

'He often slats one sort of wood into the other,' Gareth said. 'Makes a sort of stripe. His things don't actually look bad. People buy them all the time.'

'I'm not surprised,' I said.

'Aren't you?' He seemed pleased, as if he'd been afraid I wouldn't be impressed, but I was, considerably.

As we turned to leave I said, 'Was it in their sitting-room that that poor girl died?'

'Gruesome,' Gareth said, nodding. 'I didn't see her. Perkin did, though. He went in just after Mackie and Harry and found it all happening. And, I mean, disgusting . . . there was a mess on the carpet where she'd been lying and by the time they were allowed to clean it up, they couldn't. So they got a new carpet from insurance but Perkin acts as if the mess is still there and he's moved a sofa to cover the place. Bonkers, I think.'

I thought I might easily have done the same. Whoever would want to walk every day over a deathbed? We went back to the sitting-room and one could see, if one knew, just which of the three chintz-covered sofas wasn't in a logical place.

We stayed only a short while before returning to the family room where Tremayne was safely awake and yawning, getting ready to walk round his yard at evening stables. He invited me to go with him, which I did with pleasure, and afterwards I made cauliflower cheese for supper which Tremayne ate without a tremor.

When he went out at bedtime for a last look round, he came back blowing on his hands cheerfully and smiling broadly.

'It's thawing,' he said. 'Everything's dripping. Thank God.'

The world indeed turned from white to green during the night, bringing renewed life to Shellerton and racing.

Out in the melting woodlands, Angela Brickell spent her last night in the quiet undergrowth among the small scavenging creatures that had blessedly cleaned her bones. She was without odour and without horror, weather-scrubbed, long gone into everlasting peace.

CHAPTER EIGHT

Tremayne promoted me from Touchy to a still actively racing steeplechaser that Monday morning, a nine-year-old gelding called Drifter. I was also permitted to do a regular working gallop and by great good fortune didn't fall off. Neither Tremayne nor Mackie made any comment on my competence or lack of it, only on the state of fitness of the horse. They were taking me for granted, I realised, and was flattered and glad of it.

When we returned from the newly greenish-brownish Downs there was a strange car in the yard and a strange man drinking coffee in the kitchen; but strange to me only. Familiar to everyone else.

He was young, short, thin, angular and bold, wearing self-assurance as an outer garment. He was, I soon found, almost as foul-mouthed as Nolan but, unlike him, funny.

'Hello, Sam,' Tremayne said. 'Ready for work?'

'Too sodding right. I'm as stiff as a frigging virgin.'

I wondered idly how many virgins he had personally

introduced to frigging: there was something about him that suggested it.

Tremayne said to me, 'This is Sam Yaeger, our jockey.' To Sam Yaeger he explained my presence and said I'd been riding out.

Sam Yaeger nodded to me, visibly assessing what threat or benefit I might represent to him, running a glance over my jodhpurs and measuring my height. I imagined that because of my six feet alone he might put away fears that I could annex any of his racing territory.

He himself wore jodhpurs also, along with a brilliant yellow sweatshirt. A multi-coloured anorak, twin of Gareth's, hung over the back of his chair, and he had brought his own helmet, bright turquoise, with YAEGER painted large in red on the front. Nothing shy or retiring about Sam.

Dee-Dee, appearing for her coffee, brightened by fifty watts at the sight of him.

'Morning, Lover-boy,' she said.

Lover-boy made a stab at pinching her bottom as she passed behind him, which she seemed not to mind. Well, well, well, I thought, there was a veritable pussy-cat lurking somewhere inside that self-contained, touch-me-not secretarial exterior. She made her coffee and sat at the table beside the jockey, not overtly flirting but very aware of him.

I made the toast, which had become my accepted

job, and put out the juice, butter, marmalade and so on. Sam Yaeger watched with comically raised eyebrows.

'Didn't Tremayne say you were a writer?' he asked.

'Most of the time. Want some toast?'

'One piece, light brown. You don't look like a sodding writer.'

'So many people aren't.'

'Aren't what?'

'What they look like,' I said. 'Sodding or not.'

'What do I look like?' he demanded, but with, I thought, genuine curiosity.

'Like someone who won the Grand National among eighty-nine other races last year and finished third on the jockeys' list.'

'You've been peeking,' he said, surprised.

'I'll be interviewing you soon for your views on your boss as a trainer.'

Tremayne said with mock severity, 'And they'd better be respectful.'

'They bloody well would be, wouldn't they?'

'If you have any sense,' Tremayne agreed, nodding.

I dealt out the toast and made some more. Sam's extremely physical presence dominated breakfast throughout and I wondered briefly how he got on with Nolan, the dark side of the same coin.

I asked Dee-Dee that question after Sam and Tremayne had gone out with the second lot; asked her in the office while I checked some facts in old form books.

'Get on?' she repeated ironically. 'No, they do not.'

She paused, considered whether to tell me more, shrugged and continued. 'Sam doesn't like Nolan riding so many of the stable's horses. Nolan rides most of Fiona's runners, he accepts that, but Tremayne runs more horses in amateur races than most trainers do. Wins more, too, of course. The owners who bet, they like it, because whatever else you can say about Nolan, no one denies he's a brilliant jockey. He's been top of the amateurs' list for years.'

'Why doesn't he turn professional?' I asked.

'The very idea of that scares Sam rigid,' Dee-Dee said calmly, 'but I don't think it will happen. Especially not now, since the conviction. Nolan prefers his amateur status, anyway. He thinks of Sam as blue collar to his white. That's why . . .' she stopped abruptly as if blocking a revelation that was already on its way from brain to mouth, stopped so sharply that I was immediately interested, but without showing it asked, 'Why what?'

She shook her head. 'It's not fair to them.'

'Do go on,' I said, not pressing too much. 'I won't repeat it to anyone.'

'It wouldn't help you with the book,' she said.

'It might help me to understand the way the stable works and where its success comes from, besides Tremayne's skill. It might come partly, for instance, from rivalry between two jockeys each of whom wants to prove himself better than the other.'

She gazed at me. 'You have a twisty mind. I'd never

167

have thought of that.' She paused for decision and I simply waited. 'It isn't just riding,' she said finally. 'It's women.'

'*Women*?'

'They're rivals there, too. The night Nolan – I mean, the night Olympia died . . .'

They all said, I'd noticed, 'when Olympia died', and never 'when Nolan killed Olympia', though Dee-Dee had just come close.

'Sam set out to seduce Olympia,' Dee-Dee said, as if it were only to be expected. 'Nolan brought her to the party and of course Sam made a bee-line for her.' Somewhere in her calm voice was indulgence for Sam Yaeger, censure for Nolan, never mind that Nolan seemed to be the loser.

'Did Sam . . . er . . . know Olympia?'

'Never set eyes on her before. None of us knew her. Nolan had been keeping her to himself. Anyway, he brought her that night and she took one look at Sam and *giggled*. I know, I was there. Sam has that effect on females.' She raised her eyebrows. 'Don't say it. I respond to him too. Can't help it. He's fun.'

'I can see that,' I said.

'Can you? Olympia did. Putty in his hands which of course were all over her the minute Nolan went to fetch her a drink. When he came back, she'd gone off with Sam. Like I told you, she had on a low-cut long scarlet dress slit up the thigh . . . next best thing to a written invitation. Nolan seemed to think that Sam and

Olympia would have headed for the stables and he went looking for them there, but without results.'

She stopped again as if doubting the wisdom of telling me these things, but it seemed harder for her to stop than to start.

'Nolan came back into the house cursing and swearing and telling me he would strangle the . . . er . . . bitch because, you see, I think he blamed *her*, not Sam, for making him feel a fool. Him, Nolan, the white-collar amateur. He wasn't going to make it public and he shut up pretty soon, though he went on being angry. So, anyway, there you are, that's really what happened.'

'Which no one,' I said slowly, 'brought up at the trial.'

'Of course not. I mean, not many people knew, and it gave Nolan a *motive*.'

'Yes, it did.'

'But he didn't mean to kill her. Everyone knows that. If he'd attacked and killed *Sam*, it would have been a different matter.'

I said, frowning, 'It wasn't you, though, who said at the trial they'd heard him say he would strangle the bitch.'

'No, of course not. Some other people heard him before he reached me, and they didn't know *why* he was saying it. It didn't seem important at that time. Of course, no one ever asked me if *I* knew why he'd said it, so no one found out.'

'But the prosecution must have asked *Nolan* why he said it?'

169

DICK FRANCIS

'Yes, sure, but he said it was because he couldn't find her, nothing else. Extravagant language but not a threat.'

I sighed. 'And *Sam* wasn't for saying why, as it would further torpedo his shaky reputation?'

'Yes. And anyway he didn't believe Nolan meant to kill her. He told me that. He said it wasn't the first time he and Nolan had bedded the same girl, and sometimes Nolan had pinched one of his, and it was a bit of a lark on the whole, not a killing matter.'

'More a lark to Sam than to Nolan,' I suggested.

'Probably.' She shook herself. 'I'm getting no work done.'

'You've done some of mine.'

'Don't put it in the book,' she insisted, alarmed.

'I promise I won't,' I said.

I retired to the dining-room and, since the shape of Tremayne's passage through life was becoming more and more clear, I began to map out the book into sections, giving each a tentative title with subheadings. I still hadn't put an actual sentence on paper and was feeling tyrannised by all the blank pages lying ahead. I'd heard of writers who leaped to their typewriters as to a lover. There were days when I'd do any chore I could think of rather than pick up a pencil, and it was never easy, ever, to dig words and ideas from my brain. Half the time I couldn't believe I'd chosen this occupation; half of the time I longed for the easier solitude under the stars.

I scribbled 'Find something you like doing and spend your life doing it' at the end of the outline plan and decided it was enough for one day. If tomorrow it looked all right, maybe I'd let it stand, and go on.

Out in the woodland Detective Chief Inspector Doone looked morosely at Angela Brickell's jumbled bones while the pathologist told him they were those of a young female, dead probably less than a year.

The photographer took photographs. The game-keeper marked the spot on a large-scale map. The pathologist said it was impossible to determine the cause of death without a detailed autopsy, and very likely not even then.

With sketchy reverence for whoever they had been, the skull and other bones were packed into a coffin-shaped box, carried to a van, and driven to the mortuary.

Detective Chief Inspector Doone, seeing there was no point in looking for tyre tracks, footprints or ciga-rette ends, set two constables to searching the under-growth for clothes, shoes, or anything not rotted by time; and it was in this way that under a blanket of dead leaves they came across some wet filthy jeans, a small-sized bra, a pair of panties and a T-shirt with the remains of a pattern on the front.

Detective Chief Inspector Doone watched his men pack these sad remnants into a plastic bag and reflected that none of the clothes had been on or even near the bones.

The girl, he reckoned, had been naked when she died.

He sighed deeply. He didn't like these sorts of cases. He had daughters of his own.

Tremayne came back from the second lot in a good mood, whistling between his teeth. He wheeled straight into the office, fired off a fresh barrage of instructions to Dee-Dee and made several rapid phone calls himself. Then he came into the dining-room to let me know the state of play and to ask a favour or two, taking it (correctly) for granted that I would oblige.

The ditched jeep had gone to the big scrap heap in the sky: a replacement had been found in Newbury, a not new but serviceable Land Rover. If I would go to Newbury in the Volvo with Tremayne, I could drive the substitute home to Shellerton.

'Of course,' I said.

The racing industry was scrambling back into action, with Windsor racecourse promising to be operational on Wednesday. Tremayne had horses entered, four of which he proposed to run. He would like me to come with him, he said, to see what his job entailed.

'Love to,' I said.

He wished to go out for the evening to play poker

with friends, and he'd be back late: would I stay in for Gareth?

'Sure,' I said.

'He's old enough to be safe on his own, but . . . well . . .'

'Company,' I said. 'Someone around.'

He nodded.

'You're welcome,' I said.

'Dee-Dee thinks we take advantage of you,' he said bluntly. 'Do we?'

'No.' I was surprised. 'I like what I'm doing.'

'Cooking, baby-sitting, spare chauffeur, spare lad?'

'Sure.'

'You have the right to say no,' he said uncertainly.

'I'll tell you soon enough if I'm affronted. As for now, I'd rather be part of things, and useful. OK?'

He nodded.

'And,' I said, 'this way I get to know you better for the book.'

For the first time he looked faintly apprehensive, as if perhaps after all he didn't want his whole self publicly laid bare; but I would respect any secrecies I learned, I thought again, if he didn't want them told. This was not an investigate blast-the-lid-off exercise; this was to be the equivalent of a commissioned portrait, an affirmation of life. It might be fair to include a wart or two, but not to put every last blemish under magnification.

The day went ahead as planned and, in addition, in the Volvo on the way to Newbury, Tremayne galloped

173

through his late adolescence and his introduction (by his father, naturally) to high-stakes gambling. His father's advice, he said, was always to wager more than one could afford, otherwise one would get no thrill and feel no despair.

'He was right, of course,' Tremayne said, 'but I'm more prudent. I play poker, I back horses, I bet a little, win a little, lose a little, it doesn't flutter my pulse. I've owners who go white and shake at the races. They look on the point of dying, they stand to lose or win so much. My father would have understood it. I don't.'

'All your life's a gamble,' I said.

He looked blank for a moment. 'You mean training racehorses? True enough, I get thrills like Top Spin Lob, and true enough, great slabs of despair. You might say I wager my heartstrings, but not much cash.'

I wrote it down. Tremayne, driving conservatively, slanted a glance at my notebook and seemed pleased to be quoted. The man himself, I thought with a stirring of satisfaction, was going to speak clearly from the pages, coming alive with little help from me.

In the evening, after Tremayne had departed to his card game, Gareth asked me to teach him to cook.

I was nonplussed. 'It's easy,' I said.

'How did you learn?'

'I don't know. Maybe from watching my mother.' I looked at his face. 'Sorry, I forgot.'

'My mother makes it all difficult, not easy. And she would never let me watch her at home. She said I got under her feet.'

My own mother, I reflected, had always let me clean out raw cake mixture with my finger: had always liked to talk to me while things bubbled.

'Well,' I said, 'what do you want to eat?'

We went into the kitchen where Gareth tentatively asked for 'real' shepherd's pie, 'not that stuff in supermarket boxes that tastes of cardboard and wouldn't feed a pygmy'.

'Real, easy shepherd's pie,' I assented. 'First of all, catch your shepherd.'

He grinned and watched me assemble some minced beef, an onion, gravy powder and a jar of dried herbs.

'The gravy powder's sort of cheating,' I said. 'Your mother would be horrified, but it thickens the meat and tastes good.'

I dissolved some powder into a little water, added it to the beef, chopped the onion finely, added that, sprinkled some herbs, stirred it all around in a saucepan, put the lid on and set it to cook on a low heat.

'Next thing to decide,' I said, 'is real potatoes or dried potato granules. How are you with peeling potatoes? No? Granules then?'

He nodded.

'Follow the directions,' I said, giving him the packet.

' "Heat eight fluid ounces of water and four fluid

ounces of milk"',' he said, reading. He looked up, 'Hey, I was going to ask you . . . You know you said to boil river water before you drink it? Well, what *in*?'

I smiled. 'Best thing is a Coca-Cola can. You can usually find an empty one lying about, the litter habits of this nation being what they are. You want to just shake it up with water to wash it out a few times in case there are any spiders or anything inside, but Coke cans are pretty clean.'

'Ace,' he said emphatically. 'Well, for the potatoes we need some butter and salt . . . Will you write down all you bought last week, so I can get them again and cook when you're gone?'

'Sure thing.'

'I wouldn't mind if you stayed.'

Loneliness was an ache in his voice. I said, 'I'll be here another three weeks.' I paused. 'Would you like, say perhaps next Sunday if it's a decent day, to come out with me into some fields and perhaps some woods? I could show you a few things in the books . . . how to do them in real life.'

His face shone: my own reward.

'Could I bring Coconut?'

'Absolutely.'

'Mega cool.'

He whipped the potato granules happily into the hot liquid and we piled the fluffy result onto the cooked meat mixture in a round pie dish. Put it under the grill to brown the top. Ate the results with mutual fulfilment and cleared everything away afterwards.

'Can we take the survival kit?' he asked.

'Of course.'

'And light a fire?'

'Perhaps on your own land, if your father will let us. You can't just light fires anywhere in England. Or anyway, you shouldn't, unless it's an emergency. People do, actually, but you're supposed to get the landowner's permission first.'

'He's sure to let us.'

'Yes. I'd think so.'

'I really can't wait,' he said.

On Tuesday morning the pathologist made his report to Detective Chief Inspector Doone.

'The bones are those of a young adult female, probably five foot four or five; possible age, twenty. Could be a year or two younger or older, but not much. There was a small remaining patch of scalp, with a few hairs still adhering: the hairs are medium brown, four inches long, can't tell what length her hair was overall.'

'How long since she died?' Doone asked.

'I'd say last summer.'

'And cause of death? Drugs? Exposure?'

'As to drugs, we'll have to analyse the hairs, see what we can find. But no, you've got a problem here.'

Doone sighed. 'What problem?'

'Her hyoid bone is fractured.'

Depression settled on Doone. 'You're sure?'

'Positive. She was strangled.'

At Shellerton, Tuesday passed uneventfully with riding out, breakfast, clippings, lunch, taping, evening drinks and dinner.

In the morning I came across Dee-Dee weeping quietly into her typewriter and offered a tissue.

'It's nothing,' she said, sniffing.

'Care to unbutton?'

'I don't know why I tell you things.'

'I listen.'

She blew her nose and gave me a brief apologetic look.

'I'm old enough to know better. I'm thirty-six.' She gave her age almost in desperation, as if the figure itself were a disaster.

'Tremayne told me you'd had a disappointment in the love department,' I said hesitatingly. 'He didn't exactly say who.'

'Disappointment! Huh!' She sniffed hard. 'I loved the beast. I mean, I even ironed his shirts for him. We were lovers for ages and he dumped me from one minute to the next. And now Mackie's having a *baby*.' Her eyes filled with tears again, and I saw it was the raw ache for motherhood, that fierce instinct which could cause such unassuageable pain, that grieved her at least as much as the loss of the man.

'Do you know what?' Dee-Dee said with misery. 'That louse didn't want a child until after we were married. *After.* He never meant to marry me, I know it now, but I waited for his sake . . . and I wasted . . . *three years* . . .' She gulped, a sob escaping. 'I'll tell you, I'll take *anyone* now. I don't need a wedding ring. I want a *child.*'

Her voice died in a forlorn pining wail, a keen of mourning. With a hunger that strong she could make dreadful decisions, but who could tell which would be better for her to be in the end, reckless or barren? Either way, there would be regrets.

She dried her eyes, blew her nose again and shook herself as if straightening her emotions by force, and when I next looked in on her she was typing away collectedly in her usual self-contained manner as if our conversation had never taken place.

On Tuesday afternoon Detective Chief Inspector Doone sent his men to search the whole area where the bones had been discovered. Chiefly, he told them, they were to look for shoes. Also for anything else man-made. They could use metal detectors. They should look under dead leaves. They were to mark on the map where each artefact was found, and also tag the artefact, being careful not to destroy evidence.

This was now a murder investigation, he reminded them.

On Wednesday morning when we came in from first lot Sam Yaeger was again in the kitchen.

This time he came not in his car but with a borrowed pick-up truck in which he proposed to collect some Burma teak that Perkin had acquired for him at trade discount.

'Sam has a boat,' Tremayne told me dryly. 'An old wreck that he's slowly turning into a palace fit for a harem.'

Sam Yaeger grinned cheerfully and made no denials. 'It's already sold, or as good as,' he told me. 'Every jockey's got to have an eye to the sodding future. I buy clapped out antique boats and make them better than new. I sold the last one to one of those effing newspaper moguls. They'll pay the earth for good stuff. No fibre-glass crap.'

Life was full of surprises, I thought.

'Where do you keep the boat?' I asked, making toast.

'Maidenhead. On the Thames. I bought a bankrupt boatyard there a while back. It looks a right shambles but a bit of dilapidation's a good thing. Sodding thieves think there's nothing worth stealing. Better than a Rot-tweiler, is a bit of squalor.'

'So I suppose,' Tremayne said, 'that you're taking the wood to the boatyard on your way to the races.'

Sam looked at me in mock amazement. 'Don't know how he works these things out, do you?'

'That'll do, Sam,' Tremayne said, and one could see just where he drew the line between what he would take from Sam Yaeger, and what not. He began to discuss the horses he would be running at Windsor races that afternoon, telling Sam that 'Bluecheesecake is better, not worse, for the lay off,' and 'Give Just The Thing an easy if you feel her wavering. I don't want her ruined while she's still green.'

'Right,' Sam said, concentrating. 'What about Cashless? Do I ride him in front again?'

'What do you think?'

'He likes it better. He just got beat by faster horses, last time.'

'Go off in front, then.'

'Right.'

'Nolan rides Telebiddy in the amateur race,' Tremayne said. 'Unless the Jockey Club puts a stop to it.'

Sam scowled but spoke no evil. Tremayne told him what he would be riding on the morrow at Towcester and said he'd have no runners at all on Friday.

'Saturday, I'm sending five or six to Chepstow. You'll go there. So will I. With luck, Nolan rides Fiona's horse in the Wilfred Johnstone Hunter Chase at Sandown. Maybe Mackie will go to Sandown; we'll have to see.'

Dee-Dee came in composedly for her coffee and as before sat next to Sam. Sam might be a constant seducer, I thought, looking at them, but he wouldn't want to leave a trail of paternity problems. Dee-Dee might get him into bed but not into fatherhood. Bad luck, try again.

Tremayne gave Dee-Dee instructions about engaging transport for Saturday, which she memorized as usual.

'Remember to phone through the entries for Folkestone and Wolverhampton. I'll decide on the Newbury entries this morning before I go to Windsor.'

Dee-Dee nodded.

'Pack the colours for Windsor.'

Dee-Dee nodded.

'Phone the saddler about collecting those exercise sheets for repair.'

Dee-Dee nodded.

'Right then. That's about it.' He turned to me. 'We'll leave for Windsor at twelve-thirty.'

'Fine,' I said.

He went up to the Downs to watch the second lot, driving the newly acquired Land Rover. Sam Yaeger took the pick-up round to Perkin's half of the house and loaded up his teak. Dee-Dee took her coffee into the office and I made a determined attempt to sort each year's clippings into order of significance, the most newsworthy on top.

At about that time, Detective Chief Inspector Doone went into the formerly unused office that had been dubbed 'Incident Room' for the bones investigation and laid out on a trestle table the bits and pieces that his men had gleaned from the woodland.

There were the clothes found originally, now drying out in the centrally-heated air. There was also a pair of well-worn and misshapen trainers, still sodden, which might once have been white.

Apart from those, there were four old, empty and dirty soft drink cans, a heavily rusted toy fire-engine, a pair of broken sunglasses, a puckered leather belt with split stitches, a gin bottle, a blue plastic comb uncorrupted by time, a well-chewed rubber ball, a gold-plated ball-point pen, a pink lipstick, chocolate bar wrappers, a pitted garden spade and a broken dog collar.

Detective Chief Inspector Doone walked broodingly round the table staring at the haul from all angles.

'Speak to me, girl,' he said. 'Tell me who you are.'

The clothes and the shoes made no answer.

He called in his men and told them to go back to the woods and widen the search, and he himself, as he had the day before, went through the lists of missing persons, trying to make a match.

He knew it was possible the young woman had been a far stranger to the area but thought it more likely that she was within fifty miles of her home. They usually were, these victims. He decided automatically to beam in on the locally lost.

He had a list of twelve persistent adolescent run-aways: all possibles. A list of four defaulters from youth custody. A short list of two missing prostitutes. A list of six missing for 'various reasons'.

One of those was Angela Brickell. The reason given was: 'Probably doped a racehorse in her charge. Skipped out.'

Doone's attention passed over her and fastened thoughtfully on the wayward daughter of a politician. Reason for being missing: 'Mixed with bad crowd. Unmanageable.'

It might do his stalled career a bit of good, Doone reckoned, if it turned out to be *her*.

CHAPTER NINE

Tremayne told me that the only place that he couldn't take me on Windsor racecourse was into the Holy of Holies, the weighing room. Everywhere else, he said, I should stay by his side. He wouldn't forever be looking back to make sure I was with him: I was to provide my own glue.

Accordingly I followed him doggedly, at times at a run. Where he paused briefly to talk to other people he introduced me as a friend, John Kendall, not as Boswell. He left me to sort out for myself the information bombarding me from all sides, rarely offering explanations, and I could see that explanations would have been a burden for him when he was so busy. His four runners, as it happened, were in four consecutive races. He took me for a quick sandwich and a drink soon after our arrival on the racecourse and from then on began a darting progress: into the weighing room to fetch his jockey's saddle and weight cloth containing the correct amount of lead; off at a trot to the saddling boxes to do up the girths himself and straighten the tack to send the horse out looking good; into the parade ring to join the owners and give last-minute orders to the jockey; off up to the stands to watch the horse run; down again to the unsaddling areas, hoping to greet a winner, otherwise to listen to the why-not story from the jockey, and then off to the weighing room to pick up another saddle and weight cloth to start all over again.

Nolan was there, anxiously asking if Tremayne had received any thumbs-down from the Jockey Club.

'No,' Tremayne said. 'Have you?'

'Not an effing peep.'

'You ride, then,' Tremayne said. 'And don't ask questions. Don't invite a no. They'll tell you quickly enough if they want you off. Apply your mind to winning. Telebiddy's owners are here with their betting money burning holes in their pockets, so deliver the goods, eh?'

'Tell them I want a better effing present than last time.'

'Win the race first,' Tremayne said.

He made one of his dives into the weighing room, leaving me outside with Nolan who had come dressed to stifle criticism. All the same he complained to me bitterly that the effing media had snapped him coming through the main gate and he could do without their sodding attentions, the obscene so and sos.

The filth of Nolan's language tended to wash over one, I found: the brain tended finally to filter it out.

Much the same could be said about Sam Yaeger who slouched up beside us and annoyed Nolan by patting him on the back. Sam, too, was transformed by tidiness and I gradually observed that several of the jockeys arrived and departed from the racecourse dressed for the boardroom. Their working clothes might be pink, purple and the stuff of fantasy but they were saying they were businessmen first.

The physical impact of each of Nolan and Sam was diluted and dissipated by the open air that incidentally was still as cold as their relationship.

'Go easy on Bluecheesecake,' Nolan said. 'I don't want him effing loused up before the Kim Muir at Cheltenham.'

Sam answered, 'I'm not nannying any sodding amateur.'

'The Kim Muir is his main effing target.'

'Eff his sodding target.'

Did anyone ever grow up, I wondered. The school playground had a lot to answer for.

Away from each other, as I discovered during the afternoon, they were assured, sensible and supremely expert.

Sam made no concessions on Bluecheesecake. Through a spare pair of Tremayne's binoculars I watched his gold cap from start to finish, seeing the smooth pattern of his progress along the rails, staying in third or fourth place while others surged forward and fell back on his outside.

The steeplechase course at Windsor proved to be a winding figure-of-eight, which meant that tactics were important. At times one saw the runners from head-on; difficult to tell who was actually in front. Coming round the last of several bends Bluecheesecake made a mess of one head-on-view fence, his nose going down to the ground, Sam's back wholly visible from shoulders down to bottom up. Tremayne beside me let go of a Nolan-strength curse, but both horse and jockey righted themselves miraculously without falling and lost, Sam said afterwards, no more than three or four lengths.

Perhaps because of having to make up for those lengths in limited time before the winning post, Sam, having given his mount precious extra seconds for recovery of balance, rode over the last two fences with what even I could see was total disregard for his own safety and pressed Bluecheesecake unceremoniously for every ounce of effort.

Tremayne put down his glasses and watched the rocketing finish almost impassively, giving no more than a satisfied grunt when in the last few strides Bluecheese-cake's nose showed decisively in front.

Before the cheers had died, Tremayne had set off at a run to the winners' enclosure with me in pursuit, and after he'd received his due congratulations, inspected his excited, sweating, breathless charge for cuts and damage (none), and talked briefly to the press he followed Sam into the weighing room to fetch the saddle again for Just The Thing.

When he came out he was escorted by Nolan who fell into step beside him complaining ferociously that Sam had given Bluecheesecake a viciously hard race and spoiled his, Nolan's, chances at Cheltenham.

'Cheltenham is six weeks off,' Tremayne said calmly. 'Plenty of time.'

Nolan repeated his gripe.

Tremayne said with amazing patience, 'Sam did exactly right. Go and do the same with Telebiddy.'

Nolan stalked away still looking more furious than was sensible in his position and Tremayne allowed himself a sigh but no comment. He took a lot more from Nolan, I reflected, than he would allow from Sam, even though it seemed to me that he liked Sam better. A lot of things were involved there: status, accent, connections; all the signal flags of class.

Sam rode Just The Thing in the next event, a hurdle race, with inconspicuous gallantry, providing the green mare with a clear view of the jumps and urging her on at the end to give her a good idea of what was expected. She finished a respectable third to Tremayne's almost tangible pleasure: and it was fascinating to me to have heard the plans beforehand and see them put into exact effect.

While Tremayne was on his way from weighing room to saddling boxes for Telebiddy in the next race he handed me an envelope and asked me to put the contents for him on the Tote; Telebiddy, all to win.

'I don't like people to see me bet,' he said, 'because

189

for one thing it shows them I'm pretty confident, so they put their money on too and it shortens the odds. I usually bet by phone with a bookmaker, but today I wanted to judge the state of the ground first. It can be treacherous, after snow. You don't mind, do you?'

'Not at all.'

He nodded and hurried off, and I made my way to the Tote windows and disposed of enough to keep me in food for a year. Small, as in Tremayne's 'small bet', was a relative term, I saw.

I joined him in the parade ring and asked if he wanted the tickets.

'No. If he wins, collect for me, will you?'

'OK.'

Nolan was talking to the owners, exercising his best charm and moderating his language. In jockey's clothes he still looked chunky, strong and powerfully arrogant, but the swagger seemed to stop the moment he sat on the horse. Then professionalism took over and he was concentrated, quiet and neat in the saddle.

I tagged along behind Tremayne and the owners and, from the stands, watched Nolan give a display of razor-sharp competence that made most of the other amateurs look like Sunday drivers.

He saved countable seconds over the fences, his mount gaining lengths by always seeming to take off at the right spot. Judgment, not luck. The courage that Mackie loved was still there, unmistakable.

The owners, mother and daughter, were tremblers.

They weren't entirely white and near to dying, but from what they said the betting money was out of their pockets and on the horse in a big way and there was a good deal of lip- and knuckle-biting from off to finish.

Nolan, as if determined to outride Sam Yaeger, hurled himself over the last three fences and won by ten lengths pulling up. Tremayne let out a deep breath and the owners hugged each other, hugged Tremayne and stopped shaking.

'You could give Nolan a good cash present for that,' Tremayne said bluntly.

The owners thought Nolan would be embarrassed if they gave him such a present.

'Give it to me, to give to him. No embarrassment.'

The owners said they'd better run down and lead in their winner, which they did.

'Stingy cats,' Tremayne said in my ear as we watched them fuss over the horse and have their picture taken.

'Won't they really give Nolan anything?' I asked.

'It's against the rules, and they know it. Amateurs aren't supposed to be given money for winning. Nolan will have backed the horse anyway, he always does with a hot chance like this. And I get one hundred per cent commitment from my jockey.' His voice was dry with humour. 'I often think the Jockey Club has it wrong, not letting professional jockeys bet on their own mounts.'

He returned to the weighing room to fetch Sam's saddle and weight cloth for Cashless, and I went off to the Tote and collected his Telebiddy winnings, which approximately equalled his stake. Nolan, it appeared, had been riding the hot favourite.

When I commented on it to Tremayne in the parade ring as we watched Cashless being led round, he told me that Nolan's presence on any horse shortened its odds, and Telebiddy had won twice for him already this season. It was a wonder, Tremayne said, that the Tote had paid evens: he'd expected less of a return. I would do him a favour, he added, if I would give him his winnings on the way home, not in public, so I walked around with a small fortune I had no hope of repaying if I lost it, keeping it clutched in my left-hand trouser pocket.

We went up to the stands for the race and watched Cashless set off in front as expected, a position he easily held until right where it mattered, the last fifty yards. Then three jockeys who had been waiting behind him stepped on the accelerator, and although Cashless didn't in any way give up, the three others passed him.

Tremayne shrugged. 'Too bad.'

'Will you run him in front again next time?' I asked, as we went down off the stands.

'I expect so. We've tried keeping him back and he runs worse. He's one-paced in a finish, that's his trouble. He's game enough, but it's hard to find races he can win.'

We reached the parade ring where the unsuccessful runners were being unsaddled. Sam, looping girths over his arm, gave Tremayne a rueful smile and said Cashless had done his best.

'I saw,' Tremayne agreed. 'Can't be helped.' We watched Sam walk off towards the weighing room and Tremayne remarked thoughtfully that he might try Cashless in an amateur race, and see what Nolan could do.

'Do you play them off against each other on purpose?' I asked.

Tremayne gave me a flickering glance. 'I do the best for my owners,' he said. 'Like a drink?'

It appeared he had arranged to meet the owners of Telebiddy in the Club bar and when we arrived they were already celebrating with a bottle of champagne. Nolan, too, was there, being incredibly nice to them but without financial results.

When the two women had left in a state of euphoria, Nolan asked belligerently whether Tremayne had told them to give him a present.

'I suggested it,' Tremayne said calmly, 'but you'll be lucky. Better settle for what you took from the bookmakers yourself.'

'Damn little,' Nolan said, or words to that effect, 'and the bloodsucking lawyers will get the lot.' He shouldered his way out of the bar in self-righteous outrage, which seemed to be his uppermost state of mind oftener than not.

With non-commital half-lowered eyelids Tremayne watched him go, then transferred his gaze to me.

'Well,' he asked, 'what have you learned?'

'What you intended me to, I expect.'

He smiled. 'And a bit more than I intended. I've noticed you do that all the time.' With a contented sigh he put down his empty glass. 'Two winners,' he said. 'A better than average day at the races. Let's go home.'

At about the same time we were driving home with Tremayne's winnings safely stowed in his own pockets, not mine, Detective Chief Inspector Doone was poring over the increased pickings from the woodland.

The Detective Chief Inspector could be said to be purring. Among some insignificant long-rusted detritus lay the star of the whole collection, a woman's handbag. Total satisfaction had been denied him, as the prize had been torn open on one side, probably by a dog, whose toothmarks still showed, so that most of the contents had been lost. All the same, he was left with a shoulder strap, a corroded buckle and at least half of a brown plastic school-style bag which still held, in an intact inner zipped pocket, a small mirror and a folded photograph frame.

With careful movements Doone opened the frame and found inside, water-stained along one edge but otherwise sharply clear, a coloured snapshot of a man standing beside a horse.

Disappointed that there was still no easy identifi-

cation of the handbag's past owner, Doone took a telephone call from the pathologist.

'You were asking about the teeth,' the pathologist
said. 'The dental records you gave me are definitely
not those of our bones. Our girl had good teeth. One
or two missing, but no fillings. Sorry.'

Doone's disappointment deepened. The politician's
daughter had just been ruled out. He mentally reviewed
his list again, skipped the prostitutes and provisionally
paused on Angela Brickell, stable lad. Angela
Brickell . . . horse.

The bombshell burst on Shellerton on Thursday.

Tremayne was upstairs showering and dressing
before going to Towcester races when the doorbell
rang. Dee-Dee went to answer it and presently came
into the dining-room looking mystified.

'It's two men,' she said. 'They say they're policemen.
They flashed some sort of identity cards, but they won't
say what they want. I've put them in the family room
until Tremayne comes down. Go and keep an eye on
them, would you mind?'

'Sure,' I said, already on the move.

'Thanks,' she said, returning to the office. 'Whatever
they want it looks boring.'

I could see why she thought so. The two men might
have invented the word grey, so characterless did they
appear at first sight. Ultimate plain clothes, I thought.

'Can I help you?' I said.

'Are you Tremayne Vickers?' one of them asked.

'No. He'll be down soon. Can I help?'

'No, thank you, sir. Can you fetch him?'

'He's in the shower.'

The policeman raised his eyebrows. Trainers, however, didn't shower before morning exercise, they showered after, before going racing. That was Tremayne's habit, anyway. Dee-Dee had told me.

'He's been up since six,' I said.

The policeman's eyes widened, as if I'd read his mind.

'I am Detective Chief Inspector Doone, Thames Valley Police,' he said. 'This is Detective Constable Rich.'

'How do you do,' I said politely. 'I'm John Kendall. Would you care to sit down?'

They perched gingerly on chairs and said no to an offer of coffee.

'Will he be long, sir?' Doone asked. 'We must see him soon.'

'No, not long.'

Doone, on further inspection, appeared to be about fifty, with grey-dusted light brown hair and a heavy medium-brown moustache. He had light brown eyes, big bony hands and, as we all slowly discovered, a habit of talking a lot in a light Berkshire accent.

This chattiness wasn't at all apparent in the first ten minutes before Tremayne came downstairs buttoning the blue and white striped cuffs of his shirt and carrying his jacket gripped between forearm and chest.

'Hello,' he said, 'who's this?'

Dee-Dee appeared behind him, apparently to tell him, but Doone introduced himself before either she or I could do so.

'Police?' Tremayne said, unworried. 'What about?'

'We'd like to speak to you alone, sir.'

'What? Oh, very well.'

He asked me with his eyes to leave with Dee-Dee, shutting the door behind us. I returned to the dining-room but presently heard the family room door open and Tremayne's voice calling.

'John, come back here, would you?'

I went back. Doone was protesting about my presence, saying it was unnecessary and inadvisable.

Tremayne said stubbornly, 'I want him to hear it. Will you repeat what you said?'

Doone shrugged. 'I came to inform Mr Vickers that some remains have been found which may prove to be those of a young woman who was once employed here.'

'Angela Brickell,' Tremayne said resignedly.

'Oh.'

'What does "Oh" mean, sir?' Doone enquired sharply.

'It means just oh,' I said. 'Poor girl. Everyone thought she'd just done a bunk.'

'They have a photograph,' Tremayne said. 'They're trying to identify the man.' He turned to Doone. 'Show

197

it to him.' He nodded in my direction. 'Don't take my word for it.'

Unwillingly Doone handed me a photograph enclosed in a plastic holder.

'Do you know this man, sir?' he asked.

I glanced at Tremayne who was not looking concerned.

'You may as well tell him,' he said.

'Harry Goodhaven?'

Tremayne nodded. 'That's Fiona's horse, Chickweed, the one they said was doped.'

'How can you recognise a horse?' Doone asked.

Tremayne stared at him. 'Horses have faces, like people. I'd know Chickweed anywhere. He's still here, out in the yard.'

'Who is this man, this Harry Goodhaven?' Doone demanded.

'The husband of the owner of the horse.'

'Why would Angela Brickell be carrying his photograph?'

'She wasn't,' Tremayne said. 'Well, I suppose she was, but it was the *horse*'s photograph she was carrying. She looked after it.'

Doone looked completely unconvinced.

'To a lad,' I said, 'the horses they look after are like children. They love them. They defend them. It makes sense that she carried Chickweed's picture.'

Tremayne glanced at me with half-stifled surprise, but I'd been listening to the lads for a week.

'What John says,' Tremayne nodded, 'is absolutely true.'

The attendant policeman, Constable Rich, was all the time taking notes, though not at high speed: not shorthand.

Doone said, 'Sir, can you give me the address of this Harry Goodhaven?'

With slight irritation Tremayne answered, 'This Harry Goodhaven, as you call him, is Mr Henry Goodhaven who owns the Manor House, Shellerton.'

Doone very nearly said 'Oh' in his turn, and made a visible readjustment in his mind.

'I'm already running late,' Tremayne said, making moves to leave.

'But sir . . .'

'Stay as long as you like,' Tremayne said, going. 'Talk to John, talk to my secretary, talk to whoever you want.'

'I don't think you understand, sir,' Doone said with a touch of desperation. 'Angela Brickell was *strangled*.'

'*What?*' Tremayne stopped dead, stunned. 'I thought you said . . .'

'I said we'd found some remains. Now that you've recognised the . . . er . . . horse, sir, we're pretty sure of her identity. Everything else fits; height, age, possible time of death. And, sir . . .' he hesitated briefly as if to summon courage, 'only last week, sir, we had a Crown Court case about another young woman who was strangled . . . strangled here in this house.'

There was silence.

Tremayne said finally, 'There can't be any connection. The death that occurred in this house was an accident, whatever the jury thought.'

Doone said doggedly, 'Did Mr Nolan Everard have any connections with Angela Brickell?'

'Yes, of course he did. He rides Chickweed, the horse in that photograph. He saw Angela Brickell quite often in the course of her work.' He paused for thought. 'Where did you say her . . . remains . . . were found?'

'I don't think I said, sir.'

'Well, where?'

Doone said, 'All in good time, sir,' a shade uncomfortably, and it occurred to me that he was hoping someone would *know*, and anyone who knew would very likely have strangled her.

'Poor girl,' Tremayne said. 'But all the same, Chief Inspector, I do now have to go to the races. Stay as long as you like, ask whatever you want. John here will explain to my assistant and head lad. John, tell Mackie and Bob what's happened, will you? Phone the car if you need me. Right, I'm off.'

He continued purposefully and at good speed on his way and one could see and hear the Volvo start up and depart. In some bemusement Doone watched him go: his first taste of the difficulty of deflecting Tremayne from a chosen course.

'Well, Chief Inspector,' I said neutrally, 'where do you want to begin?'

'Your name, sir?'

I gave it. He was a good deal more confident with me, I noticed: I didn't have a personality that over-shadowed his own.

'And your . . . er . . . position here?'

'I'm writing a history of the stables.'

He seemed vaguely surprised that someone should be engaged on such an enterprise and said lamely, 'Very interesting, I'm sure.'

'Yes, indeed.'

'And . . . er . . . did you know the deceased?'

'Angela Brickell? No, I didn't. She vanished last summer, I believe, and I've been here only a short time, roughly ten days.'

'But you knew about her, sir,' he said shrewdly.

'Let me show you how I knew,' I said. 'Come and look.'

I led him into the dining-room and showed him the piles of clippings, explaining they were the raw materials of my future book.

'This is my workroom,' I said. 'Somewhere in *that* pile of cuttings,' I pointed, 'is an account of Angela Brickell's disappearance. That's how I know about her, and that's all I know. No one has mentioned her outside of this room since I've been here.'

He looked through the past year's cuttings and found the pieces about the girl. He nodded a few times and laid them back carefully where he'd found them, and seemed reassured about me personally. I got the first hint of the garrulity to come.

'Well, sir,' he said, relaxing, 'you can start introducing me to all the people here and explain why I'm asking questions and, as I've found on other cases when only remains are found that people tend to think the worst and imagine all sorts of horrors so that it makes them feel sick and wastes a good deal of time altogether, I'll tell you, sir, and you can pass it on, that what was found was *bones*, sir, quite clean and no smell, nothing horrible, you can assure people of that.'

'Thank you,' I said, a shade numbly.

'Animals and insects had cleaned her, you see.'

'Don't you think that fact alone will make people feel sick?'

'Then don't stress it, sir.'

'No.'

'We have her clothes and shoes and her handbag and lipstick back at the police station ... they were scattered around her and I've had my men searching ...' He stopped, not telling me then where the search had occurred; except that if she'd been scavenged it had to have been out of doors. Which for a stable girl, in a way, made sense.

'And if you don't mind, sir, will you please just tell everyone she's been found, not that she was strangled.'

'How do you know that she was strangled, if there's nothing much left?'

'The hyoid bone, sir. In the throat. Fractured. Only

a direct blow or manual pressure does that. Fingers usually, from behind.'

'Oh, I see. All right, I'll leave it to you. We'd better start with Mr Vickers' secretary, Dee-Dee.'

I steered him into the office and introduced him. Detective Constable Rich followed everywhere like a shadow, a non-speaking taker of notes. I explained to Dee-Dee that Angela Brickell had probably been found.

'Oh good,' she said spontaneously, and then, seeing it wasn't good at all, 'Oh dear.'

Doone asked to use the telephone, Dee-Dee at once assenting. Doone called his people back at base.

'Mr Vickers identified the horse as one that Angela Brickell tended in his stable, and the man as the owner of the horse, or rather the owner's husband. I'd say it's fairly sure we have Angela Brickell in the mortuary. Can you arrange to send round a WPC to her parents? They live out Wokingham way. The address is in my office. Do it pronto. We don't want anyone from Shellerton upsetting them first. Break it to them kindly, see? Ask if they could recognise any clothes of hers, or handbag. Ask Mollie to go to them, if she's on duty. She makes it more bearable for people. She mops up their grief. Get Mollie. Tell her to take another constable with her, if she wants.'

He listened for a moment or two and put down the receiver.

'The poor lass has been dead six months or more,' he said to Dee-Dee. 'All that's left is sweet clean bones.'

Dee-Dee looked as if that thought were sick-making enough, but I could see that Doone's rough humanity would comfort in the end. He was like a stubby-fingered surgeon, I thought: delicate in his handiwork against the odds.

He asked Dee-Dee if she knew of any reason for Angela Brickell's disappearance. Had the girl been unhappy? Having rows with a boyfriend?

'I've no idea. We didn't find out until after she'd gone that she must have given chocolate to Chickweed. Stupid thing to do.'

Doone looked lost. I explained about the theobromine. 'That's in those clippings, too,' I said.

'We found some chocolate bar wrappers with the lass,' Doone said. 'No chocolate. Is that what was meant in our notes by "possibly doped horse in her charge"?'

'Spot on,' I said.

'Chocolate!' he said disgustedly. 'Not worth dying for.'

I said, enlightened, 'Were you looking for a big conspiracy? A doping ring?'

'Have to consider everything.'

Dee-Dee said positively, 'Angela Brickell wouldn't have been in a doping ring. You don't know what you're talking about.'

Doone didn't pursue it but said he'd like to talk to the rest of the stable staff, asking Dee-Dee meanwhile not to break the news to anyone else as he would prefer to do it himself. Also he didn't want anyone springing the tragedy prematurely onto the poor parents.

'Surely I can tell Fiona,' she protested.

'Who's Fiona?' He frowned, perhaps trying to remember.

'Fiona Goodhaven, who owns Chickweed.'

'Oh, yes. Well, not her either. *Especially* not her. I like to get people's first thoughts, first impressions, not hear what they think after they've spent hours discussing something with all their friends. First thoughts are clearer and more valuable, I've found.'

He said it with more persuasion than command, with the result that Dee-Dee agreed to stay off the grapevine. She didn't ask how the girl had died. If she realised Doone's remarks best fitted a murder scenario, she didn't say so. Perhaps she simply shied away from having to know.

Doone asked to be taken out to the stables. On the way I asked him to remember, if he met Mackie, Tremayne's daughter-in-law and assistant trainer, that she was newly pregnant.

He gave me a sharp glance.

'You're considerate,' I said mildly. 'I thought you might want to modify the shocks.'

He looked disconcerted but made no promise either way and, as it happened, by the time we reached the yard, Mackie had gone home and Bob Watson was alone there, beavering away with saw, hammer and nails, making a new saddle-horse to hold the saddles in the tack room. We found him outside the tack-room door, not too pleased to be interrupted.

I introduced Bob to Doone, Doone to Bob. Doone told him that some human remains discovered by chance were thought to be those of Angela Brickell.

'No!' Bob said. 'Straight up? Poor little bitch. What did she do, fall down a quarry?' He looked absent-mindedly at a piece of wood he held as if he'd temporarily forgotten its purpose.

'Why should you say that, sir?' Doone asked attentively.

'Manner of speaking,' Bob said, shrugging. 'I always thought she'd just scarpered. The guv'nor swore she'd given Chickweed chocolate, but I reckon she didn't. I mean, we all know you mustn't. Anyway, who found her? Where did she go?'

'She was found by chance,' Doone said again. 'Was she unhappy over a boyfriend?'

'Not that I know of. But there's twenty lads and girls here, and they come and go all the time. Truth to tell, I can't remember much about her, except she was sexy. Ask Mrs Goodhaven, she was always kind to her. Ask the other girls here, some of them lived in a hostel with her. Why did you want to know about a boyfriend? She didn't take a high jump, did she? Is that what she did?'

Doone didn't say yes or no, and I understood what he'd meant by preferring to listen to unadulterated first thoughts, to the first pictures and conclusions that minds leaped to when questioned.

He talked to Bob for a while longer but as far as I could see learned nothing much.

'You want to see Mackie,' Bob said in the end. 'That's young Mrs Vickers. The girls tell her things they'd never tell me.'

Doone nodded and I led him and the ubiquitous Rich round the house to Mackie and Perkin's entrance, ringing the bell. It was Perkin himself who came to the door, appearing in khaki overalls, looking wholly artisan and smelling, fascinatingly, of wood and linseed oil.

'Hello,' he said, surprised to see me. 'Mackie's in the shower.'

Doone took it in his stride this time, introducing himself formerly.

'I came to let Mrs Vickers know that Angela Brickell's been found,' he said.

'Who?' Perkin said blankly. 'I didn't know anyone was lost. I don't know any Angela . . . Angela who did you say?'

Doone patiently explained she'd been lost for seven or more months. Angela Brickell.

'Good Lord. Really? Who is she?' A thought struck him. 'I say, is she the stable girl who buggered off sometime last year? I remember a bit of a fuss.'

'That's the one.'

'Good then, my wife will be glad she's found. I'll give her the message.'

He made as if to close the door but Doone said he
would like to see Mrs Vickers himself.

'Oh? All right. You'd better come in and wait. John?
Come in?'

'Thanks,' I said.

He led the way into a kitchen-dining room where I
hadn't been before and offered us rattan armchairs
round a table made of a circular slab of glass resting
on three gothic plaster pillars. The curtains and chair
covers were bright turquoise overprinted with blowsy
grey, black and white flowers, and all the kitchen fitments were faced with grey-white streaked Formica;
thoroughly modern.

Perkin watched my surprise with irony and said,
'Mackie chose everything in a revolt against good taste.'

'It's happy,' I said. 'Light-hearted.'

The remark seemed somehow to disturb him, but
Mackie herself arrived with damp hair at that point
looking refreshed and pleased with life. Her reaction to
Doone's first cautious words was the same as everyone
else's. 'Great. Where is she?'

The gradual realisation of the true facts drained the
contentment and the colour from her face. She listened
to his questions and answered them, and faced the
implications squarely.

'You're telling us, aren't you,' she said flatly, 'that
either she killed herself . . . or somebody killed her?'

'I didn't say that, madam.'

'As good as.' She sighed desolately. 'All these ques-

tions about doping rings . . . and boyfriends. Oh God.'
She closed her eyes briefly, then opened them to look
at Doone and me.

'We've just had months and months of trouble and
anxiety over Olympia and Nolan, we've had the TV
people and reporters in droves, driving us mad with
their questions, we're only just beginning to feel free
of it all . . . and I can't bear it . . . I can't bear it . . . it's
starting all over again.'

CHAPTER TEN

I borrowed the Land Rover and at Doone's request led him down to the village and into Harry and Fiona's drive. I was surprised that he still wanted me with him and said so, and he explained a little solemnly that he found people felt less *threatened* by a police officer if he turned up with someone they knew.

'Don't you want them to feel threatened?' I asked. 'Many police seem to like it that way.'

'I'm not many policemen.' He seemed uninsulted. 'I work in my own way, sir, and if sometimes it's not how my colleagues work then I get my results all the same and it's results that count in the end. It may not be the best way to the highest promotion,' he smiled briefly, 'but I do tend to solve things, I assure you.'

'I don't doubt it, Chief Inspector,' I said.

'I have three daughters,' he said, sighing, 'and I don't like cases like this one.'

We were standing in the drive looking at the noble façade of a fine Georgian manor.

'Never make assumptions,' he said absent-mindedly,

as if giving me advice. 'You know the two most pathetic words a policeman can utter when his case falls apart around him?'

I shook my head.

'I assumed,' he said.

'I'll remember.'

He looked at me calmly in his unthreatening way and said it was time to trouble the Goodhavens.

As it happened, only Fiona was there, coming to the kitchen door in a dark blue tailored suit with a white silk blouse, gold chains, high-heeled black shoes and an air of rush. She smiled apologetically when she saw me.

'John,' she said. 'What can I do for you? I'm going out to lunch. Can you make it quick?'

'Er . . .' I said, 'this is Detective Chief Inspector Doone, Thames Valley Police. And Constable Rich.'

'Policemen?' she asked, puzzled, and then in terrible flooding anxiety, 'Nothing's happened to Harry?'

'No, no. Nothing. It's not about Harry. Well, not exactly. It's about Angela Brickell. They've found her.'

'Angela . . .? Oh yes. Well, I'm glad. Where did she go?'

Doone was very adroit, I thought, at letting silence itself break the bad news.

'Oh my dear,' Fiona said, after a few quiet revelationary seconds, 'is she dead?'

'Yes, I'm afraid so, madam.' Doone nodded. 'I need to ask you a few questions.'

'Oh, but . . .' She looked at her watch. 'Can't it wait? It's not just a lunch, I'm the guest of honour.'

We were still standing on the doorstep. Doone without arguing produced the photograph and asked Fiona to identify the man, if she could.

'Of course. It's Harry, my husband. And that's my horse, Chickweed. Where did you get this?'

'From the young woman's handbag.'

Fiona's face was full of kindness and regret. 'She loved Chickweed,' she said.

'Perhaps I could come back when your husband's at home?' Doone suggested.

Fiona was relieved. 'Oh, yes, do that. After five tonight or tomorrow morning. He'll be here until about . . . um . . . eleven, I should think, tomorrow. Bye, John.'

She hurried back into the house, leaving the door open, and presently, from beside our own cars, we saw her come out, lock the back door, hide the key under the stone (Tut, tut, Doone said disapprovingly) and drive away in a neat BMW, her blond hair shining, cheerful hand waving goodbye.

'If you had to describe her in one word,' Doone said to me, 'what would it be?'

'Staunch,' I said.

'That was quick.'

'That's what she is. Steadfast, I'd say.'

'Have you known her long?'

'Ten days, like the others.'

'Mm.' He pondered. 'I won't have ten days, not living in their community, like you do. I might ask you again what people here are really like. People sometimes don't act natural when they're with policemen.'

'Fiona did. Surely everyone did who you've met this morning?'

'Oh yes. But there's some I haven't met. And there are loyalties . . . I read the transcript of part of that trial before I came here. Loyalty is strong here, wouldn't you agree? Staunch, steadfast loyalty, wouldn't you say?'

Doone might look grey, I thought, and his chatty almost sing-song Berkshire voice might be disarming, but there was a cunningly intelligent observer behind the waffle, and I did suddenly believe, as I hadn't entirely before, that usually he solved his cases.

He said he would like to speak to all the other stable girls before they heard the news from anyone else, and also the men, but the women first.

I took Doone and Rich to the house in the village which I knew the girls called their hostel, though I'd never been in it. It was a small modern house in a cul-de-sac, bought cheaply before it was built, Tremayne had told me, and appreciating nicely with the years. I explained to Doone that I didn't know all the girls' names: I saw them only at morning exercise and sometimes at evening stables.

'Fair enough,' he said, 'but they'll all know *you*. You can tell them I'm not an ogre.'

I wasn't any longer so sure about that but I did what

213

he asked. He sat paternally on a flower-patterned sofa in the sitting-room, at home among the clutter of pot plants, satin cushions, fashion magazines and endless photographs of horses, and told them without drama that it looked possible Angela Brickell had died the day she hadn't returned for evening stables. They had found her clothes, her handbag and her bones, he said, and naturally they were having to look into it. He asked the by now familiar questions: did they think Angela had been deeply involved in doping horses, and did they know if she'd had rows with her boyfriend.

Only four of the six girls had been employed at the yard in Angela's time, they said. She definitely hadn't been doping horses; they found the idea funny. She wasn't bright enough, one of them said unflatteringly. She hadn't been their close friend. She was moody and secretive, they all agreed, but they didn't know of any one steady boyfriend. They thought Sam had probably had her, but no one should read much in that. Who was Sam? Sam Yaeger, the stable jockey, who rode more than the horses.

There were a few self-conscious giggles. Doone, father of three daughters, interpreted the giggles correctly and looked disillusioned.

'Did Angela and Sam Yaeger quarrel?'

'You don't quarrel with Sam Yaeger,' the brightest of them said boldly. 'You go to bed with him. Or in the hay.'

Gales of giggles.

They were all in their teens, I thought. Light-framed, hopeful, knowing.

The bold girl said, 'But no one takes Sam seriously. It's just a bit of fun. He makes a joke of it. If you don't want to, you just say no. Most of us say no. He'd never try to force anyone.'

The others looked shocked at the idea. 'It's casual with him, like.'

I wondered if Doone were thinking that maybe with Angela it hadn't been casual after all.

The bold girl, whose name was Tansy, asked when they'd found the poor little bitch.

'When?' Doone considered briefly. 'Someone noticed her last Sunday morning. Mind you, he wasn't in a great hurry to do anything because he could see she'd been lying there peacefully a long time, but then he phoned us and the message reached me late Sunday afternoon while I was sleeping off my wife's Yorkshire pudding – great grub, that is – so Monday I went to see the lass and we started trying to find out who she was, because we have lists of missing people, runaways mostly, you see? Then yesterday we found her handbag, and it had this photo in it, so I came over this morning to check if she was the missing stable girl on our missing persons list. So I should think you could say we really found her this morning.'

His voice had lulled them into accepting him on friendly terms and they willingly looked at the photograph he passed around.

'That's Chickweed,' they said, nodding.

'You're sure you can tell one horse from another?'

'Of course you can,' they said, 'when you see them every day.'

'And the man?'

'Mr Goodhaven.'

Doone thanked them and tucked the photo away again. Rich took slow notes, none of the girls paying him any attention.

Doone asked if by any chance Angela Brickell had owned a dog. The girls, mystified, said no. Why would he think so? They'd found a dog's collar near her, he explained, and a well-chewed ball. None of them had a dog, Tansy said.

Doone rose to go and told them if anything occurred to them, to send him a message.

'What sort of thing?' they asked.

'Well now,' he said kindly. 'We know she's dead, but we want to know how and why. It's best to know. If you were found dead one day, you'd want people to know what happened, wouldn't you?'

Yes, they nodded, they would.

'Where did she go?' Tansy asked.

Doone as near as dammit patted her head, but not quite. I thought that that would have undone all his good fatherly work. Willing they might be, but feminists all, too smart to be patronised.

'We have to do more tests first, miss,' he said obscurely. 'But soon we hope to make a statement.'

They all accepted that easily enough and we said our goodbyes, travelling back through the village to a bungalow nearer Bob Watson's house, where the unmarried lads lived.

The living-room in the lads' hostel, in sharp contrast to the girls', was plantless, without cushions and was grubbily scattered with newspapers, empty beer cans, pornography, dirty plates and muddy boots. Only the televisions and video players in both places looked the same.

The lads all knew that Angela Brickell had been found dead as one of them had learned it from Bob Watson. None of them seemed to care about her personally (exactly like the girls) and they too had no information and few opinions about her.

'She rode all right,' one of them said, shrugging.

'She was a bit of a hot pants,' said another.

They identified Chickweed's picture immediately and one of them asked if he could have the photo when the police had done with it.

'Why?' Doone asked.

'Because I look after the old bugger now, that's why. Wouldn't mind having a snap of him.'

'Better take another one,' Doone advised him. 'By rights this belongs to the lass's parents.'

'Well,' he later demanded of me, after we'd left. 'What do you think?'

'It's *your* job to think,' I protested.

He half smiled. 'There's a long way to go yet. If you

217

think of anything, you tell me. I'll listen to everything anyone wants to say. I'm not proud. I don't mind the public telling me the answers. Make sure everyone knows that, will you?'

'Yes,' I said.

The telephone in Shellerton House began ringing that afternoon in a clamour that lasted for days. However reticent Doone had been, the news had spread at once like a bush fire through the village that *another* young woman connected with Tremayne Vickers' house and stables had been found dead. Newspapers, quickly informed, brusquely demanded to be told where, when and why. Dee-Dee repeated and repeated that she didn't know until she was almost in tears. I took over from her after a while and dispensed enormous courtesy and goodwill but no facts, of which, at the time anyway, I knew very few.

I worked on the book and answered the phone most of Friday and didn't see Doone at all, but on Saturday I learned that he had spent the day before scattering fear and consternation.

Tremayne had asked if I would prefer to go to Sandown with Fiona, Harry and Mackie, saying he thought I might find it more illuminating: he himself would be saddling five runners at Chepstow and dealing with two lots of demanding owners besides. 'To be frank, you'd be under my feet. Go and carry things for Mackie.'

With old-fashioned views, which Mackie herself tolerated with affection, he persisted in thinking pregnant women fragile. I wondered if Tremayne understood how little Perkin would like my carrying things for Mackie and determined to be discreet.

'Fiona and Harry are taking Mackie,' Tremayne said, almost as if the same thought had occurred to him. I'll check that they'll take you too, though it's a certainty if they have room.'

They had room. They collected Mackie and me at the appointed time and they were very disturbed indeed.

Harry was driving. Fiona twisted round in the front seat to speak to Mackie and me directly and with deep lines of worry told us that Doone had paid two visits to them the day before, the first apparently friendly and the second menacing in the extreme.

'He seemed all right in the morning,' Fiona said. 'Chatty and easy-going. Then he came back in the evening . . .' She shivered violently, although it was warm in the car, '. . . and he more or less accused Harry of strangling that bloody girl.'

'*What?*' Mackie said. 'That's ridiculous.'

'Doone doesn't think so,' Harry said gloomily. 'He says she was definitely strangled. And did he show you that photo of me with Chickweed?'

Mackie and I both said yes.

'Well, it seems he got it enlarged. I mean, blown up really big. He said he wanted to see me alone, without Fiona, and he showed me the enlargement which was just of me, not the horse. He asked me to confirm that I was wearing my own sunglasses in the photo. I said of course I was. Then he asked me if I was wearing my own belt, and I said of course. He asked me to look carefully at the buckle. I said I wouldn't be wearing anyone else's things. Then he asked me if the pen clipped onto the racecard I was holding in the photo was mine also . . . and I got a bit shirty and demanded to know what it was all about.' He stopped for a moment, and then in depression went on. 'You won't believe it . . . but they found my sunglasses and my belt and my gold pen lying with that girl, wherever she was, and Doone won't *tell* us where for some God-silly reason. I don't know how the hell those things got there. I told Doone I hadn't seen any of them for ages and he said he believed it. He thought they'd been with Angela Brickell all these months . . . that I'd dropped them when I was with her.'

He stopped again, abruptly, and at that point added no more.

Fiona, in a strong mixture of indignation and alarm, said, 'Doone demanded to know precisely where Harry had been on the day that girl went missing and also he said he might want to take Harry's *fingerprints.*'

'He thinks I killed her,' Harry said. 'It's obvious he does.'

'It's ridiculous,' Mackie repeated. 'He doesn't know you.'

'Where *were* you on that day?' I asked. 'I mean, you might have a perfect alibi.'

'I might have,' he said, 'but I don't know where I was. Could you say for certain what you were doing on the Tuesday afternoon of the second week of June last year?'

'Not for sure,' I said.

'If it had been the *third* week,' Harry said, 'we'd have been at Ascot races. Royal Ascot. Tarted up in top hats and things.'

'We keep a big appointments diary,' Fiona said fiercely. 'I dug up last year's. There's nothing listed at all on that second Tuesday. Neither of us can remember what we were doing.'

'No work?' I suggested. 'No meetings?'

Harry and Fiona simultaneously said no. Fiona was on a couple of committees for good causes, but there'd been no meetings that day. Harry, whose personal fortune seemed to equal Fiona's in robust good health, had in the past negotiated the brilliant sale of an inherited tyre-making company (so Tremayne had told me) and now passed his time lucratively as occasional consultant to other private firms looking for a golden corporate whale to swallow them. He couldn't remember any consultations for most of June.

'We went to see Nolan ride Chickweed at Uttoxeter near the end of May,' Fiona said worriedly. 'Angela was there looking after the horse. That was the day someone fed him theobromine and caffeine, and if she didn't give Chickweed chocolate herself then she must have let someone else do it. Sheer negligence, probably. Anyway, Chickweed won and Angela went back to Shellerton with him and we saw her a few days later and gave her an extra present, as we were so pleased with the way she looked after the horse. I mean, a horse's success is always partly due to whoever cares for it and grooms it. And I can't remember seeing the wretched girl again after that.'

'Nor can I,' Harry said.

They went over and over the same old ground all the way to Sandown and it was clear they had spoken of little else since Doone's devastating identification of Harry's belongings.

'Someone must have put those things there to incriminate Harry,' Mackie said unhappily.

Fiona agreed with her, but it appeared that Doone didn't.

Harry said, 'Doone believes it was an unpremeditated murder. I asked him why and he just said that most murders were unpremeditated. Useless. He said people who commit unpremeditated murder often drop things from extreme agitation and don't know they've dropped them. I said I couldn't even remember ever talking to the girl except in the company of my wife and he simply stared at me, not believing me. I'll tell you, pals, it was unnerving.'

'Awful,' Mackie said vehemently. '*Wicked.*'

Harry, trying to sound balanced, was clearly horribly

disconcerted and was driving without concentration, braking and accelerating jerkily. Fiona said they had thought of not going to Sandown as they weren't in a fun-day mood, but they had agreed not to let Doone's suspicions ruin everything. Doone's suspicions were nevertheless conspicuously wrecking their equilibrium and it was a subdued little group that stood in the parade ring watching Fiona's tough hunter, the famous Chickweed, walk round before the Wilfred Johnstone Hunter Chase.

No one, one hoped, had given him chocolate.

Fiona had told Nolan about Doone's accusations. Nolan told Harry that now he, Harry, knew what it was like to have a charge of murder hanging over him he would in retrospect have more sympathy for him, Nolan. Harry didn't like it. With only vestiges of friendliness he protested that he, Harry, had not been found with a dead girl at his feet.

'As good as, by the sound of things,' Nolan said, rattled.

'Nolan!' Fiona wasn't amused. 'Everyone, stop talking about it. Nolan, put your mind on the race. Harry, not another word about that *bloody* girl. Everything will be sorted out. We'll just have to be patient.'

Harry gave her a fond but rueful glance and, over her shoulder, caught my eye. There was something more in his expression, I thought, and after a moment identified it as fear: maybe faint, but definitely present. Harry and fear hadn't, until then, gone together in my mind, particularly not since his controlled behaviour in a frozen ditch.

Mackie, *in loco* Tremayne, saw Nolan into the saddle and the four of us walked towards the stands to see the race. With Mackie and Fiona in front, Harry fell into step beside me.

'I want to tell you something,' he said, 'but not Fiona.'

'Fire away.'

He looked quickly around him, checking no one could hear.

'Doone said ... Christ ... he said the girl had no clothes on when she died.'

'God, Harry.' I felt my mouth still open, and closed it consciously.

'I don't know what to do,' he said.

'Absolutely nothing.'

'Doone asked what I was doing there with my belt off.'

The shock still trembled in his voice.

'The innocent aren't found guilty,' I protested.

He said miserably, 'Oh, yes, they are. You know they are.'

'But not on such flimsy evidence.'

'I haven't been able to tell Fiona. I mean, we've always been fine together, but she might start *wondering* ... I don't honestly know how I'd bear that.'

We reached the stands and went up to watch, Harry falling silent in his torturing troubles amid the raucous calls of bookmakers and the enfolding hubbub of the gathering crowd. The runners cantered past on their way to the starting gate, Nolan looking professional as usual on the muscly chestnut that Fiona had ridden all autumn out hunting. Chickweed, Mackie had told me, was Fiona's especial pet: her friend as much as her property. Chickweed, circling and lining up, running in the first hunter chase of the spring season, was going to win three or four times before June, Tremayne hoped.

We were joined at that point by pudgy unfit Lewis, who panted that he had only just arrived in time and asked if the Jockey Club had said anything about Nolan going on riding.

'Not a word,' Fiona said. 'Fingers crossed.'

'If they were going to stop him,' Lewis opined judiciously, taking deep breaths, 'they'd surely have let him know by today, so perhaps the expletive sod's got away with it.'

'Brotherly love,' Fiona remarked ironically.

'He owes me,' Lewis said darkly and with such growling intensity that all of us, I thought, recognised the nature of the debt, even if some hadn't wanted to believe it earlier.

'And will you collect?' Harry asked, his sarcasm showing.

'No thanks to you,' Lewis replied sharply.

'Perjury's not my best act.'

Lewis smiled like a snake, all fangs.

'I,' he said, 'am the best bleep bleep actor of you all.'

Fiona starkly faced the certainty that Lewis had not

after all been too drunk to see straight when Olympia died. Mackie's clear face was pinched with dismay. Harry, who had known all along, would have shrugged off Lewis's admission philosophically were it not for his own ominous future.

'What would you have me do?' Lewis demanded, seeing the general disapproval. 'Say he called her every filthy name in the book and shook her by the neck until her eyes popped out?'

'Lewis!' Fiona exclaimed, not believing him. 'Shut up.'

Lewis gave me a mediumly hostile glance and wanted to know why I was always hanging around. No one answered him, me included.

Fiona said, 'They're off' a split second before the official announcement and concentrated through her raceglasses.

'I asked you an expletive question,' Lewis said to me brusquely.

'You know why,' I replied, watching the race.

'Tremayne isn't here,' he objected.

'He sent me to see Sandown.'

Chickweed was easy to spot, I discovered, with the white blaze down his chestnut face that so clearly distinguished him in the photograph nodding away on the rails at every galloping step. The overall pace seemed slower to me than the other races I'd watched, the jumping more deliberate; but it wasn't, as Tremayne had warned me, an easy track even for the sport's top performers, and for hunters a searching test. 'Watch them jump the seven fences down the far side,' he'd said. 'If a horse meets the first one right, the others come in his stride. Miss the first, get it wrong, legs in a tangle, you might as well forget the whole race. Nolan is an artist at meeting that first fence right.'

I watched particularly. Chickweed flew the first fence and all the next six down the far side, gaining effortless lengths. 'There's nothing like the hunting field for teaching a horse to jump,' Tremayne had said. 'The trouble is, hunters aren't necessarily fast. Chickweed is, though. So was Oxo who won the Grand National years back.'

Chickweed repeated the feat on the second circuit and then, a length in front of his nearest pursuer, swept round the long bend at the bottom end of the course and straightened himself for the third fence from home – the Pond fence, so called because the small hollow beside it had once been wet, though now held mostly reeds and bushes.

'Oh, come on,' Fiona said explosively, the tension too much. 'Chicky Chickweed . . . jump it.'

Chicky Chickweed rose to it as if he'd heard her, his white blaze showing straight on us before he veered right towards the second last fence and the uphill pull to home.

'A lot of races are lost on the hill,' Tremayne had told me. 'It's where stamina counts, where you need the reserves. Any horse that has enough left to accelerate there is going to win. Same at Cheltenham. A race at either place can change dramatically after the last fence. Tired horses just fade away, even if they're in the lead.'

Chickweed made short work of the second last fence but didn't shake off his pursuer.

'I can't bear it,' Fiona said.

Mackie put down her raceglasses to watch the finish, anxiety digging lines on her forehead.

It was only a race, I thought. What did it matter? I answered my own question astringently: I'd written a novel, what did it matter if it won or lost on its own terms? It mattered because I cared, because it was where I'd invested all thought, all effort. It mattered to Tremayne and Mackie the same way. Only a race . . . but also their skill laid on the line.

Chickweed's pursuer closed the gap coming to the last fence.

'Oh, no,' Fiona groaned, lowering her own glasses. 'Oh, Nolan, come on.'

Chickweed made a spectacular leap, leaving unnecessary space between himself and the birch, wasting precious time in the air. His pursuer, jumping lower in a flatter trajectory, landed first and was fastest away.

'*Damn*,' Harry said.

Fiona was silent, beginning to accept defeat.

Nolan had no such thoughts. Nolan, aggressive instincts in full flood, was crouching like a demon over Chickweed's withers delivering the message that losing was unacceptable. Nolan's whip rose and fell twice, his arm swinging hard. Chickweed, as if galvanised, reversed his decision to slow down now that he'd been passed and took up the struggle again. The jockey and horse in front, judging the battle won, eased up fractionally too soon. Chickweed caught them napping a stride from the winning post and put his head in front just where it mattered, the crowd cheering for him, the favourite, the fighter who never gave up.

It was Nolan, I saw, who had won that race. Nolan himself, not the horse. Nolan's ability, Nolan's character acting on Chickweed's. Through Nolan I began to understand how much more there was to riding races than fearlessness and being able to stay in the saddle. More than tactics, more than experience, more than ambition. Winning races, like survival, began in the mind.

Fiona, triumphant where all had looked lost, breathless and shiny-eyed, hurried ahead with Mackie to meet the returning warriors. Lewis, Harry and I pressed along in their wake.

'Nolan's a genius,' Harry was saying.

'The other expletive jockey threw it away,' Lewis had it.

Never assume, I thought, thinking of Doone. Never assume you've won until you hold the prize in your hand.

Doone *was* assuming things, I thought. Not taking his own advice. Or so it seemed.

We all went for a celebratory drink, though in Mackie's case it was ginger ale. Harry ordered the obligatory bubbles, his heart in his boots. Nolan was as high as Fiona, Lewis a grudging applauder. I, I supposed, an observer, still on the outside looking in. Six of us in a racecourse bar smiling in unison while the cobweb ghosts of two young women set traps for the flies.

We arrived back at Shellerton before Tremayne returned from Chepstow. Fiona dropped Mackie off at her side of the house and I walked round to Tremayne's, unlocking the door with the key he'd given me and switching on lights.

There was a message from Gareth on the family room corkboard: 'GONE TO MOVIE BACK FOR GRUB.' Smiling, I kicked the hot logs together and blew some kindling sticks to life with the bellows to revive the fire and poured some wine and felt at home.

A knock on the back door drew me from comfort to see who it was, and I didn't at first recognise the young woman looking at me with a shy enquiring smile. She was pretty in a small way, brown haired, self-effacing ... Bob Watson's wife, Ingrid.

'Come in,' I said warmly, relieved to have identified her. 'But I'm the only one home.'

'I thought maybe Mackie. Mrs Vickers ...'

'She's round in her own house.'

'Oh. Well ...' She came over the threshold tentatively and I encouraged her into the family room where she stood nervously and wouldn't sit down.

'Bob doesn't know I'm here,' she said anxiously.

'Never mind. Have a drink?'

'Oh no. Better not.'

She seemed to be screwing herself up to something, and out it all finally came in a rush.

'You were ever so kind to me that night. Bob reckons you saved me from frostbite at the least . . . and pneumonia, he said. Giving me your own clothes. I'll never forget it. Never.'

'You looked so cold,' I said. 'Are you sure you won't sit down?'

'I was *hurting* with cold.' She again ignored the chair suggestion. 'I knew you'd come back just now . . . I saw Mrs Goodhaven's car come up the road . . . I came to talk to you, really. I've got to tell someone, I think, and you're . . . well . . . easiest.'

'Go on then. Talk. I'm listening.'

She said in a small burst, unexpectedly, 'Angela Brickell was a Roman Catholic, like I am.'

'Was she?' The news meant very little.

Ingrid nodded. 'It said on the local radio news tonight that Angela's body was found last Saturday by a gamekeeper on the Quillersedge Estate. There was quite a bit about her on the news, about how the police were proceeding with their enquiries and all that. And it said foul play was suspected. They're such stupid words, foul play. Why didn't they just say someone

231

probably did her in? Anyway, after she'd vanished last year Mrs Vickers asked me to clear all her things out of the hostel and send them to her parents, and I did.'

She stopped, staring searchingly at my face for understanding.

'What,' I asked, feeling the way, 'did you find in her belongings? Something that worries you ... because she's dead?'

Ingrid's face showed relief at being invited to tell me.

'I threw it away,' she said. 'It was a do-it-yourself home kit for a pregnancy test. She'd used it. All I found was the empty box.'

CHAPTER ELEVEN

Tremayne came home and frightened Ingrid away like Miss Muffet and the spider.

'What did she want?' he asked, watching her scuttling exit. 'She always seems scared of me. She's a real mouse.'

'She came to tell me something she thinks should be known,' I said reflectively. 'I suppose she thought I could do the telling, in her place.'

'Typical,' Tremayne said. 'What was it?'

'Angela Brickell was perhaps pregnant'.

'What?' He stared at me blankly. '*Pregnant?*'

I explained about the used test. 'You don't buy or use one of those tests unless you have good reason to.'

He said thoughtfully. 'No, I suppose not.'

'So,' I said, 'there are about twenty lusty males connected with this stable and dozens more in Shellerton and throughout the racing industry; and even if she *were* pregnant – and from what Doone said about bones I don't see how they can tell yes or no, even if she were – it still might have nothing to do with her death.'

'But it might.'

'She was a Roman Catholic, Ingrid says.'

'What's that got to do with it?'

'They're against abortion.'

He stared into space.

I said, 'Harry's in trouble. Have you heard?'

'No, what trouble?'

I told him about Doone's accusations, and also about Chickweed's way of winning and about Lewis's more or less explicit admission of perjury. Tremayne poured himself a gin and tonic of suitably gargantuan proportions and told me in his turn that he'd had a rotten day at Chepstow. 'One of my runners broke down and another went crashing down arse over tip at the last fence with the race in his pocket. Sam dislocated his thumb, which swelled like a balloon, and although he's OK he won't realistically be fit again until Tuesday, which means I have to scratch around for a replacement for Monday. And one lot of owners groused and groaned until I could have knocked their heads together and all I can do is be nice to them and sometimes it all drives me up the bloody wall, to tell you the truth.'

He flopped his weight into an armchair, stretched out his legs and rested his gaze on his toecaps, thinking things over.

'Are you going to tell Doone about the pregnancy test?' he asked finally.

'I suppose so. It's on Ingrid's conscience. If I don't pass on what she's said, she'll find another mouthpiece.' He sighed. 'It won't do Harry much good.'

'Nor harm.'

'It's a motive. Juries believe in motives.'

I grunted. 'Harry won't come to trial.'

'Nolan did. And a good motive would have jailed him, you can't say it wouldn't.'

'The pregnancy test is a non-starter,' I said. 'Ingrid threw the empty box away; there's no proof it really existed; there's no saying if Angela used it or when; there's no certainty about the result; there's no knowing who she'd been sleeping with.'

'You should have been a lawyer.'

Mackie and Perkin came through for their usual drink and news-exchange and even Chickweed's win couldn't disperse the general gloom.

'Angela pregnant?' Mackie shook her head, almost bewildered. 'She didn't say anything about it.'

'She might have done, given time,' Tremayne said, 'if the test was positive.'

'Damned careless of her,' Perkin said. 'That bloody girl's nothing but trouble. It's all upsetting Mackie just when she should be feeling relaxed and happy, and I don't like it.'

Mackie stretched out a hand and squeezed her husband's in gratitude, the underlying joy resurfacing, as persistent as pregnancy itself. Perhaps Angela Brickell too, I speculated, had been delighted to be needing her test. Who could tell?

Gareth gusted in full of plans for an expedition I'd forgotten about, a fact he unerringly read on my face.

'But you said you would teach us things, and we could light a fire.' His voice rose high with disappointment.

'Um,' I said. 'Ask your father.'

Tremayne listened to Gareth's request for a patch of land for a camp fire and raised his eyebrows my way.

'Do you really want to bother with all this?'

'Actually, I suggested it, in a rash moment.'

Gareth nodded vigorously. 'Coconut's coming at ten.'

Mackie said, 'Fiona asked us to go down in the morning to toast Chickweed and cheer Harry up.'

'But John *promised*,' Gareth said anxiously.

Mackie smiled at him indulgently. 'I'll make John's excuses.'

Sunday morning crept in greyly on a near-freezing drizzle, enough to test the spirits of all would-be survivors. Tremayne, drinking coffee in the kitchen with the lights on at nine-thirty, suggested scrubbing the whole idea. His son would vehemently have none of it. They compromised on a promise from me to bring everyone home at the first sneeze, and Coconut arrived on his bicycle in brilliant yellow oilskins with a grin to match.

It was easy to see how he'd got his name. He stood in the kitchen dripping and pulled off a sou'wester to reveal a wiry tuft of light brown hair sticking straight up from the top of his head. (It would never lie down properly, Gareth later explained.)

Coconut was nearly fifteen. Below the top-knot he had bright intelligent eyes, a big nose and a sloppy loose-lipped mouth, as if his face hadn't yet synthesised with his emerging character. Give him a year, I thought, maybe two, then the shell would firm to define the man.

'There's a bit of wasteland at the top of the apple orchard,' Tremayne said. 'You can have that.'

'But, Dad . . .' Gareth began, raising objections.

'It sounds fine,' I said firmly. 'Survivors can't choose.'

Tremayne looked at me and then at Gareth thought-fully and nodded as if to confirm a private thought.

'But February's a bad month for food,' I said, 'and I suppose we'd better not steal a pheasant, so we'll cheat a bit and take some bacon with us. Bring gloves and a penknife each. We'll go in ten minutes.'

The boys scurried to collect waterproofs for Gareth, and Tremayne asked what exactly I planned to do with them.

'Build a shelter,' I said. 'Light a fire, gather some lunch and cook it. That'll be enough, I should think. Everything takes forever when you start with nothing.'

'Teach them they're lucky.'

'Mm.'

He came to the door to see off the intrepid expedition, all of us unequipped except for the survival kit (with added bacon) that I wore round my waist and the penknives in their pockets. The cold drizzle fell relentlessly but no one seemed to mind. I waved briefly to Tremayne and went where Gareth led; which was through a gate in a wall, through a patch of long-deserted garden, through another gate and up a slow gradient through about fifty bare-branched apple trees, fetching up on a small bedraggled plateau roughly fenced with ruined dry-stone walling on one side and a few trees in the remains of a hawthorn hedge full of gaps round the rest. Beyond that untidy boundary lay neat prosperous open acres of winter ploughing, the domain of the farmer next door.

Gareth looked at our terrain disgustedly and even Coconut was dismayed, but I thought Tremayne had chosen pretty well, on the whole. Whatever we did, we couldn't make things worse.

'First of all,' I said, 'we build a shelter for the fire.'

'Nothing will burn in this rain,' Gareth said critically.

'Perhaps we'd better go back indoors, then.'

They stared in faint shock.

'No,' Gareth said.

'Right.' I brought the basic survival tin out of my pocket and gave him the coil of flexible saw. 'We passed at least four dead apple trees on the way up here. Slide a couple of sticks through the loops at the ends of this saw, and you and Coconut go and cut down one of those dead trees and bring it up here. Cut it as near the ground as you can manage.'

It took them roughly three seconds to bounce off with renewed enthusiasm, and I wandered round the decrepit piece of what Tremayne had truly described as wasteland, seeing everywhere possibilities of a satisfactory camp. The whole place, for instance, was pale brown with the dead stalks of last year's unmown grass; an absolute gift.

By the time the boys returned, puffing, red-faced and dragging the results of their exertions, I'd wrenched out a few rusty old metal fence posts, cut a lot of living hawthorn switches from the hedge and harvested a pile of the dead grass stalks from a patch near the last row of apple trees. We made a short trip down to the deserted garden to reap a patch of old stinging nettles for bindings, and about an hour after setting off were admiring a free-standing four-foot-square shelter made of a metal frame with a slightly sloping roof of closely latticed hawthorn switches thickly thatched on top with endless piled-on bundles of dried grass. While we watched, the drizzle trickled down the top layer of brownish stalks and dripped off to one side, leaving a small rain-free area underneath.

After that, by themselves, the boys made a simple square frame lashed with thickly criss-crossed hawthorn which we could lean against any one side of the fire shelter to prevent the rain from blowing straight in.

Gareth understood without being told and explained it to Coconut matter-of-factly.

'OK,' I said. 'Next, we find some flat dry stones from that broken-down wall to make a floor for the fire. Don't bring very wet stones, they can explode when they get hot. Then we go around looking for anything very small and dry that will burn. Dead leaves. Bits of fluff caught on fences. Anything inside that wrecked old greenhouse in the garden. When you find some-thing, keep it dry in your pockets. When we've got enough tinder, we'll feather some kindling sticks. We also need enough dry wood, if you can find any. And bring any old cowpats you come across: they burn like peat.'

After another hour's labour we had stacked under the fire shelter the remains of an old cucumber frame from the greenhouse and enough dry tinder to take kindly to a flame. Then, working with my hands under the shelter, I showed them how to strip the bark off a wet stick and make shallow lengthwise cuts in the dry dead wood underneath so that fine shavings curled outwards and the stick looked feathered all over. They each made one with their knives: Gareth quick and neat, Coconut all thumbs.

Finally with a match, a piece of candle, the tinder of dead leaves and flower heads, the feather kindling sticks, the cucumber frame and a good deal of luck (but no cowpats) a bright little fire burned healthily against the drizzly odds and Gareth and Coconut looked as if the sun had risen where they didn't expect it.

The smoke curled up and out over the edges of the thatched roofing. I remarked that if we'd had to live there for months we could hang spare meat and fish under the roof to smoke it. Apple wood made sweet smoke. Oak would smoke some meats better.

'We couldn't live out here for months.' Coconut couldn't imagine it.

'It wasn't always sunny in Sherwood Forest,' I said.

We snapped all the smaller twigs off the felled apple tree and added them gradually to the blaze, then made the beginnings of a human-sized shelter by wedging the dead tree as a roof and rear wall between two live trees, bringing more hawthorn to weave through the branches, heaping onto the top and rear surface any boughs, dead plants and turves we could cut and thickly laying a floor below of grass stalks, the nearest thing to straw. Apart from a few drips, we were out of the rain.

Lunch, when we finally ate it after a long forage, consisted mainly of finds from the old garden: some tubers of wild parsley, comfrey and Jerusalem arti-choke, a handful of very small Brussels sprouts (ugh, Gareth said) and a rather bitter green leaf salad of plantain, dock and dandelion (double ugh). Never eat poisonous buttercups, I said, be grateful for dandelions. Coconut flatly refused to contemplate worms, the only things plentiful. Both boys fell on the bacon, threaded

241

and grilled on sharpened peeled sticks, and such was their hunger that they afterwards chewed for ages on strips of the inner sweet bark of a young birch tree that was struggling away in the hedge. Birch bark was good nourishing food, I said. Gareth said they would take my word for it.

We drank rather scummy rainwater found in an old watering can and boiled in a Coke can Gareth collected from the Shellerton House dustbin. They declined my offer to make coffee from roast dandelion root. Next time they went camping they would take tea bags, they said.

We were sitting in the shelter, the fire burning red with embers on its stone base a few feet away, the drizzle almost a permanence, the odd foods eaten, the end of the experiment not far ahead.

'How about staying out here all night?' I asked.

They both looked horrified.

'You'd survive,' I said, 'with shelter and a fire.'

'It would be miserable,' Gareth said. 'It's freezing cold.'

'Yes.'

There was a pause, then Gareth added, 'Survival isn't really much fun, is it?'

'Often not,' I agreed. 'Just a matter of life or death.'

'If we were outlaws in Sherwood Forest,' he said, 'the Sheriff's men would be hunting us.'

'Nasty.'

Coconut involuntarily looked around for enemies, shivering at the thought.

'We can't stay out all night. We have to go to school tomorrow,' he said.

The relief on both their faces was comical, and I thought that perhaps for a second or two they'd had a vision of a much older, more brutal world where every tomorrow was a struggle, where hunger and cold were normal and danger ever present and cruel. A primitive world, far back from Robin Hood, back from the Druids who'd walked the ancient Berkshire Downs, back where laws hadn't been invented or rights thought of, back before organisation, before tribes, before ritual, before duty. Back where the strong ate and the weak died, the bedrock and everlasting design of nature.

When a dark shade of iron seeped into the slate-grey light, we pulled the fire to pieces and dowsed the hot ends in wet grass. Then we stacked the remaining pile of apple wood neatly under the fire's roofing and started for home, carrying as little as we'd brought.

Gareth looked back at the intertwined tree shelter and the dead fireplace and seemed for a moment wistful, but it was with leaps and whoops that he and Coconut ran down from there to re-embrace the familiar constraints of civilisation.

'God,' Gareth said, barging in through the back door, 'lead me to a pizza. To two pizzas, maybe three.'

Laughing, I peeled off my long-suffering ski-suit and

left them to it in the kitchen, heading myself for warmth in the family room; and there I found a whole bunch of depressed souls sprawling in armchairs contemplating a different sort of disastrous tomorrow where food was no problem but danger abounded.

Harry, Fiona, Nolan, Lewis, Perkin, Mackie and Tremayne, all silent, as if everything useful had been said already. Tight-knit, interlocked, they looked at me vaguely, at the stranger within their gates, the unexpected character in their play.

'Ah . . . John,' Tremayne said, stirring, remembering, 'are both boys still living?'

'More or less.'

I poured myself some wine and sat on an unoccupied footstool, feeling the oppression of their collective thoughts and guessing that they all now knew everything I did, and perhaps more.

'If Harry didn't do it, who did?' It was Lewis's question, which got no specific reply, as if it had been asked over and over before.

'Doone will find out,' I murmured.

Fiona said indignantly, 'He's not trying. He's not looking beyond Harry. It's disgraceful.'

Proof that Doone was still casting about, however, arrived noisily at that point in the shape of Sam Yaeger, who hooted his horn outside as a preliminary and swept into the house in a high state of indignation.

'Tremayne!' he said in the doorway, and then stopped

abruptly at the sight of the gathered clan. 'Oh. You're all here.'

'You're supposed to be resting,' Tremayne said repressively.

'To hell with bloody resting. There I was, quietly nursing my bruises according to orders, when this Policeman Plod turns up on my doorstep. Sunday afternoon! Doesn't the bugger ever sleep? And d'you know what little gem he tossed at me? Your bloody stable girls told him I'd had a bit of how's-your-father with Angela effing Brickell.'

The brief silence which greeted this announcement wasn't exactly packed with disbelief.

'Well, did you?' Tremayne asked.

'That's not the point. The point is that it wasn't any Tuesday last June. So this Doone fellow asks me what I was doing that day, as if I could remember. Working on my boat, I expect. He asked if I logged the hours I worked on it. Is this man for real? I said I hadn't a bloody clue what I was doing, maybe it was a couple of willing maidens, and he has no sense of humour, it's in a permanent state of collapse, he said it wasn't a joking matter.'

'He has three daughters,' I said. 'It worries him.'

'I can't help his effing hang-ups,' Sam said. 'He said he had to check every possibility, so I told him he'd have a long job considering old Angie's opportunities, not to mention willingness.' He paused. 'She was even making goo-goo eyes at Bob Watson at one time.'

'She wouldn't have got past Ingrid,' Mackie said. 'Ingrid looks meek and mild but you should see her angry. She keeps Bob in her sight. She doesn't trust any girl in the yard. I doubt if Angela got anywhere with Bob.'

'You never know,' Sam said darkly. 'Can I have a drink? Coke?'

'In the fridge in the kitchen,' Perkin said, not stirring to fetch it.

Sam nodded, went out and came back carrying a glass, followed by Gareth and Coconut busily stoking their furnaces with pizza wedges.

Tremayne raised his eyebrows at the food.

'We're starving,' explained his younger son. 'We ate *roots*, and birch bark and dandelion leaves, and no one in their right mind would live in Sherwood Forest being chased by the Sheriff.'

Sam looked bewildered. 'What *are* you on about?' he demanded.

'Survival,' Gareth said. He marched over to a table, picked up *Return Safe from the Wilderness* and thrust it into Sam's hands. 'John wrote it,' he said, 'and five other books like it. So we built a shelter and made a fire and cooked roots and boiled water to drink . . .'

'What about Sherwood Forest?' Harry drawled, smiling but looking strained notwithstanding.

Coconut explained, 'We might be cold and hungry but there weren't any enemies lurking behind the apple trees.'

'Er . . .' Sam said.

Tremayne, amused, enlightened everyone about our day.

'Tell you what,' Gareth said thoughtfully, 'it makes you realise how lucky you are to have a bed and a pizza to come home to.'

Tremayne looked at me from under lowered lids, his mouth curving with contentment. 'Teach them they're lucky,' he'd said.

'Next time,' Coconut enquired, 'why don't we make some bows and arrows?'

'What for?' asked Perkin.

'To shoot the Sheriff's men, of course.'

'You'd wind up hanged in Nottingham,' Tremayne said. 'Better stick to dandelion leaves.' He looked at me. 'Is there going to be a next time?'

Before I could answer, Gareth said 'Yes.' He paused. 'Well, it wasn't all a laugh a minute, but we did *do* something. I could do it again. I could live out in the cold and the rain . . . I feel good about it, that's all.'

'Well done!' Fiona exclaimed sincerely. 'Gareth you're a great boy.'

It embarrassed him, of course, but I agreed with her.

'How about it?' Tremayne asked me.

'Next Sunday,' I said, 'we could go out again, do something else.'

'Do what?' Gareth demanded.

'Don't know yet.'

The vague promise seemed enough for both boys

who drifted back to the kitchen for further supplies, and Sam, leafing through the book, remarked that some of my more ingenious traps looked as if they would kill actual people, not only big animals like deer.

'Eating venison in Sherwood Forest was a hanging matter too,' Harry observed.

I said, agreeing with Sam, 'Some traps aren't safe to set unless you know you're alone.'

'If Gareth's confident after one day,' Nolan said to me without much friendliness from the depths of an armchair, 'what does that make you? Superman?'

'Humble,' I said, with irony.

'How very goody-goody,' he said sarcastically, with added obscenities. 'I'd like to see you ride in a steeplechase.'

'So would I,' Tremayne said heartily, taking the sneering words at face value. 'We might apply for a permit for you, John.'

No one took him seriously. Nolan took offence. He didn't like even a semi-humorous suggestion that anyone else should muscle in on his territory.

Monday found Dee-Dee in tears over Angela Brickell's pregnancy test. Not tears of sympathy, it seemed, but of envy.

Monday also found Doone on our doorstep, wanting to check up on the dates which Chickweed had won and Harry had been there to watch.

'Mr Goodhaven?' Tremayne echoed. 'It's Mrs Good-haven's horse.'

'Yes, sir, but it was Mr Goodhaven's photo the dead lass was carrying.'

'It was the *horse's* photo,' Tremayne protested. 'I told you before.'

'Yes, sir,' Doone agreed blandly. 'Now, about those dates . . .'

In suppressed fury, Tremayne sorted the way through the form book and his memory, saying finally that there had been no occasion that he could think of when Harry had been at the races without Fiona.

'How about the fourth Saturday in April?' Doone asked slyly.

'The what?' Tremayne looked it up again. 'What about it?'

'Your travelling head lad thinks Mrs Goodhaven had flu that day. He remembers her saying later at Stratford, when the horse won but failed the dope test later, that she was glad to be there, having missed his last win at Uttoxeter.'

Tremayne absorbed the information in silence.

'If Mr Goodhaven went alone to Uttoxeter,' Doone insinuated, 'and Mrs Goodhaven was at home tucked up in bed feeling ill . . .'

'You really don't know what you're talking about,' Tremayne interrupted. 'Angela Brickell was in charge of a *horse*. She couldn't just go off and leave it. And she came back here with it in the horse-box. I'd have

249

known if she hadn't, and I'd have sacked her for negligence.'

'But I understood from your travelling head lad, sir,' Doone said with sing-song deadliness, 'that they had to wait for Angela Brickell that day at Uttoxeter because when they were all ready to go home she couldn't be found. She *did* leave her horse unattended, sir. Your travelling head lad decided to wait another half-hour for her, and she turned up just in time, and wouldn't say where she'd been.'

Tremayne said blankly, 'I don't remember any of this.'

'No doubt they didn't trouble you, sir. After all, no harm had been done . . . had it?'

Doone left one of his silences hovering, in which it was quite easy to imagine the specific harm that could have been done by Harry.

'There's no privacy for anything odd on racecourses,' Tremayne said, betraying the path his own thoughts had taken. 'I don't believe a word of what you're hinting.'

'Angela Brickell died about six weeks after that,' Doone said, 'by which time she'd have used a pregnancy test.'

'Stop it,' Tremayne said. 'This is supposition of the vilest kind, aimed at a good intelligent man who loves his wife.'

'Good intelligent men who love their wives, sir, aren't immune to sudden passions.'

'You've got it wrong,' Tremayne said doggedly.

Doone rested a glance on him for a long time and then transferred it to me.

'What do you think, sir?' he said.

'I don't think Mr Goodhaven did anything.'

'Based on your ten days' knowledge of him?'

'Twelve days now. Yes.'

He ruminated, then asked me slowly, 'Do you yourself have any feelings as to who killed the lassie? I ask about feeling, sir, because if it were solid knowledge you would have given it to me, wouldn't you?'

'Yes, I would. And no, I have no feeling, no intuition, unless it is that it was someone unconcerned with this stable.'

'She worked here,' he said flatly. 'Most murders are close to home.' He gave me a long assessing look. 'Your loyalties, sir,' he said, 'are being sucked into this group, and I'm sorry about that. You're the only man here who couldn't have had any hand in the lassie's death, and I'll listen to you and be glad to, but only if you go on seeing straight, do you get me?'

'I get you,' I said, surprised.

'Have you asked Mr Goodhaven about the day he went racing without his wife?' Tremayne demanded.

Doone nodded. 'He denies anything improper took place. But then, he would.'

'I don't want to hear any more of this,' Tremayne announced. 'You're inventing a load of rubbish.'

'Mr Goodhaven's belongings were found with the

lassie,' Doone said without heat, 'and she carried his photograph, and that's not rubbish.'

In the silence after this sombre reminder he took his quiet leave and Tremayne, very troubled, said he would go down to the Goodhavens' house to give them support.

Fiona however telephoned while he was on his way, and I answered the call because Dee-Dee had already gone home, feeling unwell.

'John!' she exclaimed. 'Where's Tremayne?'

'On his way down to you.'

'Oh. Good. I can't tell you how awful this is. Doone thinks . . . he says . . .'

'He's been here,' I said. 'He told us.'

'He's like a bulldog.' Her voice shook with distress. 'Harry's strong, but this . . . this *barrage* is wearing him down.'

'He's desperately afraid you'll doubt him,' I said.

'What?' She sounded overthrown. 'I don't, for a minute.'

'Then tell him.'

'Yes, I will.' She paused briefly. 'Who did it, John?'

'I don't know.'

'But you'll see. You'll see what we're too close to see. Tremayne says you understand things without being told, more than most people do. Harry says it comes of all those qualities his Aunt Erica wouldn't allow you, insight through imagination and all that.'

They'd been discussing me; odd feeling.

I said, 'You might not want to know.'

'Oh.' It was a cry of admission, of revelation. 'John . . . save us all.'

She put the phone down without waiting for a response to her extraordinary plea, and I wondered seriously what they expected of me, what they saw me to be: the stranger in their midst who would solve all problems as in old-fashioned Westerns, or an eminently ordinary middling writer who was there by accident and would listen to everyone but in the end be ineffectual. Given a choice, I would without question have opted for the latter.

By Tuesday the press had been drenched with leaks from all quarters. Trial by public opinion was in full swing, the libel laws studiously skirted by a profligate scattering of the word 'alleged' but the underlying meaning plain: Harry Goodhaven had allegedly bedded a stable girl, got her pregnant, and throttled her to save his marriage to a 'wealthy heiress', without whose money he would be penniless.

Wednesday's papers, from Harry's point of view, were even worse, akin to the public pillory.

He phoned me soon after lunch.

'Did you see the bloody tabloids?'

'Yes,' I said.

'If I come and pick you up, will you just come out driving with me?'

'Sure.'

'Fine. Ten minutes.'

Without any twinges of conscience I laid aside my notes on Tremayne's mid-career. With two weeks already gone of my four-week allocation, I was feeling fairly well prepared to get going on the page, but as usual any good reason for postponing it was welcome.

Harry came in his BMW, twin of Fiona's, and I climbed in beside him, seeing more new lines of strain in his face and also rigidity in his neck muscles and fingers. His fair hair looked almost grey, the blue eyes altogether without humour, the social patina wearing thin.

'John, good of you,' he said. 'Life's bloody.'

'I'll tell you one thing,' I tried a shot at comfort, 'Doone knows there's something wrong with his case, otherwise he would have arrested you already.' I settled into the seat beside him, fastening the belt.

He glanced my way as he put the car into gear and started forward. 'Do you think so? He keeps coming back. He's on our doorstep every day. Every day, a new pin-prick, a new awkward bloody circumstance. He's building a cage round me, bar by bar.'

'He's trying to break your nerve,' I said, guessing. 'Once he'd arrested and charged you, the papers would have to leave you alone. He's letting them have a field day, waiting for someone to remember something and waiting for you to crack and incriminate yourself. I shouldn't think he's tried to stop any of the leaks since the press found out where the girl was lying and he had to make an official statement. Maybe he's even organised a leak or two himself; I wouldn't put it past him.'

Harry turned the nose of the car towards Reading to travel by the hilly route that would take us through the Quillersedge Estate. I wondered why he'd gone that way but I didn't directly ask him.

'Yesterday,' he said bitterly, 'Doone asked me what Angela Brickell had been wearing. It's been in all the papers. He asked me if she'd undressed willingly. I could have strangled him ... Oh God, what am I saying?'

'Shall I drive?' I asked.

'What? Oh yes, we nearly hit that post ... I didn't see it. No, I'm all right. Really I am. Fiona says not to let him rattle me, she's being splendid, absolutely marvellous, but he *does* rattle me, I can't help it. He tosses out these lethal questions as if they were harmless afterthoughts ... "Did she undress willingly?" How can I answer? I wasn't there.'

'That's the answer.'

'He doesn't believe me.'

'He isn't sure,' I said. 'Something's bothering him.'

'I wish it would bother him into an early grave.'

'His successor might be worse. Might prefer a conviction to the truth. Doone does at least seek the truth.'

'You can't mean you like him!' The idea was an enormity.

'Be grateful to him. Be glad you're still free.' I paused. 'Why are we going this way?'

The question surprised him. 'To get to where we're going, of course.'

'So we're not just out for a drive?'

'Well, no.'

'All around you,' I said, 'is the Quillersedge Estate.'

'I suppose so,' he said vaguely. Then: 'Dear God, we go along this road all the time. I mean, everyone in Shellerton goes to Reading this way unless it's snowing.'

A long stretch of the road was bordered on each side by mixed woodland, dripping now with yesterday's rain and looking bare-branched and bedraggled in the scrag end of winter. Part of the woodland was thinned and tamed and fenced neatly with posts and wire, policed with 'no trespassing' notices; part was wild and open to anyone caring to push through the tangle of trees, saplings and their assorted undergrowth. Five yards into that, I thought, and one would be invisible from the road. Only the strongly motivated, though, would try to go through it: it was no easy afternoon stroll.

'Anyway,' Harry said, 'the Quillersedge Estate goes on for miles. This is just the western end of it. The place where they found Angela was much nearer Bucklebury.'

'How do you know?'

'Dammit, it was in the papers. Are *you* doubting me now?' He was angered and disconcerted by my question, then shook his head in resignation. 'That was a

Doone question. How do I know? Because the Reading papers printed a map, that's how. The gamekeeper put his X on the spot.'

'I don't doubt you,' I said. 'If I doubted you I would doubt my own judgement too, and in your case I don't.'

'I suppose that's a vote of confidence.'

'Yes.'

We drove a fair way along the roads and through villages unknown to me, going across country to heaven knew where. Harry, however, knew where, and turned down a mostly uninhabited lane, through some broken gateposts into a rutted drive; this led to a large sagging barn, an extensive dump of tangled metal and wood and a smaller barn to one side. Beyond this unprepossessing mess lay a wide expanse of muddy grey water sliding sluggishly by with dark wooded hills on the far side.

'Where are we?' I asked, as the car rolled to a stop, the only bright new thing in the general dilapidation.

'That's the Thames,' Harry said. 'Almost breaking its banks, by the look of things, after all that rain and melted snow. This is Sam's boatyard, where we are now.'

'*This?*' I remembered what Sam had said about useful squalor: it had been an understatement.

'He keeps it this way on purpose,' Harry confirmed. 'We all came here for a huge barbecue party he gave to celebrate being champion jockey...eighteen months ago, I suppose. It looked different that night.

257

One of the best parties we've been to . . .' His voice tailed off, as if his thoughts had moved away from what his mouth was saying; and there was sweat on his forehead.

'What's making you nervous?' I asked.

'Nothing.' It was clearly a lie. 'Come with me,' he said jerkily. 'I want someone with me.'

'All right. Where are we going?'

'Into the boathouse.' He pointed to the smaller of the barns. 'That big place on the left is Sam's workshop and dock where he works on his boats. The boathouse isn't used much, I don't think, though Sam made it into a grotto the night of the party. I'm going to meet someone there.' He looked at his watch. 'I'm a bit early. Don't suppose it will matter.'

'Who are you going to meet?'

'Someone,' he said, and got out of the car. 'I don't know who. Look,' he went on, as I followed him, 'someone's going to tell me something which may clear me with Doone. I just . . . I wanted *support* . . . a witness, even. I suppose you think that's stupid.'

'No.'

'Come on, then.'

'I'll come, but don't put too much hope on anyone keeping the appointment. People can be pretty spiteful, and you've had a rotten press.'

'You think it's a hoax?' The idea bothered him, but he'd obviously considered it.

'How was the meeting arranged?'

'On the telephone,' he said. 'This morning. I didn't know the voice. Don't even know if it was a man or woman. It was low. Sort of careful, I suppose, looking back.'

'Why here,' I asked, 'of all places?'

He frowned. 'I've no idea. But I can't afford not to listen, if it's something which will clear me. I can't, can I?'

'I guess not.'

'I don't really like it either,' he confessed. 'That's why I wanted company.'

'All right,' I shrugged. 'Let's wait and see.'

With relief he smiled wanly and led the way across some rough ground of stones and gnarled old weeds, joining a path of sorts that ran from the big barn to the boathouse and following that to our destination.

Close to, the boathouse was if anything less attractive than from a distance, though there were carved broken eaves that had once been decorative in an Edwardian way and could have been again, given the will. The construction was mostly of weathered old brick, the long side walls going down to the water's edge, the whole built on and into the river's sloping bank.

True to Sam's philosophy the ramshackle wooden door had no latch, let alone a padlock, and pushed inwards, opening at a touch.

Windows in the walls gave plenty of light, but inside all one could see was a bare wooden floor stretching to double glass doors leading to a railed balcony over-hanging the swollen river.

'Don't boathouses have water in them?' I enquired mildly.

'The water's underneath,' Harry said. 'This room was for entertaining. There's another door down by the edge of the river for going into the boat dock. That's where the grotto was. Sam had just put coloured lights all round and some actually in the water ... it looked terrific. There was a bar up here in this room. Fiona and I went out onto the balcony with our drinks and looked at the sky full of stars. It was a warm night. Everything perfect.' He sighed. 'Perkin and Mackie were with us, smooching away in newly-wedded bliss. It all seems so long ago, when everyone was happy, everything simple. Nothing could go wrong ... Then Tremayne had a spectacular year and to crown it Top Spin Lob won the National ... and since then not much has gone right.'

'Did Sam invite Nolan to his party?'

Harry smiled briefly. 'Sam felt good. He asked Dee-Dee, Bob Watson, the lads, everyone. Must have been a hundred and fifty people. Even Angela ...' He stopped and looked at his watch. 'It's just about time.'

He turned and took a step towards the far-end balcony, the ancient floorboards creaking underfoot.

There was a white envelope lying on the floor about halfway to the balcony and, saying perhaps it was a message, he went towards it and bent to pick it up, and with a fearsome crack a whole section of the floor gave way under his weight and shot him, shouting, into the dock beneath.

CHAPTER TWELVE

It happened so fast and so drastically that I nearly slid after him, managing only instinctively to pivot on one foot and throw myself headlong back onto the boards still remaining solid behind the hole.

Harry, I thought ridiculously, was dead unlucky with cold dirty water. I wriggled until I could peer over the edge into the wet depths below and I couldn't see him at all.

Shit, I thought, peeling off my jacket. Come up for God's sake, Harry, so I can pull you out.

No sign of him. Nothing. I yelled to him. No reply.

I kicked off my boots and swung down below, holding on to a bared crossbeam that creaked with threat, swinging from one hand while I tried to see Harry and not land on top of him.

All that was visible was brownish opaque muddy water. No time for anything except getting him out. I let go of the beam and dropped with bent legs so as to splash down softly and felt the breath rush out of my lungs from the iciness of the river. Letting the water

buoy up my weight I stretched my feet down to touch
bottom and found the water came up to my ears; took
a deep breath, put the rest of my head under and
reached around for Harry, unable to see him, unable
with open eyes to see anything at all.

He had to be there. Time was short. I stood up for
a gasp of air, ducked down again, searching with fingers,
with feet, with urgency turning to appalling alarm. I
could feel things, pieces of metal, sharp spiky things,
nothing living.

Another gasp of air. I looked for bubbles rising,
hoping to find him that way, and saw not bubbles but
a red stain in the water a short way off, a swirl of colour
against drab.

At least I'd found him. I dived towards the scarlet
streaks and touched him at once, but there was no
movement in him, and when I tried to pull him to the
surface, I couldn't.

Shit ... Shit ... Stupid word kept repeating in my
brain. I felt and slid my arms under Harry's and with
my feet slipping on the muddy bottom yanked him
upwards as fiercely as I could and found him still stuck
and yanked again twice more with increasing desperation until finally whatever had been holding him
released its grasp and he came shooting to the surface,
only to begin falling sluggishly back again as a dead
weight.

With my own nose barely above water I held him
with his head just higher than mine, but he still wasn't

breathing. I laced my arms round his back, under his own arms, letting his face fall on mine, and in that awkward position I blew my own breath into him, not in the accepted way with him lying flat with most things in control, but into his open nostrils, into his flaccid mouth, into either or both at once, as fast as I could, trying to pump his chest in unison, to do what his own intercostal muscles had stopped doing, pulling his ribcage open for air to flow in.

They tell you to go on with artificial respiration for ever, for long after you've given up hope. Go on and on, I'd been told. Don't give up. Don't ever give up.

He was heavy in spite of the buoyancy from the water. My feet went numb down on the mud. I blew my breath into him rhythmically, faster than normal breathing, squeezing him, telling him, ordering him in my mind to take charge of himself, come back, come back ... Harry, come back ...

I grieved for him, for Fiona, for all of them, but most for Harry. That humour, that humanity; they couldn't be lost. I gave him my breath until I was dizzy myself and I still wouldn't accept it was all useless, that I might as well stop.

I felt the jolt in his chest as I hugged it in rhythm against mine and for a second couldn't believe it, but then he heaved again in my arms and coughed in my face and a mouthful of dirty water shot out in a spout and he began coughing in earnest and choking and gasping for air ... gasping, gulping air down, wheezing

264

in his throat, whooping like whooping cough, struggling
to fill his functioning lungs.

He couldn't have been unconscious for long, looking
back, but it seemed an eternity at the time. With coughing, he opened his eyes and began groaning which was
at least some sign of progress, and I started looking
about to see how we were going to get out of what
appeared to be uncomfortably like a prison.

Another door, Harry had said, down by the river's
edge: and in fact, when I looked I could see it, a once-
painted slab of wood set in brickwork, its bottom edge
barely six inches above the water.

Across the whole end of the building, stretching from
the ceiling down into the river, was a curtain of linked
metal like thick over-sized chicken wire, presumably
originally installed to keep thieves away from any boat
in the dock. Beyond it flowed the heavy mainstream,
with small eddies curling along and through the wire
on the surface.

The dock itself, I well understood, was deeper than
usual because of the height of the river. The door was
still six inches above it, though . . . it didn't make sense
to build a door high if the water was usually lower . . .
not unless there was a step somewhere . . . a step or
walkway even, for the loading and unloading of
boats . . .

Taking Harry gingerly with me I moved to the left,
towards the wall, and with great relief found that there
was indeed a walkway there at about the height of my

waist. I lifted Harry until he was sitting on the walkway and then, still gripping him tightly, wriggled up beside him so that we were both sitting there with our heads wholly above water, which may not sound a great advance but which was probably the difference between life and death.

Harry was semi-conscious, confused and bleeding. The only good thing about the extreme cold of the water, I thought, was that whatever the damage, the blood loss was being minimised. Apart from that, the sooner we were out of there, the better.

The hole through which Harry had fallen was in the centre of the ceiling. If I stood up on the walkway, I thought, I could probably stretch up and touch the ceiling, but wouldn't be able to reach the hole. Might try jumping . . . might pull more of the floor down. It didn't look promising. There seemed to be part of a beam missing in the area. Rotted through, no doubt.

Meanwhile I had to get Harry well propped so that he wouldn't fall forward and drown after all, and to do that I reckoned we needed to be in the corner. I tugged him gently along the walkway, which was made of planks, I discovered, with short mooring posts sticking up at intervals, needing me to lift his legs over one at a time. Still, we reached the end in a while, and I stood up and tugged him back until he was sitting wedged in the corner, supported by the rear and side walls.

He had stopped coughing, but still looked dazed. The blood streaking scarlet was from one of his legs, now stretched out straight before him but still not in view on account of the clouded water. I was debating whether to try to stop the bleeding first or to leave him in his uncertain state while I found a way out, trusting he wouldn't totally pass out, when I heard the main door creak open directly above our heads; the way Harry and I had come in.

My first natural impulse was to shout, to get help from whoever had come: and between intention and voice a whole stream of thoughts suddenly intruded and left me silent, open-mouthed to call out but unsure of the wisdom.

Thoughts. Harry had come to this place to meet someone. He didn't know who. He'd been given a meeting place he knew of. He'd gone there trustingly. He'd walked into the boathouse and tried to pick up an envelope and the floor had given way beneath him and a piece of beam was missing; and if I hadn't been there with him he would certainly have drowned in the dock, impaled on something lurking beneath the surface.

Part of my later training had been at the hands of an ex-SAS instructor whose absolute priority for survival was evading the enemy; and with doubt but also awareness of danger I guessed at an enemy above our heads, not a saviour. I waited for exclamations of horror from above, for someone to call Harry's name in alarm, for some natural, innocent reaction to the floor's collapse.

Instead there was silence. Then the creak of a step or two, then the sound of the door being quietly closed.

Eerie.

All sounds from outside were muffled because of the dock being partly below ground level, set into the slope of the bank, but in a short while I heard the sound of a car door slamming and after that the noise of an engine starting up and being driven away.

Harry suddenly said, 'Bloody hell.' A couple of sweet words. Then he said, 'What the hell's happening?' and then, 'God, my leg hurts.'

'We came through the boathouse floor.' I pointed to the hole. 'The floorboards gave way. You landed on something that pierced your leg.'

'I'm f . . . freezing.'

'Yes, I know. Are you awake enough to sit here on your own for a bit?'

'John, for God's sake . . .'

'Not long,' I said hastily. 'I'll not leave you long.'

As I stood on the walkway, the water level reached above my knees, and I waded along beside the wall in the direction of the lower door and the river. There were indeed steps by the door, three steps and a flat landing along below the door itself. I went up the steps until the water barely covered my ankles and tried the doorlatch.

This time, no easy exit. The door was solid as rock.

On the walls beside the door there was a row of three electric switches. I pressed them all without any results from the electric light bulbs along the ceiling. There was also a control box with cables leading to the top of the metal curtain: I opened the box and pressed the red button and the green button to be found inside there but, again, nothing changed in the boathouse.

The arrangement for raising the curtain was a matter of gear wheels designed to turn a rod to wind the metal mesh up onto it like a blind. The sides of the curtain were held in tracks to help it run smoothly. Without electricity, however, it wasn't going to oblige. On the other hand, because of its construction, the whole barrier had to be reasonably light in weight.

'Harry?' I called.

'God, John . . .' His voice sounded weak and strained.

'Sit there and don't worry. I'll come back.'

'Where . . . are you going?' There was fear in his voice but also control.

'Out.'

'Well . . . hurry.'

'Yes.'

I slipped back into the water and swam a couple of strokes to the curtain. Tried standing up, but the water was much deeper there. Hung onto the wire feeling the tug of the eddies from the river.

With luck, with extreme luck, the curtain wouldn't go all the way down to the river's bed. It had no practical need to reach down further than the drought level of the river which had to leave a gap of at least

two or three feet. From the weight point of view, a gap
was sensible.

Simple.

I took a breath and pulled myself hand over hand
down the curtain, seeking to find the bottom of it with
my feet: and there was indeed a gap between the
bottom edge of the curtain and the mud, but only a
matter of inches, and there was clutter down there,
unidentifiable, pressing against the barrier, trying to get
past it.

I came up for air.

'Harry?'

'Yes.'

'There's a space under the metal curtain. I'm going
out into the river and I'll be back for you very soon.'

'All right.' More control this time: less fear.

Deep breath. Dived, pulling myself down the wire.
Came to the end of it, felt the mud below. The bottom
edge of the curtain was a matter of free links, not a
connecting bar. The links could be raised, but only
singly, not all together.

Go under it, I told myself. The temptation to return
safely back up where I'd come from was enormous. Go
under . . .

I swung down at the bottom, deciding to go head
first, face up, curling my back down into the soft river
bed, praying . . . *praying* that the links wouldn't catch
on my clothes . . . in my knitted sweater . . . should have
stripped . . . head under, metal laying on my face, push

the links up with hands, full strength, take care, don't rush, don't snag clothes, get free of the jumble of things on the mud around me, hold onto the wire outside, don't let go, the current in the river was appreciable, tugging, keep straight, *hang on*, shoulders through, raise the links, back through, bottom through, legs . . . links . . . short of breath . . . lungs hurting . . . careful, careful . . . unknown things round my ankles, hampering . . . *had* to breathe soon . . . feet catching . . . feet . . . *through*.

The river immediately floated my free legs away as if it would have them, and I had to grab the wire fiercely to avoid going with the current. But I was through and not stuck in the dreadful clutch of metal links, not grasped by debris, not drowning without any chance of rescue.

I came up into the air gasping deeply, panting, aching lungs swelling, feeling a rush of suppressed terror, clinging onto the curtain in a shaky state.

'Harry?' I called.

The dock looked dark beyond the curtain and I couldn't see him, but he could indeed see me.

'Oh John . . .' His relief was beyond measure. 'Thank God.'

'Not long now,' I said, and heard the strain in my own voice too.

I edged along the curtain in the upstream direction of the shut door and by hauling my way up the links at the side managed to scramble round the boathouse

271

wall and up out of the water to roll at last onto the grassy bank. Bitterly cold, shivering violently from several causes, but *out*.

I stood up with knees that felt like buckling and tried to open the door into the dock; and it was as immovable from outside as in. It had a mortise lock, a simple keyhole and no key.

Perhaps the best thing to do, I thought despairingly, was to find a telephone and get professional help: the fire brigade and an ambulance. If I couldn't find a telephone in Sam's big workshop I could drive Harry's car to the nearest house . . .

Big snag.

Harry's car had gone.

My mind started playing the shit tape monotonously.

Before I did anything, I thought, I needed to put on my boots. Went into the boathouse through the top door.

Another big snag.

No boots.

No ski-jacket either.

Harry's voice came from below, distant and wavery, 'Is anyone there?'

'It's me, John,' I shouted. 'Just hold on.'

No reply. He was weaker, perhaps. Better hurry.

There was now no doubt about murderous intention on someone's part and the certainty made me perversely angry, stimulating renewed strength and a good deal of bloody-mindedness. I ran along the stony path to Sam's large shed in my socks and hardly felt the discomfort, and found to my relief that I could get inside easily enough – no lock on the door.

The space inside looked as much like a junkyard as the space outside. The centre, I saw briefly, was occupied by a large boat on blocks, its superstructure covered with lightweight grey plastic sheeting.

I spent a little precious time searching for a telephone, but couldn't find one. There was no office, no place partitioned off or locked. Probably Sam kept good tools somewhere, but he'd hidden them away.

All around lay old and rusting tools and equipment, but among the junk I found almost at once two perfect aids: a tyre lever and a heavy mallet for driving in mooring pegs.

With those I returned at speed to the boathouse and attacked the lower door, first hammering the toe of the tyre lever into a non-existent crack between the wooden door frame and the surrounding brickwork at a level just below the keyhole, then bashing the far end of that iron to put heavy leverage against the door frame, then wrenching out the lever and repeating the whole process above the lock, this time with fury.

The old wood of the door frame gave up the struggle and splintered, freeing the tongue of the lock, and without much more trouble I pulled the door open towards me, swinging it wide. I left the tyre lever and mallet on the grass and stepped down into the boathouse, the shocking chill of the water again a teeth-gritter.

At least, I thought grimly, it was a calm day. No wind-chill to speak of, to polish us off.

I waded along to Harry who was sagging back against the corner, his head lolling only just above the surface.

'Come on,' I said urgently. 'Harry, wake up.'

He looked at me apathetically through a mist of weakness and pain and one could see he'd been in that water a lot too long. Apathy, like cold, was a killer. I bent down and turned him until I had my hands under his arms, his back towards me, and I floated him along in the water to the steps and there strained to pull him up them and out onto the grass.

'My leg,' he said, moaning.

'God, Harry, what do you weigh?' I asked, lugging.

'None of your bloody business,' he mumbled.

I half laughed, relieved. If he could say that, for all his suffering, he wasn't in a dying frame of mind. It gave me enough impetus to finish the exit, though I dare say he, like me, felt only marginally warmer for being on land.

His leg seemed to have stopped bleeding, or very nearly, and he couldn't have severed an artery or he'd have bled to death by now, but all the same there had to be a pretty serious wound under the cloth of his trousers and the faster I could get him to a doctor the better.

As far as I remembered from our arrival, the boatyard lay down a lane with no houses nearby: I'd have a fair run in my socks to find help.

On the other hand, among the general clutter, only a few feet off, I could see the upturned keel of an old clinker-built rowing boat. Small. Maybe six feet overall. A one-man job, big enough for two. If it weren't full of holes . . .

Leaving Harry briefly I went to the dinghy and heaved it over right side up. Apart from needing varnish and loving care it looked seaworthy, but naturally there were no rowlocks and no oars.

Never mind. Any piece of pole would do. Plenty lying about. I picked up a likely length and laid it in the boat.

The dinghy had a short rope tied to its bow: a painter.

'Harry, can you hop?' I asked him.

'Don't know.'

'Come on. Try. Let's get you into the boat.'

'Into the *boat*?'

'Yes. Someone's taken your car.'

He looked bewildered, but the whole afternoon must have seemed so unbelievable to him that hopping into a boat would seem to be all of a piece. In any case, he made feeble efforts to help me get him to his left foot, and with my almost total support he made the few hops to reach the boat, though I could see it hurt him sorely. I helped him sit down on the one centre thwart and arranged his legs as comfortably as possible, Harry cursing and wincing by turns.

'Hang on tight to the sides,' I said. 'Tight.'

'Yes.'

He didn't move, so I pulled his hands out and positioned them on the boat's edges.

'Grip,' I said fiercely.

'Fine.' His voice was vague, but his hands tightened.

I tugged and lugged the dinghy until it was sliding backwards down the bank, and then held on to the painter, digging my heels in, leaning back to prevent too fast and splashy a launch. At the last minute, when the stern hit the swollen water and the dinghy's progress flattened out, I jumped in myself and simply hoped against all reasonable hope that we wouldn't sink at once.

We didn't. The current took the dinghy immediately and started it on its way downstream, and I edged past Harry into the stern space behind him and retrieved my piece of pole.

'What's that?' Harry asked weakly, trying to make sense of things.

'Rudder.'

'Oh.'

I made a crook of my left elbow on the back of the boat and laid the pole across it, the shorter end in my right hand, the longer end trailing behind in the water. The steering was rudimentary, but enough to keep us travelling bow-first downstream.

Downstream was always the way to people . . . Bits of

the guide books floated familiarly to the surface. *Some of your traps are horrific.*

Some of the traps described how to arrange for the prey to fall through seemingly firm ground into a pit full of spikes beneath.

Everyone had read the guides.

'John?' Harry said. 'Where are we going?'

'Maidenhead, possibly. I'm not quite sure.'

'I'm bloody cold.'

There was some water in the boat now, sloshing about under our feet.

Shit.

Nowhere on the Thames was far from civilisation, not even Sam's boatyard. The wide river narrowed abruptly with a notice on our left saying DANGER in huge letters, and smaller notice saying LOCK with an arrow to the right.

I steered the dinghy powerfully to the right. DANGER led to a weir. A lock would do just fine. Locks had keepers.

At about then I took note that there weren't in fact any other boats moving on the river and I remembered that often the locks closed for maintenance in winter and maybe the lock-keeper would have gone shopping . . .

Never mind. There were houses in sight on the right.

They proved to be summer cottages, all closed.

We floated on as if in a timeless limbo. The water in the bottom of the boat grew deeper. The current away from the mainstream, was much weaker. The lock cut seemed to last for ever, narrowing though, with high dark trees on the left; finally, blessedly, on the right, there were moorings for boats wanting passage through the lock to the lower level of the river below. No boats there, of course. No helping hands. Never mind.

I took the dinghy as far as we could go, right up near to the lock gates. Tied the painter to a mooring post and stepped up out of the boat.

'Won't be long,' I told Harry.

He nodded merely. It was all too much.

I climbed the steps up onto the lock and knocked on the door of the lock-keeper's house, and through great good fortune found him at home. A lean man: kind eyes.

'Fell in the river, did you?' he asked cheerfully, observing my soaked state. 'Want to use the phone?'

CHAPTER THIRTEEN

I went with Harry in the ambulance to Maidenhead hospital, both of us swathed in blankets, Harry also in a foil-lined padded wrap used for hypothermia cases; and from then on it was a matter of phoning and reassuring Fiona and waiting to see the extent of Harry's injuries, which proved to be a pierced calf, entry and exit wounds both clean and clotted, with no dreadful damage in between.

While Fiona was still on her way the medics stuffed Harry full of antibiotics and other palliatives and put stitches where they were needed, and by the time she'd wept briefly in my arms he was warm and responding nicely in the recovery room somewhere.

'But why,' she asked, half cross, half mystified, 'did he go to Sam's boatyard in the first place?' Like a mother scolding her lost child, I thought, after he's come back safe: just like Perkin with Mackie.

'He'll tell you about it,' I said. 'They say he's doing fine.'

'You're damp!' She disengaged herself and held me at arm's length. 'Did you fall through the floor too?'

'Sort of.' The hospital's central heating had been doing a fine job of drying everything on me and I felt like one of those old-fashioned clothes-horses, steaming slightly in warm air. Still no shoes or boots; couldn't be helped.

Fiona looked at my feet dubiously.

'I was going to ask you to drive Harry's car home,' she said, 'but I suppose you can't.'

I explained that Harry's car had already been driven away.

'Where is it, then?' she asked, bewildered. 'Who took it?'

'Maybe Doone will find out.'

'That man!' She shivered. 'I hate him.'

Before I could comment, a nurse came to fetch her to see Harry, and she went anxiously, calling over her shoulder for me to wait for her; and when she returned half a hour later she looked dazed.

'Harry's sleepy,' she said. 'He kept waking up and telling me silly things . . . How could he possibly get to this hospital in a *boat*?'

'I'll tell you on the way home. Would you like me to drive?'

'But . . .'

'It's quite easy with bare feet. I'll take off my socks.'

She unlocked the car herself and handed me the keys without comment. We arranged ourselves in the seats and as we headed for Shellerton in the early dark I told her calmly, incompletely and without terrors, the gist of what had befallen us in Sam's boatyard.

She listened with a frown, adding her own worry.

'Turn right here,' she said once, automatically, and another time, 'Sorry, we should have turned left there, we'll have to go back,' and finally, 'Go straight to Shellerton House. I'll drive home from there. I'm all right, really. It's just so upsetting. It made me shaky, seeing Harry dopey like that, pumped full of drugs.'

'I know.'

I pulled up outside Tremayne's house and while I put on my socks again she said she would come in for a while for company, 'to cure the trembles'.

Tremayne, Mackie and Perkin were all in the family room for the usual evening drinks. Tremayne made more than his usual fuss over Fiona, sensing some sort of turmoil, telling her comfortably that Mackie had just come back from Ascot races where he'd sent a runner for the apprentice race which had proved a total waste of time.

The note I'd left for Tremayne, 'GONE OUT WITH HARRY, BACK FOR GRUB', was still pinned to the corkboard. He took my arrival with Fiona as not needing comment.

'I think someone tried to kill Harry,' Fiona said starkly, cutting abruptly through Tremayne's continuing Ascot chat.

'What?'

281

There was an instant silence and general shock on all the faces, including Fiona's own.

'He went to Sam's boatyard and fell through some floorboards and was nearly drowned . . .' She told it to them much as I'd told her myself. 'If John hadn't been with him to help . . .'

Tremayne said robustly, 'My dearest girl, it must have been the most dreadful accident. Whoever would want to kill Harry?'

'No one,' Perkin said, his voice an echo of Tremayne's. 'I mean, what for?'

'Harry's a dear,' Mackie said, nodding.

'You'd never think so to read the papers recently,' Fiona pointed out, lines creasing her forehead. 'People can be incredibly vicious. Even people in the village. I went into the shop this morning and everyone stopped talking and stared at me. People I've known for years. I told Harry and he was furious, but what can we do? And now this . . .'

'Did Harry say someone tried to kill him?' Perkin asked.

Fiona shook her head. 'Harry was too dopey.'

'Does John think so?'

Fiona glanced at me. 'John didn't actually say so. It's what I think myself. What I'm afraid of. It scares me to think of it.'

'Then don't, darling,' Mackie put an arm round her and kissed her cheek. 'It's a frightening thing to have happened, but Harry *is* all right.'

'But someone stole his car,' Fiona said, hollow-eyed.

'Perhaps he left the key in the ignition,' Tremayne guessed, 'and a passer-by saw an opportunity.'

Fiona agreed unwillingly. 'Yes, he would have left his keys. He trusts people. I've told him over and over again that you simply *can't* these days.'

They all spent time reassuring Fiona until the worst of the worry unwound from her body and I watched the movement of her silver-blond hair in the soft lights and made no attempt to throw doubts because it would have achieved nothing good.

With Doone, early the next afternoon, it was a different matter. He'd had my bald account of events over the telephone in the morning, his first knowledge of what had happened. Now he came into the dining-room where I was working and sat down opposite me at the table.

'I hear you're a proper little hero,' he said dryly.

'Oh, really, who says so?'

'Mr Goodhaven.'

I stared back blandly with the same expression that he was trying on me. The morning's bulletin on Harry had been good, the prognosis excellent, his memory of events reportedly clarifying fast.

'Accident or attempted murder?' Doone asked, apparently seeking a considered answer.

I gave him one. 'The latter, I'd say. Have you found his car?'

'Not yet.' He frowned at me with a long look in which I read nothing. 'Where would you search for it?' he asked.

After a pause I said, 'At the top of a cliff.'

He blinked.

'Don't you think so?' I said.

'Beachy Head? Dover?' he suggested. 'A long drive to the sea.'

'Maybe a metaphorical cliff,' I said.

'Go on, then.'

'Is it usual,' I asked, 'for policemen to ask for theories from the general public?'

'I told you before, I like to hear them. I don't always agree, but sometimes I do.'

'Fair enough. Then what would you have thought if Harry Goodhaven had disappeared for ever yesterday afternoon and you'd found his car later by a cliff, real or metaphorical?'

'Suicide,' he said promptly. 'An admission of guilt.'

'End of investigation? Books closed?'

He stared at me sombrely. 'Perhaps. But unless we eventually found a body, there would also be the possibility of simple flight. We would alert Australia . . . look for him round the world. The books would remain open.'

'But you wouldn't investigate anyone else, because you would definitely consider him guilty.'

'The evidence points to it. His flight or suicide would confirm it.'

'But something about that evidence bothers you.'

I was beginning to learn about his expressions, or lack of them. The very stillness of his muscles meant that I'd touched something he'd thought hidden.

'Why do you say so?' he asked eventually.

'Because you've made no arrest.'

'That simple.'

'Without your knowledge, I can only guess.'

'Guess away,' he invited.

'Then I'd say perhaps Harry's sunglasses and pen and belt were with Angela Brickell because she took them there herself.'

'Go on,' he said neutrally. It wasn't, I saw, a new idea to him.

'Didn't you say her handbag had been torn open, the contents gone except for the photo in a zipped pocket?'

'I did say so, yes.'

'And you found chocolate wrappings lying about?'

'Yes.'

'And traces of dogs?'

'Yes.'

'And any dog worth his salt would bite open a handbag to get to the chocolate?'

'It's possible.' He made a decision and a big admission. 'There were toothmarks on the handbag.'

'Suppose then,' I said, 'that she did in fact have a

thing about Harry. He's a kind and attractive man. Suppose she did carry his photo with the horse, not Fiona's, who's the owner after all. Suppose she'd managed to acquire personal things of Harry's, his sunglasses, a pen, even a belt, and wore them or carried them with her, as young people do. They'd only be evidence of her crush on Harry, not of his presence at her death.'

'I considered all that, yes.'

'Suppose someone couldn't understand why you didn't arrest Harry, particularly in view of all the hounding in the papers, and decided to remove any doubts you might be showing?'

He sat for a while without speaking, apparently debating how many of his thoughts to share. Not many more, it transpired.

'Whoever took Harry's car,' I said, 'removed my jacket and boots as well. I took them off before I went through the floor into the dock.'

'Why didn't you tell me that?' He seemed put out, severe.

'I'm telling you now.' I paused. 'I would think that whoever took those things is very worried indeed now to find that I was with Harry and that he is alive. I'd say there wasn't supposed to be any reason to think Harry had gone to Sam's boatyard. No one would ever have looked for him there. I'd say it was an attempt to confirm Harry's guilt that went disastrously wrong, leaving you with bristling new doubts and a whole lot more to investigate.'

He said formally, 'I would like you to be present at the boatyard tomorrow morning.'

'What do you think of the place?' I asked.

'I've taken statements from Mr and Mrs Goodhaven and others,' he said stiffly. 'I haven't been to the boatyard yet. It has, however, been cordoned off. Mr Yaeger is meeting me there tomorrow at nine a.m. I would have preferred this afternoon but it seems he is riding in three races at Wincanton.'

I nodded. Tremayne had gone there, also Nolan. Another clash of the Titans.

'You know,' Doone said slowly, 'I had indeed started to question others besides Mr Goodhaven.'

I nodded. 'Sam Yaeger for one. He told us. Everyone knew you'd begin casting wider.'

'The lass had been indiscriminate,' he said regretfully.

Tremayne lent me his Volvo to go to the boatyard in the morning, reminding me before I set off that it was the day of the awards dinner at which he was to be honoured.

I'd seen the invitation pinned up prominently by Dee-Dee in the office: most of the racing world, it seemed, would be there to applaud. For Tremayne, though he had a few self-deprecating jokes about it,

the event gave proof of the substance of his life, much
like the biography.

Sam and Doone were already in the boatyard by the
time I'd found my way there, neither of them radiating
joy, Sam's multicoloured jacket only emphasising the
personality clash with grey plain clothes. They'd been
waiting for me, it seemed, in a mutual absence of
civility.

'Right, sir,' Doone said, as I stood up out of the car,
'we've done nothing here so far. Moved nothing. Please
take us through your actions of Wednesday afternoon.'

Sam said crossly, 'Asking for sodding trouble, coming
here.'

'As it turned out,' Doone said placidly. 'Go on, Mr
Kendall.'

'Harry said he was due to meet someone in the
boathouse, so we went over there.' I walked where we'd
gone, the others following. 'We opened this main door.
It wasn't locked.'

'Never is,' Sam said.

I pushed open the door and we looked at the hole
in the floor.

'We walked in,' I said. 'Just talking.'

'What about?' Doone asked.

'About a great party Sam gave here once. Harry was
saying there had been a bar here in the boathouse and
a grotto below. He began to walk down to the windows
and saw an envelope on the floor and when he bent to
pick it up, the floor creaked and gave way.'

Sam looked blank.

'Is that likely?' Doone asked him. 'How long ago was the floor solid enough to hold a party on it?'

'A year last July,' Sam said flatly.

'Quick bit of rot,' Doone commented, in his sing-song voice.

Sam made no answer, in itself remarkable.

'Anyway,' I said, 'I took off my boots and jacket and left them up here and I dropped into the water, because Harry hadn't come up for air, like I told you.'

'Yes,' Doone said.

'You can see better from the lower door,' I remarked, turning to go down the path. 'This door down here leads into the dock.'

Sam disgustedly fingered the splintered door frame.

'Did you sodding do this?' he demanded. 'It wasn't locked.'

'It was,' I said. 'With no key in sight.'

'The key was in the keyhole on the inside.'

'Absolutely not,' I said.

Sam pulled the door open and we looked into the scene that was all too familiar to my eyes; an expanse of muddy water, the hole in the ceiling overhead and the curtain of iron mesh across the exit to the river; a dock big enough for a moderate-sized cabin cruiser or three or four smaller boats. The water smelled dankly of mud and winter, which I hadn't seemed to notice when I'd been in it.

'There's a sort of walkway along this right-hand wall,'

I told Doone. 'You can't see it now because of the floodwater.'

Sam nodded. 'A mooring dock, with bollards.'

'If you care to walk along there,' I suggested, deadpan, 'I'll show you an interesting fact about that hole.'

They both stared at the water with reluctance stamped all over their faces, then Sam's cleared as he thought of a more palatable solution.

'We'll go and look in a boat.'

'How about the curtain?'

'Roll it up, of course.'

'Now, wait,' Doone said. 'The boat can wait. Mr Kendall, you came through the hole, found Mr Goodhaven and brought him to the surface. You sat him on the dock, then dived out under the curtain and climbed onto the bank. Is that right?'

'Yes, except that while I was pulling Harry along to that far corner to give him better support, someone opened the main door above our heads, like I told you, and then went away without saying anything, and I heard a car drive off, which might have been Harry's.'

'Did you hear any car *arriving*?' Doone asked.

'No.'

'Why didn't you call out for help?'

'Harry had been enticed here ... It all felt like a trap. People who set traps come back to see what they've caught.'

Doone gave me another of his assessments.

Sam said, frowning, 'You can't have dived out under the curtain, it goes right down to the river bed.'

'I sort of slithered under it.'

'You took a sodding risk.'

'So do you,' I said equably, 'most days of the week. And I didn't have much choice. If I hadn't found a way out we'd both eventually have died of cold or drowning, or both. Certainly by now. Most likely Wednesday night.'

After a short thoughtful silence Doone said, 'You're out on the bank. What next?'

'I saw the car had gone. I went to collect my boots and jacket, but they'd gone too. I called to Harry to reassure him, then I went out to that big shed to find a telephone, but I couldn't.'

Sam shook his head. 'There isn't one. When I'm here I use the portable phone from my car.'

'I couldn't find any decent tools, either.'

Sam smiled. 'I hide them.'

'So I used a rusty tyre lever and a mallet, and I'm sorry about your woodwork.'

Sam shrugged.

'Then what?' Doone asked.

'Then I got Harry out here and put him in a dinghy and we . . . er . . . floated down to the lock.'

'My sodding dinghy!' Sam exclaimed, looking at the imitation scrapyard. 'It's gone!'

'I'm sure it's safe down at the lock,' I said. 'I told the lock-keeper it was yours. He said he'd look after it.'

'It'll sink,' Sam said. 'It leaks.'

'It's out on the bank.'

'You'll never make a writer,' he said.

'Why not?'

'Too sodding sensible.'

He read my amusement and gave me a twisted grin.

I said, 'What happens to the rubbish lying in the dock when you roll up the curtain?'

'Sodding hell!'

'What are you talking about?' Doone asked us.

'The bed of this dock is mud, and it slopes downwards towards the river,' I said. 'When the curtain's rolled up, there's nothing to stop things drifting out by gravity into the river and being moved downstream by the current. Bodies often float to the surface, but you of all people must know that those who drown in the Thames can disappear altogether and are probably taken by undercurrents down through London and out to sea.' Sometimes from my high Chiswick window I'd thought about horrors down below the surface, out of sight. Like hidden motives, running deadly, running deep.

'Everyone in the Thames Valley knows they disappear,' Doone nodded. 'We lose a few holidaymakers every year. Very upsetting.'

'Harry's leg was impaled on something,' I said mildly. 'He was stuck underwater. He'd have been dead in a very few minutes. Next time Sam rolled the curtain up, Harry would have drifted quietly out of there, I should think, and no one would ever have known he'd been here. If his body were found anywhere downstream, well then, it could be suicide. If it wasn't found, then he'd escaped justice.' I paused, and asked Sam directly, 'How soon would you have rolled up the curtain?'

He answered at once. 'Whenever I'd found the hole in the floor. I'd have gone to take a look from beneath. Like we're going to now. But I hardly ever come over here. Only in summer.' He gave Doone a sly look. 'In the summer I bring a mattress.'

'And Angela Brickell?' Doone asked.

Sam, silenced, stood with his mouth open. A bull's-eye, I thought, for the Detective Chief Inspector.

I asked Sam, 'What's under the water in the dock?'

'Huh?'

'What did Harry get stuck on?'

He brought his mind back from Angela Brickell and said vaguely, 'Haven't a clue.'

'If you raise the curtain,' I said, 'we may never know.'

'Ah,' Doone stared judiciously at Sam, all three of us still clustered round the open door. 'It's a matter for grappling irons, then. Can we get a light inside there?'

'The main switch for here is over in the shed,' Sam said as if automatically, his mind's attention elsewhere. 'There's nothing in the dock except maybe a couple of beer cans and a radio some clumsy bimbo dropped when she was teetering out of a punt in high heels. I ask you . . .'

'Harry wasn't impaled on a radio,' I said.

Sam turned away abruptly and walked along the path to his workshop. Doone made as if to go after him, then stopped indecisively and came back.

'This could have been an accident, sir,' he said uneasily.

I nodded. 'A good trap never looks like one.'

'Are you quoting someone?'

'Yes. Me. I've written a good deal about traps. How to set them. How to catch game. The books are lying about all over the place in Shellerton. Everyone's dipped into them. Follow the instructions and kill your man.'

'You're not joking by any chance, are you, sir?'

I said regretfully, 'No, I'm not.'

'I'll have to see those books.'

'Yes.'

Sam came back frowning and, stretching inside without stepping into the water, pressed the three switches that had been unresponsive two days earlier. The lights in the ceiling came on without fuss and illuminated the ancient brick walls and the weathered old grey beams which crossed from side to side, holding up the planks of the floor above: holding up the planks, except where the hole was.

Doone looked in briefly and made some remark about returning with assistance. Sam looked longer and said to me challengingly, 'Well?'

'There's a bit of beam missing,' I said, 'isn't there?'

He nodded unwillingly. 'Looks like it. But I didn't know about it. How could I?'

Doone, in his quiet way a pouncer, said meaningfully, 'You yourself, sir, have all the knowledge and the tools for tampering with your boathouse.'

'I didn't.' Sam's response was belligerence, not fear. 'Everyone knows this place. Everyone's been here. Everyone could cut out a beam that small, it's child's play.'

'Who, precisely?' Doone asked. 'Besides you?'

'Well . . . anybody. Perkin! He could. Nolan . . . I mean, most people can use a saw, can't they? Can't you?'

Doone's expression assented but he said merely, 'I'll take another look upstairs now, if you please, sir.'

We went in gingerly but as far as one could tell the floor was solid except for the one strip over the missing bit of beam. The floorboards themselves were grey with age, and dusty, but not worm-eaten, not rotten.

Sam said, 'The floorboards aren't nailed down much. Just here and there. They fit tightly most of the time because of the damp, but when we have a hot dry summer they shrink and you can lift them up easily. You can check the beams for rot.'

'Why are they like that?' Doone asked.

'Ask the people who built it,' Sam said, shrugging. 'It was like this when I bought it. The last time I took the floorboards up was for the party, installing coloured spotlights and strobes in the ceiling underneath.'

'Who knew you took the floorboards up?' Doone asked.

Sam looked at him as if he were retarded. 'How do I know?' he demanded. 'Everyone who asked how I'd done the lighting. I told them.'

I went down on my knees and edged towards the hole.

'Don't do that,' Doone exclaimed.

'Just having a look.'

The way the floorboards had been laid, I saw, had meant that the doctored beam had been a main load-bearer. Several of the planks, including those that had given way under Harry's weight, had without that beam's support simply been hanging out in space, resting like a seesaw over the previous beam but otherwise supported only by the tight fit of each plank against the next. The floorboards hadn't snapped, as I'd originally thought; they'd gone down into the dock with Harry.

I tested a few planks carefully with the weight of my hand, then retreated and stood up on safer ground.

'Well?' Doone said.

'It's still lethal just each side of the hole.'

'Right.' He turned to Sam. 'I'll have to know, sir, when this tampering could have been carried out.'

Sam looked as if he'd had too much of the whole thing. With exasperation, he said, 'Since when? Since Christmas?'

Doone said stolidly. 'Since ten days ago.'

Sam briefly gave it some thought. 'A week last Wed-

nesday I dropped off a load of wood here on my way
to Windsor races. Thursday I raced at Towcester. Friday
I spent some time here, half a day. Saturday I raced at
Chepstow and had a fall and couldn't ride again until
Tuesday. So Sunday I was nursing myself until you
came knocking on my door, and Monday I spent here,
pottering about. Tuesday I was back racing at Warwick.
Wednesday I went to Ascot, yesterday Wincanton,
today Newbury . . .' He paused. 'I've never been here
at night.'

'What races did you ride in on Wednesday afternoon?' Doone asked. 'At Ascot.'

'What races?'

'Yes.'

'The two-mile hurdle, the novice hurdle, novice
chase.'

I gathered from Doone's face that it wasn't the type
of answer he'd expected, but he pulled out a notebook
and wrote down the reply as given, checking that he'd
got it right.

Sam, upon whom understanding had dawned, said,
'I wasn't here driving Harry's sodding car away, if that's
what you're thinking.'

'I'll need to ascertain a good many people's whereabouts on Wednesday afternoon,' Doone said placidly
in a flourish of jargon. 'But as for now, sir, we can
proceed with our investigations without taking any
more of the time of either of you two gentlemen, for
the present.'

'Class dismissed?' Sam said with irony.

Doone, unruffled, said we would be hearing from him later.

Sam came with me to where I'd parked Tremayne's car on stone-strewn grass. The natural jauntiness remained in his step but there was less confidence in his thoughts, it seemed.

'I like Harry,' he said, as we reached the Volvo.

'So do I.'

'Do you think I set that trap?'

'You certainly could have.'

'Sure,' he said. 'Dead easy. But I didn't.'

He looked up into my face, partly anxious, partly still full of his usual machismo.

'Unless you killed Angela Brickell,' I said, 'you wouldn't have tried to kill Harry. Wouldn't make sense.'

'I didn't do the silly little bimbo any harm.' He shook his head as if to free her from his memory. 'She was too intense for me, if you want to know. I like a bit of a giggle, not remorse and tears afterwards. Old Angie took everything seriously, always going on about mortal sin, and I got sodding tired of it, and of her, tell the truth. She wanted me to marry her!' His voice was full of the enormity of such a thought. 'I told her I'd got my sights set on a high-born heiress and she damned near scratched my eyes out. A bit of a hell-cat, she could be, old Angie. And hungry for it! I mean, she'd whip her clothes off before you'd finished the question.'

I listened with fascination to this insider viewpoint,

and the moody Miss Brickell suddenly became a real person; not a pathetic collection of dry bones, but a mixed-up pulsating young woman full of strong urges and stronger guilts who'd piled on too much pressure, loaded her need of penitence and her heavy desires and perhaps finally her pregnancy onto someone who couldn't bear it all, and who'd seen a violent way to escape her.

Someone, I thought with illumination, who knew how easily Olympia had died from hands round the neck.

Angela Brickell had to have invited her own death. Doone, I supposed, had known that all along.

'What are you thinking?' Sam asked, uncertainly for him.

'What did she look like?' I said.

'Angie?'

'Mm.'

'Not bad,' he said. 'Brown hair. Thin figure, small tits, round bottom. She agonised about having breast implants. I told her to forget bloody implants, what would her babies think? That turned on the taps, I'll tell you. She bawled for ages. She wasn't much fun, old Angie, but effing good on a mattress.'

What an epitaph, I thought. Chisel it in stone.

Sam looked out over the flooding river and breathed in the damp smell of the morning as if testing wine for bouquet, and I thought that he lived through his senses to a much greater degree than I did and was intensely alive in his direct approach to sex and his disregard of danger.

He said cheerfully, as if shaking off murder as a passing inconvenience, 'Are you going to this do of Tremayne's tonight?'

'Yes. Are you?'

He grinned. 'Are you kidding? I'd be shot if I wasn't there to cheer. And anyway,' he shrugged as if to disclaim sentiment, 'the old bugger deserves it. He's not all bad, you know.'

'I'll see you there, then,' I said, agreeing with him.

'If I don't break my neck.' It was flippantly said, but an insurance against fate, like crossed fingers. 'I'd better tell this sodding policeman where the main electric switch is. I've got it rigged so no one can find it but me, as I don't want people being able to walk in here after dark and turn the lights on. Inviting vandalism, that is. When the force have finished here, they can turn the electric off.'

He bounced off towards Doone, who was writing in his notebook, and they were walking together to the big boatshed as I drove away.

Even after having done the week's shopping en route, I was back at Shellerton House as promised in good time for Tremayne to drive his Volvo to Newbury races. He had sent three runners off in the horse-box and was taking Mackie to assist, leaving me to my slowly grow-ing first chapter in the dining-room.

When they'd gone Dee-Dee came in, as she often did now, to drink coffee over the sorted clippings.

I said, 'I hope Tremayne won't mind my taking all these with me when I go home.'

'Home . . .' Dee-Dee smiled. 'He doesn't want you to go home, didn't you know? He wants you to write the whole book here. Any day now he'll probably make you an offer you can't refuse.'

'I came for a month. That's what he said.'

'He didn't know you then.' She took a few mouthfuls of coffee. 'He wants you for Gareth, I think.'

That made sense, I thought; and I wasn't sure which I would choose, to go or to stay, if Dee-Dee was right.

When she'd returned to the office I tried to get on with the writing but couldn't concentrate. The trap in Sam's boathouse kept intruding and so did Angela Brickell; the cold threat of khaki water that could rush into aching lungs to bring oblivion and the earthy girl who'd been claimed back by the earth, eaten clean by earth creatures, become earth-digested dirt.

Under the day-to-day surface of ordinary life in Shel-lerton the fish of murder swam like a shark, silent, unknown, growing new teeth. I hoped Doone would net him soon, but I hadn't much faith.

Fiona telephoned during the afternoon to say that she'd brought Harry home and he wanted to see me,

DICK FRANCIS

so with a sigh but little reluctance I abandoned the empty page and walked down to the village.

Fiona hugged me as a long-lost brother and said Harry still couldn't be quite clear in his mind as he was saying now that he remembered drowning. However could one remember drowning?

'Quite hard to forget, I should think.'

'But he didn't drown!'

'He came close.'

She led me into the pink-and-green chintzy sitting-room where Harry, pale with blue shadows below the eyes, sat in an armchair with his bandaged leg elevated on a large upholstered footstool.

'Hello,' he said, raising a phantom smile. 'Do you know a cure for nightmares?'

'I have them awake,' I said.

'Dear God.' He swallowed. 'What's true, and what isn't?'

'What you remember is true.'

'Drowning?'

'Mm.'

'So I'm not mad.'

'No. Lucky.'

'I told you,' he said to Fiona. 'I tried not to breathe, but in the end I just did. I didn't mean to. Couldn't help it.'

'No one can,' I said.

'Sit down,' Fiona said to me, kissing Harry's head. 'What's lucky is that Harry had the sense to take you with him. And what's more, everyone's apologising all over the place except for one vile journalist who says it's possible a misguided vigilante thought getting rid of Harry the only path to real justice, and I want Harry to sue him, it's truly vicious.'

'I can't be bothered,' Harry said in his easy-going way. 'Doone was quite nice to me! That's enough.'

'How's the leg?' I asked.

'Lousy. Weighs a couple of tons. Still, no gangrene as yet.'

He meant it as a joke but Fiona looked alarmed.

'Darling,' he said placatingly, 'I'm bloated with anti-biotics, punctured with tetanus jabs and immunised against cholera, yellow-spotted mountain fever and athlete's foot. I have it on good authority that I'm likely to live. How about a stiff whisky?'

'No. It'll curdle the drugs.'

'For John, then.'

I shook my head.

'Take Cinderella to the ball,' he said.

'What?'

'Fiona to Tremayne's party. You're going, aren't you?'

I nodded.

'I'm not leaving you,' Fiona protested.

'Of course you are, love. It wouldn't be the same for Tremayne if you weren't there. He dotes on you. John can take you. And,' his eyes brightened mischievously with reawakening energy, 'I know who'd love to use my ticket.'

'Who?' his wife demanded.

'Erica. My sainted aunt.'

CHAPTER FOURTEEN

The Lifetime Award to Tremayne was the work of a
taken-over, revitalised hotel chain aiming to crash the
racing scene with sponsorship in a big way. They, Castle
Houses, had put up the prize for a steeplechase and
had also taken over a prestigious handicap hurdle race
already in the programme for Saturday.

The cash on offer for the hurdle race had stretched
the racing world's eyes wide and excited owners into
twisting their trainers' arms so that the entries had
been phenomenal (Dee-Dee said). The field would be
the maximum allowed on the course for safety and
several lightweights had had to be balloted out.

As a preliminary to their blockbuster, Castle Houses
had arranged the awards dinner and subsidized the
tickets so that more or less everyone could afford them.
The dinner was being held on the racecourse, in the
grandstand with its almost limitless capacity; and the
whole affair, Mackie had told me, was frankly only a
giant advertisement, but everyone might as well enjoy
it.

Before we went we met in the family room, Tremayne pretending nonchalance and looking unexpectedly sophisticated in his dinner jacket: grey hair smooth in wings, strong features composed, bulky body slimmed by ample expert tailoring. Perkin's jacket by contrast looked a shade too small for him and in hugging his incipient curves diminished the difference between the sizes of father and son.

Gareth's appearance surprised everyone, especially Tremayne: he made a bravado entrance to cover shyness in a dinner jacket no one knew he had, and he looked neat, personable and much older than fifteen.

'Where did you get that?' his father asked, marvelling.

'Picked it off a raspberry bush.' He smiled widely. 'Well, actually, Sam said I was the same height as him now and he happened to have two. So he's lent it to me. OK?'

'It's great,' Mackie said warmly, herself shapely in a shimmering black dress edged with velvet. 'And John's jacket, I see, survived the plunge into the ditch.'

The ditch seemed a long time ago: two weeks and three days back to the lonely silent abandoned struggle in the attic, to the life that seemed now to be the dream, with Shellerton the reality. Shellerton the brightly-lit stage; Chiswick the darkened amphitheatre where one sat watching from the gods.

'Don't get plastered tonight, John,' Tremayne said. 'I've a job for you in the morning.'

'Do you know how to avoid a hangover for ever?' Gareth asked me.

'How?' I said.

'Stay drunk.'

'Thanks a lot,' I said, laughing.

Tremayne, happy with life, said, 'You feel confident riding Drifter now, don't you?'

'More or less,' I agreed.

'Tomorrow you can ride Fringe. I own a half-share in him. He's that five-year-old in the corner box. You can school him over hurdles.'

I must have looked as astonished as I felt. I glanced at Mackie, saw her smiling, and knew she and Tremayne must have discussed it.

'Second lot,' Tremayne said. 'Ride Drifter first lot as usual.'

'If you think so,' I said a shade weakly.

'If you stay here a bit longer,' Tremayne said, 'and if you ride schooling satisfactorily, I don't see why you shouldn't eventually have a mount in an amateur race, if you put your mind to it.'

'*Cool*,' Gareth said fervently.

'I shouldn't think he wants to,' Perkin remarked as I hadn't answered in a rush. 'You can't make him.'

An offer I couldn't refuse, Dee-Dee had said; and I'd thought only of money. Instead, he was holding out like a carrot a heart-stopping headlong plunge into a new dimension of existence.

'Say you will,' Gareth begged.

Here goes impulse again, I thought. To hell with the helium balloon, it could wait a bit longer.

'I will.' I looked at Tremayne. 'Thank you.'

He nodded, beaming and satisfied, saying, 'We'll apply for your permit next week.'

We all loaded into the Volvo and went down to Shellerton Manor where everyone trooped in to see Harry. Tired but cheerful he held court from his chair and accepted Mackie's heartfelt kiss with appreciative good humour.

'I'm so glad you're alive,' she said, with a suspicion of tears, and he stroked her arm and said lightly that he was too, on the whole.

'What did it feel like?' Perkin said curiously, glancing at the bandaged leg.

'It happened too fast to feel much,' Harry said, smiling lopsidedly. 'If John hadn't been there I'd have died without knowing it, I dare say.'

'Don't!' Fiona exclaimed. 'I can't bear even to think of it. Tremayne, off you go or you'll be late. John and I will pick up Erica and see you soon.' She swept them out, following them, fearing perhaps that they would add to Harry's fatigue; and he and I looked at each other across the suddenly empty room in a shared fundamental awareness.

'Do you know who did it?' he asked, weariness and perhaps despair returning, stress visible.

I shook my head.

'Couldn't be someone I know.' He meant that he didn't want it to be. 'They meant to *kill* me, dammit.'

'Dreary thought.'

'I don't want to guess. I try not to. It's pretty awful to know someone hates me enough . . .' He swallowed. 'That hurts more than my leg.'

'Yes.' I hesitated. 'It was maybe not hate. More like a move in a chess game. And it went wrong, don't forget. The strong presumption of guilt has changed to a stronger presumption of innocence. Entirely and diametrically the wrong result. That can't be bad.'

'I'll hang onto that.'

I nodded. 'Better than a funeral.'

'Anything is.' He dredged up a smile. 'I've got a neighbour coming in to be with me tonight while you're all out. I feel a bit of a coward.'

'Rubbish. Bodyguards make good sense.'

'Do you want a permanent job?'

Fiona returned, pulling on a fluffy white wrap over her red silk dress, saying she really didn't want to go to the dinner and being persuaded again by her husband. He would be fine, he said, his friend would be there in a moment and goodbye, have a good time, give Tremayne the evening of his life.

Fiona drove her own car, the twin of Harry's (still lost), and settled Erica Upton in the front beside her when we collected her on a westerly detour. The five-star novelist gave me an unfathomable glimmer when I closed the car door for her and remarked that she'd had a long chat with Harry that afternoon on the telephone.

'He told me to lay off, as you'd saved his life,' she announced badly. 'A proper spoilsport.'

I said in amusement, 'I don't suppose you'll obey him.'

I heard the beginning of a chuckle from the front seat, quickly stifled. The battle lines, it seemed, had already been drawn. Hostilities however were in abeyance during arrival at the racecourse, disrobing, hair-tidying and first drinks. Half the racing world seemed to have embraced the occasion, for which after the last race that afternoon there had been much speedy unrolling of glittering black and silver ceiling-to-floor curtaining, transforming the workaday interior of the grandstand into something ephemerally magnificent.

'Theatrical,' Erica said disapprovingly of the décor, and so it was, but none the worse for that. It lifted the spirits, caused conversation, got the party going. Background music made a change from bookies' cries. Fiona looked at the seating plan and said to meet at table six. People came and surrounded her and Erica, and I drifted away from them and around, seeing a few people I knew by sight and hundreds I didn't. Like being at a gravediggers' convention, I thought, when one had marked out one's first plot.

My thoughts ran too much on death.

Bob Watson was there, dapper in a dark grey suit, with Ingrid shyly pretty in pale blue.

LONGSHOT

'Couldn't let down the guv'nor,' Bob said cheerfully. 'Anyway, he gave us the tickets.'

'Jolly good,' I said inanely.

'You're riding Fringe tomorrow,' he said, halfway between announcement and question. 'Schooling. The guv'nor just told me.'

'Yes.'

'Fringe will look after you,' he said inscrutably, looking around. 'Done this place up like an Egyptian brothel, haven't they?'

'I don't really know.'

'Oh, very funny.'

Ingrid giggled. Bob quelled her with a look, but I noticed slightly later and indeed all evening that she stuck very closely to his side; this could have been interpreted as her own insecurity if I hadn't remembered Mackie saying that meek little Ingrid never gave Bob much chance to stray with the likes of Angela Brickell and God help him if he did.

Sam Yaeger, ever an exhibitionist, had come in a white dinner jacket, having lent Gareth his black. He also had a frilled white shirt, a black shoestring tie and a definite air of strain under the confident exterior. Doone, it appeared, had more or less accused him straight out of sabotaging his own boathouse.

'He says I had the tools, the knowledge, the opportunity and the location, and he looked up those races I rode at Ascot and worked out that I could have had time between the first two and the last to drive to

311

Maidenhead and remove Harry's car. I asked why should I bother to do that when presumably if I had set the trap I would expect Harry's car still to be there *after* the races, and he just wrote down my answer as if I'd made a confession.'

'He's persistent.'

'He listens to you,' Sam said. 'We've all noticed. Can't you tell him I didn't sodding do it?'

'I could try.'

'And he whistled up his cohorts after you'd gone,' Sam complained, 'and they came with wet-suits and grappling irons and a heavy magnet and dredged up a lot of muck from the dock. An old broken bicycle frame, some rusted railings, an old disintegrating metal gate . . . it had all been lying here and there on the property. They clammed up after a bit and wouldn't show me everything, but he thinks I put it all in the water hoping Harry would get tangled in it.'

'Which he did.'

'So I'm asking you, how come *you* didn't get spiked when you went down there after him?'

'I learned how to jump into shallow water very young. So I didn't go down far. Put my feet down cautiously after I was floating.'

He stared. 'How the sod do you do that?'

'Jump shallow? The second your feet touch the water you raise your knees and crumple into a ball. The water itself acts as a brake. You must have done it

312

yourself some time or other. And I had the air in my clothes to hold me up, don't forget.'

'Doone asked me if I'd left your jacket and boots in Harry's car. Tricky bastard. I know now how Harry's been feeling. You get that flatfoot looking to tie you in knots and it's like being squeezed by coils and coils of a sodding boa constrictor. Everything you say, he takes it in the wrong way. And he looks so damned harmless. He got me so riled I lost a race this afternoon I should have won. Don't say I said that. I don't bloody know why we all tell you things. You don't belong here.'

'Perhaps that's why.'

'Yeah, perhaps.'

He seemed to have let out sufficient steam and resentment for the moment and turned to flirt obligingly with a middle-aged woman who touched his arm in pleased anticipation. Owners, Tremayne had said, either loved or hated Sam's manner: the women loved it; the men put up with it in exchange for winners.

Nolan, glowering routinely at Sam from a few feet away, switched his ill-humour to me.

'I don't want you treading on my effing toes,' he said forcefully. 'Why don't you clear off out of Shellerton?'

'I will in a while.'

'I told Tremayne there'll be trouble if he gives you any of my rides.'

'Ah.'

'He has the effing gall to say I suggested it myself and he knows bloody well I was taking the piss.' He glared at me. 'I don't understand what Fiona sees in you. I told her you're just a bag of shit with a pretty face who needs his arse kicked. You keep away from her horses, understand?'

I understand that he like everyone else was suffering from the atmospheric blight cast by Angela Brickell; he perhaps most because the strain of his own trial and conviction was so recent. There was no way I was ever going to ride as well as he did and he surely knew it. Fiona would never jock him off, in racing's descriptive phrase.

He stomped away, his place almost immediately taken by his brother, who gave me a malicious imitation of a smile and said, 'Nolan doesn't expletive like you, dear heart.'

'You don't say.'

Lewis was sober, so far. Also unaccompanied, like Nolan, though Harry had mentioned at one time that Lewis was married: his reclusive wife preferred to stay at home to avoid the fuss and fracas of Lewis drunk.

'Nolan likes to be the centre of attention and you've usurped his pinnacle,' Lewis said.

'Rubbish.'

'Fiona and Mackie look to you, now, not to him. And as for Tremayne, as for Gareth . . .' He gave me a sly leer. 'Don't put your neck within my brother's reach.'

'Lewis!' His lack of fraternal feeling shocked me more than his suggestion. 'You stuck *your* neck out for him, anyway.'

'Sometimes I hate him,' he said with undoubted truth, and wheeled away as if he had said enough.

Glasses in hand, the chattering groups mixed and mingled, broke and re-formed, greeted each other with glad cries as if they hadn't seen each other for years, not just that afternoon. Tremayne, large smile a permanence, received genuinely warm congratulations with believable modesty and Gareth, appearing eel-like at my elbow, said with gratification, 'He deserves it, doesn't he?'

'He does.'

'It makes you think a bit.'

'What about?'

'I mean, he's just Dad.' He struggled to get it right. 'Everyone's two people, aren't they?'

I said with interest, 'That's profound.'

'Get away.' He felt awkward at the compliment. 'I'm glad for him, anyway.'

He snaked off again and within minutes the throng began moving towards dinner, dividing into ten to a table, lowering bottoms onto inadequate chairs, fingering menus, peering at the print through candlelight, scanning their allotted neighbours. At table number six I found myself placed between Mackie and Erica Upton, who were already seated.

Erica was inevitable, I supposed, though I suspected Fiona had switched a few place cards before I reached there: a certain bland innocence gave her away.

'I did ask to sit next to you,' Erica remarked, as if

reading my thoughts as I sat down, 'once I knew you'd be here.'

'Er . . . why?'

'Do you have so little self-confidence?'

'It depends who I'm with.'

'And by yourself?'

'In a desert, plenty. With pencil and paper, little.'

'Quite right.'

'And you?' I asked.

'I don't answer that sort of question.'

I listened to the starch in her voice, observed it in the straightness of her backbone, recognised the ramrod will that made no concessions to hardship.

'I could take you across a desert,' I said.

She gave me a long piercing inspection. 'I hope that's not an accolade.'

'An assessment,' I said.

'You've found your courage since I met you last.'

She had a way of leaving one without an answer. She turned away, satisfied, to talk to Nolan on her other side, and I, abandoned, found Mackie on my right smiling with enjoyment.

'She's met her match,' she said.

I shook my head regretfully. 'If I could write like her . . . or ride like Sam or Nolan . . . if I could do *anything* that well, I'd be happy.'

Her smile sweetened. 'Try cooking.'

'Dammit . . .'

She laughed. 'I hear the power of your banana flam-bées made Gareth oversleep.'

Perkin, on her other side, murmured something to get her attention and for a while I watched Tremayne make the best of our table having been graced by the sponsor's wife, a gushing froth of a lady in unbecoming lemon. He would clearly have preferred to be talking to Fiona on his other side, but the award was having to be paid for with politeness. He glanced across the table, saw me smiling, interpreted my thought and gave me a slow ironic blink.

He soldiered manfully through the salmon soufflé and the beef Wellington while Lewis on the lady's other side put away a tumbler full of vodka poured from a half-bottle in his pocket. Fiona watched him with a frown: Lewis's drinking, even to my eyes, was increasingly without shame. Almost as if, having proclaimed himself paralytic in court, he was setting about proving it over and over again.

Glumly fidgeting between Lewis and Perkin, Gareth ate everything fast and looked bored. Perkin with brotherly bossiness told him to stop kicking the table leg and Gareth uncharacteristically sulked. Mackie made a placatory remark and Perkin snapped at her too.

She turned her head my way and with a frown asked, 'What's wrong with everyone?'

'Tension.'

'Because of Harry?' She nodded to herself. 'We all

pretend, but no one can help *wondering* . . . This time
it's much worse. Last time at least we knew how Olympia died. Angela Brickell's on everyone's nerves.
Nothing feels safe any more.'

'You're safe,' I said. 'You and Perkin. Think about
the baby.'

Her face cleared as if automatically: the thought of
the baby could diminish to trivia the grimmest fore-
bodings.

Perkin on her other side was saying contritely, 'Sorry,
darling, sorry,' and she turned to him with ever-ready
forgiveness, the adult of the pair. I wondered fleetingly
if Perkin, as a father, would be jealous of his child.

Dinner wound to a close: speeches began. Cultured
gents, identified for me by Mackie as being the Hima-
layan peaks of the Jockey Club, paid compliments to
Tremayne from an adjacent table and bowed low to the
sponsor. He, the lemon lady's husband, eulogised Tremayne, who winced only slightly over Top Spin Lob
being slurred to Topsy Blob, and a minion in the livery
of Castle Houses brought forth a tray bearing the award
itself, a silver bowl rimmed by a circle of small galloping
horses, an award actually worthy of the occasion.

Tremayne was pink with gratification. He accepted
the bowl. Everyone cheered. Photos flashed. Tremayne
made a brief speech of all-round thanks: thanks to the
sponsors, to his friends, his staff, his jockeys, to racing
itself. He sat down, overcome. Everyone cheered him
again and clapped loudly. I began to wonder how many

of them would buy Tremayne's book. I wondered whether after that night Tremayne would need the book written.

'Wasn't that great?' Mackie exclaimed, glowing.

'Yes, indeed.'

The background music became dance music. People moved about, flocking round Tremayne, patting his back. Perkin took Mackie to shuffle on the square of dance floor adjoining the table. Nolan took Fiona, Lewis got drunker, Gareth vanished, the sponsor retrieved his lady: Erica and I sat alone.

'Do you dance?' I asked.

'No.' She looked out at the still-alive party. 'The Duchess of Richmond's Ball,' she said.

'Do you expect Waterloo tomorrow?'

'Sometime soon. Who is Napoleon?'

'The enemy?'

'Of course.'

'I don't know,' I said.

'Use your brains. What about insight through imagination?'

'I thought you didn't believe in it.'

'For this purpose, I do. Someone tried to kill Harry. That's extremely disturbing. What's disturbing about it?'

It seemed she expected an answer, so I gave it. 'It was premeditated. Angela Brickell's death may or may not have been, but the attack on Harry was vastly thought out.'

She seemed minutely to relax.

'My God!' I said, stunned.

'What? What have you thought of?' She was alert again, and intent.

'I'll have to talk to Doone.'

'Do you know who did it?' she demanded.

'No, but I know what he knew.' I frowned. 'Everyone knows it.'

'What? Do explain.'

I looked at her vaguely, thinking.

'I don't believe it's very important,' I said in the end.

'Then what is it?' she insisted.

'Wood floats.'

She looked bemused. 'Well, of course it does.'

'The floorboards that went down to the water with Harry, they stayed under. They didn't float.'

'Why not?'

'Have to find out,' I said. 'Doone can find out.'

'What does it matter?'

'Well,' I said, 'no one could be absolutely certain that Harry would be spiked and drown immediately. So suppose he's alive and swimming about. He's been in that place before, at Sam's party, and he knows there's a mooring dock along one wall. He knows there's a door and he had daylight and can see the river through the metal curtain. So how does he get out?'

She shook her head. 'Tell me.'

'The door opens outwards. If you're inside, and you're standing in only six inches of water, not six feet, and you've got three or four floorboards floating about, you use one of them as a ram to break the lock or batter the door down. You're big and strong like Harry and also wet, cold, desperate and angry. How long does it take you to break out?'

'I suppose not long.'

'When Napoleon came to the boathouse,' I said, 'there wasn't any sound of Harry battering his way out. In fact,' I frowned, 'there's no saying how long the enemy had been there, waiting. He might have been hiding . . . heard Harry's car arrive.'

Erica said, 'When your book's published, send me a copy.'

I looked at her open-mouthed.

'Then I can tell you the difference between invention and insight.'

'You know how to pierce,' I said, wincing.

She began to say something else but never completed it. Instead our heads turned in unison towards the dancers, among whom battle seemed already to have started. There was a crash and a scream and bizarrely against the unrelentingly cheerful music two figures could be seen fighting.

Sam . . . and Nolan.

Sam had blood on his white jacket and down the white ruffles. Nolan's shirt was ripped open, showing a lot of hairy chest. They were both reeling about exchanging swinging blows not ten feet from table six and I stood up automatically, more in defence than interference.

Perkin tried to pull them apart and got smartly knocked down by Nolan, quick and tough with his fists as with his riding. I stepped without thinking onto the polished square and tried words instead.

'You stupid fools,' I said: not the most inventive sentence ever.

Nolan took his attention off Sam for a split second, lashed out expertly at my face and whirled back to his prime target in time to parry Sam's wildly lunging arm and kick him purposefully between the legs. Sam's head came forward. Nolan's fist began a descent onto the back of Sam's vulnerable neck.

With instinct more than thought, I barged into Nolan bodily, pushing him off line. He turned a face of mean-eyed fury in my direction and easily transferred his hatred.

I was vaguely aware that the dance floor had cleared like morning mist and also acutely conscious that Nolan knew volumes more about bare-knuckle fisticuffs than I did.

Racing people were extraordinary, I thought. Far from piling into Nolan in a preventative heap, they formed an instant ring around us and, as the band came to a straggling sharp-flat unscheduled halt, Lewis's drunken aristocratic voice could be heard drawling, 'Five to four the field.'

Everyone laughed. Everyone except Nolan. I

doubted if he'd heard. He was high on the flooding wave from the bursting dam of his dark nature, all the anxiety, guilt, hate and repressions sweeping out in a reckless torrent, no longer containable.

In a straight fight I wasn't going to beat him. All I would be was a punchbag for his escaping fury, the entity he saw as a new unbearable threat to his dominance in Tremayne's stable; the interloper, usurper, legitimate target.

I turned my back on him and took a step or two away. All I knew about fighting was ruse and trickery. I could see from the onlooking faces that he was coming for me and at what speed, and when I felt the air behind me move and heard the brush of his clothes I went down fast on one knee and whirled and punched upwards hard into the bottom of his advancing rib cage and then shifted my weight into his body and upwards so as to lift him wholesale off the floor, and before he'd got that sorted out I had one of his wrists in my hand and he ended up on his feet with me behind him, his arm in a nice painful lock and my mouth by his ear.

'You stupid shit,' I said intensely. 'The Jockey Club are here. Don't you care about your permit?'

For answer, he kicked back and caught me on a shin.

'Then I'll ride all your horses,' I said unwisely.

I gave him a hard releasing shove in the general direction of Sam, Perkin and an open-mouthed Gareth and at last watched a dozen restraining hands clutch and keep him from destroying himself entirely, but he struggled against them and turned his vindictive face my way and shouted in still exploding rage, '*I'll kill you.*'

I stood unmoving and listened to those words, and thought of Harry.

CHAPTER FIFTEEN

I apologized to Tremayne.

'Nolan started it,' Mackie said.

She peered anxiously at the reddening bruise on Perkin's cheek, a twin to one on mine.

Perkin sat in angry confusion at table six while the racing crowd, entertaining skirmish over, drifted away and got the band re-started.

Nolan was nowhere in sight. Sam took off his stained jacket, wined his bloody nose, sucked his knuckles and began making jokes as a form of released tension.

'I bumped into him, that's all I did,' he proclaimed with tragicomic gestures. 'Well, say I then took Fiona off him and maybe I told him to go find himself another filly and the next thing was he got a pincer-hold on my ear and was bopping me one on the nose and there I was bleeding fit to fill the Frenchy furrows so naturally I gave him one back.'

He collected an appreciative audience which definitely didn't include Tremayne. The shambles at the end of his splendid evening was aggravating him sorely and he propelled Fiona into a seat at the table with some of the disgruntled force he'd shown in Ronnie Curzon's office.

Fiona said anxiously, 'But, Tremayne, Sam meant it as a joke.'

'He should have had more sense,' Tremayne's voice was rough. Gareth, next to Perkin, looked at his father with apprehension, knowing the portents.

'Nolan's been through a lot,' Fiona said excusingly.

'Nolan's a violent man,' Tremayne stated with fierce irritation. 'You don't go poking a stick at a rattlesnake if you don't want to get bitten.'

'Tremayne!' She was alarmed at his brusqueness, which he immediately softened.

'My dear girl, I know he's your cousin. I know he's been through a lot, I know you're fond of him, but he and Sam shouldn't be in the same room together just now.' He looked from her to me. 'Are you all right?'

'Yes.'

'John was splendid!' Mackie explained, and Perkin scowled.

Erica grinned at me like a witch, saying, 'You're much too physical for the literati.'

'Let's go home,' Tremayne said abruptly. He stood, kissed Fiona, picked up the box containing his silver bowl and waited for obedience from his sons, his daughter-in-law and his prospective biographer. We stood. We followed him meekly. He made a stately, somewhat forbidding exit, his displeasure plainly visible to all around, his mien daring unkind souls to snigger.

No one did. Tremayne was held in genuine respect and I saw more sympathy than smirks: yet he in many respects was the stoker of the ill-feeling between his warring jockeys, and putting me among them wasn't a recipe for a cease-fire.

'Perhaps I'd better not ride schooling in the morning,' I suggested, as we reached the gate to the car park.

'Are you scared?' he demanded, stopping dead.

I stopped beside him as the other three went on ahead.

'Nolan and Sam don't like it, that's all,' I said.

'You bloody well ride. I'll get you that permit. I'll tame Nolan by threats. Understand?'

I nodded.

He stared at me intently. 'Is that why Nolan said he would kill you? Besides your making a public fool of him?'

'I think so.'

'Do you want to ride in a race or two, or don't you?'

'I do.'

'School Fringe tomorrow, then. And as for now, you'd better go back with Fiona. Make sure she gets home safe. Harry won't want Nolan pestering her and he's quite capable of it.'

'Right.'

He nodded strongly and went on towards his Volvo, and I returned to find Fiona arguing with Nolan in the

entrance hall. She and Erica beside her saw me with
relief, Nolan with fresh fury.

'I was afraid you'd gone,' Fiona said.

'Thank Tremayne.'

Nolan said angrily, 'Why is this bag of slime always
hanging about?'

He made no move, though, to attack me.

'Harry asked him to see me home,' Fiona said placatingly. 'Get some rest, Nolan, or you won't be fit for
Groundsel tomorrow.'

He heard, as I did, the faint threat in the cousinly
concern, and at least it gave him an excuse for a face-
saving exit. Fiona watched his retreating back with a
regret neither Erica nor I shared.

I rode Drifter with the first lot in the morning and
crashed off on to the wood chippings halfway up the
gallop.

Tremayne showed a modicum of anxiety but no sympathy, and the anxiety was for the horse. He sent a lad
after it to try to catch it and with disgust watched me
limp towards him rubbing a bruised thigh.

'Concentrate,' he said. 'What the hell do you think
you were doing?'

'He swerved.'

'You weren't keeping him straight. Don't make
excuses, you weren't concentrating.'

The lad caught Drifter and brought him to join us.

'Get up,' Tremayne said to me testily.

I wriggled back into the saddle. I supposed he was right about not concentrating: a touch of the morning afters.

They'd all gone to bed the night before when I'd returned from a last noggin with Harry. I'd walked up from the village under a brilliantly starry sky, breathing cold shafts of early-morning air, thinking of murder. Sleep had come slowly with anxiety dreams. I felt unsettled, not refreshed.

I rode Drifter back with the rest of the string and went in to breakfast, half expecting to be told I wouldn't be allowed to ride Fringe. Tremayne's own mood appeared to be a deepening depression over the evening's finale, and I was sorry because he deserved to look back with enjoyment.

He was reading a newspaper when I went in, and scowling heavily.

'How did they get hold of this so damned fast?'

'What?'

'This.' He pushed the opened paper violently across the table and I read that a brace of brawling jockeys had climaxed the prestigious award dinner with a bloody punch-up. Ex-champion Yaeger and amateur champion Nolan Everard (recently convicted of manslaughter) had been restrained by friends. Tremayne Vickers had said 'no comment'. The sponsor was furious. The Jockey Club were 'looking into it'. End of story.

'It's rubbish,' Tremayne snorted. 'I never said "no comment". No one asked me for any comment. The sponsor had left by the time it happened, so how can he be furious? So had the Jockey Club members. They went after the speeches. I talked to some of them as they were leaving. They congratulated me. Huh!'

'The fuss will die down,' I assured him.

'Makes me look a bloody fool.'

'Make a joke of it,' I suggested.

He stared. 'I don't feel like joking.'

'No one does.'

'It's this business about Harry, isn't it? Upsets everyone. Bloody Angela Brickell.'

I made the toast.

He said, 'Are you fit enough to ride Fringe?'

'If you'll let me.'

He studied me, some of his ill-feeling fading. 'Concentrate, then.'

'Yes.'

'Look,' he said a touch awkwardly, 'I don't mean to take my bad temper out on you. If you hadn't been here we'd all be in a far worse pickle. Best thing I ever did, getting you to come.'

In surprise, I searched for words to thank him but was forestalled by the telephone ringing. Tremayne picked up the receiver and grunted, 'Hello?', not all his vexation yet dissipated.

His face changed miraculously to a smile. 'Hello, Ronnie. Calling to find out how the book's going? Your boy's been working on it. What? Yes, he's here. Hold on.' He passed me the receiver, saying unnecessarily, 'It's Ronnie Curzon.'

'Hello, Ronnie,' I said.

'How's it going?'

'I'm riding a good deal.'

'Keep your mind on the pages. I've got news for you.'

'Good or bad?'

'My colleague in America phoned yesterday evening about your book.'

'Oh.' I felt apprehensive. 'What did he say?'

'He says he likes *Long Way Home* very much indeed. He will gladly take it on, and he is certain he can place it with a good publisher.'

'Ronnie!' I swallowed, unable to get my breath. 'Are you sure?'

'Of course, I'm sure. I always told you it was all right. Your English publisher is very enthusiastic. She told my American colleague the book is fine and he agrees. What more do you want?'

'Oh . . .'

'Come down from the ceiling. A first novel by an unknown British writer isn't going to be given a huge advance.' He mentioned a sum which would pay my rent until I'd finished the helium balloon and leave some over for sandwiches. 'If the book takes off like they hope it will, you'll get royalties.' He paused. 'Are you still there?'

'Sort of.'

331

He laughed. 'It's all beginning. I have faith in you.'

Ridiculously, I felt like crying. Blinked a few times instead and told him in a croaky voice that I'd met Erica Upton twice and had sat next to her at dinner.

'She'll destroy you!' he said, horrified.

'I don't think so. She wants a copy of the book when it's published.'

'She'll tear it apart. She likes making mincemeat of new writers.' He sounded despairing. 'She does hatchet jobs, not reviews.'

'I'll have to risk it.'

'Let me talk to Tremayne.'

'OK, and Ronnie . . . thanks.'

'Yes, yes . . .'

I handed back the receiver and heard Ronnie being agitated on the other end.

'Hold on,' Tremayne said, 'she likes him.'

I distinctly heard Ronnie's disbelieving '*What?*'

'Also she's very fond of her nephew, Harry, and on Wednesday John saved Harry's life. I grant you she may write him a critical review, but she won't demolish him.' Tremayne listened a bit and talked a bit and then gave me the receiver again.

'All right,' Ronnie said more calmly, 'any chance you get, save her life too.'

I laughed, and with a sigh he disconnected.

'What happened?' Tremayne asked. 'What did he tell you?'

'I'm going to be published in America. Well . . . probably.'

'Congratulations.' He beamed, pleased for me, his glooms lifting. 'But that won't change things, will it? I mean here, between us. You will still write my book, won't you?'

I saw his anxiety begin to surface and promptly allayed it.

'I will write it. I'll do the very best I can and just hope it does you justice. And will you excuse me if I run and jump and do handsprings? I'm bursting . . . Ronnie said it's all beginning. I don't know that I can bear it.' I looked at him. 'Did you feel like this when Top Spin Lob won the National?'

'I was high for days. Kept smiling. Topsy Blob, I ask you!' He stood up. 'Back to business. You'll come up with me in the Land Rover. Fringe's lad can ride him up, then change with you.'

'Right.'

Ronnie's news, I found, had given me a good deal more confidence in Fringe than I had had on Drifter, illogical though it might be.

It's all beginning . . .

Concentrate.

Fringe was younger, whippier and less predictable than Drifter: rock music in place of classical. I gathered the reins and lengthened the stirrup leathers a couple of holes while Fringe made prancing movements, getting used to his new and heavier rider.

'Take him down below the three flights of hurdles,' Tremayne said, 'then bring him up over them at a useful pace. You're not actually racing. Just a good half-speed gallop. Bob Watson will be with you for company. Fringe jumps well enough but he likes guidance. He'll waver if you don't tell him when to take off. Don't forget, it's you that's schooling the horse, not the other way round. All ready?'

I nodded.

'Off you go, then.'

He seemed unconcerned at letting me loose on his half-share investment and I tried telling myself that ahead lay merely a quick pop over three undemanding obstacles, not the first searching test of my chances of racing. I'd ridden over many jumps before, but never on a racehorse, never fast, never caring so much about the outcome. Almost without being aware of it I'd progressed from the hesitancy of my first few days there to a strong positive desire to go down to the starting gate: any starting gate, anywhere. I had to admit that I envied Sam and Nolan.

Bob was circling on his own horse, waiting for me. Both his horse and Fringe, aware they would be jumping, were stimulated and keen.

'Guv'nor says you're to set off on the side nearest him,' Bob said briefly. 'He wants to see what you're doing.'

I nodded, slightly dry-mouthed. Bob expertly trotted his mount into position, gave me a raised-eye query about readiness and kicked forward into an accelerating gallop. Fringe took up his position alongside with familiarity and eagerness, an athlete doing what he'd been bred for, and enjoyed.

First hurdle ahead. Judge the distance . . . give Fringe the message to shorten his stride . . . I gave it to him too successfully, he put in a quick one, got too near the hurdle, hopped over it nearly at a standstill, lost lengths on Bob.

Damn, I thought. *Damn.*

Second hurdle, managed it a bit better, gave him the signal three strides from the jump, felt him lift off at the right time, felt his assurance flow back and his faith in me revive, even if provisionally.

Third hurdle, I left him too much to his own devices as the distance was awkward. I couldn't make up my own mind whether to get him to lengthen or shorten and in consequence I didn't make his mind up to do either and we floundered over it untidily, his hooves rapping the wooden frames, my weight too far forward . . . a mess.

We pulled up at the end of the schooling stretch and trotted back to where Tremayne stood with his binoculars. I didn't look at Bob; didn't want to see his disapproval, all too wretchedly aware that I hadn't done very well.

Tremayne with pursed lips offered no direct opinion. Instead he said, 'Second pop, Bob. Off you go,' and I gathered we were to go back to the beginning and start again.

I seemed to have more time to get things together the second time and Fringe stayed beside Bob fairly smoothly to the end. I felt exalted and released and newly alive in myself, but also I'd watched Sam Yaeger in a schooling session one morning and knew the difference.

Tremayne said nothing until we were driving back to the stable and then all he did was ask me if I were happy with what I'd done. Happy beyond expression in one way, I thought, but not in another. I knew for certain I wanted to race. Knew I had elementary skill.

'I'll learn,' I said grimly, and he didn't answer.

When we reached the house, however, he rummaged about in the office for a while complaining that he could never find anything on Dee-Dee's days off and eventually brought a paper into the dining-room, plonked it on the table and instructed me to sign.

It was, I saw, an application for a permit to race as an amateur jockey. I signed it without speaking, incredibly delighted, grinning like a maniac.

Tremayne grunted and bore the document away, coming back presently to say I should stop working and go with him to Newbury races, if I didn't mind. Also Mackie would be coming with us and we'd be picking up Fiona.

'And frankly,' he said, coming to the essence of the

matter, 'those two don't want to go without you, and Harry wants you to be there and . . . well . . . so do I.'

'All right,' I said.

'Good.'

He departed again and, after a moment's thought, I went into the office to put through a call to Doone's police station. He was off duty, I was told. I could leave my name and a message.

I left my name.

'Ask him,' I said, 'why the floorboards in the boathouse didn't float.'

'Er . . . would you repeat that, sir?'

I repeated it and got it read back with scepticism.

'That's right,' I confirmed, amused. 'Don't forget it.'

We went to the races and watched Nolan ride Fiona's horse Groundsel and get beaten by a length into second place, and we watched Sam ride two of Tremayne's runners unprofitably and then win for another trainer.

'There's always another day,' Tremayne said philosophically.

Fiona told us on the way to the races that the police had phoned Harry to say they'd found his car in the station car park at Reading.

'They said it looks OK but they've towed it off somewhere to search for clues. I never knew people really said "search for clues", but that's what they said.'

'They talk like their notebooks,' Tremayne nodded. From Reading station one could set off round the world. Metaphorical cliff, I thought. A guilty disappearance had been the intended scenario, not a presumption of suicide. Unless of course the car had been moved again after Harry had made his unscheduled reappearance.

The racecourse was naturally buzzing with accounts of the row at Tremayne's dinner, most of the stories inflamed and inaccurate because of the embroidery by the press. Tremayne bore the jokes with reasonable fortitude, cheered by the absence of enquiry or even remarks from the Jockey Club, not even strictures about 'bringing racing into disrepute' which I'd learned was the yardstick for in-house punishment.

By osmosis of information, both Sam and Nolan knew details of Fringe's schooling. Sam said, 'You'll be taking my sodding job next,' without meaning it in the least, and Nolan, bitter-eyed and cursing, saw Tremayne's warning glare and subsided with festering rancour.

'How on earth do they know?' I asked, mystified.

'Sam phoned Bob to find out,' Tremayne said succinctly. 'Bob told him you did all right. Sam couldn't wait to tell Nolan. I heard him doing it. Bloody pair of fools.'

All afternoon Fiona kept me close by her side, looking around for me any time I fell a step behind. She tried unsuccessfully to hide what she described as 'preposterous fear', and I understood that her fear had no focus and no logic, but was becoming a state of mind. Tremayne, sensing it also, fussed over her even more than usual and Fiona herself made visible efforts to act normally and as she said 'be sensible'.

Whenever Mackie wasn't actively helping Tremayne she stayed close also to Fiona, and although I tried I couldn't dislodge the underlying anxiety in their eyes. Silver-blond and red-head, they clung to each other occasionally as long-time friends, and spoke to Nolan, cousin of one, ex-fiancé of the other, with an odd mixture of dread, exasperation and compassion.

Nolan was disconcerted by having lost on Groundsel though I couldn't see that he'd done anything wrong. Tremayne didn't blame him, still less Fiona, but the non-success intensified if possible his ill-will towards me. I was truly disconcerted myself to have acquired so violent an enemy without meaning to and could see no resolution short of full retreat; and the trouble was that since that morning's schooling any inclination to retreat had totally vanished.

I looked back constantly to the morning with huge inward joy; to Ronnie's phone call, to the revelation over hurdles. Doors opening all over the place. All beginning.

The afternoon ending, we took Fiona home and went on to Shellerton House where Perkin came through for drinks, Tremayne went out to see the horses and Gareth returned from a football match. An evening like most others in that house, but to me the first of a changed life.

*

The next day, Sunday, Gareth held me to my promise to take him and Coconut out on another survival trip.

The weather was much better; sunny but cold still with a trace of breeze, a good day for walking. I suggested seven miles out, seven miles back; Gareth with horror suggested two. We compromised on borrowing the Land Rover for positioning, followed by walking as far as their enthusiasm took them.

'Where are you going?' Tremayne asked.

'Along the road over the hills towards Reading,' I said. 'There's some great woodland there, unfenced, no signs saying "keep out".'

Tremayne nodded. 'I know where you mean. It's all part of the Quillersedge Estate. They only try to keep people out just before Christmas, to stop them stealing the fir trees.'

'We'd better not light a fire there,' I said, 'so we'll take our food and water with us.'

Gareth looked relieved. 'No fried worms.'

'No, but it will be survival food. Things you could pick or catch.'

'OK,' he said with his father's brand of practical acceptance. 'How about chocolate instead of dandelion leaves?'

I agreed to the chocolate. The day had to be bearable. We set off at ten, collected Coconut and bowled along to the woods.

There were parking places all along that road, not planned, official, tarmacked areas but small inlets of beaten earth formed by the waiting cars of many walkers. I pulled into one of them, put on the handbrake and, when the boys were out, locked the doors.

Gareth wore of course his psychedelic jacket. Coconut's yellow oilskins had been superseded by an equally blinding anorak and I, in the regrettable absence of my ski-suit jacket, looked camouflaged against the trees in stone-washed jeans and a roomy olive-drab Barbour borrowed from Tremayne.

'Right,' I said, smiling, as they slid the straps of bright blue nylon knapsacks over their shoulders, 'we'll take a walk into the Berkshire wilderness. Everyone fit?'

They said they were, so we stepped straight into the tangled maze of alder, hazel, birch, oak, pine, fir and laurel and picked out steps over dried grass, scratchy brambles and the leafless knee-high branching shoots of the wood's next generation. None of this had been cleared or replanted; it was scrub woodland as nature had made it, the real thing as far as the boys were concerned.

I encouraged them to lead but kept them going towards the sun by suggesting detours round the obstructing patches, and I identified the trees for them, trying to make it interesting.

'We're not eating the bark again, are we?' Coconut said, saying ugh to a birch tree.

'Not today. Here is a hazel. There might still be some nuts lying round it.'

They found two. Squirrels had been there first.

DICK FRANCIS

We went about a mile before they tired of the effort
involved, and I didn't mean to go much further in any
case because according to the map I had in my pocket
we were by then in about the centre of the western
spur of the Quillersedge woods. We'd come gently up
and down hill, but not much further on the ground fell
away abruptly, according to the map's contour lines,
with too hard a climb on the return.

Gareth stopped in one of the occasional small clear-
ings and mentioned food hopefully.

'Sure,' I said. 'We can make some reasonable seats
with dead twigs to keep our bottoms off the damp
ground, if you like. No need today for a shelter.'

They made flat piles of twigs, finishing them off with
evergreen, then emptied their rucksacks and spread the
blue nylon on top. We all sat fairly comfortably and
ate things I'd bought for the occasion.

'Smoked trout!' Gareth exclaimed. 'That's an
advance on roots.'

'You could catch trout and smoke them if you had
to,' I said. 'The easiest way to catch them is with a
three-pronged spear, but don't tell that to fishermen.'

'How do you smoke them?'

'Make a fire with lots of hot embers. Cover the
embers thickly with green fresh leaves: they'll burn
slowly with billows of smoke. Make a latticed frame to
go over the fire and put the trout on it or otherwise
hang them over the smoke, and if possible cover it all
with branches or more leaves to keep the smoke inside.

342

The best leaves for smoking are things like oak or beech. The smell of the smoke will go into the fish to some extent, so don't use anything you don't like the smell of. Don't use holly or yew, they're poisonous. You can smoke practically anything. Strips of meat. Bits of chicken.'

'Smoked salmon!' Coconut said. 'Why not?'

'First catch your salmon,' said Gareth dryly.

He had brought a camera and he took photos of everything possible; the seats, the food, ourselves.

'I want to remember these days when I'm old like Dad,' Gareth said. 'Dad wishes he'd had a camera when he went round the world with his father.'

'Does he?' I asked.

He nodded. 'He told me when he gave me this one.'

We ate the trout with unleavened bread and healthy appetites and afterwards filled up with mixed dried fruit and pre-roasted chestnuts and almonds. The boys declared it a feast compared with the week before and polished off their chocolate as a bonus.

Gareth said casually, 'Was it in a place like this that someone killed Angela Brickell?'

'Well . . . I should think so. But five miles or so from here,' I said.

'And it was summer,' he commented. 'Warm. Leaves on the trees.'

'Mm.' Imaginative of him, I thought.

'She wanted to kiss me,' he said with a squirm.

Both Coconut and I looked at him in astonishment.

'I'm not as ugly as all that,' he said, offended.

'You're not ugly,' I assured him positively, 'but you're young.'

'She said I was growing up.' He looked embarrassed, as did Coconut.

'When did she say that?' I asked mildly.

'In the Easter holidays, last year. She was always out there in the yard. Always looking at me. I told Dad about it, but he didn't listen. It was Grand National time and he couldn't think of anything but Top Spin Lob.' He swallowed. 'Then she went away and I was really glad. I didn't like going out into the yard when she was there.' He looked at me anxiously. 'I suppose it's wrong to be glad someone's dead.'

'Is glad what you feel?'

He thought about it.

'Relieved,' he said finally. 'I was afraid of her.' He looked ashamed. 'I used to think about her, though. Couldn't help it.'

'It won't be the last time someone makes a pass at you,' I said prosaically. 'Next time, don't feel guilty.'

Easier said than done, I supposed. Shame and guilt tormented the innocent more than the wicked.

Gareth seemed liberated by having put his feelings into words and he and Coconut jumped up and ran around, throwing mock punches at each other, swinging on tree branches, getting rid of bashfulness with shouts and action and shows of strength. I supposed I'd been like that too, but I couldn't remember.

'Right,' I said, as they subsided onto the seats and panted while I packed away our food wrappings (which would have started a dinky fire). 'Which way to the Land Rover?'

'That way,' said Gareth immediately, pointing east.

'That way,' Coconut said, pointing west.

'Which way is north?' I asked.

They both got it instinctively wrong, but then worked it out roughly by the sun, and I showed them how to use a watch as a compass, which Gareth half remembered, having learned before.

'Something to do with pointing the hands at the sun,' he guessed.

I nodded. 'Point the hour hand at the sun, then halfway between the hand and twelve o'clock is the north-south line.'

'Not in Australia,' Gareth said.

'We're not in Australia,' Coconut objected. He looked at his watch and around him. 'That way is north,' he said, pointing. 'But which way is the Land Rover?'

'If you go north you'll come to the road,' I said.

'What do you mean "you"?' Gareth demanded. 'You're coming too. You've got to guide us.'

'I thought,' I said, 'that it would be more fun for you to find your own way back. And,' I went on as he tried to interrupt, 'so as you don't get lost if the sun goes in, you can paint the trees as you go with luminous paint. Then you can always come back to me.'

'*Cool*,' he said, entranced.

345

'What?' Coconut wanted to know.

Gareth told him about finding one's way back to places by blazing the trail.

'I'll follow you,' I said, 'but you won't see me. If you go really badly wrong, I'll tell you. Otherwise, survival's up to you.'

'Ace,' Gareth said happily.

I unzipped the pouch round my waist and gave him the small jar of paint and the sawn-off paintbrush.

'Don't forget to paint so you can see the splash from both directions, coming and going, and don't get out of sight of your last splash.'

'OK.'

'Wait for me when you hit the road.'

'Yes.'

'And take the whistle.' I held it out to him from the pouch. 'It's just a back-up in case you get stuck. If you're in trouble, blow it, and I'll come at once.'

'It's only a mile,' he protested, slightly hurt, not taking it.

'What do I say to your father if I mislay you?'

He grinned in sympathy, giving way, and put the best of all insurances in his pocket.

'Let's go back the way we came,' Coconut said to Gareth.

'Easy!' Gareth agreed.

I watched them decide on the wrong place and paint the first mark carefully round a sapling's trunk. They might just possibly have been able to find the morning's path if they'd been starting again from the road, but tracking backwards was incredibly difficult. All the identifiable marks of our passage, like broken twigs and flattened grass, pointed forward into the wood, not out of it.

They consulted their watches and moved north through the trees, looking back and painting as they went. They waved once and I waved back, and for some time I could see the bright jackets in the dappled shade of the afternoon sun. Then, when they had gone, I began to slowly follow their splashes.

I could go much faster than they could. When I saw them again I dropped down on one knee, knowing that even though they were constantly looking back they wouldn't see me at that low level, in my nature-coloured clothes.

Besides the map I'd brought along my faithful compass, and by its reckoning checked the boys' direction all the time. They wandered off to the north-east a bit but not badly enough to get really lost, and after a while made a correction to drift back to north.

The pale cream splashes were easy to spot, never far apart. Gareth had intelligently chosen smooth-barked saplings all the way and all the marks were at the same height, at about waist level, where painting came to him most naturally, it seemed.

I kept the boys in sight intermittently all the way. They were talking to each other loudly as if to keep lurking wood-spirits at bay, and I did vividly remember that teenage spooky feeling of being alone in wild woodland and at the mercy of supernatural eyes. Even in sunshine one could be nervous. At night a couple of times at fifteen I'd been terrified.

On that day, as I slowly followed the trail, I simply felt at home and at peace. There were birds singing, though not yet many, and apart from the boys' voices the quiet was as old and deep as the land. The woods still waited the stirring of spring, lying chilly and patient with sleeping buds and butterflies in cocoons. The smells of autumn, of compost and rot, still faintly lingered into the winter thaw, only the pines and firs remaining fragrant if one brushed them. Pine resin, collected by tapping, dried to lumps that made brilliant firelighters.

It was a slow-going mile, but towards the end one could hear occasional cars along the road ahead and Gareth and Coconut with whoops crashed through the last few yards, again, as the week before, relieved to be back in the space age.

I speeded up and stepped out behind them, much to Gareth's surprise.

'We thought you were miles back,' he exclaimed.

'You laid an excellent trail.'

'The paint's nearly finished.' He held it up to show me and the jar slipped out of his hand, rolling the remains of its contents onto the earth. 'Hey, sorry,' he said. 'But there wasn't much left.'

'Doesn't matter.' I picked up the jar which was slip-

pery on the outside from dripped paint and, screwing
its lid on, dropped it with the brush into a plastic bag
before stowing it again in my pouch.

'Can we get some more?' Coconut asked.

'Sure. No problem. Ready to go home?'

The boys, both pumped up by their achievement, ran
and jumped all along the road to the Land Rover that
we found round the next bend, and rode back in
euphoric good spirits.

'Terrific,' Gareth told Tremayne, bursting into the
family room after we'd dropped Coconut and returned
to Shellerton. 'Fantastic.'

Whether they wanted to or not, Tremayne, Mackie
and Perkin received a minute-by-minute account of the
whole day with the sole exception of the discussion
about Angela Brickell. Tremayne listened with veiled
approval, Mackie with active interest, Perkin with
boredom.

'It's a real wilderness,' Gareth said. 'You can't hear
anything. And I took lashings of photos—' He stopped,
suddenly frowning. 'Hold on a minute.'

He sped out of the room and came back with his
blue knapsack, searching the contents worriedly.

'My camera's not here!'

'The one I gave you for Christmas?' Tremayne asked,
not over-pleased.

'Perhaps Coconut's got it,' Perkin suggested lan-
guidly.

'Thanks.' Gareth leaped to the telephone in hopes

that were all too soon dashed. 'He says he didn't see it after lunchtime.' He looked horrified. 'We'll have to go back at once.'

'No, you certainly won't,' Tremayne said positively. 'It sounds a long way and it'll be getting dark soon.'

'But it's *luminous* paint,' Gareth begged. 'That's the whole point, you can see it in the dark.'

'No,' said his father.

Gareth turned to me. 'Can't we go back?'

I shook my head. 'Your father's right. We could get lost in those woods at night, paint or no paint. You've only got to miss one mark and you'd be out there till morning.'

'*You* wouldn't get lost.'

'I might,' I said. 'We're not going.'

'Did you drop it on the path back?' Mackie asked sympathetically.

'No . . .' He thought about it. 'I must have left it where we had lunch. I hung it on a branch to keep it from getting damp. I just forgot it.'

He was upset enough for me to say, 'I'll get it tomorrow afternoon.'

'Will you?' Disaster swung back to hope. 'Oh, *great*.'

Tremayne said doubtfully, 'Will you find one little camera hanging in all those square miles of nothing?'

'Of course he will,' Gareth told him confidently. 'I told you, we left a *trail*. And oh!' He thought of something. 'Isn't it lucky I dropped all the paint, because

350

now you can see where the trail starts, because we didn't paint any trees once we could see the road.'

'Do explain,' Mackie said.

Gareth explained.

'Will you really find the trail?' Mackie asked me, shaking her head.

'As long as someone hasn't parked on the patch of paint and taken it all away on their tyres.'

'Oh, no,' Gareth said, anguished.

'Don't worry,' I told him. 'I'll find your camera if it's still in the clearing.'

'It is. I'm sure. I remember hanging it up.'

'All right then,' Tremayne said. 'Let's talk about something else.'

'Grub?' Gareth asked hopefully. 'Pizza?'

CHAPTER SIXTEEN

On Monday morning, first lot, I was back on Drifter.

'He's entered in a race at Worcester the day after tomorrow,' Tremayne said, as we walked out to the yard at seven in the half-dawn. 'Today's his last training gallop before that, so don't fall off again. The vet's been here already this morning to test his blood.'

Tremayne's vet took small blood samples of all the stable's runners prior to their last training gallop before they raced, the resulting detailed analysis being able to reveal a whole host of things from a raised lymphocyte count to excreted enzymes due to muscle damage. If there were too many contra-indications in the blood the vet would advise Tremayne that the horse was unlikely to run well or win. Tremayne said the process saved the owners from wasting money on fruitless horsebox expenses and jockey fees and also saved himself a lot of inexplicable and worrying disappointments.

'Are you going to Worcester yourself?' I asked.

'Probably. Might send Mackie. Why?'

'Er . . . I wondered if I could go to see Drifter race.'

He turned his head to stare at me as if he couldn't at once comprehend my interest, but then, understanding, said of course I could go if I wanted to.

'Thanks.'

'You can gallop Fringe this morning, second lot.'

'Thanks again.'

'And thanks to you for giving Gareth such a good day yesterday.'

'I enjoyed it.'

We reached the yard and stood watching the last preparations as usual.

'That's a good camera,' Tremayne said regretfully. 'Stupid boy.'

'I'll get it back.'

'Along his precious trail?' He was doubtful.

'Maybe. But I had a map and a compass with me yesterday. I know pretty well where we went.'

He smiled, shaking his head. 'You're the most competent person. Like Fiona says, you put calamities right.'

'It's not always possible.'

'Give Drifter a good gallop.'

We went up to the Downs and at least I stayed in the saddle, and felt indeed a new sense of being at home there, of being at ease. The strange and difficult was becoming second nature in the way that it had when I'd learned to fly. Racehorses, helicopters; both needed hands responsive to messages reaching them,

and both would usually go where you wanted if you
sent the right messages back.

Drifter flowed up the gallop in a smooth fast rhythm
and Tremayne said he would have a good chance at
Worcester if his blood was right.

When I'd left the horse in the yard and gone in for
breakfast I found both Mackie and Sam Yaeger sitting
at the table with Tremayne, all of them discussing that
day's racing at Nottingham. The horse that Tremayne
had been going to run had gone lame, and another of
Sam's rides had been withdrawn because its owner's
wife had died.

'I've only got a no-hoper left,' Sam complained. 'It's
not bloody worthwhile going. Reckon I'll catch flu and
work on the boat.' He telephoned forthwith, made
hoarse-voiced excuses and received undeserved sympathy. He grinned at me, putting down the receiver.
'Where's the toast, then?'

'Coming.'

'I hear you played Cowboys and Indians all over
Berkshire with Gareth and Coconut yesterday.'

'News travels,' I said resignedly.

'I told him,' Mackie said, smiling. 'Any objections?'

I shook my head and asked her how she was feeling.
She'd stopped riding out with the first lot because of
nausea on waking, and Tremayne, far from minding,
continually urged her to rest more.

'I feel sick,' she said to my enquiry. 'Thank goodness.'

'Lie down, my dear girl,' Tremayne said.

'You all fuss too much.'

Sam said to me, 'Doone spent all Saturday afternoon at the boatyard.'

'I thought he was off duty.'

'He got a message from you, it seems.'

'Mm. I did send one.'

'What message?' Tremayne asked.

'I don't know,' Sam answered. 'Doone phoned me yesterday to say he'd been to the boatyard and taken away some objects for which he would give me a receipt.'

'What objects?' asked Tremayne.

'He wouldn't say.' Sam looked at me. 'Do you know what they were? You steered him to them, it seems. He sounded quite excited.'

'What was the message?' Mackie asked me.

'Um . . .' I said. 'I asked him why the floorboards didn't float.'

Tremayne and Mackie appeared mystified but Sam immediately understood and looked thunderstruck.

'Bloody hell, how did you think of it?'

'Don't know,' I said. 'It just came.'

'Do explain,' Mackie begged.

I told her what I'd told Erica at Tremayne's dinner, and said it might not lead to anything helpful.

'But it certainly might,' Mackie said.

Sam said to me thoughtfully, 'If you hadn't stopped me, I'd have rolled up the curtain so as to go into the dock in a boat, and all that stuff under the water would have slithered away into the river and no one would have been any the wiser.'

'Fiona's sure John will find out, before Doone does, who set that trap for Harry,' Mackie said.

I shook my head. 'I don't know who it was. Wish I did.'

'Matter of time,' Tremayne said confidently. He looked at his watch. 'Talking of time, second lot.' He stood up. 'Sam, I want a trial of that new horse Roydale against Fringe. You ride Roydale, John's on Fringe.'

'OK,' Sam said easily.

'John,' Tremayne turned to me, 'don't try to beat Sam as if it were a race. This is a fact-finder. I want you to see which has most natural speed. Go as fast as you can but if you feel Fringe falter don't press him, just ease back.'

'Right.'

'Mackie, talk to Dee-Dee or something. I'm not taking you up there to vomit in the Land Rover.'

'Oh, Tremayne, as if I would.'

'Not risking it,' he said gruffly. 'Don't want you bouncing about on those ruts.'

'I'm not an invalid,' she protested, but she might as well have argued with a rock. He determinedly left her behind and drove Sam and me up to the gallops.

On the way, Sam said to me dryly, 'Nolan usually rides any trials. He'll be furious.'

'Thanks a lot.'

Tremayne said repressively, 'I've told Nolan he won't be riding work here again until he cools off.'

Sam raised his eyebrows comically. 'Do you want John shot? Nolan's a whiz with a gun.'

'Don't talk nonsense,' Tremayne said a shade uneasily, and bumped the Land Rover across the ruts of the track and onto the smooth upland grass before drawing to a halt. 'Keep your mind on Roydale. He belongs to a new owner. I want your best judgment. His form's not brilliant, but nor is the trainer he's come from. I want to know where we're at.'

'Sure,' Sam said.

'Stay upsides Fringe as long as you can.'

Sam nodded. We took Roydale and Fringe from the lads and, when Tremayne had driven off and positioned himself on his hillock, we started together up the all-weather gallop, going the fastest I'd ever been. Fringe, flat out at racing pace, had a wildness about him I couldn't really control and I guessed it was that quality which won him races. Whenever Roydale put his nose in front, Fringe found a bit extra, but it seemed there wasn't much between them, and with the end of the wood chippings in sight the contest was still undecided. I saw Sam sit up and ease the pressure, and copied him immediately, none too soon for my taxed muscles and speed-starved lungs. I finished literally breathless but Sam pulled up nonchalantly and trotted back to Tremayne for a report in full voice.

'He's a green bugger,' he announced. 'He has a

mouth like elephant skin. He shies at his own shadow and he's as stubborn as a pig. Apart from that, he's fast, as you saw.'

Tremayne listened impassively. 'Courage?'

'Can't tell till he's on a racecourse.'

'I'll enter him for Saturday. We may as well find out. Perhaps you'd better give him a pop over hurdles tomorrow.'

'OK.'

We handed the horses back to their respective lads and went down the hill again with Tremayne and found Doone waiting for us, sitting in his car.

'That man gives me the sodding creeps,' Sam said as we disembarked.

The greyly persistent Detective Chief Inspector emerged like a turtle from his shell when he saw us arrive, and he'd come alone for once: no silent note-taker in his shadow.

'Which of us do you want?' Tremayne enquired bullishly.

'Well, sir.' The sing-song voice took all overt menace away, yet there was still a suggestion that collars might be felt at any minute. 'All of you, sir, if you don't mind.'

Just the same if we did mind, he meant.

'You'd better come in, then,' Tremayne offered, shrugging.

Doone followed us into the kitchen, removed a grey tweed overcoat and sat by the table in his much-lived-in grey suit. He felt comfortable in kitchens, I thought.

LONGSHOT

Tremayne vaguely suggested coffee, and I made a mug of instant for us each.

Mackie came through from having breakfasted with Perkin saying she wanted to know how the trial had gone. She wasn't surprised to see Doone, only resigned. I made her some coffee and she sat and watched while Doone picked a piece of paper out of his breast pocket and handed it to Sam.

'A receipt, sir,' he said, 'for three lengths of floor-board retrieved from the dock in your boathouse.'

Sam unfolded the paper and looked at it dumbly.

'Why didn't they float?' Tremayne asked bluntly.

'Ah. So everyone knows about that?' Doone seemed disappointed.

'John just told us,' Tremayne nodded.

Doone gave me a sorrowful stare, but I hadn't given a thought to his wanting secrecy.

'They didn't float, sir, because they were weighted.'

'With what?' Sam asked.

'With pieces of paving stone. There are similar pieces of paving stone scattered on a portion of your boatyard property.'

'*Paving* stone?' Sam sounded bemused, then said doubtfully, 'Do you mean broken slabs of pink and grey marble?'

'Is that what it is, sir, marble?' Doone didn't know much about marble, it appeared.

'It might be.'

Doone pondered, made up his mind, went out to his

359

car and returned carrying a five-foot plank which he laid across the kitchen table. The old grey wood, though still dampish, looked as adequate for its purpose as its fellows still forming the boathouse floor and didn't seem to have been weakened in any way. Slightly towards one end, on the surface that was now uppermost on the table, rested a long, unevenly shaped darkish slab of what I might have thought was rough-faced granite.

'Yes,' Sam said, glancing at it. 'That's marble.' He stretched out his hand and tried to pick it up, and the plank came up an inch with it. Sam let it drop, frowning.

'It's stuck on,' Doone said, nodding. 'From the looks of the other pieces lying about, the surface that's stuck to the wood is smooth and polished.'

'Yes,' Sam said.

'Superglue, we think,' Doone said, 'would make a strong enough bond.'

'A lot of plastic adhesives would,' Sam said, nodding.

'And how do you happen to have chunks of marble lying about?' Doone asked, though not forbiddingly.

'It came with a job-lot of stuff I bought from a demolition firm,' Sam explained without stress. 'They had some panelling I wanted for a boat I did up, and some antique bathroom fittings. I had to take a lot of oddments as well, like the marble. It came from a mansion they were pulling down. They sell off things, you know. Fireplaces, doors, anything.'

Doone asked conversationally, 'Did you stick the marble on to the floorboards, sir?'

'No, I sodding well did *not*,' Sam said explosively.

'On to the underside of the floorboards,' I said. 'There were no slabs of marble in sight when Harry and I went into the upstairs room of the boathouse. I expect, if there are some other blocks still in place, that you can see them from underneath, in the dock.'

Doone with slight reluctance admitted that there seemed to be marble stuck to the underside of one more floorboard on each side of the hole.

The plank on the table was about eight inches across. Harry had taken three of them down with him; five altogether had been doctored. The trap with its missing section of beam had been three and a half feet across, and Harry, taking the envelope bait, had gone through its centre.

'Have you finished snooping round my place now?' Sam demanded, and Doone shook his head.

'I want to work on my boat,' Sam objected.

'Go ahead, sir. Never mind my men, if they're there.'

'Right.' Sam stood up with bouncing energy, quite unlike a patient suddenly stricken with flu. 'Bye, Tremayne. Bye, Mackie. See you, John.'

He went out to his car carrying his jazzy jacket and tooted as he drove away. The kitchen seemed a lot less alive without him.

'I'd like to talk to Mr Kendall alone,' Doone said placidly.

Tremayne's eyebrows rose but he made no objection. He suggested I took Doone into the dining-room while he told Mackie about Roydale's gallop, and Doone followed me docilely, bringing the plank.

The formality of the dining-room furnishings seemed at first to change his mood from ease to starch, but it appeared to me after a short while that he was troubled rather by indecision as to which side I was now on, them or us.

He seemed to settle finally for us, us being the police, or at least the fact-seekers and, clearing his throat, he told me that his men with grappling irons and magnets had missed finding the floorboards the first time, probably because the floorboards weren't magnetic. Did I, he wanted to know, think the trap-setter had taken magnetism into account.

I frowned. 'Stretching it a bit,' I said. 'I should think he looked around for something heavy that would take glue, and with all that junk lying around there was bound to be something. The marble happened to be perfect. But the whole thing was so thoroughly thought out, you really can't tell.'

'Do you know who did it?' he asked forthrightly.

'No,' I said truthfully.

'You must have opinions.' He shifted on his chair, looking around him. 'I'd like to hear them.'

'They're negative more than positive.'

'Often just as valuable.'

'I'd assume the trap-setter had been a guest at Sam

Yaeger's boatyard party,' I said, 'only you warned me never to assume.'

'Assume it,' he said, almost smiling and in some inner way contented.

'And,' I went on, 'I'd assume it was the person who killed Angela Brickell who wanted to fix the blame for ever on Harry by making him disappear, only . . .'

'Assume it,' he said.

'Anyone could have killed Angela Brickell, but only a hundred and fifty or so people went to Sam's party, and half of those were women.'

'Don't you think a woman could have set that trap?' he asked neutrally.

'Sure, a woman could have thought it out and done the carpentering. But what woman could have lured Angela Brickell and persuaded her to take all her clothes off in the middle of a wood?'

He sucked his teeth.

'All right,' he said, 'I agree, a man killed her.' He paused, 'Motive?'

'I'd guess . . . to keep a secret. I mean, suppose she was pregnant. Suppose she went out into the woods with . . . *him*, and they were going to make love . . . or they'd done it . . . and she said "I'm pregnant, you're the father, what are you going to do about it?" She was full of jumbled religious guilts but it was she who was the seducer . . .' I paused. 'I'd think perhaps she was killed because she wanted too much . . . and because she wouldn't have an abortion.'

He made a sound very like a purr in his throat.

'All right,' he said again. 'Method: strangulation. Guaranteed to work, as everyone around here knew, after the death of that other girl, Olympia.'

'Yes.'

'Opportunity?' he said.

'No one can remember what they were doing the day Angela Brickell disappeared.'

'Except the murderer,' he observed. 'What about opportunity on the day Mr Goodhaven fell through the floor?'

'Someone was there to drive his car away ... no fingerprints, I suppose?'

'Gloves,' he said succinctly. 'Too few of Mr Goodhaven's prints are still there. No palm print on the gear lever, for instance. I don't know if we'd have worried about that if we'd thought he'd done a bunk. It was a cold day, after all. He might have worn gloves himself.'

'You might have guessed at collusion,' I suggested.

'Did you ever consider police work?'

'Not good at that sort of discipline.'

'You don't like taking orders, sir?'

'I prefer giving them to myself.'

He smiled without criticism. 'You'd be no good in uniform.'

'None at all.'

He was entitled, I supposed, to his small exploratory excursion around my character; and if he himself, I thought, had been wholly fulfilled by uniform, he would still be in it.

Perkin in his overalls appeared in the open doorway, hovering.

'Is Mackie over here?' he said. 'I can't find her.'

'In the kitchen with Tremayne,' I said.

'Thanks.' He swept a gaze over Doone and the plank and said with irony, 'Sorting it out, then?'

Doone said a shade heavily, 'Mr Kendall's always helpful,' and Perkin made a face and went off to join Mackie.

'About Harry's car,' I said to Doone. 'There must have been just a small problem of logistics. I mean, perhaps our man parked his own car in Reading station car park, then took a train to Maidenhead station and a bus from there to near the river, and went on foot from there to the boatyard ... wouldn't that make sense?'

'It would, but so far we haven't found anyone who noticed anything useful.'

'Car park ticket?'

'There wasn't one in the car. We don't know when the car arrived in the car park. It could have been parked somewhere else on Wednesday and repositioned when our man discovered Mr Goodhaven was still alive.'

'Mm. It would mean that our man had a lot of time available for manoeuvring.'

DICK FRANCIS

'Racing people do have flexible hours,' he observed, 'and they mostly have free afternoons.'

'I don't suppose there's a hope that my jacket and boots were still in the car?' I asked.

'No sign of them. Sorry. They'll be in a dump somewhere, shouldn't wonder.' He was looking round the room again, and this time revealed his purpose. 'About those guide books of yours, I'd like to see them.'

They were in the family room. I went to fetch them and returned with only three I'd found, *Jungle*, *Safari* and *Ice*. The others, I explained, could be anywhere, as everyone had been reading them.

He opened *Jungle* and quickly flipped through the opening chapters, which were straightforward advice for well-equipped jungle holidays: 'Never put a bare foot on the earth. Shower in slip-ons. Sleep with your shoes inside your mosquito netting. Never drink untreated water ... never brush your teeth with it ... don't wash fruit or vegetables in it, avoid suspect ice-cubes.'

' "Never get exhausted"!' Doone said aloud. 'What sort of advice is that?'

'Exhausted people can't be bothered to stick to life-saving routines. If you don't drive yourself too hard you're more likely to survive. For instance, if you've a long way to go, it's better to get there slowly than not at all.'

'That's weak advice,' he said, shaking his head.

I didn't argue, but many died from exhaustion every

366

year through not understanding the strengths of weakness. It was better to stop every day's travel early so as to have good energy for raising a tent, digging an igloo, building a platform up a tree. Dropping down exhausted without shelter could bring new meaning to the expression 'dead tired'.

' "Food",' Doone read out. ' "Fishing, hunting, trapping." ' He flicked the pages. ' "In the jungle, hang fishhooks to catch birds. Don't forget bait. You always need bait." ' He looked up. 'That envelope was bait, wasn't it?'

I nodded. 'Good bait.'

'We haven't found it. That water's like liquid mud. You can't see an inch through it, my men say.'

'They're right.'

He stared for a second. 'Oh, yes. I'd forgotten you'd been in it.' He went back to the book. ' "It's possible to bring down game with a spear or a bow and arrow, but these take considerable practice and involve hours spent lying in wait. Let a trap do the waiting . . ." ' He read on. ' "The classic trap for large animals is a pit with sharpened staves pointing upwards. Cover the pit with natural-looking vegetation and earth, and suspend the bait over the top." ' He looked up. 'Very graphic illustrations and instructions.'

'Afraid so.'

Eyes down again to the book, he went on, ' "All sharpened staves for use in traps (and also spears and arrows) can be hardened to increase their powers of

penetration by being charred lightly in hot embers, a process which tightens and toughens the wood fibres." '
Doone stopped reading and remarked, 'You don't say anything about sharpening old bicycle frames and railings.'

'There aren't many bicycle frames in the jungle. Er ... were they sharpened?'

He sighed. 'Not artificially.' He read on. ' "If digging or scraping out a pit is impracticable because of hard or waterlogged ground, try netting. Arrange a net to entangle game when it springs the trap. To make a strong net you can use tough plant fibres ..." ' He silently read several pages, occasionally shaking his head, not, I gathered, in disagreement with the text, but in sorrow at its availability.

' "How to skin a snake",' he read. 'Dear God.'

'Roast rattlesnake tastes like chicken,' I said.

'You've eaten it?'

I nodded. 'Not at all bad.'

' "First aid. How to stop heavy bleeding. Pressure points ... To close gaping wounds, use needle and thread. To help blood clot, apply cobwebs to the wound." *Cobwebs!* I don't believe it.'

'They're organic,' I said, 'and as sterile as most bandages.'

'Not for me, thanks.' He put down *Jungle* and flipped through *Safari* and *Ice*. Many of the same suggestions for traps appeared in all the books, modified only by terrain.

' "Don't eat polar bear liver," ' Doone read in amazement, ' "it stores enough vitamin A to kill humans." ' He smiled briefly. 'That would make a dandy new method for murder.'

First catch your polar bear . . .

'Well, sir,' Doone said, laying the books aside, 'we can trace the path of ideas about the trap, but who do you think put them into practice?'

I shook my head.

'If I throw names at you,' he said, 'give your reasons for or against.'

'All right,' I said, cautiously.

'Mr Vickers.'

'Tremayne?' I must have sounded astonished. 'All against.'

'Why, exactly?'

'Well, he's not like that.'

'As I told you before, I don't know these people the way you do. So give me reasons.'

I said, thinking, 'Tremayne Vickers is forceful, a bit old-fashioned, straightforward, often kind. Angela Brickell would not have been to his taste. If – and to my mind it's a colossal if – *if* she managed to seduce him and then told him he was the father-to-be, and if he believed it, it would have been more his style to pack her off home to her parents and provide for her. He doesn't shirk responsibility. Also, I can't imagine him taking any woman out into deep woods for sex.

Impossible. As for trying to kill Harry . . .' Words failed me.

'All right,' Doone said. He brought out a notebook and methodically wrote 'KENDALL'S ASSESSMENTS' at the top of the page. Underneath he wrote 'Tremayne Vickers', followed by a cross, and under Tremayne, 'Nolan Everard'.

'Nolan Everard,' he said.

Not so easy. 'Nolan is brave. He's dynamic and determined . . . and violent.'

'And he threatened to kill you,' Doone said flatly.

'Who told you that?'

'Half the racing world heard him.'

Sighing, I explained about my riding.

'And when he attacked you, you picked him up like a baby in front of all those people,' Doone said. 'A man might not forgive that.'

'We're talking about Angela Brickell and Harry,' I pointed out mildly.

'Talk about Nolan Everard then. *For*, first.'

'*For* . . . Well, he killed Olympia, not really meaning to, but definitely by putting her life at risk. He couldn't afford another scandal while waiting for trial. If Angela Brickell had seduced him – or the other way round – and she threatened a messy paternity suit . . . I don't know. That's again a big if, but not as impossible as Tremayne. Nolan and Sam Yaeger often bed the same girl, more or less to spite each other, it seems. Nolan regularly rides the horse, Chickweed, that Angela

Brickell had care of, and there would have been opportunities for sex at race meetings, like in a horse-box, if
he wanted to take the risk. He could sue me for slander
over this.'

'He won't hear of it,' Doone said positively. 'This
conversation is just between you and me. I'll deny I
ever discussed the case with you if anyone asks.'

'Fair enough.' I thought a bit. 'As for the trap for
Harry, Nolan would be mentally and physically
capable.'

'But? I hear your but.'

I nodded. '*Against.* He's Fiona's cousin, and they're
close. He depends on Fiona's horses to clinch his ama-
teur-champion status. He couldn't be sure she would
have the heart to go on running racehorses if she were
forced to believe Harry a murderer . . . if she thought
he had left her without warning, without a note, if she
were worried sick by not knowing where he'd gone,
and was also haunted by the thought of Harry with
Angela Brickell.'

'Would Everard have stopped to consider all that?'
he mused doubtfully.

'The trap was well thought out.'

Doone wrote a question mark after Nolan's name.

'Doesn't *anyone* have a solid alibi for Wednesday
afternoon?' I asked. 'That's the one definite time our
man has to explain away.'

'And don't think we don't know it,' Doone nodded.
'Not many of the men connected with this place can

DICK FRANCIS

account for every hour of that afternoon, though the
women can. We've been very busy this morning,
making enquiries. Mrs Goodhaven went to a committee
meeting, then home in time to be there when you
telephoned. Mrs Perkin Vickers was at Ascot races,
vouched for by saddling a horse in the three-mile chase.
Mr Vickers' secretary Dee-Dee made several telephone
calls from the office here and Mrs Ingrid Watson went
shopping in Oxford with her mother and can produce
receipts.'

'Ingrid?'

'She can't vouch for what her husband did.'

He wrote 'Bob Watson' under Nolan.

'*For* him being our man,' I said dubiously, 'is, I suppose, Ingrid herself. She wouldn't put up with shenani-
gans with Angela Brickell. But whether Bob would kill
to stay married to Ingrid . . .' I shook my head. 'I don't
know. He's a good head lad, Tremayne trusts him, but
I wouldn't stake my life on his loyalty. Also he's an
extremely competent carpenter, as you saw yourself.
He was serving drinks at the party when Olympia
died. He went to the boatyard party as a guest.'

'*Against?*'

I hesitated. 'Killing Angela Brickell might have been
a moment's panic. Setting the trap for Harry took cunning and nerve. I don't know Bob Watson well enough
for a real opinion. I don't know him like the others.'

Doone nodded and put a question mark after his
name also.

372

'Gareth Vickers,' he wrote.

I smiled. 'It can't be him.'

'Why not?' Doone asked.

'Angela Brickell's sexuality frightened him. He would never have gone into the woods with her. Apart from that, he hasn't a driving licence, and he was at school on Wednesday afternoon.'

'Actually,' Doone said calmly, 'he is known to be able to drive his father's jeep on the Downs expertly, and my men have discovered he was out of school last Wednesday afternoon on a field trip to Windsor Safari Park. That's not miles from the boatyard. The teacher in charge is flustered over the number of boys who sloped off to buy food.'

I considered Gareth as a murderer. I said, 'You asked me for my knowledge of these people. Gareth couldn't possibly be our man.'

'Why are you so sure?'

'I just am.'

He wrote a cross against Gareth's name, and then as an afterthought, a question mark also.

I shook my head. Under Gareth's name he wrote 'Perkin Vickers'.

'What about *him*?' he asked.

'Perkin . . .' I sighed. 'He lives in another world half the time. He works hard. *For*, I suppose, is that he makes furniture, he's good with wood. I don't know that it's *for* or *against* that he dotes on his wife. He's very possessive of her. He's a bit childlike in some

ways. She loves him and looks after him. *Against*...
he doesn't have much to do with the horses. Seldom
goes racing. He didn't remember who Angela Brickell
was, the first morning you were here.'

Doone pursed his lips judiciously, then nodded and
wrote a cross against Perkin, and then again a question
mark.

'Keeping your options open?' I asked dryly.

'You never know what we don't know,' he said.

'Deep.'

'It might be reasonable to assume that Mr Goodhaven didn't set the trap himself, to persuade me of his
innocence,' he said, writing 'Henry Goodhaven' on the
list.

'A hundred per cent,' I agreed.

'However, he took you along as a witness.' He
paused. 'Suppose he planned it and it all went wrong?
Suppose he needed you there to assert he'd walked
into a trap?'

'Impossible.'

He put a question mark against Harry, all the same.

'Who drove his car away?' I said, a shade aggres-
sively.

'A casual thief.'

'I don't believe it.'

'You like him,' Doone said. 'You're unreliable.'

'That page is headed "KENDALL'S ASSESSMENTS".' I
protested. 'My assessment of Harry merits a firm cross.'

He looked at what he'd written, shrugged and

changed the question mark to a negative. Then he made a question mark away to the right on the same line. 'My assessments,' he said.

I smiled a little ruefully and said reflectively, 'Have you worked out when the trap was set? Raising the floorboards, finding the marble and sticking it on, cutting out the bit of beam – and I bet that went floating down the river – remembering to lock the lower door . . . It would all have taken a fair time.'

'When would *you* say it was done, then?' he asked, giving nothing away.

'Any time Tuesday, or Wednesday morning, I suppose.'

'Why, exactly?'

'Anti-Harry fever was publicly at its height on Monday, Tuesday and Wednesday, but by the Sunday before, at least, you'd begun to spread your investigation outwards . . . which must horribly have alarmed our man. Sam Yaeger spent Monday at the boatyard because he'd been medically stood down from racing as a result of a fall, but by Tuesday he was racing again; on Wednesday he rode at Ascot, so the boathouse was vulnerable all day Tuesday and again Wednesday morning.'

Doone looked at me from under his eyelids.

'You're forgetting something,' he said, and added 'Sam Yaeger' to his list.

CHAPTER SEVENTEEN

'Put a cross,' I said.

Doone shook his head. 'You admire him. You could be blinded.'

I thought it over. 'I do in many ways admire him, I admit. I admire his riding, his professionalism. He's courageous. He's a realist.' I paused. 'I'll agree that on the *For* side you could put the things you listed the other day, that he has all the skills to set the trap and the perfect place to do it.'

'Go on,' Doone nodded.

'You'd begun actively investigating him,' I said.

'Yes, I had.'

'He'd rolled around a bit with Angela Brickell,' I said, 'and that's where we come to the biggest *Against*.'

'You're not saying he couldn't have had the irritation, the nerve, the strength to strangle her?'

'No, I'm not, though I don't think he did it. What I'm saying is that he wouldn't have taken her out into the woods. He told you himself he moves a mattress into the boathouse on such occasions. If he'd strangled her on impulse it would have been *there*, and he could have slid her weighted body into the river, no one the wiser.'

Doone listened with his head on one side. 'But what if he'd deliberately planned it? What if he'd suggested the woods as being far away from his own territory?'

'I wouldn't think he'd need to cover his sins with strangulation,' I said. 'Everyone knows he seduced anything that moves. He would pass off an Angela Brickell sort of scandal with a laugh.'

Doone disapproved, saying, 'Unsavoury,' and maybe thinking of his assailable daughters.

'We haven't got very far,' I said, looking at his list. All my own assessments were a cross except the question mark against Nolan. Not awfully helpful, I thought.

Doone clicked his pen a few times, then at the bottom wrote Lewis Everard.

'That's a long shot,' I said.

'Give me some *Fors* and *Againsts*.'

I pondered. '*Against* first. I don't think he's bold enough to have set that trap, but then . . .' I hesitated, 'there's no doubt he's both clever and cunning. I wouldn't have thought he would have gone into the woods with Angela Brickell. Can't exactly say why, but I'd think he'd be too fastidious, especially when he's sober.'

'*For?*' Doone prompted, when I stopped.

'He gets drunk . . . I don't know if he'd tumble Angela Brickell in that state or not.'

'But he knew her.'

'Even if not in the biblical sense,' I agreed.

'Sir!' he said with mock reproach.

'He would have seen her at the races,' I said, smiling. 'And *For* . . . he is a good liar. According to him, he's the best actor of the lot.'

'A question mark, then?' Doone's pen hovered.

I slowly shook my head. 'A cross.'

'The trouble with you,' Doone said with disillusion, looking at the column of negatives, 'is that you haven't met enough murderers.'

'None,' I agreed. 'You can't exactly count Nolan Everard.'

'And you wouldn't know a murderer if you tripped over one.'

'Your list is too short,' I said.

'It seems so.' He put away the notebook and stood up. 'Well, Mr Kendall, thank you for your time. I don't discount your impressions. You've helped me clarify my thoughts. Now we'll have to step up our enquiries. We'll get there in the end.'

The sing-song accent came to a stop and he shook my hand and let himself out, a grey man in grey clothes following his own informal, idiosyncratic path towards the truth.

I sat for a while thinking of what I'd said and of what he'd told me, and I still couldn't believe that any of the people I'd come to know so well was really a murderer.

No one was a villain, not even Nolan. There had to be someone else, someone we hadn't begun to consider.

I worked on and off on Tremayne's book for the rest of the morning but found it hard to concentrate.

Dee-Dee drifted in and out, offering coffee and company, and Tremayne put his head in to say he was going to Oxford to see his tailor, and to ask if I wanted an opportunity to shop.

I thanked him and declined. I would probably have liked to replace my boots and ski-jacket, but I still hadn't much personal money. It was easy at Shellerton House to get by without any. Tremayne would doubtless have lent me some of the quarter-advance due at the end of the month but my lack was my own choice, and as long as I could survive as I was, I wouldn't ask. It was all part of the game.

Mackie came through from her side to keep company with Dee-Dee, saying Perkin had gone to Newbury to collect some supplies, and presently the two women went out to lunch together, leaving me alone in the great sprawling house.

I tried again and harder to work and felt restless and uneasy. Stupid, I thought. Being alone never bothered me: in fact, I liked it. That day, I found the size of the silent house oppressive.

I went upstairs, showered and changed out of riding clothes into the more comfortable jeans and shirt I'd worn the day before and pulled on sneakers and the red sweater for warmth. After that I went down to the kitchen and made a cheese sandwich for lunch and wished I'd gone with Tremayne if only for the ride. It was the usual pattern of finding something to do – *anything* – rather than sit down and face the empty page, except that that day the uneasiness was extra.

I wandered in a desultory fashion into the family room which looked dead without the fire blazing and began to wonder what I could make for dinner. Gareth's 'BACK FOR GRUB' message was still pinned to the corkboard, and it was with a distinct sense of release that I remembered I'd said that I would go back for his camera.

The unease vanished. I found a piece of paper and left my own message: 'I'VE BORROWED THE LAND ROVER TO FETCH GARETH'S CAMERA. BACK FOR COOKING THE GRUB!' I pinned it to the corkboard with a red drawing pin and a light heart, and went upstairs again to change back into jodhpur boots to deal with the terrain and to pick up the map and the compass in case I couldn't find the trail. Then I skipped downstairs and went out to the wheels, locking the back door behind me.

It was a good day, sunny like the day before but with more wind. With a feeling of having been unexpectedly let out of school, I drove over the hills on the road to Reading and coasted along the unfenced part of the Quillersedge Estate until I thought I'd come more or less to where Gareth had dropped the paint: parked off the road there and searched more closely for the place on foot.

No one had driven the paint away on their tyres. The splash was dusty but still visible and, without much trouble, I found the beginning of the trail about twenty feet straight ahead in the wood and followed it as easily through the tangled trees and undergrowth as on the day before.

Gareth a murderer . . . I smiled to myself at the absurdity of it. As well suspect Coconut.

The pale paint splashes, the next one ahead visible all the time, weren't all that marked the trail: it showed signs in broken twigs and scuffed ground of our passage the day before. By the time I came back with the camera it would be almost a beaten track.

Wind rattled and swayed the trees and filled my ears with the old songs of the land, and the sun shone through the moving boughs in shimmering ever-changing patterns. I wound my slow way through the maze of unpruned growth and felt at one with things there and inexpressibly happy.

The trail strayed round and eventually reached the small clearing. Our improvised seats were frayed by the wind but still identified the place with certainty, and almost at once I spotted Gareth's camera, prominently hanging, as he'd said, from a branch.

I walked across to collect it and something hit me very hard indeed in the back.

Moments of disaster are disorientating. I didn't know

what had happened. The world had changed. I was
falling. I was lying face down on the ground. There
was something wrong with my breathing.

I had heard nothing but the wind, seen nothing but
the moving trees but, I thought incredulously, *someone
had shot me.*

From total instinct as much as from injury I lay
as dead. There was a zipping noise beside my ear as
something sped past it. I shut my eyes. There was
another jolting thud in my back.

So this was death, I thought numbly; and I didn't
even know who was killing me, and I didn't know why.

Breathing was terrible. My chest was on fire. A wave
of clammy perspiration broke out on my skin.

I lay unmoving.

My face was on dead leaves and dried grass and
pieces of twig. I could smell the musty earth. Earth-
digested, come to dust.

Someone, I thought dimly, was waiting to see if I
moved: and if I moved there would be a third thud and
my heart would stop. If I didn't move someone would
come and feel for a pulse and, finding one, finish me
off. Either way, everything that had been beginning was
now ending, ebbing away without hope.

I lay still. Not a twitch.

I couldn't hear anything but the wind in the trees.
Could hear no one moving. Hadn't heard even the
shots.

Breathing was dreadful. A shaft of pain. Minimum

air could go in, trickle out. Too little. In a while . . . I would go to sleep.

A long time seemed to pass, and I was still alive.

I had a vision of someone standing not far behind me with a gun, waiting for me to move. He was shadowy and had no face, and his patience was for ever.

Clammy nausea came again, enveloping and ominous. My skin sweated. I felt cold.

I didn't exactly try to imagine what was happening in my body.

Lying still was anyway easier than moving. I would slide unmoving into eternity. The man with the gun could wait for ever, but I would be gone. I would cheat him that way.

That's delirium, I thought.

Nothing happened in the clearing. I lay still. Time drifted.

After countless ages I seemed to come back to a real realization that I was continuing to breathe, even if with difficulty, and didn't seem in immediate danger of stopping. However ghastly I might feel, however feeble, I wasn't drowning in blood. Wasn't coughing it up. Coughing was a bleak thought, the way my chest hurt.

My certainty of the waiting gun had begun to fade. He wouldn't be there after all this time. He wouldn't stand for ever doing nothing. He hadn't felt my pulse. He must have thought it unnecessary.

He believed I was dead.

He had gone. I was alone.

It took me a while to believe those three things utterly and another while to risk acting on the belief.

If I didn't move I would die where I lay.

With dread, but in the end inevitability, I moved my left arm.

Christ, I thought, that *hurt*.

Hurt it might, but nothing else happened.

I moved my right arm. Just as bad. Even worse.

No more thuds in the back, though. No quick steps, no pounce, no final curtain.

Perhaps I really was alone. I let the thought lie there for comfort. Wouldn't contemplate a cat-and-mouse cruelty.

I put both palms flat on the decaying undergrowth and tried to heave myself up on to my knees.

Practically fainted. Not only could I not do it but the effort was so excruciating that I opened my mouth to scream and couldn't breathe enough for that either. My weight settled back on the earth and I felt nothing but staggering agony and couldn't think connectedly until it abated.

Something was odd, I thought finally. It wasn't only that I couldn't lift myself off the ground but that I was stuck to it in some way.

Cautiously, sweating, with fiery stabs in every inch, I wormed my right hand between my body and the earth and came to what seemed like a rod between the two.

I must have fallen on to a sharp stick, I thought.

Perhaps I hadn't been shot. But yes, I had. Hit in the back. Couldn't mistake it.

Slowly, trying to ration the pain into manageable portions, I slid my hand out again, and then after a while, hardly believing it, I bent my arm and felt round my back and came to the rod there also, and faced the grim certainty that someone had shot me not with a bullet but an *arrow*.

I lay for a while simply wrestling with the enormity of it.

I had an arrow right through my body from back to front somewhere in the region of my lower ribs. Through my right lung, which was why I was breathing oddly. Not, miraculously, through any major blood vessels, or I would by now have bled internally to death. About level with my heart, but to one side.

Bad enough. Awful. But I was still alive.

I'd been hit twice, I remembered. Maybe I had two arrows through me. One or two, I was still alive.

'*Survival begins in the mind.*'

I'd written that, and knew it to be true. But to survive an arrow a mile from a road with a killer around to make sure I didn't make it ... where in one's mind did one search for the will to survive that? Where, when just getting to one's knees loomed as an unavoidable torture and to lie and wait to be rescued appeared to be merely common sense.

I thought about rescue. A long long way off. No one

would start looking for me for hours; not until after dark. The sun on my back was warm, but the February nights were still near zero and I was wearing only a sweater. Theoretically the luminous trail should lead rescuers to the clearing even at night . . . but any sensible murderer would have obliterated the road end of it after he'd found his own way out.

I couldn't realistically be rescued before tomorrow. I thought I might die while I waited: might die in the night. People died of injuries sometimes because their bodies went into shock. General trauma, not just the wound, could kill.

One thought, one decision at a time.

Better die trying.

All right. Next decision.

Which way to go?

The trail seemed obvious enough, but my intended killer had come and gone that way – must have done – and if he should return for any reason I wouldn't want to meet him.

I had a compass in my pocket.

The distant road lay almost due north of the clearing and the straightest line to the road lay well to the left of the paint trail.

I waited for energy, but it didn't materialise.

Next decision: get up anyway.

The tip of the arrow couldn't be far into the earth, I thought. I'd fallen with it already through me. It could be only an inch or so in. No more than a centimetre, maybe.

I shut my mind to the consequences, positioned my hands, and pushed.

The arrow tip came free and I lay on my side in frightful suffering weakness, looking down at a sharp black point sticking out from scarlet wool.

Black. The length of a finger. Hard and sharp. I touched the needle tip of it and wished I hadn't.

Only one arrow. Only one all the way through, at least.

Not much blood, surprisingly. Or perhaps I couldn't tell, blood being the same colour as the jersey, but there was no great wet patch.

A mile to the road seemed an impossible distance. Moving an inch was taxing. Still, inches added up. Better get started.

First catch your compass . . .

With an inward smile and a mental sigh I retrieved the compass carefully from my pocket and took a bearing on north. North, it seemed, was where my feet were.

I rolled with effort to my knees and felt desperately, appallingly, overwhelmingly ill. The flicker of humour died fast. The waves of protest were so strong that I almost gave up there and then. Outraged tissues, invaded lungs, an overall warning.

I stayed on my knees, sitting back on my heels, head bowed, breathing as little as possible, staring at the protruding arrow, thinking the survival programme was too much.

There was a pale slim rod sticking into the ground beside me. I looked at it vaguely and then with more attention, remembering the thing that had sung past my ear.

An arrow that had missed me.

It was about as long as an arm. A peeled fine-grained stick, dead straight. A notch in its visible end, for slotting onto a bowstring. No feather to make a flight.

The guide books all gave instructions for making arrows.

'Char the tips in hot embers to shrink and toughen the fibres for better penetration . . .'

The charred black tip had penetrated all right.

'Cut two slots in the other end, one shallow one for the bowstring, one deep one to push a shaped feather into, to make a flight so that the arrow will travel straighter to the target.'

Illustrations thoughtfully provided.

If the three arrows had all had flights . . . if there'd been no wind . . .

I closed my eyes weakly. Even without flights, the aim had been deadly enough.

Gingerly, sweating, I curled my left hand behind my back and felt for the third arrow, and found it sticking out of my jersey though fairly loose in my hand. With trepidation I took a stronger hold of it and it came away altogether but with a sharp dagger of soreness, like digging out a splinter.

The black tip of that arrow was scarlet with blood, but I reckoned it hadn't gone in further than a rib or my spine. I only had the first one to worry about.

Only the one.

Quite enough.

It would have been madness to pull it out, even if I could have faced doing it. In duels of old, it hadn't always been the sword going *into* the lungs that had killed so much as the drawing of it out. The puncture let air rush in and out, spoiling nature's enclosed vacuum system. With holes to the outer air, the lungs collapsed and couldn't breathe. With the arrow still in place, the holes were virtually blocked. With the arrow in place, bleeding was held at bay. I might die with it in. I'd die quicker with it out.

The first rule of surviving a disaster, I had written, was to accept that it had happened and make the best of what was left. Self-pity, regrets, hopelessness and surrender would never get one home. Survival began, continued and was accomplished in the mind.

All right, I told myself, follow your own rules.

Accept the fact of the arrow. Accept your changed state. Accept that it hurts, that every moment will hurt for the foreseeable future. Take that for granted. Go on from there.

Still on my knees I edged round to face north.

The clearing was all mine: no man with a gun. No archer with a bow.

The day in some respects remained incredibly the same. The sun still threw its dappled mantle and the trees still creaked and resonantly vibrated in the oldest of symphonies. Many before me, I thought, had been shot by arrows in ancient woodland and faced their mortality in places that had looked like this before man started killing man.

But I, if I stirred myself, could reach surgeons and antibiotics and hooray for the National Health Service. I slowly shifted on my knees across the clearing, aiming to the left of the painted trail.

It wasn't so bad . . .

It was awful.

For God's sake, I told myself, ignore it. Get used to it. Think about north.

It wasn't possible to go all the way to the road on one's knees: the undergrowth was too thick, the saplings in places too close together. I would have to stand up.

So, OK, hauling on branches, I stood up.

Even my legs felt odd. I clung hard to a sapling with my eyes closed, waiting for things to get better, telling myself that if I fell down again it would be much much *much* worse.

North.

I opened my eyes eventually and took the compass out of my jeans pocket, where I'd stowed it to have hands free for standing up. Holding on still with one hand, I took a visual line ahead from the north needle to mark into memory the furthest small tree I could see, then put the compass away again and with infinite slowness clawed a way forward by inches and after a while reached the target and held on to it for dear life.

I had travelled perhaps ten yards. I felt exhausted.

'Never get exhausted', I had written. Dear God.

I rested out of necessity, out of weakness.

In a while I consulted the compass, memorised another young tree and made my way there. When I looked back I could no longer see the clearing.

I was committed, I thought. I wiped sweat off my forehead with my fingers and stood quietly, holding on, trying to let the oxygen level in my blood climb back to a functioning state.

A functioning mode, Gareth might have said.

Gareth . . .

Sherwood Forest, I thought, eight hundred years ago. Whose face should I pin on the Sheriff of Nottingham . . .

I went another ten yards, and another, careful always not to trip, holding onto branches as onto railings. My breath began wheezing from the exertion. Pain had finally become a constant. Ignore it. Weakness was more of a problem, and lack of breath.

Stopping again for things to calm down I began to do a few unwelcome sums. I had travelled perhaps fifty yards. It seemed a marathon to me but realistically it was roughly one thirty-fifth of a mile, which left thirty-four thirty-fifths still to go. I hadn't timed the fifty yards but it had been no sprint. According to my watch it was already after four o'clock, a rotten piece of information borne out by the angle of the sun. Darkness lay ahead.

I would have to go as fast as I could while I could still see the way, and then rest for longer, and then probably crawl. Sensible plan, but not enough strength to go fast.

Fifty more yards in five sections. One more thirty-fifth of the way. Marvellous. It had taken me fifteen minutes.

More sums. At a speed of fifty yards in fifteen minutes it would take me another eight hours to reach the road. It would then be half-past midnight, and that didn't take into account long rest or crawling.

Despair was easy. Survival wasn't.

To hell with despair, I thought. Get on and walk.

The shaft of the arrow protruding from my back occasionally knocked against something, bringing me to a gasping halt. I didn't know how long it was, couldn't feel as far as the end, and I couldn't always judge how much space I needed to keep it clear.

I'd come out on the simple camera-fetching errand without the complete zipped pouch of gadgets but I did have with me the belt holding my knife and the multi-purpose survival tool, and on the back of that tool there was a mirror. After the next fifty yards I drew it out and took a look at the bad news.

The shaft, straight, pale and rigid, stuck out about eighteen inches. There was a notch in the end for the bowstring, but no flight.

I didn't look at my face in the mirror. Didn't want to confirm how I felt. I returned the small tool to the pouch and went another fifty yards, taking care.

North. Ten yards visible at a time. Go ten yards. Five times ten yards. Short rest.

The sun sank lower on my left and the blue shadows of dusk began gathering on the pines and firs and creeping in among the sapling branches and the alders. In the wind, the shadows threw barred stripes and moved like prowling tigers.

Fifty yards, rest. Fifty yards, rest. Fifty yards, rest. Think of nothing else.

There would be moonlight later, I thought. Full moon was three days back. If the sky remained clear, I could go on by moonlight.

Dusk deepened until I could no longer see ten yards ahead, and after I'd knocked the shaft of the arrow against an unseen hazard twice within a minute I stopped and sank slowly down to my knees, resting my forehead and the front of my left shoulder against a young birch trunk, drained as I'd never been before.

Perhaps I would write a book about this one day, I thought.

Perhaps I would call it . . . Longshot.

A long shot with an arrow.

Perhaps not so long, though. No doubt from only a

few yards out of the clearing, to get a straight view. A short shot, perhaps.

He'd been waiting there for me, I concluded. If he'd been following me he would have to have been close because I had gone straight to the camera, and I would have heard him, even in the wind. He'd been there first, waiting, and I'd walked up to the carefully prominent bait and presented him with a perfect target, a broad back in a scarlet sweater, an absolute cinch.

Traps.

I'd walked into one, as Harry had.

I leaned against the tree, sagging into it. I did feel comprehensively dreadful.

If I'd been the archer, I thought, I would have been waiting in position, crouched and camouflaged, endlessly patient, arrow notched on a bow. Along comes the target, happily unaware, going to the camera, putting himself in position. Stand up, aim . . . a whamming direct hit, first time lucky.

Shoot twice more at the fallen body. Pity to waste the arrows. Another nice hit.

Target obviously dead. Wait a bit to make sure. Maybe go near for a closer look. All well. Then retreat along the trail. Mission accomplished.

Who was the Sheriff of Nottingham . . . ?

I tried to find a more comfortable position but there wasn't one, really. To save my knees a bit I slid down onto my left hip, leaning my head and my left side against the tree. It was better than walking, better than fighting the tangle of woodland, but whether it was better than lying in the clearing I couldn't decide. Yet he, the archer, might have gone back there to check again after all and if he had he would know I was alive, but he would never find me where I was now, deep in impenetrable shadow along a path he couldn't follow in the dark.

It was ironic, I thought, that for the expedition for Gareth and Coconut I'd deliberately chosen to aim for a spot on the map that looked as remote from any road as possible. I should have had more sense.

The darkness intensified down in the wood though I could see stars between the boughs. I listened to the wind. Grew cold. Felt extremely alone.

I let go of things a bit. Simply existed. Let thoughts drift. I felt formless, part of time and space, an essence, a piece of cosmos. The awareness of the world's antiquity which was often with me seemed to intensify, to be a solace. Everything was one. Every being was integral, but alone. One could dissolve and still exist . . . I hovered on the edge of consciousness, semi-asleep, making nonsense.

I relaxed too far. My weight shifted against the tree, slipping downwards, and the shaft of the arrow hit the ground. The explosive pain of it brought me hellishly back to full savage consciousness and to a revived desire not to become part of the eternal mystery just yet. I struggled back into equilibrium and tried to ride the pulverising waves of misery and found to my desperate dismay that the finger of arrow in front was almost an inch longer.

I'd pushed the arrow further through. I'd done hell knew what extra damage to my lung. I didn't know how to bear what my body felt.

I went on breathing. Went on living. That's all one could say.

The worst of it got better.

I sat for what seemed a long time in the cold darkness, breathing shallowly, not moving at all, just waiting, and eventually there was a lightening of the shadows and a luminosity in the wood, and the moon rose clear and bright in the east. To eyes long in the dark, it was as daylight.

Time to go. I pulled out the compass, held it horizontally close to my eyes, let the needle settle onto north, looked that way and mapped the first few feet in my mind.

Putting thought into action was an inevitable trial. Everything was sore, every muscle seemed wired directly to the arrow. Violent twinges shot up my nerves like steel lightning.

So what, I told myself. Stop bellyaching. Ignore what it feels like, concentrate on the journey.

Concentrate on the Sheriff . . .

I pulled myself to my feet again, rocked a bit, sweated, clung onto things, groaned a couple of times, gave myself lectures. Put one foot in front of the other, the only way home.

Knocking the arrow seemed after all not to have been the ultimate disaster. Moving seemed to require the same amount of breath as before, which was to say more than could be easily provided.

I couldn't always see so far ahead by moonlight and needed to consult the compass more often. It slowed things up to keep slipping it in and out of my jeans pocket so after a while I tucked it up the sleeve of my jersey. That improvement upset the old fifty-yard rhythm but it didn't much matter. I looked at my watch instead and stopped every fifteen minutes for a rest.

The moon rose high in the sky and shone unfalteringly into the woods, a silver goddess that I felt like worshipping. I became numb again to discomfort to a useful degree and plodded on methodically taking continual bearings, breathing carefully, aiming performance just below capability so as to last out to the end.

The archer had to have a face.

If I could think straight, if every scrap of attention didn't have to be focused on not falling, I could probably get nearer to knowing. Things had changed since the arrow. A whole lot of new factors had to be considered. I tripped over a root, half lost my balance, shoved the new factors into oblivion.

Slowly, slowly, I went north. Then one time when I put my hand in my sleeve to bring out the compass, it wasn't there.

I'd dropped it.

I couldn't go on without it. Had to go back. Doubted

if I could find it in the undergrowth. I felt swamped with liquefying despair, weak enough for tears.

Get a bloody grip on things, I told myself. Don't be stupid. Work it out.

I was facing north. If I turned precisely one hundred and eighty degrees I would be facing where I'd come from.

Elementary.

Think.

I stood and thought and made the panic recede until I could work out what to do, then I took my knife out of its sheath on my belt and carved an arrow in the bark of the tree I was facing. An arrow pointing sky-wards. I had arrows on the brain as well as through the lungs, I thought.

The tree pointed north.

The compass had to be somewhere in sight of that arrow. I would have to crawl to have any hope of finding it.

I went down on my knees carefully and as carefully turned to face the other way, south. The tangle of brown foot-long dried grass and dead leaves and the leafless shoots of new growth filled every space between saplings and established trees. Even in daylight with every faculty at full steam it wouldn't have been an easy search, and as things were it was abysmal.

I crawled a foot or two, casting about, trying to part the undergrowth, hoping desperate hopes. I looked back to the arrow on the tree, then crawled another foot. Nothing. Crawled another and another. Nothing. Crawled until I could see the arrow only because it was pale against the bark, and knew I was already further away than when I'd taken the last bearing.

I turned round and began to crawl back, still sweeping one hand at a time through the jumbled growth. Nothing. Nothing. Hope became a very thin commodity. Weakness was winning.

The compass had to be *somewhere*.

If I couldn't find it I would have to wait for morning and steer north by my watch and the sun. If the sun shone. If I lasted that long. The cold of the night was deepening and I was weaker than I'd been when I set out.

I crawled in a fruitless search all the way back to the tree and then turned and crawled away again in a slightly different line, looking, looking, hope draining away yard by yard in progressive debility, resolution ebbing with failure.

One time when I turned to check on the arrow on the tree, I couldn't see it. I no longer knew which way was north.

I stopped and slumped dazedly back on my heels, facing utter defeat.

Everything hurt unremittingly and I could no longer pretend I could ignore it. I was wounded to death and dying on my knees, scrabbling in dead grass, my time running out with the moonlight, shadows closing in.

I felt that I couldn't endure any more. I had no will

left. I had always believed that survival lay in the mind
but now I knew there were things one couldn't survive.
One couldn't survive unless one could believe one
could, and belief had leaked out of me, gone with sweat
and pain and weakness into the wind.

CHAPTER EIGHTEEN

Time . . . unmeasured time . . . slid away.

I moved in the end from discomfort, from stiffness: made a couple of circling shuffles on my knees, an unthought-out search for a nest to lie in, to die in, maybe.

I looked up and saw again the arrow cut into the tree. It hadn't been and wasn't far away, just out of sight behind a group of saplings.

Apathetically, I thought it of little use. The arrow pointed in the right direction, but ten feet past it, without a compass, which way was north?

The arrow on the tree pointed upwards.

I looked slowly in that direction, as if instructed. Looked upwards to the sky: and there, up there, glimpsed now and then between the moving boughs, was the constellation of the great bear . . . and the pole star.

No doubt from then on my route wasn't as straight or as accurate as earlier, but at least I was moving. It wasn't possible after all to curl up and surrender, not with an alternative. Clinging onto things, breathing little, inching a slow way forwards, I achieved again a sort of numbness to my basic state and in looking upwards to the stars at every pause felt lighter and more disembodied than before.

Light-headed, I dare say.

I looked at my watch and found it was after eleven o'clock, which meant nothing really. I couldn't reach the road by half past midnight. I didn't know how long I'd wasted looking for the compass or how long I'd knelt in capitulation. I didn't know at what rate I was now travelling and no longer bothered to work it out. All I was really clear about was that this time I would go on as long as my lungs and muscles would function. Survival or nothing. It was settled.

The face of the archer . . .

In splinters of thought, unconnectedly, I began to look back over the past three weeks.

I thought of how I must seem to them, the people I'd grown to know.

The writer, a stranger, set down in their midst. A person with odd knowledge, odd skills, physically fit. Someone Tremayne trusted and wanted around. Someone who'd been in the right place a couple of times. Someone who threatened.

I thought of Angela Brickell's death and of the attacks on Harry and me and it seemed that all three had had one purpose, which was to keep things as they were. They were designed not to achieve but to prevent.

One foot in front of the other . . .

Faint little star, half hidden, revealed now and then by the wind; flickering pin-point in a whirling galaxy, the prayer of navigators . . . see me home.

Angela Brickell had probably been killed to close her mouth. Harry was to have died to cement his guilt. I wasn't to be allowed to do what Fiona and Tremayne had both foretold, that I would find the truth for Doone.

They all expected too much of me.

Because of that expectation, I was half dead.

All guesses, I thought. All inferences. No actual objects that could prove guilt. No statements or admissions to go on, but only probability, only likelihood.

The archer had to be someone who knew I was going to go back for Gareth's camera. It had to be someone who knew how to find the trail. It had to be someone who could follow instructions to make an effective bow and sharp arrows, who had time to lie in wait, who wanted me gone, who had a universe to lose.

The way information zoomed round Shellerton, anyone theoretically could have heard of the lost camera and the way to find it. On the other hand the boys' expedition had occurred only yesterday . . . dear God, only *yesterday* . . . and if . . . *when* . . . I got back, I could find out for certain who had told who.

One step and another. There was fluid in my lungs,

rattling and wheezing at every breath. People lived a long time with fluid ... asthma ... emphysema ... years. Fluid took up air space ... you never saw anyone with emphysema run upstairs.

Angela Brickell had been small and light; a pushover.

Harry and I were tall and strong, not easy to attack at close quarters. Half the racing world had seen me pick up Nolan and knew I could defend myself. So, sharp spikes for Harry and arrows for John, and it was only luck in both cases that had saved us. I'd been there for Harry and the arrow had by-passed my heart.

Luck.

The clear sky was luck.

I didn't want to see the face of the archer.

The sudden admission was a revelation in itself. Even with his handiwork through me, I thought of the sadness inevitably awaiting the others; yet I would have to pursue him, for someone who had three times seen murder as a solution to problems couldn't be trusted never to try it again. Murder was habit-forming, so I'd been told.

Endless night. The moon moved in silver stateliness across the sky behind me. Left foot. Right foot. Hold on to branches. Breathe by fractions.

Midnight.

If ever this ended, I thought, I wouldn't go walking in woodland for a very long time. I would go back to my attic and not be too hard on my characters if they came to pieces on their knees.

I thought of Fringe and the Downs and wondered if I would ever ride in a race, and I thought of Ronnie Curzon and publishers and American rights and of Erica Upton's reviews and it all seemed as distant as Ursa Major but not one whit as essential to my continued existence.

Grapevine round Shellerton. A mass of common knowledge. Yet this time ... this time ...

I stopped.

The archer had a face.

Doone would have to juggle with alibis and charts, proving opportunity, searching for footprints. Doone would have to deal with a cunning mind in the best actor of them all.

Perhaps I was wrong. Doone could find out.

I tortoised onwards. A mile was sixty-three thousand three hundred and sixty inches. A mile was roughly one point six kilometres or one hundred and sixty thousand centimetres.

Who cared?

I might have travelled at almost eight thousand inches an hour if it hadn't been for the stops. Six hundred and sixty feet. Two hundred and twenty yards.

A furlong! Brilliant. One furlong an hour. A record for British racing.

Twinkle twinkle little star ...

No one but a bloody fool would try to walk a mile with an arrow through his chest. Meet J. Kendall, bloody fool.

Light-headed.

One o'clock.

The moon, I thought briefly, had come down from the sky and was dancing about in the wood not far ahead. Rubbish, it couldn't be. It certainly was. I could see it shining.

Lights. I came to sensible awareness; to incredulous understanding. The lights were travelling along the road.

The road was real, was there, was not some lost myth in a witch-cursed forest. I had actually got there. I would have shouted with joy if I could have spared the oxygen.

I reached the last tree and leaned feebly against it, wondering what to do next. The road had for so long been the only goal that I'd given no thought to anything beyond it. It was dark now; no cars.

What to do? Crawl out onto the road and risk getting run over? Hitchhike? Give some poor passing motorist a nightmare?

I felt dreadfully spent. With the trunk's support I slid down to kneeling, leaning head and left shoulder against the bark. By my reckoning, if I'd steered anything like a true course, the Land Rover was way along the road to the right, but it was pointless and impossible to reach it.

Car lights came round a bend from that direction

and seemed not to be travelling too fast. I tried waving an arm to attract attention but only a weak flap of a hand was achieved.

Have to do better.

The car braked suddenly with screeching wheels, then backed rapidly until it was level with me. It was the Land Rover itself. How could it be?

Doors opened. People spilled out. People I knew.

Mackie.

Mackie running, calling, 'John, John,' and reaching me and stopping dead and saying, 'Oh my *God*.'

Perkin behind her, looking down, his mouth shocked open in speechlessness. Gareth saying, 'What's the matter,' urgently, and then seeing and coming down scared and wide-eyed on his knees beside me.

'We've been looking for you for *ages*,' he said. 'You've got an arrow . . .' His voice died.

I knew.

'Run and fetch Tremayne,' Mackie told him and he sprang instantly to his feet and sprinted away along the road to the right, his feet impelled as if by demons.

'Surely we must take that arrow out,' Perkin said, and put his hand on the shaft and gave it a tug. He hardly moved it in my chest but it felt like liquid fire.

I yelled . . . it came out as a croak only but it was a yell in my mind . . . 'Don't.'

I tried to move away from him but that made it worse. I shot out a hand and gripped Mackie's trouser

407

leg and pulled with strength I didn't know I still had left. Strength of desperation.

Mackie's face came down to mine, frightened and caring.

'Don't ... move ... the arrow,' I said with terrible urgency. 'Don't let him.'

'Oh God.' She stood up. 'Don't touch it, Perkin. It's hurting him dreadfully.'

'It would hurt less out,' he said obstinately. The vibrations from his hand travelled through me, inducing terror as well.

'*No. No.*' Mackie pulled at his arm in a panic. 'You must leave it. You'll kill him. Darling, you *must* leave it alone.'

Without her, Perkin would have had his way but he finally took his dangerous hand off the shaft. I wondered if he believed that it would kill me. Wondered if he had any idea what force he would have needed to pull the arrow out, like a wooden skewer out of meat. Wondered if he could imagine the semi-asleep furies he'd already reawakened. The furies had claws and merciless teeth. I tried to breathe even less. I could feel the sweat running down my face.

Mackie leaned down again. 'Tremayne will get help.' Her voice was shaky with stress, with the barbarity of things.

I didn't answer: no breath.

A car pulled up behind the Land Rover and dis-gorged Gareth and then Tremayne who moved like a tank across the earthy verge and rocked to a halt a yard away.

'*Jesus Christ*,' he said blankly. 'I didn't believe Gareth.' He took charge of things then as a natural duty but also, it seemed, with an effort. 'Right, I'll call an ambulance on the car phone. Keep still,' he said to me, unnecessarily. 'We'll soon have you out of here.'

I didn't answer him either. He sped away back to the car and we could hear his urgent voice, though not the words. He returned shortly telling me to hang on, it wouldn't be for long; and the shock had made him breathless too, I noticed.

'We've looked for you for hours,' he said, anxious, I thought, to prove I hadn't been forgotten. 'We telephoned the police and the hospitals and they had no news of a car crash or anything, so then we came out here . . .'

'Because of your message,' Mackie said, 'on the corkboard.'

Oh, yes.

Gareth's camera was swinging from Perkin's hand. Mackie saw me watching it and said, 'We found the trail, you know.'

Gareth chimed in. 'The paint by the road had gone but we looked and looked in the woods. I remembered where we'd been.' He was earnest. 'I remembered pretty well where it started. And Perkin found it.'

'He went all the way along it with a torch,' Mackie

said, stroking her husband's arm, 'clever thing – and he came back after absolutely ages with Gareth's camera and said you weren't there. We didn't know what to do next.'

'I wouldn't let them go home,' Gareth said. A mixture of stubbornness and pride in his voice. Thank God for him, I thought.

'What happened exactly?' Tremayne asked me bluntly. 'How did you get like this?'

'Tell you . . . later.' It came out not much above a whisper, lost in the sound of their movements around me.

'Don't bother him,' Mackie said. 'He can hardly speak.'

They waited beside me making worried encouragements until the ambulance arrived from the direction of Reading. Tremayne and Mackie went to meet the men in uniform, to tell them, I supposed, what to expect. Gareth took a step or two after them and I called him in an explosive croak, 'Gareth,' and he stopped and turned immediately and came back, bending down.

'Yes? What? What can I do?'

'Stay with me,' I said.

It surprised him but he said, 'Oh, OK,' and stayed a pace away looking troubled.

Perkin said irritably, 'Oh, go on, Gareth.'

I said, 'No,' hoarsely. 'Stay.'

After a pause Perkin put his back towards Gareth

and his face down near mine and asked with perfect calmness, 'Do you know who shot you?' It sounded like a natural question in the circumstances, but it wasn't.

I didn't reply. I looked for the first time straight into his moonlit eyes, and I saw Perkin the son, the husband, the one who worked with wood. I looked deep, but I couldn't see his soul. Saw the man who thought he'd killed me . . . saw the archer.

'Do you really know?' he asked again.

He showed no feeling, yet my knowledge held the difference between his safety and destruction.

After a long moment, in which he read the answer for himself, I said, 'Yes.'

Something within him seemed to collapse but he didn't outwardly fall to pieces or rant and rave or even try to pull out the arrow again or finish me in any other way. He didn't explain or show remorse or produce justification. He straightened and looked across to where the men from the ambulance were advancing with his father and his wife. Looked at his brother, a pace away, listening.

He said to me, 'I love Mackie very much.'

He'd said everything, really.

I spent the night thankfully unaware of the marathon needlework going on in my chest and drifted back late in the morning to a mass of tubes and machines and techniques I'd never heard of. It seemed I was going to live: the doctors were cheerful, not cautious.

'Constitution like a horse,' one said. 'We'll have you back on your feet in no time.'

A nurse told me a policeman wanted to see me, but visitors had been barred until tomorrow.

By tomorrow, which was Wednesday, I was breathing shallowly but without mechanical help, sitting propped up sideways and drinking soup; talking, attached to drainage tubes and feeling sore. Doing just fine, they said.

The first person who came to see me wasn't Doone at all but Tremayne. He came in the afternoon and he looked white, fatigued and many years older.

He didn't ask about my health. He went over to the window of the post-operation side-ward I was occupying alone and stood looking out for a while, then he turned and said, 'Something awful happened yesterday.'

He was trembling, I saw.

'What?' I asked apprehensively.

'Perkin . . .' His throat closed. His distress was overwhelming.

'Sit down,' I said.

He fumbled his way into the chair provided for visitors and put a hand over his lips so that I shouldn't see how close he was to tears.

'Perkin,' he said after a while. 'After all these years you'd think he'd be careful.'

'What happened?' I asked, when he stopped.

'He was carving part of a cabinet, by hand . . . and he cut his leg open with the knife. He bled . . . he tried to reach the door . . . there was blood all over the floor . . . pints of it. He's had cuts sometimes before but this was an artery . . . Mackie found him.'

'Oh, no,' I said in protest.

'She's in a terrible state and she won't let them give her sedatives because of the baby.'

Despite his efforts, tears filled his eyes. He waited for his face to steady, then took out a handkerchief and fiercely blew his nose.

'Fiona's with her,' he said. 'She's been marvellous.' He swallowed. 'I didn't want to burden you with this but you'd soon have wondered why Mackie hadn't come.'

'That's the least of things.'

'I have to go back now, but I wanted to tell you myself.'

'Yes. Thank you.'

'There's so much to see to.' His voice wavered again. 'I wish you were there. The horses need to go out. I need your help.'

I wanted very much to give it but he could see I couldn't.

'In a few days,' I said, and he nodded.

'There has to be an inquest,' he said wretchedly.

He stayed for a while sitting exhaustedly as if loath to take up his burdens again, postponing the moment when he would have to go back to supporting everyone

413

else. Eventually he sighed deeply, pushed himself to his feet and with a wan smile departed.

Admirable man, Tremayne.

Doone arrived very soon after Tremayne had gone and came straight to the point.

'Who shot you?'

'Some kid playing Robin Hood,' I said.

'Be serious.'

'Seriously, I didn't see.'

He sat in the visitors' chair and looked at me broodingly.

'I saw Mr Tremayne Vickers in the car park,' he said. 'I suppose he told you their bad news?'

'Yes. Dreadful for them.'

'You wouldn't think, would you,' he added, 'that this could be another murder?'

He saw my surprise. 'I hadn't thought of it,' I said.

'It looks like an accident,' he said with a certain delicacy, 'but he was experienced with that knife, was young Mr Vickers, and after Angela Brickell, after Mr Goodhaven, after your little bit of trouble . . .' He left the thought hanging and I did nothing to bring it to earth. He sighed after a while and asked how I was feeling.

'Fine.'

'Hm.' He bent down and picked up a carrier that he'd lain on the floor. 'Thought you might like to see this.' He drew out a sturdy transparent plastic inner bag and held it up to the light to show me the contents.

An arrow, cut into two pieces.

One half was clean and pale, and the other stained and dark, with a long black section sharpened at the tip.

'We've had our lab take a look at this,' he said in his sing-song way, 'but they say there are no distinctive tool marks. It could have been sharpened by any straight blade in the kingdom.'

'Oh,' I said.

'But charring the point, now, that's in your books.'

'And in other books besides mine.'

He nodded. 'Yesterday morning, at Shellerton House, Mr Tremayne Vickers and young Mr and Mrs Perkin Vickers all told me they'd spent three or four hours looking for you on Monday night. Young Gareth didn't want them to give up, they said, but Mr Vickers senior told him you'd be all right even if you had got lost. You knew how to look after yourself, he said. They were just about to go home when they found you.'

'Lucky me.'

He nodded. 'An inch either way and you'd be history, so I hear. I told them all not to worry, I would go on working with you as soon as you were conscious and we would see our way together to a solution of the whole case.'

'Did you?' He took away what breath I still had.

'Mr Tremayne Vickers said he was delighted.' He paused. 'Did you follow that trail of paint towards the clearing they talk about?'

'Mm.'

'And was it along the trail that someone shot at you?'

'Mm.'

'We'll be taking a look at it ourselves, I shouldn't wonder.'

I made no comment and he looked disappointed.

'You should be wanting your assailant brought to justice.' Text book words again. 'You don't seem to care.'

'I'm tired,' I said.

'You wouldn't be interested then in the glue.'

'What glue?' I asked. 'Oh yes, glue.'

'For sticking marble to floorboards,' he said. 'We had it analysed. Regular impact adhesive. On sale everywhere. Untraceable.'

'And the alibis?'

'We're working on them, but everyone moved about so much except poor young Mr Vickers, who was in his workroom all the time.'

He seemed to be waiting for me to react, rather as if he'd floated a fly in front of a fish.

I smiled at him a little and displayed no interest. His moustache seemed to droop further from the lack of good results. He rose to go and told me to take care. Good advice, though a bit too late. He would proceed, he said, with his enquiries.

I wished him luck.

'You're too quiet,' he said.

When he'd gone I lay and thought for a long time about poor young Mr Vickers, and of what I should have told Doone, and hadn't.

Perkin, I thought, was one of the very few people who'd known about the camera and the trail. I'd listened to Gareth tell him in detail on Sunday evening.

Mackie had told Sam Yaeger on Monday morning.

Theoretically she could also have told Fiona on the telephone who could have told Nolan or Lewis, but it wasn't the sort of item one would naturally bother to pass on.

On Monday morning Doone had turned up at Shellerton House with the plank. Perkin knew it was I who had remembered that the floorboards should have floated, and on Monday he'd seen the plank on the dining-room table and heard Doone and me talking in close private consultation. Everything Fiona and Tremayne believed of me must have looked inevitable at that moment. John Kendall would lead Doone to the quarry, who was himself. Any quarry was entitled to take evasive action: to pre-empt discovery by striking first.

By lunchtime Perkin had driven off, going to Newbury for supplies, he'd said. Going to the Quillersedge woods, more like.

Tremayne had gone to Oxford to his tailor. Mackie was out to lunch with Dee-Dee. Gareth was at school.

I'd abandoned the empty house and walked joyfully into the woods and only by chance did I know what had hit me.

I imagined Perkin threading along that trail at night, following the paint quite easily as he'd been that way already in daylight, and being secretly pleased with himself because if he had inadvertently left any traces of his passage the first time they could be explained away naturally by the second. That satisfaction would smartly have evaporated when he reached the clearing and found me gone. A nasty shock, one might say. He might have been intending to go back to his family and appear utterly horrified while breaking the news of my death. Instead, he'd looked shocked and utterly horrified at seeing me still alive. Open-mouthed. Speechless. Too bad.

If I'd tried to walk out along the trail, I would have met Perkin face to face.

I shivered in the warm hospital room. Some things were better unimagined.

For Perkin, making arrows would have been like filing his nails, and he'd had a stove right in his work-room for the charring. He must have constructed a pretty good strong bow too (according to my detailed instructions) which would by now no doubt be broken into unidentifiable pieces in distant undergrowth, Perhaps he'd risked time to practise with a few shots before I got there. Couldn't tell unless I went back to look for spent arrows, which I wasn't going to do.

Random thoughts edged slowly into my mind for the rest of the day.

For instance, Perkin thought in wood, like a language. Any trap he made would be wooden.

Nolan had knocked Perkin down at Tremayne's dinner. I'd picked Nolan up and made a fool of him. Perkin wouldn't have risked any way to kill me that meant creeping up on me, not after what he'd seen.

Perkin had had to get over the shock of finding my familiar ski-jacket and boots in the boathouse and then the far worse shock of the cataclysmic reversal of his scheme when Harry and I both lived.

The best actor of them all, he had contained those shocks within himself with no screaming crises of nerves. Many a convicted murderer had displayed that sort of control. Maybe it was something to do with a divorce from reality. There were books on the subject. One day I might read them.

Perkin had resented Mackie's friendly feelings towards me. Not strongly enough to kill me for that, but certainly strongly enough to make killing me satisfying in that respect also.

Never assume . . .

Perkin had always been presumed to be busy in his workshop, and yet there were hours and days when he might not have been, when Mackie was out of the house seeing to the horses. On the Wednesday of Harry's trap, Mackie had been saddling Tremayne's runner in the three-mile chase at Ascot.

Perkin had made none of the classic mistakes. Hadn't scattered monogrammed handkerchiefs about or faked alibis or carelessly dropped dated train tickets or shown knowledge he shouldn't have had. Perkin had listened more than he'd talked, and he'd been cunning and careful.

I thought of Angela Brickell and of all the afternoons Perkin had spent alone in the house. She had tried to seduce even Gareth. Not hard to imagine she'd set her sights also on Perkin. Intelligent men in love with their wives weren't immune to blatantly offered temptations. Sudden arousal. Quick, casual gratification. End of episode.

Except not the end of the episode if there were a failure of a birth control measure and the result was conception. Not the end if the woman asked for money or threatened disclosure. Not the end if she could and would destroy the man's marriage.

Say Angela Brickell had definitely been pregnant. Say she was sure who the father was; and working in a racing stable with thoroughbreds she would know that proving paternity was increasingly an exact science. The father wouldn't be able to deny it. Say she enticed him into the woods and became demanding in every way and heavily emotional, piling on pressure.

Perkin had not long before seen Olympia lying dead at Nolan's feet. He'd heard over and over again how fast she'd died. Say that picture, that certainty, had

420

flashed into his mind. The quick way out of all his troubles lay in his own two strong hands.

I imagined what Perkin might have been feeling. Might have been facing.

Mackie at that time had been unable to conceive and was troubled and unhappy because of it. Angela Brickell however was devastatingly carrying Perkin's child. Perkin loved Mackie and all too probably couldn't face her knowing what he'd done. Couldn't bear to hurt her so abominably. Was perhaps ashamed. Didn't want his father to find out.

Irresistible solution: a fast death for Angela too. Easy.

Perhaps he, not she, had chosen the woods. Perhaps he'd planned it, perhaps it hadn't been a lightning urge but the first of his traps.

Impossible to know now if either scenario were right. Possible, likely, probable; no more than one of those.

I wondered if he had gone home feeling anything but relief.

Long before Doone came knocking on the door, Perkin could have decided, in case the girl's body were ever found, to say he didn't remember her. No one had thought it odd that he didn't; he was seldom seen with the horses.

His one catastrophic mistake had been to try to settle the mystery for ever by making Harry disappear.

By his actions shall you know him . . .

By his arrows.

I thought that Doone would not think of looking in Perkin's workroom for a match to the arrow's wood. Perkin hadn't had much time to hunt elsewhere for anything suitable. He would have used a common wood, not exotic; but all the same there would be more of it to be found, perhaps even in the cabinet he was making of bleached oak.

He hadn't had any handy feathers, so no flights.

Perkin would have known that a wood match could be made. He knew more about wood than anyone else.

Doone, with his promise of instant detection once I woke up, must have been the end of hope.

He did love Mackie. His universe was lost. One way out remained.

I thought of Tremayne and his pride in Perkin's work. Thought of Gareth's vulnerable age. Thought of Mackie, her face alive with the wondrous joy of discovering she was pregnant. Thought of that child growing up, loved and safe.

Nothing could be gained by trying to prove what Perkin had done. Much would be smashed. They all would suffer. The families always suffered most.

No child would become a secure and balanced adult with a known murderer for a father. Without knowledge, Mackie's grief would heal normally in time. Tremayne and Gareth wouldn't be crippled by undeserved shame. All of them would live more happily if they and the world remained in ignorance, and try to achieve that I would give them the one gift I could.

Silence.

At the short uncomplicated inquest on Perkin a week later the coroner found unhesitatingly for 'Accident' and expressed sympathy with the family. Tremayne came to collect me from the hospital afterwards and told me on the way to Shellerton that Mackie had got through the court ordeal bravely.

'The baby?' I asked.

'The baby's fine. It's what's giving Mackie strength. She says Perkin is with her, will always be with her that way.'

'Mm.'

Tremayne glanced briefly across at me and back to the road.

'Has Doone found out yet who put that arrow through you?' he asked.

'I don't think so,' I said.

'You don't know, yourself?'

'No.'

He drove for a while in silence.

'I just wondered . . .' he said uncertainly.

After a while I said, 'Doone came to see me twice. I told him I didn't know who shot me. I told him I had no ideas of any sort any more.'

I certainly hadn't told him where to look for arrow wood.

Doone had been disgustedly disillusioned with me: I had closed ranks with *them*, he said. Goodhavens, Everards, Vickers and Kendall. 'Yes,' I'd agreed, 'I'm sorry.' Doone said there was no way of proving who had killed Angela Brickell. 'Let her lie,' I said, nodding. After a silence he'd risen greyly to his feet to leave and told me to look after myself. Wryly I'd said, 'I will.' He'd gone slowly, regretfully, seeing regret in my face also, an unexpected mutual liking, slipping away into memory.

'You don't think,' Tremayne said painfully, 'I mean, it had to be someone who knew you would fetch Gareth's camera, who shot you.'

'I told Doone it was a kid playing Robin Hood.'

'I'm . . . afraid . . .'

'Block it out,' I said. 'Some kid did it.'

'John . . .'

He knew, I thought. He was no fool. He could have worked things out the same way I had, and he'd have had a hellish time believing it all of his own son.

'About my book,' he said hesitating, 'I don't know that I want to go on with it.'

'I'm going to write it,' I said positively. 'It's going to be an affirmation of your life and your worth, just as was intended. It's all the more important now, for you especially, but for Gareth, for Mackie and your new grandchild as well. For you and for them, it's essential I do it.'

'You do know,' he said.

'It was a kid.'

He drove without speaking the rest of the way.

Fiona and Harry were with Mackie and Gareth in the family room. Perkin's absence was to me almost a shock, so accustomed had I become to his being there. Mackie looked pale but in charge of things, greeting me with a sisterly kiss.

'Hi,' Gareth said, very cool.

'Hi yourself.'

'I've got the day off from school.'

'Great.'

Harry said, 'How are you feeling?' and Fiona put her arms carefully round me and let her scent drift in my senses.

Harry said his Aunt Erica sent good wishes, his eyes ironic.

I asked Harry how his leg was. All on the surface and polite.

Mackie brought cups of tea for everyone; a very English balm in troubles. I remembered the way Harry had laced the coffee after the ditch, and would have preferred that, on the whole.

It was a month yesterday, I thought, that I came here.

A month in the country . . .

Harry said, 'Has anyone found out who shot at you?'

He was asking a simple unloaded question, not like Tremayne. I gave him a simple answer, the one that eventually became officially accepted.

'Doone is considering it was a child playing out a fantasy,' I said. 'Robin Hood, Cowboys and Indians. That sort of thing. No hope of ever really knowing.'

'Awful,' Mackie said, remembering.

I looked at her with affection and Tremayne patted my shoulder and told them I would be staying on as arranged to write his book.

They all seemed pleased, as if I belonged; but I knew I would leave them again before summer, would walk out of the brightly-lit play, and go back to the shadows and solitude of fiction. It was a compulsion I'd starved for, and even if I never went hungry again I would feel that compulsion for ever. I couldn't understand it or analyse it, but it was there.

After a while I left the family room and wandered through the great central hall and on into the far side of the house, into Perkin's workroom.

It smelled aromatically and only of wood. Tools lay neatly as always. The glue-pot was cold on the stove. Everything had been cleaned and tidied and there were no stains on the polished floor to show where his life had pumped out.

I felt no hatred for him. I thought instead of the extinction of his soaring talent. Thought of consequences and seduction. What's done is done, Tremayne would say, but one couldn't wipe out an enveloping feeling of pathetic waste.

A copy of *Return Safe from the Wilderness* lay on a workbench, and I picked it up idly and looked through it.

Traps. Bows and arrows. All the familiar ideas.

I flipped the pages resignedly and they fell open as if from use at the diagram in the first-aid section showing the pressure points for stopping arterial bleeding. I stared blankly at the carefully drawn and accurate illustration of exactly where the main arteries could be found nearest the surface in the arms and wrists . . . and in the legs.

Dear God, I thought numbly. I taught him that too.

RISK

To the memory of
Lionel Vick,
first a professional steeplechase jockey,
then a certified accountant;
always a brave man.
And my thanks to his associate,
Michael Foote.

CHAPTER ONE

Thursday, March 17th, I spent the morning in anxiety, the afternoon in ecstasy, and the evening unconscious.

Thursday night, somewhere between dark and dawn, I slowly surfaced into a nightmare which would have been all right if I'd been asleep.

It took me a good long time to realize I was actually awake. Half awake, anyway.

There was no light. I thought my eyes were open, but the blackness was absolute.

There was a lot of noise. Different noises, loud and confusing. A heavy engine. Rattling noises. Creaks. Rushing noises. I lay in a muzzy state and felt battered by too much sound.

Lay . . . I was lying on some sort of mattress. On my back. Cold, sick and stiff. Aching. Shivering. Physically wretched and mentally bewildered.

I tried to move. Couldn't for some reason lift either hand to my face. They seemed to be stuck to my legs. Very odd.

An interminable time passed. I grew colder, sicker, stiffer, and wide awake.

Tried to sit up. Banged my head on something close above. Lay down again, fought a sudden spurt of panic, and made myself take it step by step.

Hands. Why couldn't I move my hands? Because my wrists seemed to be fastened to my trousers. It didn't make sense, but that was what it felt like.

Space. What of space? I stiffly moved my freezing feet, exploring. Found I had no shoes on. Only socks. On the immediate left, a wall. Close above, a ceiling. On the immediate right, a softer barrier. Possibly cloth.

I shifted my whole body a fraction to the right, and felt with my fingers. Not cloth, but netting. Like a tennis net. Pulled tight. Keeping me in. I pushed my fingers through the mesh, but could feel nothing at all on the far side.

Eyes. If I hadn't gone suddenly blind (and it didn't feel like it), I was lying somewhere where no light penetrated. Brilliant deduction. Most constructive. Ha bloody ha.

Ears. Almost the worst problem. Constant din assaulted them, shutting me close in the narrow black box, preventing me hearing any further than the powerful, nearby, racketing engine. I had a frightening feeling that even if I screamed no one would hear me. I had a sudden even more frightening feeling of *wanting* to scream. To make someone come. To make someone tell me where I was, and why I was there, and what on earth was happening.

I opened my mouth and yelled.

I yelled 'Hey' and 'Come here' and 'Bloody bastard, come and let me out', and thrashed about in useless rage, and all that happened was that my voice and fear bounded back in the confined space and made things worse. Chain reaction. One-way trip to exhaustion.

In the end I stopped shouting and lay still. Swallowed. Ground my teeth. Tried to force my mind into holding on to sense. Disorientation was the road to gibbering.

Concentrate, I told myself. *Think*.

That engine . . .

A big one. Doing a job of work. Situated somewhere close, but not where I was. The other side of a wall. Perhaps behind my head.

If it would only stop, I thought numbly, I would feel less sick, less pulverized, less panicky, less threatened.

The engine went right on hammering, its vibration reaching me through the walls. Not a turbine engine: not smooth enough, and no whine. A piston engine. Heavy duty, like a tractor . . . or a lorry. But I wasn't in a lorry. There was no feeling of movement; and the engine never altered its rate. No slowing or accelerating. No changes of gear. Not a lorry.

A generator. It's a generator, I thought. Making electricity.

I was lying tied up in the dark and on a sort of shelf near an electric generator. Cold, sick and frightened. And where?

As to how I'd got there . . . well, I knew that, up to a

point. I remembered the beginning, well enough. I would never forget Thursday, March 17th.

The most shattering questions were those to which I could think of no answer at all.

Why? What for? And *what next?*

CHAPTER TWO

That Thursday morning a client with his life in ruins kept me in the office in Newbury long after I should have left for Cheltenham races, and it seemed churlish to say, 'Yes, Mr Wells, terribly sorry about your agony, but I can't stop to help you now because I want to nip off and enjoy myself.' Mr Wells, staring-eyed and suicidal, simply had to be hauled in from his quicksand.

It took three and a half hours of analysis, sympathy, brandy, discussion of ways and means, and general pep-talk, to restore the slightest hope to his horizon, and I wasn't his doctor, priest, solicitor or other assorted hand-holder, but only the accountant he'd engaged in a frenzy the night before.

Mr Wells had bitten the dust in the hands of a crooked financial adviser. Mr Wells, frantic, desperate, had heard that Roland Britten, although young, had done other salvage jobs. Mr Wells on the telephone had offered double fees, tears, and lifelong gratitude as inducements: and Mr Wells was a confounded nuisance.

For the first and probably the only time in my life I

5

was that day going to ride in the Cheltenham Gold Cup, the race which ranked next to the Grand National in the lives of British steeplechase riders. No matter that the tipsters gave my mount little chance or the bookies were offering ante-post odds of forty-to-one, the fact remained that for a part-time amateur like myself the offer of a ride in the Gold Cup was as high as one could go.

Thanks to Mr Wells I did not leave the office calmly and early after a quick shuffle through the day's mail. Not until a quarter to one did I begin to unstick his leech-like dependence and get him moving, and only then by promising another long session on the following Monday. Halfway through the door, he froze yet again. Was I sure we had covered every angle? Couldn't I give him the afternoon? Monday, I said firmly. Wasn't there anyone else he could see, then?

'Sorry,' I said. 'My senior partner is away on holiday.'

'Mr King?' he asked, pointing to the neat notice 'King and Britten' painted on the open door.

I nodded, reflecting gloomily that my senior partner, if he hadn't been touring somewhere in Spain, would have been most insistent that I got off to Cheltenham in good time. Trevor King, big, silver-haired, authoritative and worldly, had my priorities right.

We had worked together for six years, ever since he'd enticed me, from the city office where I'd been trained, with the one inducement I couldn't refuse: flexible working hours which allowed time to go racing. He already had five or six clients from the racing world,

Newbury being central for many of the racing stables strung out along the Berkshire Downs, and, needing a replacement for a departing assistant, he'd reckoned that if he engaged me he might acquire a good deal more business in that direction. Not that he'd ever actually said so, because he was not a man to use two words where one would do; but his open satisfaction as his plan had gradually worked made it obvious.

All he had apparently done towards checking my ability as an accountant, as opposed to amateur jockey, was to ask my former employers if they would offer me a substantial raise in salary in order to keep me. They said yes, and did so. Trevor, it seemed, had smiled like a gentle shark, and gone away. His subsequent offer to me had been for a full partnership and lots of racing time; the partnership would cost me ten thousand pounds and I could pay it to him over several years out of my earnings. What did I think?

I'd thought it might turn out just fine; and it had.

In some ways I knew Trevor no better than on that first day. Our real relationship began and ended at the office door, social contact outside being confined to one formal dinner party each year, to which I was invited by letter by his wife. His house was opulent: building and contents circa nineteen twenties, with heavy plate glass cut to fit the top surfaces of polished furniture, and an elaborate bar built into the room he called his 'snug'. Friends tended to be top management types or county councillors, worthy substantial citizens like Trevor himself.

On the professional level, I knew him well. Orthodox establishment outlook, sober and traditional. Patriarchal, but not pompous. Giving the sort of gilt-edged advice that still appeared sound even if in hindsight it turned out not to be.

Something punitive about him, perhaps. He seemed to me sometimes to get a positive pleasure from detailing the extent of a client's tax liabilities, and watching the client droop.

Precise in mind and method, discreetly ambitious, pleased to be a noted local personage, and at his charming best with rich old ladies. His favourite clients were prosperous companies; his least favourite, incompetent individuals with their affairs in a mess.

I finally got rid of the incompetent Mr Wells and took my tensions down to the office car park. It was sixty miles from Newbury to Cheltenham and on the way I chewed my fingernails through two lots of roadworks and an army convoy, knowing also that near the course the crawling racegoing jams would mean half an hour for the last mile. There had been enough said already about the risks of putting up an amateur ('however good' some kind columnist had written) against the top brass of the professionals on the country's best horses in the most important race of the season's most prestigious meeting. 'The best thing Roland Britten can do is to keep Tapestry out of everyone else's way' was the offering of a less kind writer, and although I more or less agreed with him I hadn't meant to do it by not arriving in time. Of all possible unprofessional behaviour, that would be the worst.

Lateness was the last and currently the most acute of a whole list of pressures. I had been riding as an amateur in jump races since my sixteenth birthday, but was now, with thirty-two in sight, finding it increasingly difficult to keep fit. Age and desk work were nibbling away at a stamina I'd always taken for granted: it now needed a lot of effort to do what I'd once done without thought. The hour and a half I spent early every morning riding exercise for a local trainer were no longer enough. Recently, in a couple of tight finishes, I'd felt the strength draining like bathwater from my creaking muscles, and had lost at least one race because of it. I couldn't swear to myself that I was tuned up tight for the Gold Cup.

Work in the office had multiplied to the point where doing it properly was a problem in itself. Half-days off for racing had begun to feel like treachery. Saturdays were fine, but impatient clients viewed Wednesdays at Ascot or Thursdays at Stratford-upon-Avon with irritation. That I worked at home in the evenings to make up for it satisfied Trevor, but no one else. And my case load, as jargon would put it, was swamping me.

Apart from Mr Wells, there had been other jobs I should have done that morning. I should have sent an appeal against a top jockey's tax assessment; I should have signed a certificate for a solicitor; and there had been two summonses for clients to appear before the Tax Commissioners, which needed instant action, even if only evasive.

'I'll apply for postponements,' I told Peter, one of our two assistants. 'Ring both of those clients, and tell them not to worry, I'll start on their cases at once. And check that we've all the papers we need. Ask them to send any that are missing.'

Peter nodded sullenly, unwillingly, implying that I was always giving him too much work. And maybe I was.

Trevor's plans to take on another assistant had been so far halted by an offer which was currently giving both of us headaches. A big London firm wanted to move in on us, merge, amalgamate, and establish a large branch of itself on our patch, with us inside. Materially, we would benefit, as at present the steeply rising cost of overheads like office rent, electricity and secretarial wages was coming straight out of our pockets. We would also be under less stress, as at present when one of us was ill or on holiday, the burden on the other was heavy. But Trevor agonized over the prospect of demotion from absolute boss, and I over the threat of loss of liberty. We had postponed a decision until Trevor's return from Spain in two weeks' time, but at that point bleak realities would have to be faced.

I drummed my fingers on the steering wheel of my Dolomite and waited impatiently for the roadworks' traffic lights to turn green. Looked at my watch for the hundredth time. 'Come on,' I said aloud. 'Come *on*.' Binny Tomkins would be absolutely furious.

Binny, Tapestry's trainer, didn't want me on the horse. 'Not in the Gold Cup,' he'd said positively, when the owner had proposed it. They'd faced each other belligerently outside the weighing room of Newbury racecourse, where Tapestry had just obliged in the three mile 'chase: Mrs Moira Longerman, small, blonde and bird-like, versus sixteen stone of frustrated male.

' . . . just because he's your *accountant*,' Binny was saying in exasperation when I rejoined them after weighing-in. 'It's bloody ridiculous.'

'Well, he won today, didn't he?' she said.

Binny threw his arms wide, breathing heavily. Mrs Longerman had offered me the Newbury ride on the spur of the moment when the stable jockey had broken his ankle in a fall in the previous race. Binny had accepted me as a temporary arrangement with fair grace, but Tapestry was the best horse in his yard, and for a middle-ranker like him a runner in the Gold Cup was an event. He wanted the best professional jockey he could get. He did not want Mrs Longerman's accountant who rode in thirty races in a year, if he was lucky. Mrs Longerman, however, had murmured something about removing Tapestry to a more accommodating trainer, and I had not been unselfish enough to decline the offer, and Binny had fumed in vain.

Mrs Longerman's previous accountant had for years let her pay to the Inland Revenue a lot more tax than

11

DICK FRANCIS

she'd needed, and I'd got her a refund of thousands. It wasn't the best grounds for choosing a jockey to ride for you in the Gold Cup, but I understood she was thanking me by giving me something beyond price. I quite passionately did not want to let her down; and that, too, was a pressure.

I was worried about making a reasonable show, but not about falling. When one worried about falling, it was time to stop racing: it would happen to me one day, I supposed, but it hadn't yet. I worried about being unfit, unwanted, and late. Enough to be going on with.

Binny was spluttering like a lit fuse when I finally arrived, panting, in the weighing room.

'Where the hell have you been?' he demanded. 'Do you realize the first race is over already and in another five minutes you'd be fined for not turning up?'

'Sorry.'

I carried my saddle, helmet, and bag of gear through into the changing room, sat down thankfully on the bench, and tried to stop sweating. The usual bustle went on around me; jockeys dressing, undressing, swearing, laughing, accepting me from long acquaintance as a part of the scenery. I did the accounts for thirty-two jockeys and had unofficially filled in tax assessment forms for a dozen more. I was also to date employed as accountant by thirty-one trainers, fifteen stud farms, two Stewards of the Jockey Club, one racecourse, thirteen bookmakers, two horse-transport firms, one blacksmith, five forage merchants, and upwards of forty people who owned racehorses. I probably knew more about the private financial affairs of the racing world than any other single person on the racecourse.

In the parade ring Moira Longerman twittered with happy nerves, her button nose showing kittenishly just above a fluffy upstanding sable collar. Below the collar she snuggled into a coat to match, and on the blonde curls floated a fluffy sable hat. Her middle-aged blue eyes brimmed with excitement, and in the straightforward gaiety of her manner one could see why it was that so many thousands of people spent their hobby money on owning racehorses. Not just for the gambling, nor the display: more likely for the kick from extra adrenalin, and the feeling of being involved. She knew well enough that the fun could turn to disappointment, to tears. The lurking valleys made the mountaintops more precious.

'Doesn't Tapestry look *marvellous*?' she said, her small gloved hands fluttering in the horse's direction as he plodded round the ring under the gaze of the ten-deep banks of intent spectators.

'Great,' I said truthfully.

Binny scowled at the cold sunny sky. He had produced the horse with a gloss seldom achieved by his other runners: impeccably plaited mane and tail, oiled hooves, a new rug, gleamingly polished leather tack, and an intricate geometric pattern brushed into the well-groomed hairs of the hindquarters. Binny was busy telling the world that if his horse failed it would not be from lack of preparation. Binny was going to use me for evermore as his reason for not having won the Gold Cup.

I can't say that it disturbed me very much. Like Moira Longerman, I was feeling the throat-catching once-in-a-lifetime thrill of a profound experience waiting just ahead. Disaster might follow, but whatever happened I would have had my ride in the Gold Cup.

There were eight runners, including Tapestry. We mounted, walked out on to the course, paraded in front of the packed and noisy stands, cantered down to the start. I could feel myself trembling, and knew it was stupid. Only a cool head could produce a worthy result. Tell that to the adrenal glands.

I could pretend, anyway. Stifle the butterfly nerves and act as if races of this calibre came my way six times a season. None of the other seven riders looked anxious or strung up, yet I guessed that some of them must be. Even for the top pros, this was an occasion. I reckoned that their placid expressions were nearly as phoney as mine, and felt better.

We advanced to the tapes in a bouncing line, restraining the eager heads on short reins, and keeping the weight still back in the saddle. Then the starter pressed his lever and let the tapes fly up, and Tapestry took a great bite of air and practically yanked my arms out of their sockets.

Most three and a quarter mile 'chases started moderately, speeded up a mile from home, and maybe finished in a decelerating procession. The Gold Cup field that day set off as if to cover the whole distance in record Derby time, and Moira Longerman told me later that Binny used words she'd never heard before when I failed to keep Tapestry close in touch.

By the time we'd swept over the first two fences, by the stands, I was last by a good six lengths, a gap not much in itself but still an I-told-you-so sort of distance so early in the proceedings. I couldn't in fact make up my mind. Should I go faster? Stick closer to the tails in front? Tapestry had set off at a greater speed already than when he'd won with me at Newbury. If I let him zip along with the others he could be exhausted and tailed off at half-way. If I held him up, we might at least finish the race.

Over the third fence and over the water I saw the gap lengthening and still dithered about tactics. I hadn't expected the others to go off so fast. I didn't know if they hoped to maintain that speed throughout, or whether they would slow and come back to me later. I couldn't decide which was more likely.

But what would Binny say if I guessed wrong and was last the whole way? What wouldn't he say?

What was I doing in this race, out of my class?

Making an utter fool of myself.

Oh God, I thought, why did I try it?

Accountants are held to be cautious by nature but at that point I threw caution to the winds. Almost anything would be better than starting last and staying last.

Prudence would get me nowhere. I gave Tapestry a kick which he didn't expect and he shot forward like an arrow.

'Steady,' I gasped. 'Steady, dammit.'

Shorten the gap, I thought, but not too fast. Spurt too fast and I'd use the reserves we'd need for the last stretch uphill. If we ever got there. If I didn't fall off. If I didn't let Tapestry meet a fence wrong, or run out, or refuse to jump at all.

Only a mile done, and I'd lived a couple of lifetimes.

I was still last by the end of the first circuit, but no longer a disgrace. Once more round . . . and maybe we'd pass one or two before we'd done. I began at that point to enjoy myself, a background feeling mostly smothered by anxious concentration, but there all the same, and I knew from other days that it would be the enjoyment I remembered most afterwards, not the doubts.

Over the water-jump, still last, the others all in a group just ahead. Open ditch next; Tapestry met it just right and we pegged it back a length in mid-air. Landed nose to tail with the horse in front. Stayed there to the next fence, and again won ground in flight, setting off that time beside the next horse, not behind.

Great. I was no longer last. Just joint last. Whatever I might fear about Tapestry staying to the end, he was surging over the jumps meanwhile with zest and courage.

It was at the next fence, on the far side of the course, that the race came apart. The favourite fell, and the second favourite tripped over him. Tapestry swerved violently as he landed among the rolling bodies and crashed into the horse alongside. The rider of that horse fell off.

It happened so fast. One second, an orderly Gold Cup. Next second, a shambles. Three down, the high hopes of owners, trainers, lads and punters blown to the wind. Tapestry forged his way out like a bull, but when we tackled the hill ahead, we again lay last.

Never try to accelerate uphill, they say, because the horses you pass will pass you again on the way down. Save your strength, don't waste it. I saved Tapestry's strength in last place up the hill and it seemed to me that at the crest the others suddenly swooped away from me, piling on every ounce of everything they had, shooting off while I was still freewheeling.

Come on, I thought urgently, come on, it's now or never. Now, or absolutely never. Get on, Tapestry. Get going. I went down the hill faster than I'd ever ridden in my life.

A fence half-way down. A fractional change of stride. A leap to shame the chamoix.

Another jockey lay on the ground there, curled in a ball to avoid being kicked. Hard luck . . . Too bad . . .

Three horses in front. Two fences to go. I realized abruptly that the three horses in front were all there were. Not far in front, either. My God, I thought, almost laughing, just supposing I can pass one, I'll finish third. Third in the Gold Cup. A dream to last till death.

I urged Tapestry ever faster, and amazingly, he responded. This was the horse whose finishing speed was

17

doubtful, who had to be nursed. This horse, thundering along like a sprinter.

Round the bend ... only one fence to go ... I was approaching it faster than the others ... took off alongside the third horse, landed in front ... with only the last taxing uphill stretch to the post. I'm third, I thought exultantly. I'm *bloody* third.

Some horses find the Cheltenham finish a painful struggle. Some wander sideways from tiredness, swish their tails and falter when in front, slow to a leaden all-spent pace that barely takes them to the post.

Nothing like that happened to Tapestry, but it did to both of the horses in front. One of them wavered up the straight at a widening angle. The other seemed to be stopping second by second. To my own and everyone else's disbelief, Tapestry scorched past both of them at a flat gallop and won the Gold Cup.

I didn't give a damn that everyone would say (and did say) that if the favourite and second favourite hadn't fallen, I wouldn't have had a chance. I didn't care a fig that it would go down in history as a 'bad' Gold Cup. I lived through such a peak of ecstasy on the lengthy walk round from the winning post to the unsaddling enclosure that nothing after, I thought, could ever match it.

It was impossible ... and it had happened. Mrs Longerman's accountant had brought her a tax-free capital gain.

A misty hour later, changed into street clothes, with champagne flowing in the weighing room and all the hands I'd ever want slapping me on the shoulder, I was still so wildly happy that I wanted to run up the walls and laugh aloud and turn hand-springs. Speeches, presentations, Moira Longerman's excited tears, Binny's incredulous embarrassment, all had passed in a jumble which I would sort out later. I was high on the sort of glory wave which would put poppies out of business.

Into this ball of a day came a man in a St John's Ambulance uniform, asking for me.

'You Roland Britten?' he said.

I nodded over a glass of bubbles.

'There's a jockey wanting you. In the ambulance. Says he won't go off to hospital before he's talked to you. Proper fussed, he is. So would you come?'

'Who is it?' I asked, putting my drink down.

'Budley. Fell in the last race.'

'Is he badly hurt?'

We walked out of the weighing room and across the crowded stretch of tarmac towards the ambulance which stood waiting just outside the gates. It was five minutes before the time for the last race of the day, and thousands were scurrying about, making for the stands, hurrying to put on the last bet of the meeting. The ambulance man and I walked in the counter-current of those making for the car park before the greater rush began.

'Broken leg,' said the ambulance man.

'What rotten luck.'

19

I couldn't imagine what Bobby Budley wanted me for. There had been nothing wrong with his last annual accounts and we'd had them agreed by the Inspector of Taxes. He shouldn't have had any urgent problems.

We reached the back doors of the white ambulance, and the St John's man opened them.

'He's inside,' he said.

Not one of the big ambulances, I thought, stepping up. More like a white van, with not quite enough headroom to stand upright. They were short of regular ambulances, I supposed, on race days.

Inside there was a stretcher, with a figure on it under a blanket. I went a step towards it, head bent under the low roof.

'Bobby?' I said.

It wasn't Bobby. It was someone I'd never seen before. Young, agile, and in no way hurt. He sprang upwards off the stretcher shedding dark grey blanket like a cloud.

I turned to retreat. Found the ambulance man up beside me, inside the van. Behind him the doors were already shut. His expression was far from gentle and when I tried to push him out of the way he kicked my shin.

I turned again. The stretcher case was ripping open a plastic bag which seemed to contain a hand-sized wad of damp cotton wool. The ambulance man caught hold of one of my arms and the stretcher case the other, and despite fairly desperate heavings and struggles on my part they managed between them to hold the damp cotton wool over my nose and mouth.

It's difficult to fight effectively when you can't stand up straight and every breath you draw is pure ether. The last thing I saw in a greying world was the ambulance man's peaked cap falling off. His light brown hair tumbled out loose into a shaggy mop and turned him from an angel of mercy into a straightforward villain.

I had left racecourses once or twice before on a stretcher, but never fast asleep.

Awake in the noisy dark I could make no sense of it.

Why should they take me? Did it have anything to do with winning the Gold Cup? And if so, what?

It seemed to me that I had grown colder, and still sicker, and that the peripheral noises of creaks and rushing sounds had grown louder. There was also now an uncoordinated feeling of movement: yet I was not in a lorry.

Where, then? In an aeroplane?

The sickness suddenly identified itself into being not the aftermath of ether, as I'd vaguely thought, but a familiar malaise I'd suffered on and off from childhood.

I was seasick.

On a boat.

CHAPTER THREE

I was lying, I realized, on a bunk. The tight net across the open side on my right was to prevent me from falling off. The rushing noises were from the waves washing against the hull. The creaks and rattles were the result of a solid body being pushed by an engine through the resistance of water.

To have made at least some sense of my surroundings was an enormous relief. I could relate myself to space again, and visualize my condition. On the other hand, sorting out the most disorientating part of the mystery left me feeling more acutely the physical discomforts. Cold. Hands tied to legs. Muscles stiff from immobility: and knowing I was on a boat, and knowing boats always made me sick, was definitely making me feel a lot sicker.

Ignorance was a great tranquillizer, I thought. The intensity of a pain depended on the amount of attention one gave it, and one never felt half as bad talking to people in daylight as alone in the dark. If someone would come and talk to me I might feel less cold and less miserable and less quite horribly sick.

No one came for a century or so.

The motion of the boat increased, and my queasiness with it. I could feel my weight rolling slightly from side to side, and had an all too distinct impression that I was also pitching lengthwise, first toe down, then head down, as the bows lifted and fell with the waves.

Out at sea, I thought helplessly. It wouldn't be so rough on a river.

I tried for a while with witticisms like 'Press-ganged, by God', and 'Shanghaied!' and 'Jim lad, Long John Silver's got you', to put a twist of lightness into the situation. Not a deafening success.

In time also I gave up trying to work out why I was there. I gave up feeling apprehensive. I gave up feeling cold and uncomfortable. Finally I was concentrating only on not actually vomiting, and the fact that I'd eaten nothing since breakfast was all that helped.

Breakfast . . .? I had lost all idea of time. I didn't know how long I'd been unconscious, or even how long I'd lain awake in the dark. Unconscious long enough to be shipped from Cheltenham to the coast, and to be carried on board. Awake long enough to long for sleep.

The engine stopped.

The sudden quiet was so marvellous that I only fully realized then how exhausting had been the assault of noise. I actively feared that it would start again. And was this, I wondered, the basis of brainwashing?

23

There was a new noise, suddenly, from overhead. Dragging sounds, and then metallic sounds, and then, devastatingly, a shaft of daylight.

I shut my dark-adjusted eyes, wincing, and opened them again slowly. Above my head, the shaft had grown to a square. Someone had opened a hatch.

Fresh air blew in like a shower, cold and damp. Without much enthusiasm I glanced around, seeing a small world through a wide-meshed white net.

I was in what one might call the sharp end. In the bows. The bunk where I lay grew narrower at my feet, the side walls of the cabin angling to meet in the centre, like an arrowhead.

The bunk was about two feet wide, and had another bunk above it. I was lying on a cloth-covered mattress; navy blue.

Most of the rest of the cabin was taken up by two large, open-topped, built-in, varnished wooden bins. For stowing sails, I thought. I was in the sail locker of a sailing boat.

Behind my right shoulder a door, now firmly shut, presumably led back to warmth, life, the galley and the saloon.

The matter of my wrists, too, became clear. They were indeed tied to my trousers, one on each side. From what I could see, someone had punched a couple of holes through the material in the region of each side pocket, threaded something which looked like bandage through

24

the holes, and effectively tied each of my wrists to a bunch of cloth.

A good pair of trousers ruined: but then all disasters were relative.

A head appeared above me, framed by the hatch. Indistinctly, seeing him through the net and silhouetted against the grey sky, I got the impression he was fairly young and uncompromisingly tough.

'Are you awake?' he said, peering down.

'Yes,' I said.

'Right.'

He went away, but presently returned, leaning head and shoulders into the hatch.

'If you act sensible, I'll untie you,' he said.

His voice had the bossy strength of one accustomed to dictate, not cajole. A voice which had come up the hard way, gathering aggression on the journey.

'Have you got any dramamine?' I asked.

'No,' he said. 'There's a toilet in the cabin. You can throw up into that. You're going to have to agree you'll act quiet if I come down and untie you. Otherwise I won't. Right?'

'I agree,' I said.

'Right.'

Without more ado he lowered himself easily through the hatch and stood six feet three in his canvas shoes, practically filling all available space. His body moved in effortless balance in the boat's tossing.

'Here,' he said, lifting the lid of what had looked like a

built-in varnished box. 'Here's the head. You open the
stop-cock and pump sea water through with that lever.
Turn the water off when you've done, or you'll have a
flood.' He shut the lid and opened a locker door on the
wall above. 'In here there's a bottle of drinking water and
some paper cups. You'll get your meals when we get
ours.' He fished deep into one of the sail bins, which
otherwise seemed empty. 'Here's a blanket. And a
pillow.' He lifted them out, showed them to me, both
dark blue, dropped them back.

He looked upwards to the generous square of open
sky above him.

'I'll fix you the hatch so you'll have air and light. You
won't be able to get out. And there's nothing to get out
for. We're out of sight of land.'

He stood for a moment, considering, then began to
unfasten the net, which was held simply by chrome hooks
slotted into eyelets on the bunk above.

'You can hook the net up if it gets rough,' he said.

Seen without intervening white meshes, he was not
reassuring. A strong face with vigorous bones. Smallish
eyes, narrow-lipped mouth, open air skin and straight
brown floppy hair. My own sort of age: no natural
kinship, though. He looked down at me without any hint
of sadistic enjoyment, for which I was grateful, but also
without apology or compassion.

'Where am I?' I said. 'Why am I here? Where are we
going? And who are you?'

He said, 'If I untie your hands and you try anything, I'll bash you.'

You must be joking, I thought. Six foot three of healthy muscle against a cold, stiff, seasick five foot ten. No thank you very much.

'What *is* this all about?' I said. Even to my ears, it sounded pretty weak. But then, pretty weak was exactly how I felt.

He didn't answer. He merely bent down, leaned in and over me, and unknotted the bandage from my left wrist. Extracting himself from the small space between the bunks, he repeated the process on the right.

'Stay lying down until I'm out of here,' he said.

'Tell me what's going on.'

He put a foot on the edge of the sail bins, and his hands on the sides of the hatch, and pulled himself halfway up into the outside world.

'I'll tell you,' he said unemotionally, looking down, 'that you're a bloody nuisance to me. I'm having to stow all the sails on deck.'

He gave a heave, a wriggle, and a kick, and hauled himself out.

'Tell me,' I shouted urgently. 'Why am I here?'

He didn't answer. He was fiddling with the hatch. I swung my feet over the side of the bunk and rolled in an exceedingly wobbly fashion to my feet. The pitching of the boat promptly threw me off balance and I ended in a heap on the floor.

'Tell me,' I shouted, pulling myself up again and holding on to things. 'Tell me, God dammit.'

The hatch cover slid over and shut out most of the sky. This time, though, it was not clamped down tight, but rested on metal stays, which left a three-inch gap all round: like a lid held three inches above a box.

I put a hand up through the gap and yelled again 'Tell me.'

The only reply I got was the sound of the hatch being made secure against any attempt of mine to dislodge it. Then even those sounds ceased, and I knew he'd gone away; and a minute or two later the engine started again.

The boat rolled and tossed wildly, and the sickness won with a rush. I knelt on the floor with my head over the lavatory bowl and heaved and retched as if trying to rid myself of my stomach itself. I hadn't eaten for so long that all that actually came up was bright yellow bile, but that made nothing any better. The misery of seasickness was that one's body never seemed to realize that there was nothing left to vomit.

I dragged myself onto the bunk and lay there both sweating and shivering, wanting to die.

Blanket and pillow, I thought. In the sail bin.

A terrible effort to get up and get them. I leaned down to pick them up, and my head whirled alarmingly.

Another frightful session over the bowl. Curse the blanket and pillow. But I was so cold.

I got them at the second attempt. Wrapped myself closely in the thick navy wool and put my head thankfully on the navy pillow. There was mercy somewhere, it seemed. I had a bed and a blanket and light and air and a water closet, and a lot of shipboard prisoners before me would have given their souls for all that. It seemed unreasonable to want an explanation as well.

The day passed with increasing awfulness. Anyone who has been comprehensively seasick won't need telling. Head ached and swam, skin sweated, stomach heaved, entire system felt unbelievably ill. If I opened my eyes it was worse.

How long, I thought, will this be going on? Were we crossing the Channel? Surely this relentless churning would soon end. Wherever we were going, it couldn't be far.

At some point he came back and undid the hatch.

'Food,' he said, shouting to be heard against the engine's din.

I didn't answer; couldn't be bothered.

'Food,' he shouted again.

I flapped a weak hand in the air, making go away signals.

I could swear he laughed. Extraordinary how funny seasickness is to those who don't have it. He pushed the hatch into place again and left me to it.

The light faded to dark. I slid in and out of dreams which were a good deal more comforting than reality; and during one of those brief sleeps someone came and fastened the hatch. I didn't care very much. If the boat had sunk, I would have looked upon drowning as a blessed release.

The next time the engine stopped it was only a minor relief compared with the general level of misery. I had supposed it was only in my imagination that the boat was tossing in a storm, but when the engine stopped I rolled clean off the bunk.

Climbing clumsily to my feet, holding on with one hand to the upper bunk, I felt for the door and the light switch beside it. Found the switch, and pressed it. No light. No damned light. Bloody stinking sods, giving me no light.

I fumbled my way back to the lower bunk in the blackness. Tripped over the blanket. Rolled it around me and lay down, feeling most insecure. Felt around for the net: fastened a couple of the hooks, groaning and grunting; not tidily, but enough to do the job.

From the next lot of noises from the outside world, I gathered that someone was putting up sails. On a sailing boat that merely made sense. There were rattlings and flappings and indistinct shouts, about none of which I cared a drip. It seemed vaguely strange someone should be sluicing the decks with buckets of water at such a time, until it dawned on me that the heavy intermittent splashes were made by waves breaking over the bows. The tight-closed hatch made sense. I had never wished for anything more passionately than to get my feet on warm, steady, dry land.

I entirely lost touch of time. Life became merely a matter of total wretchedness, seemingly without end. I would quite have liked a drink of water, but partly couldn't raise the energy to search for it, and partly feared to spill it in the dark, but mostly I didn't bother because every time I lifted my head the whirling bouts of sickness sent me retching to my knees. Water would be no sooner down than up.

He came and undid the hatch: not wide, but enough to let in grey daylight and a flood of fresh air. He did not, it seemed, intend me to die of suffocation.

It was raining hard outside: or maybe it was spray. I saw the bright shine of his yellow oilskins as a shower of heavy drops spattered in through the narrow gap.

His voice came to me, shouting. 'Do you want food?'

I lay apathetically, not answering.

He shouted again. 'Wave your hand if you are all right.'

I reckoned all right was a relative term, but raised a faint flap.

He said something which sounded like 'Gale', and shut the hatch again.

Bloody hell, I thought bitterly. Where were we going that we should run into gales? Out into the Atlantic? And *what for*?

The old jingle about seasickness ran through my head: 'One minute you're afraid you're dying, next minute you're afraid you're not.' For hours through the storm I groaned miserably into the pillow, incredibly ill from nothing but motion.

*

31

I woke from a sunny dream, the umpteenth awakening into total darkness.

Something different, I thought hazily. Same wild weather outside, the bows crashing against the seas and shipping heavy waves over the deck. Same creaking and slapping of wind-strained rigging. But inside, in me, something quite different.

I breathed deeply from relief. The sickness was going, subsiding slowly like an ebb tide, leaving me acclimatized to an alien environment. I lay for a while in simple contentment, while normality crept back like a forgotten luxury: but then, insistently, other troubles began to surface instead. Thirst, hunger, exhaustion, and an oppressive headache which I eventually put down to dehydration and a dearth of fresh air. A sour taste. An itching stubble of beard. A sweaty feeling of having worn the same clothes for a month. But worse than physical pinpricks, the mental rocks.

Confusion had had its points. Clarity brought no comfort at all. The more I was able to think straight, the less I liked the prospects.

There had to be a reason for any abduction, but the most usual reason made least sense. Ransom... it couldn't be. There was no one to pay a million for my release: no parents, rich or poor. Hostage... but hostages were mostly taken at random, not elaborately, from a public place. I had no political significance and no special knowledge: I couldn't be bartered, didn't know any secrets, had no access to Government papers or defence plans or scientific discoveries. No one would care more than a passing pang whether I lived or died, except perhaps Trevor, who would count it a nuisance to have to find a replacement.

I considered as dispassionately as possible the thought of death, but eventually discarded it. If I was there to be murdered, it would already have been done. The cabin had been made ready for a living prisoner, not a prospective corpse. Once out at sea, a weighted heave-ho would have done the trick. So, with luck, I was going to live.

However unrealistic it seemed to me, the only reason I could raise which made any sense at all was that I was there for revenge.

Although the majority of mankind think of auditing accountants as dry-as-dust creatures burrowing dimly into columns of boring figures, the dishonest regard them as deadly enemies.

I had had my share of uncovering frauds. I'd lost a dozen people their jobs and set the Revenue onto others, and seen five embezzlers go to prison, and the spite in some of those eyes had been like acid.

If Connaught Powys, for instance, had arranged this trip, my troubles had hardly started. Four years ago, when I'd last seen him, in court and newly convicted, he'd sworn to get even. He would be out of Leyhill about now. If by getting even he meant the full four years in a sail locker . . . well, it couldn't be that. It couldn't. I swallowed, convincing myself that from the solely practical viewpoint, it was impossible.

My throat was dry. From thirst, I told myself firmly: not from fear. Fear would get me nowhere.

I eased myself out of the bunk and onto the small patch of floor, holding on tight to the upper bunk. The black world went on corkscrewing around, but the vertigo had really gone. The fluid in my ears' semi-circular canals had finally got used to sloshing about chaotically: a pity it hadn't done it with less fuss.

I found the catch of the wall locker, opened it, and felt around inside. Paper cups, as promised. Bottle of water, ditto. Big plastic bottle with a screw cap. It was hopeless in the dark to use one of the cups: I wedged myself on the only available seat, which was the lowered lid of the loo, and drank straight from the bottle. Even then, with the violent rolling and pitching, a good deal of it ran down my neck.

I screwed the cap on again carefully and groped my way back to the bunk, taking the bottle with me. Hooked up the net again. Lay on my back with my head propped up on the pillow, holding the water on my chest and whistling 'Oh Susanna' to prove I was alive.

A long time passed during which I drank a good deal and whistled every tune I could think of.

After that I stood up and banged on the cabin door with my fists and the bottle, and shouted at the top of my voice that I was awake and hungry and furious at the whole bloody charade. I used a good deal of energy and the results were an absolute zero.

Back in the bunk I took to swearing instead of whistling. It made a change.

The elements went on giving the boat a bad time. I speculated fruitlessly about where we were, and how big the boat was, and how many people were sailing it, and whether they were any good. I thought about hot sausages and crusty bread and red wine, and for a fairly cheerful hour I thought about winning the Gold Cup.

At about the time that I began to wonder seriously if everyone except me had been washed overboard, the hatch-opening noises returned. He was there, still in his oilskins. I gulped in the refreshing blast of cold air and wondered just how much of a stinking fug was rushing out to meet him.

I unhooked the net and stood up, holding on and swaying. The wind outside shrieked like starlings.

He shouted, 'Do you want food?'

'Yes,' I yelled. 'And more water.' I held the nearly empty bottle up to him, and he reached down for it.

'Right.'

He shut the hatch and went away, but not before I had a terrifying glimpse of the outside world. The boat rolled heavily as usual to one side, to the left, and before it rolled back to the right I saw the sea. A huge uneven wave, towering to obliterate the sky, charcoal grey, shining, swept with gusts of spray. The next heavy crash of water over the hatch made me think happier thoughts of my dry cabin.

He came back, opened the hatch a few inches, and

lowered in a plastic carrier bag on a loop of rope. He shouted down at me.

'Next time I bring you food, you give me back this carrier. Understand?'

'Yes,' I shouted back, untying the rope. 'What time is it?'

'Five o'clock. Afternoon.'

'What day?'

'Sunday.' He pulled the rope up and began to shut the hatch.

'Give me some light,' I yelled.

He shouted something which sounded like 'Batteries' and put me back among the blind. Yes, well . . . one could live perfectly well without sight. I slid back onto the bunk, fastened the net, and investigated the carrier bag.

The water bottle, full; an apple; and a packet of two thick sandwiches, faintly warm. They turned out to be hamburgers in bread, not buns; and very good too. I ate the lot.

Five o'clock on Sunday. Three whole damned days since I'd stepped into the white van.

I wondered if anyone had missed me seriously enough to go to the police. I had disappeared abruptly from the weighing room, but no one would think it sinister. The changing room valet might be surprised that I hadn't collected from him my wallet and keys and watch, which he'd been holding as usual in safe keeping while I raced, and that I hadn't in fact paid him, either; but he would have put my absent-mindedness down to excitement. My car would still, I supposed, be standing in the jockeys' car park, but no one yet would have begun to worry about it.

I lived alone in a cottage three miles outside Newbury: my next-door neighbour would merely think I was away celebrating for the weekend. Our two office assistants, one boy, one girl, would have made indulgent allowances, or caustic allowances perhaps, when I hadn't turned up for work on Friday. The clients I had been supposed to see would have been irritated, but no more.

Trevor was away on his holidays. So no one, I concluded, would be looking for me.

On Monday morning, the bankrupt Mr Wells might make a fuss. But even if people began to realize I had vanished, how would they ever find me? The fact had to be faced that they wouldn't. Rescue was unlikely. Unless I escaped, I would be staying in the sail locker until someone chose to let me out.

Sunday to Monday was a long, cold, wild, depressing night.

CHAPTER FOUR

On Monday, March 21st the hatch opened twice to let in air, food, sprays of water, and brief views of constantly grey skies. On each occasion I demanded information, and got none. The oilskins gave merely an impression that the crew had more than enough to do with sailing the boat in those conditions, and had no time to answer damn fool questions.

I was used to being alone. I lived alone and to a great extent worked alone; solitary by nature, and seldom lonely. An only child, long accustomed to my own company, I tended often to feel oppressed by the constant companionship of a large number of people, and to seek escape as soon as possible. All the same, as the hours dragged on, I found life alone in the sail locker increasingly wearing.

Limbo existence, I thought. Lying in a black capsule, endlessly tossing. How long did it take for the human mind to disintegrate, left alone in uncertainty in the rattling, corkscrewing dark?

A bloody long time, I answered myself rebelliously. If

the purpose of all this incarceration was to reduce me to a crying wreck, then it wasn't going to succeed. Tough thoughts, tough words . . . I reckoned more realistically that it depended on the true facts. I could survive another week of it passably, and two weeks with difficulty. After that . . . unknown territory.

Where could we be going? Across the Atlantic? Or, if the idea really was to break me up, maybe just up and down the Irish Sea? They might reckon that any suitable stretch of rough water would do the trick.

And who were 'they'?

Not him in the oilskins. He looked upon me as a nuisance, not a target for malice. He probably had instructions regarding me, and was carrying them out. How unfunny if his instructions were to take me home once I'd gone mad.

Dammit, I thought. Dammit to bloody hell. He'd have a bloody long job. Bugger him. Bugger and sod him.

There was a great sane comfort to be found in swearing.

At some long time after my second Monday glimpse of the outside, it seemed that the demented motion of the boat was slowly steadying. Standing up out of the bunk was no longer quite such a throw-around affair. Holding on was still necessary, but not holding on for dear life. The bows crashed more gently against the waves. The thuds of water over the hatch diminished in number and weight. There were shouts on deck and a good deal of pulley noise, and I guessed they were resetting the sails.

I found also that for the first time since my first awakening, I was no longer cold.

I was still wearing the clothes I had put on in the far off world of sanity: charcoal business suit, sleeveless waistcoat-shaped pullover underneath, pale blue shirt, underpants, and socks. Somewhere on the floor in the dark was my favourite Italian silk tie, worn to celebrate the Gold Cup. Shoes had vanished altogether. From being inadequate even when reinforced by a blanket, the long-suffering ensemble was suddenly too much.

I took off my jacket and rolled it into a tidy ball. As gent's natty suiting it was already a past number: as an extra pillow it added considerably to life's luxuries. Amazing how deprivation made the smallest extras marvellous.

Time had become a lost faculty. Drifting in and out of sleep with no external references was a queer business. I mostly couldn't tell whether I'd been asleep for minutes or hours. Dreams occurred in a semi-waking state, sometimes in such short snatches that I could have counted them in seconds. Other dreams were deeper and longer, and I knew that they were the product of sounder sleep. None of them seemed to have anything to do with my present predicament, and not one came up with any useful subconscious information as to why I should be there. In my innermost soul, it seemed, I didn't know.

Tuesday morning – it must have been Tuesday

morning – he came without the oilskins. The air which flowed in through the open hatch was as always fresh and clean, but now dry and faintly warm. The sky was pale blue. I could see a patch of white sail and hear the hissing of the hull as it cut through the water.

'Food,' he said, lowering one of the by now familiar plastic carriers.

'Tell me why I'm here,' I said, untying the knot.

He didn't answer. I took the carrier off, and tied on the empty one, and held on to the rope.

'Who are you? What is this boat? Why am I here?' I said.

His face showed no response except faint irritation.

'I'm not here to answer your questions.'

'Then what *are* you here for?' I said.

'None of your business. Let go of the rope.'

I held on to it. 'Please tell me why I'm here,' I said.

He stared down, unmoved. 'If you ask any more questions, and you don't leave go of the rope, you'll get no supper.'

The simplicity of the threat, and the simplicity of the mind that made it, was a bit of a stunner. I let go of the rope, but I made one more try.

'Then please just tell me how long you're going to keep me here.'

He gave me a stubborn scowl as he pulled up the carrier.

'You'll get no supper,' he said, withdrawing his head out of sight, and beginning to shut the hatch.

'Leave the hatch open,' I shouted.

I got no joy from that either. He firmly fastened me back in the dark. I stood swaying with the boat, holding onto the upper bunk, and trying to fight down a sudden overwhelming tide of furious anger. How *dared* they abduct me and imprison me in this tiny place and treat me like a naughty child. How dared they give me no reasons and no horizons. How dared they thrust me into the squalor of my own unwashed, unbrushed, unshaven state. There was a great deal of insulted pride and soaring temper in the fiery outrage with which I literally shook.

I could go berserk and smash up the place, I thought, or calm down again and eat whatever he'd brought in the carrier: and the fact that I'd recognized the choice made it certain I'd choose the latter. The bitter, frustrated fury didn't exactly go away, but at least with a sigh I had it back under control.

The intensity of what I'd felt, and its violent, unexpected onset, both alarmed me. I would have to be careful, I thought. There were so many roads to destruction, and rage, it seemed, was one of them.

If a psychiatrist had been shut up like this, I wondered, would he have had any safety nets that I hadn't? Would his knowledge of what might happen to the mind of someone in this position help him to withstand the symptoms when they occurred? Probably I should have studied psychology, not accountancy. More useful if one were kidnapped. Stood to reason.

The carrier contained two shelled hard-boiled eggs, an apple, and three small foil-wrapped triangles of processed cheese. I saved one of the eggs and two pieces of cheese for later, in case he meant it about no supper.

He did mean it. Uncountable hours passed. I ate the second egg and the rest of the cheese. Drank some water. As the day's total entertainment, hardly a riot.

When the hatch was next opened, it was dark outside, though dark with a luminous greyness quite unlike the black inside the cabin. No carrier of food materialized, and I gathered that the respite was only so that I shouldn't asphyxiate. He had opened the hatch and gone before I got round to risking any more questions.

Gone.

The hatch was wide open. Out on the deck there were voices and a good deal of activity with ropes and sails.

'Let go.'

'You're letting the effing thing fall into the sea . . .'

'Catch that effing sheet . . . Move, can't you . . .'

'You'll have to stow the gennie along the rail . . .'

Mostly his voice, from close by, directing things.

I put one foot on the thigh-high rim of the sail bin, as he had done, and hooked my hands over the side of the hatch, and heaved. My head popped out into the free world and it was about two whole seconds before he noticed.

'Get back,' he said brusquely, punctuating his remark by stamping on my fingers. 'Get down and stay down.' He kicked at my other hand. 'Do you want a bash on the head?' He was holding a heavy chromium winch handle, and he swung it in an unmistakable gesture.

'There's no land in sight,' he said, kicking again. 'So get down.'

I dropped back to the floor, and he shut the hatch. I hugged my stinging fingers and counted it fortunate that no one went sailing in hob-nailed boots.

Two seconds' uninterrupted view of the boat had been worth it, though. I sat on the lid of the loo with my feet on the side of the lower bunk opposite, and thought about the pictures still alive on my retinas. Even in night light, with eyes adjusted to a deeper darkness, I'd been able to see a good deal.

For a start, I'd seen three men.

The one I knew, who seemed to be not only in charge of me but of the whole boat. Two others, both young, hauling in a voluminous sail which hung half over the side, pulling it in with outstretched arms and trying to stop it billowing again once they'd got it on deck.

There might be a fourth one steering: I hadn't been able to see. About ten feet directly aft of the hatch the single mast rose majestically skywards, and with all the cleats and pulleys and ropes clustered around its base it had formed a block to any straight view towards the stern. There might have been a helmsman and three or four crewmen resting below. Or there might have been automatic steering and all hands visible on deck. It seemed a huge boat, though, to be managed by three.

From the roughest of guesses and distant gleams from

chromium winches I would have put it at about a cricket pitch long. Say sixty-five feet. Or say, if you preferred it, nineteen point eight one metres. Give or take an octave.

Not exactly a nippy little dinghy for Sunday afternoons on the Thames. An ocean racer, more like.

I had had a client once who had bought himself a second-hand ocean racer. He'd paid twenty-five thousand for thirty feet of adventure, and beamed every time he thought of it. His voice came back over the years: 'The people who race seriously have to buy new boats every year. There's always something new. If they don't get a better boat they can't possibly win, and the possibility of winning is what it's all about. Now me, all I want is to be able to sail round Britain comfortably at weekends in the summer. So I buy one of the big boys' cast-offs, because they're well-built boats, and just the job.' He had once invited me to Sunday lunch on board. I had enjoyed looking over his pride and joy, but privately had been most relieved when a sudden gale had prevented us leaving the moorings at his yacht club for the promised afternoon's sail.

Highly probable, I thought, that I was now being entertained on some other big boy's cast-off. The great question was, at whose expense?

The improvement in the weather was a mixed blessing, because the engine started again. The din seemed an even worse assault on my nerves than it had at the beginning. I lay on the bunk and tried to shut my ears with the pillow and my fingers, but the roaring vibration easily by-passed such frivolous barriers. I'd either got to get used to it and ignore it, I thought, or go raving, screaming bonkers.

I got used to it.

Wednesday. Was it Wednesday? I got food and air twice. I said nothing to him, and he said nothing to me. The constant noise of the engine made talking difficult. Wednesday was a black desert.

Thursday. I'd been there a week.

When he opened the hatch, I shouted, 'Is it Thursday?'

He looked surprised. Hesitated, then shouted back, 'Yes.' He looked at his watch. 'Quarter to eleven.'

He was wearing a blue cotton tee shirt, and the day outside seemed fine. The light tended to hurt my eyes.

I untied the carrier and fastened on the previous one, which as usual contained an empty water bottle. I looked up at him as he pulled it out, and he stared down at my face. He looked his normal unsmiling self: a hard young man, unfeeling rather than positively brutal.

I didn't consciously ask him, but after a pause, during which he seemed to be inspecting the horizon, he began to fix the hatch as he had done on the first day, so that it was a uniform three inches above the deck, letting in continuous air and light.

The relief at not being locked back in the dark was absolutely shattering. I found I was trembling from head to foot. I swallowed, trying to guard against the possibility that he would change his mind. Trying to tell myself that even if it proved to be only for five minutes, I should be grateful for that.

He finished securing the hatch and went away. I took some shaky deep breaths and gave myself an ineffective lecture about stoical responses, come dark, come shine.

After a while I sat on the lid of the loo and ate the first shipboard meal that I could actually see. Two hard-boiled eggs, some crispbread, three triangles of cheese and an apple. Never much variety in the diet, but at least no one intended me to starve.

He came back about half an hour after he'd gone away.

Hell, I thought. Half an hour. Be grateful for that. I had at least talked myself into facing another dose of darkness without collapsing into rubble.

He didn't, however, shut the hatch. Without altering the way it was fixed, he slid another plastic carrier through the gap. It was not this time tied to a rope, because when he let go of it, it fell to the floor; and before I could raise any remark, he had gone again.

I picked up the carrier, which seemed light and almost empty, and looked inside.

For God's sake, I thought. Laugh. Laugh, but don't bloody snivel. An ounce of kindness was more devastating than a week of misery.

He'd given me a pair of clean socks and a paperback novel.

I spent a good deal of the day trying to look out of the gap. With one foot on the rim of the sail bins, and my hands grasping the hatch opening, I could get my head up to the top well enough, but the view would have been more comprehensive if either the gap had been a couple of inches deeper or my eyes had been located halfway up my forehead. What I did see, mostly by tilting my head and applying one eye at a time, was a lot of ropes, pulleys, and rolled up sails, a lot of green sea, and a dark line of land on the horizon ahead.

None of these things changed all day except that the smudge of land grew slowly thicker, but I never tired of looking.

At closer quarters I also looked at the fittings of the hatch itself, which, I realized after a time, had been modified slightly for my visit. The metal props which held it open were hinged, and folded down inside the cabin when the hatch was closed. Out on deck the hatch cover was mounted on two heavier extending hinges, which allowed it to open outwards completely and lie flat on its back.

Inside the cabin there were two sturdy clips for securing the hatch shut from below, and outside there were two others, for securing the hatch from above.

So far, all as planned by the ship builders. What had been added, though, was extra provision to prevent someone inside the cabin from pushing the hatch wide open after releasing it from the hinged props. Normally, one could have done this. Sail locker hatches were supposed to open easily and wide, so that the sails could be pulled in and out. There was no point in ordinary circumstances in making things difficult. But now, outside, crossing from fore to aft and from port to starboard over the top of the hatch cover, were two lengths of chain, each secured at both ends to cleats which to my eyes looked newly screwed to the deck. The chains held the hatch cover down on the props like guy ropes, taut and forceful. If I could dislodge those chains, I thought, I could get out. If I had anything to dislodge them with. A couple of Everest-sized ifs. I could get my hands out through the three inch gap, but not much arm. Not enough to reach the cleats, let alone undo the chains. As for levers, screwdrivers, hammers and files, all I had were paper cups, a flimsy carrier and a plastic water bottle. Tantalizing, all those hours looking out at unreachable freedom.

In between the long bouts of balancing up by the ceiling I sat on the loo lid and read the book, which was an American private-eye thriller with a karate-trained hero who would have chopped his way out of a sail locker in five minutes.

Inspired by him, I had another go at the cabin door. It withstood my efforts like a stolid wall. Obviously I should have studied karate as well as psychiatry. Better luck next time.

The day whizzed past. The light began to fade. Outside the smudge of land had grown into an approaching certainty, and I had no idea what land it was.

He came back, lowered the carrier, and waited while I tied on the empty ones.

'Thank you,' I shouted, as he pulled them up, 'for the book and socks.'

He nodded, and began to close the hatch.

'Please don't,' I shouted.

He paused and looked down. It seemed to be still be-kind-to-prisoners day, because he provided his first explanation.

'We are going into port. Don't waste your breath making a noise when we stop. We'll be anchored. No one will hear you.'

He shut the hatch. I ate sliced tinned ham and a hot baked potato in the noisy stupefying dark, and to cheer myself up thought that now that the journey was ending they surely wouldn't keep me there much longer. Tomorrow, perhaps, I would be out. And after that I might get some answers.

I stifled the gloomy doubts.

*

The engine slowed, the first time it had changed its note. There were footsteps on deck, and shouts, and the anchor went over with a splash. The anchor chain rattled out, sounding as if it were passing practically through the sail locker; behind the panelling, no doubt.

The engine was switched off. There was no sound from anywhere. The creakings and rushing noises had stopped. No perceptible motion any more. I had expected the peace to be a relief, but as time passed it was the opposite. Even aggravating stimuli, it seemed, were better than none at all. I slept in disjointed snatches and lay emptily awake for hours and hours wondering if one really could go mad from too much nothing.

When he next opened the hatch it was full daylight outside. Friday; mid-morning. He lowered the carrier, waited for the exchange, raised the rope, and began to close the hatch.

I made involuntarily a vague imploring gesture with my hands. He paused, looking down.

'I can't let you see where we are,' he said.

It was the nearest he had come to an apology, the nearest to admitting that he might have treated me better, if he didn't have his orders.

'Wait,' I yelled, as he pulled the hatch over.

He paused again: prepared at least to listen.

'Can't you put screens round if you don't want me to see the land?' I said. 'Leave the hatch open . . .'

He considered it. 'I'll see,' he said, 'later.'

It seemed an awfully long time later, but he did come

51

back, and he did open the hatch. While he was fastening it, I said, 'When are you going to let me out?'

'Don't ask questions.'

'I *must*,' I said explosively. 'I have to know.'

'Do you want me to shut the hatch?'

'No.'

'Then don't ask questions.'

It may have been spineless of me, but I didn't ask any more. He hadn't given me one useful answer in eight days, and if I persevered, all I would get would be no light and no supper and an end to the new era of partial humanity.

When he'd gone I climbed up for a look, and found he had surrounded the hatch area with bulging bolsters of rolled sails. My field of vision had come down to about eighteen inches.

I lay on the top bunk for a change, and tried to imagine what it was about the port, so hopelessly near, that I might recognize. The sky was pale blue, with sun shining through high, hazy cloud. It was warm, like a fine spring day. There were even seagulls.

It evoked in me such a strong picture that I became convinced that if I could only see over the sail bolsters, I would be looking at the harbour and beaches where I'd played as a child. Maybe all that frantic sailing had been nowhere but up and down the English Channel, and we were now safe back home in Ryde, Isle of Wight.

I shook the comforting dream away. All one could

actually tell for sure was that it was not in the Arctic Circle.

There were occasional sounds from outside, but all distant, and nothing of any use. I read the American thriller again, and thought a good deal about escape.

When the day was fading he came back with supper, but this time, after I'd swopped the carriers, he didn't shut the hatch. That evening I watched the light die to dusk and night, and breathed sweet air. Small mercies could be huge mercies, I thought.

Saturday, March 26th. The morning carrier contained fresh bread, fresh cheese, fresh tomatoes: someone had been shopping ashore. It also contained an extra bottle of water and a well-worn piece of soap. I looked at the soap and wondered if it was there from kindness or because I stank; and then with wildly leaping hope wondered if it was there so that I should at least be clean when they turned me loose.

I took off all my clothes and washed from head to foot, using a sock as a sponge. After the week's desultory efforts with salt water from the loo, the lather was a fantastic physical delight. I washed my face and ears and neck and wondered what I looked like with a beard.

After that, dressed in shirt and underpants which were both long overdue for the same treatment, I ate the morning meal.

After that, I tidied the cabin, folding the blanket and my extra clothes and stacking everything neatly.

After that, I still couldn't face for a long time that my soaring hope was unfounded. No one came to let me out.

It was odd how soon the most longed-for luxury became commonplace and not enough. In the dark, I had ached for light. Now that I had light, I took it for granted and ached for room to move.

The cabin was triangular, its three sides each about six feet long. The bunks on the port side, and the loo and sail bins on the starboard side, took up most of the space. The floor area in the centre was roughly two feet wide by the cabin door, but narrowed to a point about four feet in, where the bunks and the forward sail bin met. There was room to take two small paces, or one large. Any attempt at knees-bend-arms-stretch involved unplanned contact with the surrounding woodwork. There was more or less enough space to stand on one's head by the cabin door. I did that a couple of times. It just shows how potty one can get. The second time I bashed my ankle on the edge of the sail bin coming down, and decided to give Yoga a miss. If I'd tried the Lotus position, I'd have been wedged for life.

I felt a continuous urge to scream and shout. I knew that no one would hear me, but the impulse had nothing to do with reason. It stemmed from frustration, fury and induced claustrophobia. I knew that if I gave way to it, and yelled and yelled, I would probably end up sobbing.

The thought that maybe that was precisely what someone wanted to happen to me was an enormous support. I couldn't stop the screaming and shouting from going on inside my head, but at least it didn't get out.

After I'd finally come to terms with the thought that it wasn't Exodus day, I spent a good deal of time contemplating the loo. Not metaphysically: mechanically.

Everything in the cabin was either built-in, or soft. From the beginning I'd been given no possible weapons, no possible implements. All the food had been for eating with my fingers, and came wrapped only in paper or plastic, if at all. No plates. Nothing made of metal, china or glass. The light bulb had not only been unscrewed from its socket, but the glass cover for it, which I guessed should be there, was not.

The pockets of my suit had been emptied. The nail file I usually carried in my breast pocket was no longer there: nor were my pens clipped inside: and my penknife had gone from my trousers.

I sat on the floor, lifted the lid, and at close quarters glared at the loo's mechanics.

Bowl, flushing lever, pump. A good deal of tubing. The stopcock for turning the sea water on and off. Everything made with the strength and durability demanded by the wild motions of the sea, which shook flimsy contraptions to pieces.

The lever was fastened at the back, hinged to the built-in casing of the fitment. At the front, it ended in a wooden handle. Attached at about a third of the way back was the rod which led directly down into the pump, to pull the piston there up and down. The whole lever, from handle to hinge, measured about eighteen inches.

I lusted for that lever like a rapist, but I could see no way, without tools, of getting it off. The hinge and the piston linkage were each fastened with a nut and bolt, and appeared to have been tightened by Atlas. Nut versus thumb and finger was no contest. I had tried on and off for two days.

A spanner. My kingdom for a spanner, I thought.

Failing a spanner, what else?

I tried with my shirt. The cloth saved the pressure on skin and bones, but gave no extra purchase. The nuts sat there like rocks. It was like trying to change a wheel with only fingers and a handkerchief.

Trousers? The cloth itself tended to slip more easily than my shirt. I tried the waistband, and found it a great deal better. Around the inside of the waist was a strip with two narrow rows of rough-surfaced rubber let into it. The real purpose of the strip was to help belt-less trousers stay up by providing a friction grip against a tucked-in shirt. Applying trouser-band to nut gave a good grip and slightly more hope, but despite a lot of heavy effort, no results.

The day ground on. I went on sitting on the floor futilely trying to unscrew nuts which wouldn't unscrew, simply because there was nothing else to do.

*

Tinned ham again for supper. I carefully peeled off all the fat, and ate the lean.

The hatch stayed open.

I said thanks for the soap, and asked no questions.

Sunday. Another Sunday. How *could* anyone keep me locked up so long without explanation? The whole modern world was churning along outside, and there I was cooped up like the man in the iron mask, or as near as dammit.

I applied the strips of ham fat to the nuts, to see if grease would have any effect. I spent most of the day warming the piston-rod nut in my fingers, rubbing fat round its edges, and hauling at it with my trousers.

Nothing happened.

Now and again I stood up and stretched, and climbed up to see if the sail bolsters were still obstructing the view, which they always were. I read bits of the thriller again. I closed the loo lid and sat on it, and looked at the walls. I listened to the seagulls.

My ordinary life seemed far removed. Reality was inside the sail locker. Reality was a mystery. Reality was mind-cracking acres of empty time.

Sunday night drifted in and darkened and slowly became Monday. He came much earlier than usual with my breakfast, and when he had lifted out the exchange carrier, he began to close the hatch.

'Don't,' I yelled.

He paused only briefly, staring down unmoved.

'Necessary,' he said.

I went on yelling for him to open it for a long time after he'd gone away and left me in the dark. Once I'd started making a noise, I found it difficult to stop: all the stifled screams and shouts were trying to burst out through the hole in the dam. If the dam broke up, so would I. I stuffed the pillow into my mouth to make myself shut up, and resisted a desire to bang my head against the door instead.

The engine started. Din and vibration and darkness, all as before. It's too much, I thought. Too much. But there were only two basic alternatives. Stay sane or go crazy. Sanity was definitely getting harder.

Think rational thoughts, I told myself. Repeat verses, do mental arithmetic, remember all the tricks that other solitary prisoners have used to see them through weeks and months and years.

I tore my mind away from such impossible periods and directed it to the present.

The engine ran on fuel. It had used a good deal of fuel on the journey. Therefore if the boat was going far, it would need more.

Engines were always switched off during refuelling. If I made the most colossal racket when we refuelled, just possibly someone might hear. I didn't honestly see how any noise I could make would attract enough attention, but I could try.

The chain rattled back through its hidden chute as the anchor came up, and I presumed the boat was moving, although there was no feeling of motion.

Then someone came and put a radio on top of the hatch, and turned the volume up loud. The music fought a losing battle against the engine for a while, but shortly I felt the boat bump, and almost at once the engine switched off.

I knew we were refuelling. I could hear only loud pop music. And no one on the quayside, whatever I did, could possibly have heard *me*.

After a fairly short while the engine started again. There were a few small thuds outside, felt through the hull, and then nothing. Someone came and collected the radio: I yelled for the hatch to be opened, but might as well not have bothered.

Motion slowly returned to the boat, bringing hopeless recognition with it.

Going out to sea again.

Out to sea, in the noise and the dark. Still not knowing why I was there, or for how long. Growing less fit from lack of exercise and less able to deal with mental pressure. Starting last week's torments all over again.

I sat on the floor with my back against the cabin door, and folded my arms over my knees, and put my head on my arms, and wondered how I could possibly endure it.

Monday I spent in full-blown despair.

On Tuesday, I got out.

CHAPTER FIVE

Monday night the boat was anchored somewhere, but it stopped after I got my supper and started again before Tuesday mid-morning. It rained most of the time, drumming on the hatch. I was glad of the respite from the engine but in general the misery level was a pain.

When he brought the morning food he fixed the hatch open. The extent of my relief was pathetic.

Shortly after, they stopped the engine and put up the sails, and the grey sky outside slowly cleared to blue.

I ate the hard boiled eggs and the apple and thought about the thick slice of bread, upon which, for the first time, he had given me butter. Then I pulled a button off my shirt to use as a scraper, and transferred as much of the butter as I could to the stubborn nuts and bolts on the flushing lever. Then I ate the bread. Then I sat on the floor and one after the other warmed the nuts with my hand in the hope that the butter and ham fat would melt into the screw threads.

After that I ripped a length of the rubberized waistband from my trousers, and fished out of the bottom of one of the sail bins the white net which I had stored there after the storms.

It was activity for activity's sake, more than any real hope. I wound the waistband twice round the piston-rod nut, because it was the nearest, and fitted over that the chromium hook which had attached the net to the upper berth. Then I tugged the net.

After a second of gripping, the hook slid round on the cloth and fell off. I tried again, folding the waistband so that it had an elasticated side against the hook as well as against the nut. That time the hook stayed in place; but so did the nut.

I tugged several times. If I tugged very hard, hook, waistband and all came off. Nothing else happened. I slung the net back into the sail bin in depression.

After that I sat for ages with my hand on the piston-rod nut, until it was as warm as a handful of pennies clutched by a child. Then I wound the strip of waistband round quickly three times, to make the nut larger to grip, and then I tried it with all my remaining muscle power.

The waistband turned in my hand.

Damn it to hell, I thought hopelessly. I pulled it off and wound it on again, trying to grip it more tightly.

It turned again.

It may seem ridiculous, but it was not until it turned more easily the third time that I realized I was turning the nut on the bolt, not the waistband on the nut.

Unbelievable. I sat there looking idiotic, with my

mouth open. Excitement fluttered in my throat like a stifled laugh. If I could get one off, what about the other?

Time hadn't mattered for the first one. I'd had nothing else to do. For the second one, the hinge, I was feverishly impatient.

I warmed the nut, and wound on the waistband, and heaved; and nothing happened.

Heaved again.

A blob.

It had to move, I thought furiously. It simply had to. After several more useless attempts, I went back to basics.

Perhaps after all the tugging session with the hook had had some effect. I scooped out the net and applied it to the hinge nut, and tugged away with enthusiasm, replacing the hook every time it fell off. Then I made myself warm the nut as thoroughly as I had the other one, so that the heat from my hand was conducted right to the inside, where the melted grease and the minute heat-expansion of the metal could do their work. Then I wound on the waistband again and practically tore all the ligaments in my arm and back with a long and mighty heave.

And that time, the waistband turned. That time again I couldn't be sure until the third turn, when the nut started moving more freely, that I'd really done it.

I climbed up on the sail bin and squinted out at the free world. To the left all I could see was sky and a sparkle of sun on the water. I turned my head to the right and nearly fell off my perch. To the right there was a sail, and shining below it, green and rocky and moderately close, there was land.

I thought that if he came along at that moment to shut the hatch I would perversely be grateful.

Only desperation made me do what I did next, because I was sure that if he caught me in mid-escape he'd tie my hands and leave me in the dark on starvation rations.

The risk that I wouldn't get out unseen was appalling. My present conditions were just about bearable; my future afterwards wouldn't be.

Yet if I hadn't meant to risk it, why had I laboured so long on the nuts?

I went back to the loo and unscrewed the nuts completely. I knocked the bolts out, and pulled the whole lever free.

Without it, no one could flush the loo. I thought grimly that it would be an added complication if I found myself back in the cabin with it gone.

There was no sign of anyone on deck, and as usual I couldn't see if the boat was on automatic steering or whether there was anyone at the helm.

Hesitation was only in my mind. Looking back, it seemed as if I did everything very fast.

I pulled the hinged props of the hatch down inside the cabin, which one would do in the normal way if one wanted to shut the hatch oneself from the inside. This had the effect of slackening the guy-rope action of the chains crossed over the top.

Through the much reduced gap, little more than a slit, I poked the lever, aiming at where a link of chain was hooked over the top.

Long hours of inspection had given me the impression that those chains had no other fastening. Putting a link over the hook of the cleat must have seemed safe enough, because they were certain I had no means of dislodging them. I stuck the lever into the chain on the right, wedged it securely, and pushed. With almost miraculous elegance the whole chain slid loosely outwards, and the link fell off the cleat.

Without pausing for anything but mental hip-hoorays I applied the lever again, this time to where the fore and aft chain was fastened on the bow side. Again, with no more fuss, the link slid off.

I was committed. I couldn't get the chains back on again. I had to open the hatch now, and climb out. There was no retreat.

I took the lever with me as a last resort against recapture, putting it out first onto the deck. Then with both hands I released the hatch from the hinged props and pushed it wide. Eased it down gently until it lay flat, fearing to let it crash open and bring them running.

I snaked out onto the deck on my stomach. Rolled to the right, under the jib sail. Reached the railing, grabbed it with both hands, and bunny-hopped fast over the side, going down into the sea straight and feet first, like a pillar.

It wasn't the safest way of disembarking, but I survived it, staying down under the surface until my lungs protested. Surfacing was one of the most anxious moments of my life, but when I cautiously lifted mouth, nose and eyes above the water, there was the boat a hundred yards away, steadily sailing on.

With a great intake of air I sank down again and began to swim underwater towards the shore; gently, so as to make no notice-attracting splash.

The water was chilly, but not as cold as I'd expected. The shore, when I came up again, looked about a mile away, though distances at sea were deceptive.

The boat sailed on peacefully. It must have had a name on it, I supposed, though in the flurry I hadn't seen one. I wondered how long it would be before they found I had gone. Supper time, with luck.

The land ahead looked a most promising haven. To the left it was rocky, with grassy cliffs, but straight ahead lay a much greener part, with houses and hotels, and a strip of sand. Civilization, hot baths, freedom and a razor. I swam towards them steadily, taking rests. A mile was a long way for a moderate swimmer, and I was nothing like as strong as I had been twelve days earlier.

I looked back at the boat. It had gone a good way along the coast: growing smaller.

The big mainsail was sagging down the mast.

God, I thought, my heart lurching, if they're taking down the sails they'll see the open hatch.

Time had run out. They knew I had gone.

I ploughed for the shore until I felt dizzy with the effort. Swam until I had grey dots before the eyes and even greyer dots in the mind.

I wasn't going back into that dark hole. I absolutely couldn't.

When I next looked back all the sails were down and the boat was turning.

The hotels ahead were in a sandy bay. Two big hotels, white, with rows of balconies, and a lot of smaller buildings all around. There were some people on the beach, and four or five standing in the water.

Five hundred yards, perhaps.

It would take me years to swim five hundred yards.

I pushed my absolutely useless muscles into frantic efforts. If I could only reach the other bathers, I would be just one more head.

The boat had not been travelling very fast under sail. They would motor back faster. I feared to look around; to see them close. My imagination heard him shouting and pointing, and steering the boat to intercept me, felt them grabbing me with boathooks and pulling me in. When in the end I did nerve myself for a look, it was bad enough, but still too far to distinguish anyone clearly.

Next time I looked, it was alarming. They were catching up like hares. The nearest point of land was still about three hundred yards away, and it was uneven rock, not easy shelving beach. The sand lay in the centre of the bay: the curving arms were shallow cliffs. I would never reach the sand, I thought.

And yet . . . sailing boats had deep keels. They wouldn't be able to motor right up to the beach. Perhaps, after all, I could get there.

I had never felt so tired, so leaden. The hardest steeplechase had never demolished me so completely, even those I'd lost from being unfit. My progress through the water grew slower and slower, when speed was all that mattered. In the end it took me all my time to stay afloat.

There was a current, which I hadn't noticed at first, carrying me to the left, drifting me off my line to the beach. Nothing fierce; but simply sapping. I hadn't enough kick left to overcome it.

Another look back.

Literally terrifying. I could see him on deck, standing in the bows, shading his eyes with his hand. He had come back on a course closer to the shore than when I'd jumped, and it was the shoreline he seemed to be scouring most closely.

I swam on with feeble, futile strokes. I could see that I was not going to reach the sand. The current was taking me inexorably towards the higher, left hand side of the bay, where there were trees to within ten feet of the waterline, and rocks below the trees.

When I'd got to the numb stage of thinking drowning would be preferable to recapture, and doubting if one *could* drown oneself in cold blood, I found suddenly that I could no longer see for miles along the coast. I had at last got within the embracing arms of the bay. When I looked back, I couldn't see the boat.

It didn't stay out of sight long. It crept along in a straight line until it reached the centre of the bay, and there dropped anchor. I watched it in sick glimpses over my shoulder. Saw them unbuckle a black rubber dinghy and lower it over the side. Caught an impression of them lowering an outboard engine, and oars, and of two of them climbing down into the boat.

I heard the outboard splutter into life. Only about thirty feet to go to touch the land. It seemed like thirty miles.

There was a man-made strip of concrete set into the rocks ahead of me at the water's edge. I glanced along the shore towards the beach, and saw that there were others. Aids to bathers. The most heartening aid in the world to the bather approaching at snail's pace with the hounds of hell at his back.

The dinghy pulled away from the anchored boat and pointed its bulky black shape towards the shore.

I reached the strip of concrete. It was a flat step, set only inches above the water.

No grips for hauling oneself out. Just a step. I put one hand flat on it and raised a foot to it, and used jelly muscles to flounder up onto my stomach.

Not enough. Not enough. The dinghy would come while I was lying there.

69

My heart was pounding. Effort and fear in equal measures. Utter desperation took me to hands and knees and set me crawling up the rocks to find shelter.

Ordinarily it would have been easy. It was a gentle shore, undemanding. A child could have jumped where I laboured. I climbed up about six feet of tumbled rocks and found a shallow gully, half full of water. I rolled into the hollow and lay there panting, hopelessly exhausted, listening to the outboard engine grow steadily louder.

They must have seen me, I thought despairingly. Seen me climbing up out of the sea. Yet if I'd stayed at the water's edge they would have found me just as surely. I lay in defeated misery and wondered how on earth I could live through whatever was coming.

The dinghy approached. I kept my head down. They were going to have to come and find me and carry me, and if I could raise enough breath I'd yell until some of the people on the beach took notice, except that they were far enough away to think it was all a game.

The engine died and I heard his voice, raised but not exactly shouting.

He said, 'Excuse me, but have you seen a friend of ours swim in from the sea? We think he fell overboard.'

A woman's voice answered him, from so close to me that I almost fainted.

'No, I haven't seen anybody.'

He said, 'He takes drugs. He might have been acting funny.'

'Serves him right, then,' she said, sanctimoniously.

'I've been reading. I haven't seen him. Have you come from that boat?'

'That's right. We think he fell overboard about here. We heard a splash, but we thought it was just a fish. Till after.'

'Sorry,' she said. 'Why don't you ask along the beach?'

'Just starting this side,' he said. 'We'll work round.'

There was a noise of oars being fitted into rowlocks, and the splash and squeak as they pulled away. I stayed where I was without moving, hoping she wouldn't have hysterics when she saw me, dreading that she would call them back.

I could hear him, away along the shore, loudly asking the same question of someone else.

Her voice said, 'Don't be frightened. I know you're there.'

I didn't answer her. She'd taken away what was left of my breath.

After a pause she said, 'Do you take drugs?'

'No,' I said. It was little more than a whisper.

'What did you say?'

'No.'

'Hm. Well, you'd better not move. They're methodical. I think I'll go on reading.'

Incredulously, I took her advice, lying half in and half out of the water, feeling heart and lungs subside slowly to a more manageable rhythm.

'They've landed on the beach,' she said.

My heart stirred up again. 'Are they searching?' I said anxiously.

'No. Asking questions, I should think.' She paused. 'Are they criminals?'

'I don't know.'

'But . . . would they take you from here by force? With people watching?'

'Yes. You heard them. If I shouted for help, they'd say I was crazy with drugs. No one would stop them.'

'They're walking round the far side of the bay,' she said. 'Asking people.'

'My name is Roland Britten,' I said. 'I live in Newbury, and I'm an accountant. I was kidnapped twelve days ago, and they've kept me on that boat ever since, and I don't know why. So please, whoever you are, if they do manage to get me back there, will you tell the police? I really do most desperately need help.'

There was a short silence. I thought that I must have overdone it; that she didn't believe me. Yet I'd had to tell her, as a precaution.

She apparently made up her mind. 'Well then,' she said briskly, 'time for you to vanish.'

'Where to?'

'My bedroom,' she said.

She was a great one for punches in the mental solar plexus. In spite of the grimness of things in general, I almost laughed.

'Can you see me?' I said.

'I can see your feet. I saw all of you when you climbed out of the sea and scrambled up here.'

'And how do I get to your bedroom dressed in a wet shirt and underpants and nothing else?'

'Do you want to avoid those men, or don't you?'

There was no answer to that.

'Stay still,' she said sharply, though I had not in fact moved. 'They're looking this way. Someone over there seems to be pointing in this direction.'

'Oh God.'

'Stay still.' There was a longish pause, then she said, 'They are walking back along the beach, towards their boat. If they don't stop there, but come on this way, we will go.'

I waited dumbly, and more or less prayed.

'There's a path above us,' she said. 'I will hand you a towel. Wrap it round you, and climb up to the path.'

'Are they coming?'

'Yes.'

A triangle of brightly striped bathing towel appeared over the rock by my head. There was little I'd ever wanted to do less than stand up out of my secure hiding place. My nerves were all against it.

'Hurry up,' she said. 'Don't look back.'

I stood up, dripping, with my back to the sea. Pulled the towel towards me, wrapped it round like a sarong, and tackled the rocky upgrade to the path. The respite in the gully had given me back a surprising amount of energy: or perhaps it was plain fear. In any case I climbed the second stage a great deal more nimbly than the first.

'I'm behind you,' her voice said. 'Don't look back. Turn right when you reach the path. And don't run.'

'Yes ma'am,' I said under my breath. Never argue with a guardian angel.

The path was fringed on both sides with trees, with a mixture of sand and bare rock underfoot. The sunshine dappled through the branches and at any other time would have looked pretty.

When the path widened she fell into step beside me, between me and the sea.

'Take the branch path to the left,' she said, drawing level. 'And don't walk too fast.'

I glanced at her, curious to see what she looked like. She matched her voice: a no-nonsense middle-aged lady with spectacles and a practical air. Self-confident. Tall: almost six feet. Thin, and far from a beauty.

She was wearing a pale-pink blouse, fawn cotton trousers, and sandshoes, and she carried a capacious canvas beach bag.

Beach. Swimming. In March.

'Where is this place?' I said.

'Cala St Galdana.'

'Where's that?'

'Minorca, of course.'

'*Where*?'

'Don't stop walking. Minorca.'

'Island next to Majorca?'

'Of course.' She paused. 'Didn't you know?'

I shook my head. The branch path reached the top of a shallow gradient and began to descend through more trees on the far side.

She peered to the right as we went over the brow.

'Those men are just coming along the lower path, heading towards where I was sitting. I think it would be a good idea to hurry a little now, don't you?'

'Understatement,' I said.

Hurrying meant stubbing my bare toes on various half-buried stones and feeling the dismal weakness again make rubber of my legs.

'While they are looking for you on the rocks, we will reach my hotel,' she said.

I shuffled along and saved my breath. Glanced over my shoulder. Only empty path. No pursuing furies. So why did I feel that they could see through earth and trees and know exactly where to find me?

'Over that little bridge, and across the road. Over there.' She pointed. 'That's the hotel.'

It was one of the two big white ones. We reached the wide glass doors and went inside. Made it unchallenged across the hall and into the lift. Rose to the fifth floor. She scooped some keys out of her beach bag, and let us into 507.

We had seen almost nobody on the way. Still enough warm sun for holidaymakers to be out on the beach and for the staff to be sleeping.

507 had a sea-view balcony, twin beds, two armchairs,

a yellow carpet, and orange and brown curtains. Regulation hotel room, with almost none of my saviour's belongings in sight.

She walked over to the glass door, which was wide open, and half stepped onto the balcony.

'Do you want to watch?' she said.

I looked cautiously over her shoulder. From that height one could see the whole panorama of the bay. There was the boat, anchored in the centre. There was the dinghy on the sand. The headland where I'd crawled out of the sea was to the right, the path leading to it from the beach showing clearly through the trees like a dappled yellow snake.

Along the path came the two men, my familiar warder in front, making for the sand. They trudged slowly across to the dinghy, still looking continually around, and pushed it into the sea.

They both climbed in. They started the outboard. They steered away from the beach.

I felt utterly drained.

'Do you mind if I sit down?' I said.

CHAPTER SIX

Thanks to telephones, consul, bank, and friends, I flew back to England the following evening, but not before I had collected further unforgettable memories of Miss Hilary Margaret Pinlock.

She asked me my measurements, descended to the local boutiques, and returned with new clothes.

She lent me her bathroom, inspected me cleaned and dressed, and decided to go shopping for a razor. I protested. She went. It was as easy to stop Miss Pinlock as an avalanche.

With some relief I scratched the twelve days' scruffy dark stubble off my face, one glance in the looking glass having persuaded me that I was not going to look better in a beard. The twelve days of indoor life had left me thin and pale, with grey hollows in cheeks and eye sockets which I didn't remember having before. Nothing that a little freedom wouldn't fix.

On her second expedition she had also bought bread, cheese and fruit, explaining that she was there on a package holiday, and that the hotel didn't cater for random visitors.

'I'll go down to dinner at seven as usual,' she said. 'You can eat here.'

Throughout all her remarks and actions ran the positive decision-making of one accustomed to command.

'Are you a children's nurse?' I asked curiously.

'No,' she said, unsmiling. 'A headmistress.'

'Oh.'

The smile came, briefly. 'Of a girls-only comprehensive, in Surrey.'

With a touch of sardonic humour she watched me reassess her in the light of that revelation. Not a do-gooding bossy spinster, but a fulfilled career woman of undoubted power.

'Yes. Well . . .' she shrugged. 'If you give me the numbers, I'll ask the switchboard for your calls.'

'And I need a bedroom,' I said.

'Your friends might return and ask about strangers needing bedrooms,' she said.

It had occurred to me too. 'Yes, but . . .' I said.

She pointed to one of the twin beds. 'You can sleep there. I am here alone. The friend who was coming with me had to cry off at the last minute.'

'But . . .' I stopped.

She waited calmly.

'All right,' I said. 'Thank you.'

When she returned from dinner she brought with her a piece of news and a bottle of wine.

'Your friend from the boat was downstairs in the lobby, asking everyone who speaks English if they saw a crazy young man come ashore today. Everyone said no. He looks extremely worried.'

'Probably thinks I drowned.'

The boat had gone from the bay. He must have reached another mooring and returned to Cala St Galdana by road. I wondered how long and how thoroughly he would persevere in his search: the more he feared whoever he was working for, the less he would give up.

The evening air was chilly. Miss Pinlock shut the glass door against the night sky and expertly opened her bottle of Marqués de Riscal.

'Tell me about your journey,' she said, handing me a glass.

I told her the beginning and the end, and not much of the middle.

'Extraordinary,' she said.

'When I get home I'll have a go at finding out what it was all about . . .'

She looked at me gravely. 'It may not be over.'

She had an uncomfortable habit of putting my worst fears into speech.

We drank the excellent wine and she told me a little of her busy life.

'I enjoy it,' she said positively.

'Yes, I see that.'

There was a pause. She looked carefully at the wine in her glass.

She said, 'Will you go to bed with me?'

I suppose I sat in an ungentlemanly heap with my mouth open. I closed it, conscious of the insult it conveyed.

When I'd got over the first shock, she looked up. Her face was calm and businesslike as before, but also suddenly there was vulnerability and self-consciousness. A blush started on her neck, and spread painfully upwards.

She was between forty-two and forty-six, I guessed. She had dark brown wavy hair, going grey, cut with shape but not much style. A broad, lined forehead, large nose, mouth turning down naturally at the corners, and small chin. Behind her glasses her eyes were brown and looked small, probably the effect of the lenses. Wrinkles grew where wrinkles grow; and there was no glow to her skin. A face of character, but not sexually attractive, at least not to me.

'Why?' I said, which was a pretty stupid question.

She blushed a little deeper and shook her head.

'Look,' I said, 'it isn't as simple as that. I can't . . . I mean, one can't just sort of switch that sort of thing on and off, like a tap.'

We sat in awkward silence. She put down her glass, and said, 'I'm sorry. It was a ridiculous thing to say. Please try and forget it.'

'You said it because it was in your mind. So . . . well . . . you must have meant it.'

80

She half smiled, ruefully. 'It's been in my mind, now and again, for a long time. You will find it extraordinary, but I have never . . . so to speak, slept with a man.'

'In this permissive age?' I said.

'There you are, you see. You find it hard to believe. But I've never been pretty, even as a child. And also I've always been, well . . . able to do things. Learn. Teach. Organize. Administrate. All the unfeminine things. All my life people have relied on me, because I was capable. I've always had health and energy, and I've enjoyed getting on, being given senior posts, and five years ago, being offered a headship. In most ways my life has been absorbing and gratifyingly successful.'

'But?' I suggested.

She nodded. 'But. I was never interested in boys when I was in my teens, and then I thought them callow, and at university I worked all hours to get a First, and after that I've always taught in girls' schools because frankly it is usually a man who's given the headship in a mixed school, and I've never fancied the role of male-ego-massager in second place. Nothing I've ever been or done has been geared to romance.'

'So why *now*?'

'I hope you won't be angry, but it is mostly curiosity, and the pursuit of knowledge.'

I wasn't angry. Just astounded.

Her blush had subsided as fast as it had risen. She was back on surer ground.

'For some time I've thought I ought to have had the

experience. Of sexual intercourse, that is. It didn't come
my way when I was young, but I didn't expect it, you see.
I think now that I should have tried to find a man, but
then, when I was at college, I was half scared of it, and I
didn't have any great urge, and I was engrossed in my
work. Afterwards for years it didn't bother me, until I
was thirty or so, and of course by that time all the men
one meets are married, and in any case, teaching among
women, one rarely meets any men, except officials, and
so on. I go to many official functions, of course, but
people tend not to ask unmarried women to private
social occasions.'

'What changed your mind?' I asked, fascinated.

'Oh, having to cope with highly-sexed young girls. The
modern lot are so clued up. So brash and outspoken. I
like them. But I have to arrange their sex-education
lessons, and in my time I've even taught them, from text
books. I feel it would be a great deal better if I knew . . .
what the sex act felt like. I feel at a disadvantage with
many of the older girls, particularly as this last term I had
to advise a pregnant fourteen-year-old. Fourteen! She
knows more than I do. How can I advise her?'

'Catholic priests don't have this problem,' I commented.

'Catholic priests may be respected for virginity, but
school-mistresses are not.' She paused, hesitating, and
went on. 'To be honest, I also find myself at a disadvantage with the married members of my staff. Some of
them have a tendency to patronize me, even uncon-

sciously. I don't like it. I would be able to cope with it perfectly, though, if I actually knew what they know.'

'Am I,' I said slowly, 'the first man you have asked?'

'Oh yes.' She smiled slightly and drank some wine. 'There are practically no men one *can* ask. Especially if one is a headmistress, and widely known. I certainly wouldn't jeopardize my job.'

'I can see that it would be difficult,' I said, thinking about it.

'So of course holidays are the only possibility,' she said. 'I've been on archaeological cruises to Greece, and all that sort of thing, and I've seen other couples join up, but it never happened to me. And then I've heard that some lonely women throw themselves at ski-instructors and waiters and men who perform for money, but somehow that isn't what I want. I mean, I don't want to despise myself. I want knowledge without guilt or shame.'

'The dream of Eden,' I said.

'What? Oh, yes.'

'What about your friend?' I said, pointing to the second bed.

She smiled twistedly. 'No friend, just an excuse for having come alone.'

'Friends being death to the pursuit of knowledge?'

'Exactly.'

We drank some more wine.

'I've been here since last Saturday,' she said. 'I always

take a complete break straight after the end of term, and
then go back refreshed for the new work.'

'A perfect system,' I said absently. 'Why didn't you . . .
er . . . throw me back, when the men in the dinghy came
after me?'

'If you mean, did I immediately see you as a . . .
possible . . . then no, of course not. I was fascinated, in a
way. I'd never seen anyone in such terror before. I
watched you from quite a long way out. Swimming, and
looking back. It wasn't until you reached the concrete
step, though, and I saw your face clearly, that I realized
that you were being *hunted*. It would take a certain men-
tality to point the hounds at an exhausted quarry gone to
ground, and I don't have it.'

'And thank God for that,' I said.

I stood up, and opened the glass door, and went out
onto the balcony. The cool night was clear, with bright
stars over the ageless Mediterranean. Waves rippled
softly round the edges of the bay, and the gentle moonlight shone on the wide, empty expanse where the boat
had been anchored.

It was the weirdest of debts. She had saved me from
recapture. I certainly owed her my wholeness of mind, if
not life itself. If the only payment she wanted was something I didn't much want to give, then that was simply too
bad. One extreme favour, I thought sardonically,
deserved another.

I went in, and sat down. Drank some wine with a dry
mouth.

'We'll try, if you like,' I said.

She sat very still. I had a swift impression that now I'd agreed she was hastily retreating: that the half-fear of her student days was definitely still there.

'You don't have to,' she said.

'No. I want to.' Heaven forgive all liars.

She said, as if speaking to herself, and not to me: 'I'll never have another chance.'

The voice of longing teetering on the brink of the leap in the dark. Her strength of mind, I saw, would carry her through. I admired her. I determined to make Hilary Pinlock's leap something that at least she wouldn't regret: if I could.

'First of all,' I said, 'we'll switch off the lights and sit by the window for a while, and talk about it.'

We sat facing each other in dim reflected moonlight, and I asked her some fairly medical questions, to which she gave straightforward replies.

'What if you get pregnant?' I said.

'I'd solve that later.'

'You want to go ahead?'

She took a deep breath. 'If you do.'

If I *can*, I thought.

'Then I think the best thing to do first would be to get undressed,' I said. 'Do you have a nightdress? And could you lend me a dressing gown?'

I reflected, as I put on her blue candlewick in the privacy of the bathroom, that deep physical tiredness was a rotten basis for the matter in hand. I yawned. I wanted above all to go to sleep.

When I went out she was sitting by the window in a long cotton nightgown which had a frill round the neckline, but was not, of course, transparent.

'Come on,' I said. 'We'll sit on the bed.'

She stood up. The nightgown accentuated her height and thinness, and revealed long narrow feet. I pulled back the bed-clothes, sat on the white sheet, and held my hand out towards her. She came, gripped my hand, and sat beside me.

'Right,' I said. 'Now, if at any point you want to stop, you've only got to say so.'

She nodded.

'Lie down, then,' I said, 'and imagine you are twenty.'

'Why?'

'Because this is not a brain matter. It's about the stimulation of nerve endings. About feeling, not thinking. If you think all the time of who you are, you may find it inhibiting. Age doesn't exist in the dark. If you imagine you are twenty, you will be twenty, and you'll find it liberating.'

'You're a most unusual man.'

'Oh sure,' I said. 'And you're a most unusual woman. So lie down.'

She gave a small unexpected chuckle, and did as I said.

'Take off your glasses,' I said, and she put them without comment on the bedside table. In the dim light her eyes looked larger, as I'd guessed, and her big nose smaller, and her determined mouth softer. I leaned over and kissed her lips, and if it was basically a nephew-to-aunt gesture it brought a smile to her face and a grin to my own.

It was the strangest lovemaking, but it did work. I looked back afterwards to the moment when she first took pleasure in the sensation of my stroking her skin; the ripple of surprise when she felt with her hands the size of an erect man; the passion with which she finally responded; and the stunning release into gasping incredulity.

'Is that,' she said, out of breath, 'is that what every woman feels?'

I knew she had reached a most satisfactory climax. 'I guess so,' I said. 'On good days.'

'Oh my goodness,' she said in a sort of exultation. 'So now I *know*.'

CHAPTER SEVEN

Thursday morning I went back to the office and tried to take up my life where it had left off.

The same smell of typewriters, filing cabinets, reams of paper. Same bustle, adding machines, telephones. Same heaps of too much work. All familiar, all unreal.

Our two assistants, Debbie and Peter, had had a rough time, they said aggrievedly, trying to account to everyone for my unaccountable absence. They had reported my disappearance to the police, who had said I was over twenty-one and had the right to duck out if I wanted to, and that they would look for me only if I'd committed a crime, or was clearly a missing victim. They had thought I had merely gone off on a celebratory binge after winning the Gold Cup.

'We told them you wouldn't have gone away for so long,' Peter said. 'But they didn't show much interest.'

'We wanted them to get in touch with Mr King, through Interpol,' Debbie complained. 'And they laughed at the idea.'

'I expect they would,' I said. 'So Trevor is still on his holiday?'

'He's not due back until Monday,' Peter said, surprised that I should have forgotten something I knew so well.

'Oh yes . . .'

I spent the morning re-organizing the timetable and getting Peter to make new appointments to replace those I'd missed, and the afternoon discovering that as far as the police were concerned, my troubles were still of little interest. I was back home, wasn't I? Unharmed. Without having to pay a ransom? Was there any form of extortion? No. Was I starved? No. Beaten? No. Tied with ropes, straps, shackles? No. Was I sure it wasn't a practical joke? They would look into it, they said: but one of them remarked that *he* wouldn't mind a free fortnight's trip to the Mediterranean, and his colleague laughed. I gathered that if I seriously wanted to get to know, I would have to do the investigating myself.

I did want to know. Not knowing felt dangerously unsafe, like standing behind a bad-tempered horse. If I didn't know why I'd been taken the first time, how was I to stop it happening again?

Thursday evening I collected my Dolomite, which had been moved to the Cheltenham racecourse manager's front drive. ('Where on earth have you been? We traced that it was your car through the police.') Next I drove to the house of the racecourse valet to pick up my wallet and keys and racing saddle. ('Where on earth have you been? I gave the racecourse manager your car keys, I hope that's all right.') Then I drove back to my cottage (having spent the previous night in an airport hotel), and with faint-hearted caution let myself in.

No one was waiting there in the dark, with coshes or ether or one-way tickets to sail lockers. I switched on all the lights and poured myself a stiff Scotch and told myself to calm down and take a better grip.

I telephoned the trainer I regularly rode early morning exercise for ('Where on earth have you been?') and arranged to start again on Monday: and I rang a man who had asked me to ride in a hunter 'chase, to apologize for not turning up. I saw no reason not to answer the questions about where I'd been, so I told them all: abducted and taken on a boat to Minorca, and I didn't know why. I thought at least that someone might come up with a possible explanation, but everyone I told sounded as flummoxed as I felt.

There wasn't much food in the cottage, and the steak in the fridge had grown whiskers. I decided on spaghetti, with chopped up cheese melting on it, but before starting to cook I went upstairs to change new jacket for old sweater, and to make a detour to the bathroom.

I glanced casually out of the bathroom window and spent a frozen instant in pure panic.

There was a man in the garden, looking towards the downstairs rooms of the cottage. The light from the sitting-room window fell brightly on his face.

I hadn't consciously remembered him, but I knew him

at once, in one heart-stopping flash of the inner eye. He was the fake St John's Ambulance man from Cheltenham races.

Behind him, in the road, stood a car, with gleams of light edging its roof and windows. A second man was levering himself out of the passenger's seat, carrying what looked like a plastic bag containing cotton wool. A third figure, dimly seen, was heading through the garden to the back of the house.

They couldn't, I thought: surely they couldn't think they would trick me again. But with three of them, they hardly needed tricks.

The St John's man waved his arm to the man by the car, and pointed, and the two of them took up positions, one on each side of my front door, out of sight of anyone opening it from the inside. The St John's man stretched out an arm and rang my bell.

I unfroze.

Wonderful how terror sharpened the wits. There was only one place I could hide, and that was in my bedroom. The speed with which I'd gone over the side of the boat was nothing compared with my disappearance inside the cottage.

Downstairs in the sitting-room the huge old fireplace had at one side incorporated a bread oven, which the people living there before me had removed, constructing instead a head-high alcove with display shelves. Wanting a safe place in which to keep valuables, they had opened the upper part of the bread oven space into the bedroom above, where it formed a sort of box below the floor of the built-in wardrobe. Not having much in the way of valuables, I stored my two suitcases in there instead.

I opened the wardrobe door, and pulled up the hinged flap of flooring, and hauled out the cases.

The door bell rang again, insistently.

Lowering myself into the space took seconds, and I had the wardrobe door shut and the flap of floor almost in place when they burst in through the front door.

They rampaged through the place, opening and slamming doors, and shouting, and finally gathering all together downstairs.

'He must be bloody here.'

'Britten! Britten, come out, we know you're here.'

'The effing bastard's scarpered.'

I could hear every loud word through the chipboard partition between my hiding place and the sitting-room. I felt horribly vulnerable sitting there, level with the picture over the mantelshelf, practically in the room with them, hidden only by a thin piece of wall.

'He couldn't have seen us coming.'

'He never got out of the back, I'll tell you that for sure.'

'Then where the bleeding hell is he?'

'How about those suitcases of his upstairs?'

'No. He ain't in them. They're too small. And I looked.'

'He must be meaning to bleeding scarper.'

'Yeah.'

'Take another butcher's upstairs. He must be here somewhere.'

They searched the whole house again, crashing about with heavy boots.

One of them opened the wardrobe above me for the second time, and saw nothing but clothes, as before. I sat under their feet and sweated, and felt my pulse shoot up to the hundreds.

'Look under the bed,' he said.

'Can't. The bed's right on the floor.'

'How about the other bedroom, then?'

'I looked. He ain't there.'

'Well, bleeding well look again.'

The wardrobe door closed above me. I wiped the sweat out of my eyes and tried to ease my legs without scraping my shoes on the wall and making a noise. I was half sitting, half lying, in a recess about three feet long by two feet deep, and just wide enough for my shoulders. My knees were bent acutely, with my heels against the backs of my thighs. It was a bad position for every muscle I could think of.

Two of them came into the sitting-room, one after the other.

'What you got there? Here, let me see.'

'None of your bleeding business.'

'It's his wallet. You've got his wallet.'

'Yeah. Well, it was in his bedroom.'

'Well, bleeding well put it back.'

'Not likely, he's got thirty quid in it.'

'You'll effing well do as I say. You know the orders, same as I do. Don't steal nothink, don't break nothink. I told you.'

'You can have half, then.'

'Give it to me. I'll put it back. I don't trust you.' It was the St John's man talking, I thought.

'It's bloody stupid, not nicking what we can get.'

'You want the fuzz on our necks? They didn't bloody look for him last time, and they won't bloody look for him this time, either, but they will if they find his place has been turned over. Use your bloody loaf.'

'We ain't got him yet.'

'Matter of time. He's round here some place. Bound to be.'

'He won't come back if he sees us in here.'

'No, you got a point there. Tell you what, we'll turn the lights off and wait for him, and jump him, like.'

'He left all the lights on, himself. He won't come in if they're off.'

'Best if one of us waits in the kitchen, like, and the other two in the garden. Then when he gets here we can jump him from both sides, right, just as he's coming back through the door.'

'Yeah.'

Into these plans there suddenly came a fresh voice, female and enquiring.

'Mr Britten? Mr Britten, are you there?'

I heard her push the front door open and take the step into the sitting-room.

The voice of my next-door neighbour.

Yes, Mrs Morris, I'm here, I thought. And it would take more than me and a small plump senior citizen to fight off my unwanted guests.

'Who are you?' she said.

'Friends of his. Calling on him, like.'

'He's away,' she said sharply.

'No he's not. He's back. His car's round the side. And he's having a drink, see? Whisky.'

'Then where is he? Mr Britten?' she called.

'Ain't no use, lady. He's out. We're waiting for him, like.'

'I don't think you should be in here.' A brave lady, old Mrs Morris.

'We're friends of his, see.'

'You don't look like his friends,' she said.

'Know his friends, then, do yer?'

A certain nervousness crept into her voice, but the resolution was still there.

'I think you'd better wait outside.'

There was a pause, then the St John's man said, 'Where do you think he could be? We've searched all over for him.'

Let her not know about this hiding place, I prayed. Let her not think of it.

'He might've gone to the pub,' she said. 'Why don't you go down there? To the Fox.'

'Yeah, maybe.'

'Anyway, I think I'll just see you out.'

Intrepid little Mrs Morris. I heard them all go out, and shut the front door behind them. The lock clicked decisively. The cottage was suddenly still.

I lay quiet, listening for their car to start.

Nothing happened.

They were still there, I thought. Outside. Round my house. Waiting.

On the mantelshelf, the clock ticked.

I cautiously pushed up the flap over my head, and sat up, straightening knees, back and neck, with relief.

The light in my bedroom was still on, shining in a crack under the wardrobe door. I left the door shut. If they saw so much as a shadow move they would know for sure I was inside the house.

I reflected that I had had a good deal too much practice at passing uncertain hours in small dark places.

The lock clicked on my front door.

One gets to know the noises of one's own house so well that sight is unnecessary for interpretation. I heard the unmistakable sound of the hinges, and the gritty sound of a shoe on the bare flagstones of the entrance hall. Then there were quiet noises in the sitting-room itself, and low voices, and the squeak of the door to the kitchen. They had come back in a way that would not bring Mrs Morris.

I sat rigidly, wondering whether to slide down into the smaller space and risk them hearing my movements, or stay with head and shoulders above floor level and risk them searching my clothes cupboard yet again. If I coughed or sneezed, or as much as knocked the chip-board with my elbow as I slid down into the safer hiding place, they would hear me. I sat immobile, stretching my own ears and wondering despairingly how long they would stay.

Breathing evenly was difficult, controlling my heart-beat was impossible. Acute anxiety over a period of hours was highly shattering to the nerves.

From time to time I could hear them moving and murmuring, but could no longer distinctly hear their words. I supposed that they too were hiding, waiting out of sight for me to come home. It was almost funny when one thought of it: them hiding behind the furniture and me within the walls.

Unfunny if they found me. More like unfaceable.

I took a deep, shaky breath, one of many.

Someone began to come quietly upstairs. The familiar creaks of the old treads fizzed through my body like electric shocks. The risk of moving had to be taken. I tucked my elbows in and bent my knees, and eased myself back under the floor. The flap came down hard on my hair and I thought wildly that they must have heard it: but no one arrived with triumphant shouts, and the awful suspense just went on and on.

I got pains from being bent up, and I got cramps, but there was nothing I could do about that except sur-render.

One of them spent a good time in my bedroom. I could hear his footfall through the floorboards, and the small thuds of drawers shutting. Guessed he was no longer looking for me, but at what I owned. It didn't make his nearness to me any safer.

The fear seemed endless; but everything ends. I heard them murmuring again in the sitting-room, and shutting the kitchen door. The man upstairs went down again. More murmurings: a chorus. Then silence for a while. Then a step or two in the hall, and the click of the front door closing.

I waited, thinking that only one of them had gone out.

Their car started. Shifted quietly into gear. Drove off.

I still lay without moving, not trusting that it was over, that it wasn't a trick: but the absolute quietness persisted, and in the end I pushed up the flap of the floor and levered myself with much wincing and pins and needles onto my bedroom carpet.

The lights were still on, but the black square of window was grey. The whole night had passed. It was dawn.

I threw a few things into one of the suitcases and left the cottage ten minutes later.

The Yale lock on the front door showed no signs of forcing, and I guessed they must have opened it with a credit card, as I myself had done once when I'd locked myself out. My car stood untouched where I'd left it, and even my half-drunk glass of Scotch was still on the sitting-room table.

Feeling distinctly unsettled I had a wash, shave and breakfast at the Chequers Hotel, and then went to the police.

'Back again?' they said.

They listened, made notes, asked questions.

'Do you know who they were?'

'No.'

'Any evidence of a forced entry?'

'No.'

'Anything stolen?'

'No.'

'Nothing we can do, sir.'

'Look,' I said, 'these people are trying to abduct me. They've succeeded once, and they're trying again. Can't you do a damn thing to help?'

They seemed fairly sympathetic, but the answer was no. They hadn't enough men or money to mount a round-the-clock guard on anyone for an indefinite period without a very good reason.

'Isn't the threat of abduction a very good reason?'

'No. If you believe the threat, you could hire yourself a private bodyguard.'

'Thanks very much,' I said. 'But if anyone reports me missing again, I won't have gone by choice, and you might do me a favour and start looking.'

'If they do, sir, we will.'

*

99

I went to the office and sat at my desk and watched my hands shake. Whatever I normally had in the way of mental and physical stamina was at a very low ebb.

Peter came in with a cable and his usual expression of not quite grasping the point, and handed me the bad news. CAR BROKEN DOWN RETURNING WEDNESDAY APOLOGIES TREVOR.

'You read this?' I asked Peter.

'Yes.'

'Well, you'd better fetch Mr King's list, for next week, and his appointment book.'

He went on the errand and I sat and looked blankly at the cable. Trevor had sent it from some town I'd never heard of in France, and had given no return address. He wouldn't be worried, wherever he was. He would be sure I could take his extra few days in my stride.

Peter came back with the list and I laced my fingers together to keep them still. What did people take for tranquillizers?

'Get me some coffee,' I said to Peter. His eyebrows rose. 'I know it's only a quarter past nine,' I said, 'but get me some coffee . . . please.'

When he brought the coffee I sent him to fetch Debbie, so that I could share between them the most urgent jobs. Neither of them had a good brain, but they were both persistent, meticulous plodders, invaluable qualities in accountants' assistants. In many offices the assistants were bright and actively studying to become accountants themselves, but Trevor for some reason seemed always to prefer working with the unambitious sort. Peter was twenty-two, Debbie twenty-four. Peter, I thought, was a latent homosexual who hadn't quite realized it. Debbie, mousy-haired, big-busted, and pious, had a boyfriend working in a hardware shop. Peter occasionally made jokes about screws, which shocked her.

They sat opposite my desk with notebooks poised, both of them looking at me with misgiving.

'You really look awfully ill,' Debbie said. 'Worse even than yesterday. Grey, sort of.' There seemed to be more ghoulish relish in her voice than concern.

'Yes, well, never mind that,' I said. 'I've looked at Mr King's list, and there are a few accounts that won't wait until he gets back.' There were two he should have seen to before he went, but no one was perfect. 'Certificate for the solicitors, Mr Crest, and Mr Grant. I'm afraid they are already overdue. Could you bring all the papers for those two in here, Debbie? Later, I mean. Not this instant. Then there are the two summonses to appear before the Commissioners next Thursday. I'll apply for postponements for those, but you'd better bring all the books in here, Debbie, anyway, and I'll try and make a start on them.'

'That's the Axwood stables, is it? And Millrace Stud?'

'Not the stud; that's the week after. Mr King can deal with that. The Axwood stables, yes, and those corn merchants, Coley Young.'

'The Coley Young books aren't here yet,' Peter said.

'Well, for crying out loud, didn't you do what I said two weeks ago, and tell them to send them?' I could hear the scratch in my voice and did my best to stop it. 'OK,' I said slowly. 'Did you ask them to send them?'

'Yes, I did.' Peter tended to look sulky. 'But they haven't come.'

'Ring them again, would you? And what about the Axwood stables?'

'You checked those yourself, if you remember.'

'Did I?' I looked back as if to a previous existence. The two summonses to appear before the Commissioners were not particularly serious. We seldom actually went. The summonses were issued when the Inland Revenue thought a particular set of accounts were long overdue: a sort of goad to action. It meant that Trevor or I asked for a postponement, did the accounts, and sent them in before the revised date. End of drama. The two summonses in question had arrived after Trevor had left for his holidays, which was why he hadn't dealt with them himself.

'You said the petty cash book hadn't arrived,' Peter said.

'Did I? Did you ask them to send it?'

'Yes, I did, but it hasn't come.'

I sighed. 'Ring them again.'

A great many clients saw no urgency at all in getting their accounts done, and requests from us for further information or relevant papers were apt to be ignored for weeks.

'Tell them both they really will have to go before the Commissioners if they don't send those books.'

'But they won't really, will they?' Peter said. Not the brightest of boys, I thought.

'I'll get adjournments anyway,' I said patiently, 'but Trevor will need those books to hand the second he gets back.'

Debbie said, 'Mr Wells rang three times yesterday afternoon.'

'Who is Mr Wells? Oh yes. Mr Wells.'

'He says one of his creditors is applying to have him made bankrupt and he wants to know what you're going to do about it.'

I'd forgotten all the details of Mr Wells' troubles. 'Where are his books?' I asked.

'In one of those boxes,' Debbie said, pointing. A three-high row of large cardboard boxes ran along the wall under the window. Each box had the name of the client on it, in large black letters, and each contained the cash books, invoices, receipts, ledgers, paying-in books, bank statements, petty cash records, stocktakings and general paraphernalia needed for the assessment of taxes. Each of the boxes represented a task I had yet to do.

It took me an average of two working days to draw up the annual accounts for each client. Some audits took longer. I had roughly two hundred clients. The thing was impossible.

Trevor had collared the bigger firms and liked to

spend nearly a week on each. He dealt with seven clients. No wonder Commissioners' summonses fell on us like snow.

Peter and Debbie did most of the routine work, checking bank statements against cheque numbers, and against invoices paid. Someone extra to share that work would only help Trevor and me to a certain extent. Taking a third, fully equal partner would certainly reduce the pressure, but it would also entail dividing the firm's profits into three instead of two, which would mean a noticeable drop in income. Trevor was totally opposed. Amalgamation with the London firm meant Trevor not being boss and me not going racing... a fair sized impasse, all in all.

'Debbie and I didn't get our pay cheques last week,' Peter said. 'Nor did Bess.' Bess was the typist.

'And the water heater in the washroom is running cold,' Debbie added. 'And you did say I could go to the dentist this afternoon at three-thirty.'

'Sorry about all the extra work,' Peter said, not sounding it, 'but I'm afraid it's my Friday for the Institute of Accounting Staff class.'

'Mm,' I said. 'Peter, telephone to Leyhill Prison and ask if Connaught Powys is still there.'

'What?'

'Leyhill Prison. Somewhere in Gloucestershire. Get the number from directory enquiries.'

'But . . .'

'Just go and do it,' I said. 'Connaught Powys. Is he still there.'

He went out looking mystified, but then he, like Debbie, dated from after the searchingly difficult court case. Debbie went to fetch the first batch of the papers I needed, and I began on the solicitors' certificates.

Since embezzlement of clients' trust monies had become a flourishing industry, laws had been passed to ensure that auditors checked every six months to see that the cash and securities which were supposed to be in a solicitor's care actually were there. If they weren't, Nemesis swiftly struck the solicitor off the Roll. If they were, the auditor signed the certificate and pocketed his fee.

Peter returned as if he'd come from a dangerous mission, looking noble.

'The prison said he was released six weeks ago, on February 16th.'

'Thanks.'

'I had a good deal of trouble in getting through.'

'Er ... well done,' I said. He still looked as if he thought more praise was due, but he didn't get it.

If Connaught Powys had been out for six weeks, he would have had a whole month to fix me up with a voyage. I tried hard to concentrate on the checking for the certificates but the sail locker kept getting in the way.

Solicitor Grant's affair tallied at about the third shot, but I kept making errors with Denby Crest's. I realized I'd always taken clarity of mind for granted, like walking:

one of those things you don't consciously value until
you've lost it. Numbers, from my infancy, had been like a
second language, understood without effort. I checked
Denby Crest's figures five times and kept getting a fifty
thousand pounds' discrepancy, and knowing him, as he
occasionally did work for us, it was ridiculous. Denby
Crest was no crook, I thought in exasperation. It's my
useless muddle-headed thought processes. Somewhere I
was transposing a decimal point, making a mountain out
of a molehill discrepancy of probably five pounds or fifty
pence.

In the end I telephoned his office and asked to speak
to him.

'Look, Denby,' I said, 'I'm most awfully sorry, but are
you sure we've got all the relevant papers?'

'I expect so,' he said, sounding impatient. 'Why don't
you leave it for Trevor? He gets back to England
tomorrow, doesn't he?'

I explained about the broken-down car. 'He won't be
back in the office until Wednesday or Thursday.'

'Oh.' He sounded disconcerted and there was a perceptible pause. 'All the same,' he said, 'Trevor is used to
our ways. Please leave our certificate until he gets back.'

'But it's overdue,' I said.

'Tell Trevor to call me,' he said. 'And now, I'm sorry,
but I have a client with me. So if you'll excuse me . . .'

He disconnected. I shuffled his papers together thankfully and thought that if he wanted to risk waiting for
Trevor it was certainly all right by me.

At twelve-thirty Peter and Debbie went out to lunch, but I didn't feel hungry. I sat in shirtsleeves before the newly tackled sea of Mr Wells' depressing papers: put my elbows on the desk, and propped my forehead on the knuckles of my right hand, and shut my eyes. Thought a lot of rotten thoughts and wondered about buying myself a one-way ticket to Antarctica.

A voice said, 'Are you ill, asleep or posing for Rodin?'

I looked up, startled.

She was standing in the doorway. Young, fair, slender pretty.

'I'm looking for Trevor,' she said.

One couldn't have everything, I supposed.

CHAPTER EIGHT

'Don't I know you?' I said, puzzled, standing up.

'Sure.' She looked resigned, as if this sort of thing happened often. 'Cast your mind back to long hair, no lipstick, dirty jeans and ponies.'

I looked at the short bouncy bob, the fashionable make-up, the swirling brown skirt topped by a neat waist-length fur-fabric jacket. Someone's daughter, I thought; recently and satisfactorily grown up.

'Whose daughter?' I said.

'My own woman.'

'Reasonable.'

She was enjoying herself, pleased with her impact on men.

'Jossie Finch, actually.'

'Wow,' I said.

'Every grub spreads its wings.'

'To where will you fly?'

'Yes,' she said, 'I've heard you were smooth.'

'Trevor isn't here, I'm afraid.'

'Mm. Still on his hols?'

I nodded.

'Then I was to deliver the same message to you, if you were here instead.'

'Sit down?' I suggested, gesturing to a chair.

'Can't stop. Sorry. Message from Dad. What are you doing about the Commissioners? He said he was absolutely not going before any so-and-so Commissioners next Thursday, or lurid words to that effect.'

'No, he won't have to.'

'He also says he would have sent the petty cash book, or whatever, in with me this morning, but his secretary is sick, and if you ask me she's the sickest thing that ever broke fingernails on a typewriter, and she has not done something or other with petty cash receipts or vouchers, or whatever it is you need. However...' she paused, drawing an exaggerated breath. 'Dad says, if you would like to drop in this evening you could go round the yard with him at evening stables, and have a noggin afterwards, and he will personally press into your hot little palms the book your assistant has been driving him mad about.'

'I'd like that,' I said.

'Good. I'll tell him.'

'And will you be there?'

'Ah,' she said, her eyes laughing, 'a little uncertainty is the HP sauce on the chips.'

'And the spice of life to you, too.'

She gave me an excellent smile, spun on her heel so

that the skirt swirled and the hair bounced, and walked out of the office.

Jossie Finch, daughter of William Finch, master of Axwood Stables. I knew her father in the way all long-time amateur riders knew all top trainers; enough to greet and chat to at the races. Since his was one of the racing accounts which pre-dated my arrival in the firm, and which Trevor liked to do himself, I had never before actually visited his yard.

I was interested enough to want to go, in spite of all my troubles. He had approximately ninety horses in his care, both jumpers and flat racers, and winners were taken for granted. Apart from Tapestry, most of the horses I usually rode were of moderate class, owned with more hope than expectation. To see a big stableful of top performers was always a feast. I would be safe from abduction there. And Jossie looked a cherry on the top.

When Peter and Debbie came back I laid into them for going out and leaving the outer door unlocked, and they adopted put-upon expressions and said they thought it was all right, as I was there, which would stop people sneaking in to steal things.

My fault, I thought more reasonably. I should have locked it after them myself. I would have to reshape a lot of habits. It could easily have been the enemy who walked in, not Jossie Finch.

I spent part of the afternoon on Mr Wells, but more of it trying to trace Connaught Powys.

We had his original address on file, left over from the

days when he had rigged the computer and milked his firm of a quarter of a million pounds in five years. The firm's audit was normally Trevor's affair, but one year, when Trevor was away a great deal with an ulcer, I had done it instead, and by some fluke had discovered the fraud. It had been one of those things you don't believe even when it is in front of your eyes. Connaught Powys had been an active director, and had paid his taxes on a comfortable income. The solid, untaxed lolly had disappeared without trace, but Connaught himself hadn't been quick enough.

I tried his old address. A sharp voice on the telephone told me the new occupants knew nothing of the Powys' whereabouts, and wished people would stop bothering them, and regretted the day they'd ever moved into a crook's house.

I tried his solicitors, who froze when they heard who was trying to find him. They could not, they said, divulge his present address without his express permission: which, their tone added, he was as likely to give as Shylock to a church bazaar.

I tried Leyhill Prison. No good.

I tried finally a racing acquaintance called Vivian Iverson who ran a gambling club in London and always seemed to know of corruption scandals before the stories publicly broke.

'My dear Ro,' he said, 'you're fairly non gratis in that quarter, don't you know.'

'I could guess.'

111

'You put the shivers up embezzlers, my friend. They're leaving the Newbury area in droves.'

'Oh sure. And I pick the Derby winner every year.'

'You may well jest, my dear chap, but the whisper has gone round.' He hesitated. 'Those two little dazzlers, Glitberg and Ownslow, have been seen talking to Powys, who has got rid of his indoor pallor under a sun lamp. The gist, so I'm fairly reliably told, was a hate-Britten chorus.'

'With vengeance intended?'

'No information, my dear chap.'

'Could you find out?'

'I only *listen*, my dear Ro,' he said. 'If I hear the knives are out, I'll tell you.'

'You're a pet,' I said dryly.

He laughed. 'Connaught Powys comes here to play, most Fridays.'

'What time?'

'You do ask a lot, my dear chap. After dinner to dawn.'

'How about making me an instant member?'

He sighed heavily. 'If you are bent on suicide, I'll tell the desk to let you in.'

'See you,' I said. 'And thanks.'

I put down the receiver and stared gloomily into space. Glitberg and Ownslow. Six years apiece, reduced for good behaviour . . . They could have met Connaught Powys in Leyhill, and it would have been no joy to any of them that I had put them all there.

Glitberg and Ownslow had served on a local council and robbed the ratepayers blind, and I'd turned them up through some dealings they'd done with one of my clients. My client had escaped with a fine, and had removed his custom from me with violent curses.

I wondered how much time all the embezzlers and bent solicitors and corrupted politicians in Leyhill Prison spent in thinking up new schemes for when they got out. Glitberg and Ownslow must already have been out for about six months.

Debbie had gone to the dentist and Peter to his Institute of Accounting Staff class, and this time I did lock the door behind them.

I felt too wretchedly tired to bother any further with Mr Wells. The shakes of the morning had gone, but even the swift tonic of Jossie Finch couldn't lift the persistent feeling of threat. I spent an hour dozing in the armchair we kept for favoured clients and when it was time, locked the filing cabinets and my desk and every door in the office, and went down to my car.

There was no one hiding behind the front seats. No one lurking round the edges of the car park. Nothing in the boot except the suitcase I'd stowed there that morning. I started up and drove out into the road, assaulted by nothing but my own nerves.

William Finch's yard lay south-west of Newbury: a huge spread of buildings sheltering in a hollow, with a creeper-covered Victorian mansion rising on the hillside above. I arrived at the house just as Finch was

113

coming out of it, and we walked down together to the first cluster of boxes.

'Glad you could come,' he said.

'It's a treat.'

He smiled with easy charm. A tall man, going grey at about fifty, very much in command of himself and everything else. He had a broad face, fine well-shaped mouth, and the eyes of experience. Horses and owners thrived in his care, and years of success had given him a stature he plainly enjoyed.

We went from box to box, spending a couple of minutes in each. Finch told me which horse we were looking at, with some of its breeding and form. He held brief reassurance conversations in each case with the lad holding the horse's head, and with his head lad, who walked round with us. If all was well, he patted the horse's neck and fed him a carrot from a bag which his head lad carried. A practised important routine evening inspection, as carried out by every trainer in the country.

We came to an empty box in a full row. Finch gestured to it with a smile.

'Ivansky. My National runner. He's gone up to Liverpool.'

I almost gaped like an idiot. I'd been out of touch with the normal world so much that I had completely forgotten that the Grand National was due that Saturday.

I cleared my throat. 'He should ... er ... have a fair chance at the weights.' It seemed a fairly safe comment, but he disagreed.

'Ten twelve is far too much on his Haydock form. He's badly in with Wasserman, don't you think?'

I raked back for all the opinions I'd held in the safe and distant life of three weeks ago. Nothing much surfaced.

'I'm sure he'll do well,' I said.

He nodded as if he hadn't noticed the feebleness of the remark, and we went on. The horses were truly an impressive bunch, glowing with good feeding, thorough grooming and well-judged exercise. I ran out of compliments long before he ran out of horses.

'Drink?' he said, as the head lad shut the last door.

'Great.'

We walked up to the house, and he led the way into a sitting-room-cum-office. Chintz-covered sofa and chairs, big desk, table with drinks and glasses, walls covered with framed racing photographs. Normal affluent trainer ambience.

'Gin?' he said.

'Scotch, if you have it.'

He gave me a stiff one and poured gin like water for himself.

'Your health,' he said.

'And yours.'

We drank the ritual first sip, and he gestured to me to sit down.

'I've found that damned cash book for you,' he said, opening a drawer in the desk. 'There you are. Book, and file of petty cash receipts.'

'That's fine.'

'And what about these Commissioners?'

'Don't worry, I've applied for a postponement.'

'But will they grant it?'

'Never refused us yet,' I said. 'They'll set a new date about a month ahead, and we'll do your accounts and audit before then.'

He relaxed contentedly over his draught of gin. 'We can expect Trevor here next week, then? Counting hay bales and saddles?' There was humour in his voice at the thoroughness ahead.

'Well,' I said, 'maybe at the end of the week, or the one after. He won't be back until Wednesday or Thursday.' Did 'Returning Wednesday', I wondered, mean *travelling* Wednesday, or turning up for work? 'I'll do a lot of the preliminary paperwork for him, to save time.'

Finch turned to the drinks table and unscrewed the gin. 'I thought he was due back on Monday.'

'His car's broken down somewhere in France.'

'That'll please him.' He drank deeply. 'Still, if you make a start on things, the audit should get done in time.'

'Don't worry about the Commissioners,' I said; but everyone did worry when the peremptory summons dropped through their door. If one neither asked for a postponement nor attended at the due hour, the Commissioners would fix one's year's tax at whatever figure they cared to, and to that assessment there was no appeal. As such assessments were customarily far higher than the amount of tax actually due, one avoided them like black ice.

To my pleasure, the swirly brown skirt and bouncy fair hair made a swooping entrance. She was holding a marmalade cat which was trying to jump out of her arms.

'Damn thing,' she said, 'why won't he be *stroked*.'

'It's a mouser,' said her father, unemotionally.

'You'd think it would be glad of a cuddle.'

The cat freed itself and bolted. Jossie shrugged. 'Hello,' she said to me. 'So you got here.'

'Mm.'

'Well,' she said to her father, 'what did he say?'

'Eh? Oh . . . I haven't asked him yet.'

She gave him a fond exasperated smile and said to me, 'He wants to ask you to ride a horse for him.'

Finch shook his head at her, and I said, 'When?'

'Tomorrow,' Jossie said. 'At Towcester.'

'Er,' I said, 'I'm not really ultra fit.'

'Nonsense. You won the Gold Cup a fortnight ago. You must be.'

'Josephine,' her father said. 'Clam up.' He turned to me. 'I'm flying up to Liverpool in the morning, but I have this horse in at Towcester, and to be blunt he's still entered there only because someone forgot to scratch him by the eleven o'clock deadline this morning . . .'

'The chronically sick secretary,' muttered Jossie.

'So we've either got to run him after all or pay a fine, and I was toying with the idea of sending him up there, if I could get a suitable jockey.'

'Most of them having gone to the National,' Jossie added.

'Which horse?' I said.

'Notebook. Novice hurdler. Four-year-old chestnut gelding, in the top yard.'

'The one with the flaxen mane and tail?'

'That's right. He's run a couple of times so far. Shows promise, but still green.'

'Last of twenty-six at Newbury,' Jossie said cheerfully. 'It won't matter a curse if you're not fit.' She paused. 'I've been delegated to saddle it up, so you might do us a favour and come and ride it.'

'Up to you,' Finch said.

The delegated saddler was a powerful attraction, even if Notebook himself was nothing much.

'Yes,' I said weakly. 'OK.'

'Good.' Jossie gave me a flashing smile. 'I'll drive you up there, if you like.'

'I would like,' I said regretfully, 'but I'll be in London tonight. I'll go straight to Towcester from there.'

'I'll meet you outside the weighing room, then. He's in the last race, by the way. He would be.'

Novice hurdles were customarily first or last (or both), on a day's programme: the races a lot of racegoers chose to miss through lunch or leaving early to avoid the crush. The poor-relation races for the mediocre majority, where every so often a new blazing star scorched out of the ruck on its way to fame.

Running horses in novice hurdles meant starting from

118

home early or getting back late; but there were far more runners in novice hurdles than in any other type of race.

When I left it was Jossie who came back with me through the entrance hall to see me off. As we crossed a vast decrepit Persian rug I glanced at the large dark portraits occupying acres of wall space.

'Those are Nantuckets, of course,' she said, following my gaze. 'They came with the house.'

'Po-faced lot,' I said.

'You did know that Dad doesn't actually own all this?'

'Yes, I actually did know.' I smiled to myself, but she saw it.

She said defensively, 'All right, but you'd be surprised how many people make up to me, thinking that they'll marry the trainer's daughter and step into all this when he retires.'

'So you like to establish the ground rules first?'

'OK, greyhound-brain, I'd forgotten you'd know from Trevor.'

I knew in general that Axwood Stables Ltd belonged to an American family, the Nantuckets, who rarely took much personal interest in the place except as a business asset. It had been bought and brought to greatness in the fifties by a rumbustious tycoon thrown up atypically from prudent banking stock. Old Naylor Nantucket had brought his energies and enterprise to England, had fallen in love with English racing, had built a splendid modern stable yard and filled it with splendid horses. He had engaged the young William Finch to train them for him, and the middle-aged William Finch was still doing it for his heirs, except that nowadays nine tenths of the horses belonged to other owners, and the young Nantuckets, faintly ashamed of Uncle Naylor, never crossed the Atlantic to see their own horses perform.

'Doesn't your father ever get tired of training for absent owners?' I said.

'No. They don't argue. They don't ring him up in the middle of the night. And when they lose, they don't complain. He says training would be a lot easier if *all* owners lived in New York.'

She stood on the doorstep to wave me goodbye, assured and half-mocking, a girl with bright brown eyes, graceful neck, and neat nose and mouth in between.

I booked into the Gloucester Hotel, where I'd never stayed before, and ate a leisurely and much needed dinner in a nearby restaurant. I shouldn't have accepted the ride on Notebook, I thought ruefully; I'd hardly enough strength to cut up a steak.

A strong feeling of walking blindfold towards a precipice dragged at my feet all the way to Vivian Iverson's gambling club. I didn't know which way the precipice lay: ahead, behind, or all round. I only suspected that it was still there, and if I did nothing about finding it, I could walk straight over.

The Vivat Club proved as suave and well-manicured as its owner, and was a matter of interconnecting small rooms, not open expanses like casinos. There were no croupiers in eye-shades with bright dramatic spotlights over the tables, and no ladies tinkling with diamonds in half shadow. There were however two or three discreet chandeliers, a good deal of cigar smoke, and a sort of reverent hush.

Vivian, good as his word, had left a note for me to be let in, and as an extra, treated as a guest. I walked slowly from room to room, balloon glass of brandy in hand, looking for his elegant shape, and not finding it.

There were a good many businessmen in lounge suits earnestly playing chemin-de-fer, and women among them with eyes that flicked concentratedly from side to side with every delivered card. I'd never had an urge towards betting for hours on the turn of a card, but everyone to his own poison.

'Ro, my dear fellow,' Vivian said behind me. 'Come to play?'

'On an accountant's earnings?' I said, turning to him and smiling. 'What are the stakes?'

'Whatever you can afford to lose, my dear fellow.'

'Life, liberty, and a ticket to the Cup Final.'

His eyes didn't smile as thoroughly as his mouth. 'Some people lose honour, fortunes, reputation, and their heads.'

'Does it disturb you?' I asked.

He made a small waving gesture towards the chemin-de-fer. 'I provide a pastime to cater for an impulse. Like bingo.'

He put his hand on my shoulder as if we were long-lost friends and steered me towards a further room. There were heavy gold links in his cuffs, and a silk cord edging to his blue velvet jacket. Dark glossy hair on a well-shaped head, flat stomach, faint smell of fresh talc. About thirty-five, and shrewdly succeeding where others had fallen to bailiffs.

There was a green baize raised-edge gaming table in the further room, but no one was playing cards.

Behind the table, in the club's ubiquitous wooden-armed, studded-leather armchairs, sat three men.

They were all large, smoothly dressed, and unfriendly. I knew them, from way back.

Connaught Powys. Glitberg. Ownslow.

'We hear you're looking for us,' Connaught Powys said.

CHAPTER NINE

I stood still. Vivian closed the door behind me and sat in another armchair on the edge of my left-hand vision. He crossed one leg elegantly over the other and eased the cloth over the knee with a languid hand.

Ownslow watched with disfavour.

'Piss off,' he said.

Vivian's answer was an extra-sophisticated drawl. 'My dear fellow, I may have set him up, but you've no licence to knock him down.'

There were several other empty chairs, pulled back haphazardly from the centre table. I sat unhurriedly in one of them and did my best with Vivian's leg-crossing ritual, hoping that casualness would reduce the atmosphere from bash-up to boardroom. Ownslow's malevolent stare hardly persuaded me that I'd succeeded.

Ownslow and Glitberg had run a flourishing construction racket for years, robbing the ratepayers of literally millions. Like all huge frauds, theirs had been done on paper, with Glitberg in the council's Planning Office, and

Ownslow in the Works and Maintenance. They had simply invented a large number of buildings: offices, flats and housing estates. The whole council having approved the buildings in principle, Glitberg, in his official capacity, advertised for tenders from developers. The lowest good-looking tender often came from a firm called National Construction (Wessex) Ltd and the council confidently entrusted the building to them.

National Construction (Wessex) Ltd did not exist except as expensively produced lettterheads. The sanctioned buildings were never built. Huge sums of money were authorized and paid to National Construction (Wessex) Ltd, and regular reports of the buildings' progress came back as Glitberg, from Planning, made regular inspections. After the point when the buildings were passed as ready for occupation the Maintenance department took over. Ownslow's men maintained bona-fide buildings, and Ownslow also requisitioned huge sums for the maintenance of the well-documented imaginary lot.

All the paperwork had been punctiliously, even brilliantly, completed. There were full records of rents received from the imaginary buildings, and rates paid by the imaginary tenants; but as all councils took it for granted that council buildings had to be heavily subsidized, the permanent gap between revenue and expenditure was accepted as normal.

Like many big frauds it had been uncovered by accident, and the accident had been my digging a little too deeply into the affairs of one of the smaller operators sharing in the crumbs of the greater rip-off.

The council, when I'd informed them, had refused to believe me. Not, that was, until they toured their area in detail, and found weedy grass where they had paid for, among other things, six storeys of flats for low-income families, a cul-de-sac of maisonettes for single pensioners, and two roadfuls of semi-detached bungalows for the retired and handicapped.

Blind-eye money had obviously been passed to various council members, but bribery in cash was hard to prove. The council had been publicly embarrassed and had not forgiven me. Glitberg and Ownslow, who had seen that the caper could not continue for ever, had been already preparing a quiet departure when the police descended on them in force on a Sunday afternoon. They had not exactly forgiven me either.

In line with all their other attention to detail, neither of them had made the mistake of living above his legal income. The huge sums they had creamed off had been withdrawn from the National Construction (Wessex) Ltd bank account over the years as a stream of cheques and cash which had aroused no suspicion at the bank, and had then apparently vanished into thin air. Of the million-plus which they had each stolen, not a pound had been recovered.

'Whatever you want from us,' Glitberg said, 'you're not going to get.'

'You're a danger to us,' Connaught Powys said.

'And like a wasp, you'll get swatted,' said Ownslow.

I looked at their faces. All three showed the pudgy roundness of self-indulgence, and all three had the sharp, wary eyes of guilt. Separately, Connaught Powys, with his sun-lamp tan and smoothly brushed hair, looked a high-up City gent. Heavy of body, in navy blue pin-stripes. Pale grey silk tie. Overall air of power and opulence, and not a whisper of cell-fug and slopping-out in the mornings.

Ownslow in jail was an easier picture. Fairish hair straggled to his collar from a fringe round a bald dome. Thick neck, bull shoulders, hands like baseball gloves. A hard, tough man whose accent came from worlds away from Connaught Powys.

Glitberg, in glasses, had short bushy grey hair and a fanned-out spread of white side-whiskers, which made him look like a species of ape. If Connaught Powys was power, and Ownslow was muscle, Glitberg was venom.

'Have you already tried?' I said.

'Tried what?' Ownslow said.

'Swatting.'

They stared, all three of them, without expression, at some point in the air between myself and Vivian.

'Someone has,' I said.

Connaught Powys smiled very slightly. 'Whatever we have done, or intend to do, about you,' he said, 'we are not going to be so insane as to admit it in front of a witness.'

'You'll be looking over your shoulder for the rest of your life,' Glitberg said, with satisfaction.

'Don't go near building sites on a dark night,' Ownslow said. 'There's a bit of advice, free, gratis and for nothing.'

'How about a sailing boat on a dark night?' I said. 'An ocean-going sailing boat.'

I wished at once that I hadn't said it. The unfriendliness on all three faces hardened to menace, and the whole room became very still.

Into the silence came Vivian's voice, relaxed and drawling. 'Ro . . . time you and I had a drink together, don't you think?'

He unfolded himself from his chair, and I, feeling fairly weak at the knees, stood up from mine.

Connaught Powys, Glitberg, and Ownslow delivered a collective look of such hatred that even Vivian began to look nervous. His hand fumbled with the door knob, and as he left the room, behind me, he almost tripped over his own feet.

'Whew,' he said in my ear. 'You do play with big rough boys, my dear fellow.' He steered me this time into a luxurious little office; three armchairs, all safely unoccupied. He waved me to one of them and poured brandy into two balloons.

'It's not what they say,' he said, 'as how they say it.'

'And what they don't say.'

He looked at me speculatively over his glass.

127

'Did you get what you wanted? I mean, was it worth your while, running under their guns?'

I smiled twistedly. 'I think I got an answer.'

'Well then.'

'Yes. But it was to a question I didn't ask.'

'I don't follow you.'

'I'm afraid,' I said slowly, 'that I've made everything a great deal worse.'

I slept soundly at the Gloucester, but more from exhaustion than an easy mind.

From the racing page of the newspaper delivered under my door in the morning I saw that my name was down in the list of runners as the rider of Notebook in the last race at Towcester. I sucked my teeth. I hadn't thought of asking William Finch not to include me in his list for the press, and now the whole world would learn where I would be that afternoon at four-thirty. If, that was, they bothered to turn to an insignificant race at a minor meeting on Grand National day.

'You'll be looking over your shoulder for the rest of your life,' Glitberg had said.

I didn't intend to. Life would be impossible if I feared for demons in every shadow. I wouldn't climb trustingly into any ambulances at Towcester, but I would go and ride there. There was an awfully thin line, it seemed to me, between cowardice and caution.

Jossie, waiting outside the weighing room, sent the heeby-jeebies flying.

'Hello,' she said. 'Notebook is here, looking his usual noble self and about to turn in his standard useless performance.'

'Charming.'

'The trainer's orders to the jockey,' she said, 'are succinct. Stay on, and stay out of trouble. He doesn't want you getting hurt.'

'Nor do I,' I said with feeling.

'He doesn't want anything to spoil the day if Ivansky wins the National.'

'Ah,' I said. 'Does he think he will?'

'He flew off in the air-taxi this morning in the usual agonized euphoria,' she said, with affection. 'Hope zig-zagging from conviction to doubt.'

Finch had sent two horses to Towcester, the second of them, Stoolery, being the real reason for Jossie's journey. I helped her saddle it for the two mile handicap 'chase, and cheered with her on the stands when it won. The Grand National itself was transmitted on television all over the racecourse straight afterwards, so that Jossie was already consoled when Ivansky finished fifth.

'Oh well.' She shrugged. 'That's that. Dad will feel flat, the owners will feel flat, the lads will get gloomily drunk, and then they'll all start talking about next year.'

We strolled along without much purpose and arrived at the door to the bar.

'Like a drink?' I asked.

'Might pass the time.'

The bar was crowded with people dissecting the National result, and the elbowing customers jockeying for service were four deep.

'Don't let's bother,' Jossie said.

I agreed. We turned to leave, and a thin hand stretched out from the tight pressed ranks and gripped my wrist hard.

'What do you want?' a voice shouted over the din. 'I've just got served. What do you want? Quick!'

The hand, I saw, belonged to Moira Longerman, and beyond her, scowling as usual, stood Binny Tomkins.

'Jossie?' I said.

'Fruit juice. Grapefruit if poss.'

'Two grapefruit juice,' I said.

The hand let go and disappeared, shortly to reappear with a glass in it. I took it, and also the next issue, and finally Moira Longerman herself, followed by Binny, fought her way out of the throng, holding two glasses high to avoid having the expensive thimblefuls knocked flying.

'How super!' she said. 'I saw you in the distance just now. I've been trying to telephone you for weeks and now I hear some extraordinary story about you being kidnapped.'

I introduced Jossie who was looking disbelievingly at what Moira had said.

'Kidnapped?' Her eyebrows rose comically. 'You?'

'You may well laugh,' I said ruefully.

Moira handed a glass to Binny, who nodded a scant thanks. Graceless man, I thought. Extraordinary to leave any woman to fight her way to get him a drink, let alone the owner of the most important horse in his yard. She was paying, of course.

'My *dear*,' Moira Longerman said to Jossie. 'Right after Ro won the Gold Cup on my darling Tapestry, someone kidnapped him from the racecourse. Isn't that right?' She beamed quizzically up at my face, her blue eyes alight with friendly interest.

'Sure is,' I agreed.

Binny scowled some more.

'How's the horse?' I said.

Binny gave me a hard stare and didn't answer, but Moira Longerman was overflowing with news and enthusiasm.

'I do so want you to ride Tapestry in all his races from now on, Ro, so I hope you will. He's ready for Ascot next Wednesday, Binny says, and I've been trying and trying to get hold of you to see if you'll ride him.'

Binny said sourly, 'I've already engaged another jockey.'

'Then disengage him, Binny dear.' Underneath the friendly birdlike brightness there was the same touch of steel which had got me the Gold Cup ride in the first place. Moira might be half Binny's physical weight but she had twice the mental muscle.

'It might be better to let this other chap ride . . .' I began.

131

'No, no,' she interrupted. 'It's you I want, Ro. I won't have anyone else. I told Binny that, quite definitely, the very moment after you'd won the Cup. Now you're back and safe again it will either be you on my horse or I won't run him.' She glanced defiantly at Binny, impishly at Jossie, and with a determined nod of her blonde curly head, expectantly turned to me. 'Well? What do you say?'

'Er,' I said, which was hardly helpful.

'Oh go on,' Jossie said. 'You'll have to.'

Binny's scowl switched targets. Jossie caught the full blast and showed no discomfiture at all.

'He did win the Gold Cup,' she said. 'You can't say he isn't capable.'

'He does say that, my dear,' beamed Moira Longerman happily. 'Isn't it odd?'

Binny muttered something blackly of which the only audible word was 'amateurs'.

'I think that what Binny really means,' said Moira sweetly and distinctly. 'is that Ro, like most amateurs, always tries very hard to win, and won't listen to propositions to the contrary.'

Binny's face turned a dark red. Jossie practically giggled. Moira looked at me with limpid blue eyes as if not quite aware of what she'd said, and I chewed around helplessly for a sensible answer.

'Like most *jockeys*,' I said finally.

'You're so nice, Ro,' she said. 'You think everyone's honest.'

I tended, like most accountants, to think exactly the opposite, but as it happened I had never much wondered about Binny. To train a horse like Tapestry should have been enough, without trying to rig his results.

Binny himself had decided to misunderstand what Moira had said, and was pretending that he hadn't seen the chasm that was opening at his feet. Moira gave him a mischievous glance and allowed him no illusions about her power to push him in.

'Binny dear,' she said, 'I'll never desert the man who trained a Gold Cup winner for me. Not as long as he keeps turning out my horses beautifully fit, and I choose who rides them.'

Jossie cleared her throat in the following silence and said encouragingly to Binny, 'I expect you had a good bet in the Gold Cup? My father always puts a bit on in the Cup and the National. Too awful if you win, and you haven't. Makes you look such an ass, he says.'

If she had tried to rub salt into his raw wounds, it appeared she couldn't have done a better job. Moira Longerman gave a delighted laugh.

'You naughty girl,' she said, patting Jossie's arm. 'Poor Binny had so little faith, you see, that not only did he not back Tapestry to win, but I've heard he unfortunately laid it to lose. Such a pity. Poor Binny, winning the Gold Cup and ending up out of pocket.'

Binny looked so appalled that I gathered the extent of her information was a nasty shock to him.

'Never mind,' Moira said kindly. 'What's past is past.

133

And if Ro rides Tapestry next Wednesday, all will be well.'

Binny looked as if everything would be very far from well. I wondered idly if he could possibly have already arranged that Tapestry should lose on Wednesday. On his first outing after a Gold Cup win, any horse would start at short odds. Many a bookmaker would be grateful to know for certain that he wouldn't have to pay out. Binny could already have sold that welcome information, thinking that I wasn't around to upset things. Binny was having a thoroughly bad time.

I reflected that I simply couldn't afford to take Wednesday off. The mountains of undone work made me feel faintly sick.

'Ro?' Moira said persuasively.

'Yes,' I said. 'Nothing I'd like better in the world.'

'Oh goody!' Her eyes sparkled with pleasure. 'I'll see you at Ascot, then. Binny will ring you, of course, if there's a change of plan.'

Binny scowled.

'Tell me all,' Jossie demanded as we walked across to the trainers' stand to watch the next race. 'All this drama about you being kidnapped.'

I told her briefly, without much detail.

'Do you mean they just popped you on a boat and sailed off with you to the Med?'

'That's right.'

134

'What a lark.'

'It was inconvenient,' I said mildly.

'I'll bet.' She paused. 'You said you escaped. How did you do that?'

'Jumped overboard.'

Her mouth twisted with sympathy. I reflected that it was only four days since that frantic swim. It seemed another world.

Jossie was of the real, sensible world, where things were understandable, if not always pleasant. Being with her made me feel a great deal more settled, more normal, and safer.

'How about dinner,' I said, 'on the way home?'

'We've got two cars,' she said.

'Nothing to prevent them both stopping at the same place.'

'How true.'

She was again wearing swirly clothes: a soft rusty red, this time. There was nothing tailored about her, and nothing untidy. An organized girl, amusing and amused.

'There's a fair pub near Oxford,' I said.

'I'll follow you, then.'

I changed in due course for Notebook's race, and weighed out, and gave my lightest saddle to the Axwood travelling head lad, who was waiting for it by the door.

'Carrying overweight, are you?' he said sardonically.

'Four pounds.'

He made an eyes-to-heaven gesture, saying louder than words that trainers should put up professionals in

135

novice hurdle races, not amateurs who couldn't do ten stone six. I didn't mention that on Gold Cup day I'd weighed eight pounds more.

When I went out to the parade ring, he and Jossie were waiting, while a lad led the noble Notebook round and round, now wearing my saddle over a number cloth. Number thirteen. So who was superstitious?

'He bucks a bit,' said the travelling head lad, with satisfaction.

'When you get home,' Jossie said to him, 'please tell my father I'm stopping on the way back for dinner with Roland. So that he doesn't worry about car crashes.'

'Right.'

'Dad fusses,' Jossie said.

The travelling head lad gave me another look which needed no words, and which speculated on whether I would get her into bed. I wasn't so sure that I cared all that much for the travelling head lad.

A good many people had already gone home, and from the parade ring one could see a steady drift to the gate. There were few things as disheartening, I thought, as playing to a vanishing audience. On the other hand, if one made a frightful mess, the fewer who saw it, the better.

'They said "jockeys get mounted" half an hour ago,' Jossie said.

'Two seconds,' I said. 'I was listening.'

The travelling head lad gave me a leg up. Notebook gave a trial buck.

'Stay out of trouble,' Jossie said.

'It's underneath me,' I said, feeling the noble animal again try to shoot me off.

She grinned unfeelingly. Notebook bounced away, hiccupped sideways down to the start, and then kept everyone waiting while he did a circus act on his hind legs. 'Bucks a bit', I thought bitterly. I'd fall off before the tapes went up, if I wasn't careful.

The race started, and Notebook magnanimously decided to take part, setting off at an uncoordinated gallop which involved a good deal of head-shaking and yawing from side to side. His approach to the first hurdle induced severe loss of confidence in his rider, as he seemed to be trying to jump it sideways, like a crab.

As I hadn't taken the precaution of dropping him out firmly at the back, always supposing I could actually have managed it, as he was as strong as he was wilful, his diagonal crossing of the flight of hurdles harvested a barrage of curses from the other jockeys. 'Sorry' was a useless word in a hurdle race, particularly from an unfit amateur who should have known better than to be led astray by a pretty girl. I yanked Notebook's head straight at the next hurdle with a force which would have had the Cruelty to Animals people swooning. He retaliated by screwing his hindquarters sideways in mid-air and landing on all four feet at once, pointing east-north-east to the rails.

This manoeuvre at least dropped him out into last place, which he tried to put right by running away with me up the stretch in front of the stands. As we fought each other on the way outwards round the mile-and-a-half circuit I understood the full meaning of the trainer's orders to his jockey. 'Stay on, and stay out of trouble.' My God.

I was not in the least surprised that Notebook had finished last of twenty-six at Newbury. He would have been last of a hundred and twenty-six, if his jockey had had any sense. Last place on Notebook was not exactly safe, but if one had to be anywhere on him, last place was wisest. No one, however, had got the message through to the horse.

The circuit at Towcester went out downhill from the stands, flattened into a straight stretch on the far side, and ended with a stamina-sapping uphill pull to the finishing straight and the winning post. Some of the world's slowest finishes had been slogged out there on muddy days at the end of three-mile 'chases. Notebook however set off downhill on firm going at a graceless rush, roller-coastered over the most distant hurdles, and only began to lose interest when he hit the sharply rising ground on the way back.

By that time the nineteen other runners were ahead as of right, as Notebook's stop-go and sideways type of jumping lost at every flight the lengths he made up on the flat.

I suppose I relaxed a little. He met the next hurdle all wrong, ignored my bid to help him, screwed wildly in mid-air, and landed with his nose on the turf and all four feet close together behind it. Not radically different from six other landings, just more extreme.

Being catapulted off at approximately thirty miles an hour is a kaleidoscopic business. Sky, trees, rails and grass somersaulted around my vision in a disjointed jumble, and if I tucked my head in it was from instinct, not thought. The turf smacked me sharply in several places, and Notebook delivered a parting kick on the thigh. The world stopped rolling, and half a ton of horse had not come crashing down on top of me. Life would go on.

I sat up slowly, all breath knocked out, and watched the noble hindquarters charge heedlessly away.

An ambulance man ran towards me, in the familiar black St John's uniform. I felt a flood of panic. A conditioned reflex. He had a kind face: a total stranger.

'All right, mate?' he said.

I nodded weakly.

'You came a proper purler.'

'Mm.' I unclipped my helmet, and pulled it off. Speech was impossible. My chest heaved from lack of air. He put a hand under one of my armpits and helped me as far as my knees, and from there, once I could breathe properly, to my feet.

'Bones OK?'

I nodded.

'Just winded,' he said cheerfully.

'Mm.'

A Land Rover arrived beside us with a jerk, and the vet inside it said that as there were no injured horses needing his attention, he could offer me a lift back to the stands.

'You fell off,' Jossie observed, as I emerged with normal breath and clean bill of health from the doctor in the First Aid room.

I smiled, 'Granted.'

She gave me a sideways glance from the huge eyes.

'I thought all jockeys were frightfully touchy about being told they fell off,' she said. 'All that guff about it's the horse that falls, and the jockey just goes down with the ship.'

'Quite right,' I said.

'But Notebook didn't actually fall, so you fell off.' Her voice was lofty, teasing.

'I don't dispute it.'

'No, aren't you boring.' She smiled. 'They caught Notebook in the next parish, so while you change I'll go along to the stables and see he's OK, and I'll meet you in the car park.'

'Fine.'

I changed into street clothes, fixed with the valet to take my saddles, helmet, and other gear to Ascot for the following Wednesday, and walked the short distance to the car park.

The crowds had gone, and only the stragglers like me were leaving now in twos and threes. The cars still remaining stood singly, haphazardly scattered instead of in orderly rows.

I looked into the back of mine, behind the front seats.

No one there.

I wondered with a shiver what I would have done if there had been. Run a mile, no doubt. I stood leaning on my car waiting for Jossie, and no one looked in the least like trying to carry me off. A quiet spring-like Saturday evening in the Northamptonshire countryside, as friendly as beer.

CHAPTER TEN

She followed me in her pale blue Midget to the pub on the south side of Oxford, and chose a long cold drink with fruit on the top and a kick in the tail.

'Dad has schooled Notebook until he's blue in the face,' she said, pursing her lips to the straw which stuck up like a mast from the log-jam of fruit.

'Some of them never learn,' I said.

She nodded. Polite transaction achieved, I thought: she had obliquely apologized for the horse's frightful behaviour, and I had accepted that her father had done his best to teach him to jump. Some trainers, but not those of William Finch's standing, seemed to think that the best place for a green novice to learn to jump was actually in a race: rather like urging a child up the Eiger without showing him how to climb.

'What made you become an accountant?' she said. 'It's such a dull sort of job.'

'Do you think so?'

She gave me the full benefit of the big eyes. 'You obviously don't,' she said. She tilted her head a little, considering. 'You don't *look* boring and stuffy, and you don't *act* boring and stuffy, so give.'

'Judges are sober, nurses are dedicated, miners are heroes, writers drink.'

'Or in other words, don't expect people to fit the image?'

'As you say,' I said.

She smiled. 'I've known Trevor since I was six.'

A nasty one. Trevor, without any stretch of imagination, could fairly be classed as stuffy and boring.

'Carry on,' she said. 'Why?'

'Security. Steady employment. Good pay. The usual inducements.'

She looked at me levelly. 'You're lying.'

'What makes you think so?'

'People who risk their necks for nothing in jump races are not hell-bent on security, steady employment, and money.'

'Because of me Mum, then,' I said flippantly.

'She bossed you into it?'

'No.' I hesitated, because in fact I never had told anyone why I'd grown up with a fiery zeal as powerful as a vocation. Jossie waited with quizzical expectation.

'She had a rotten accountant,' I said. 'I promised her that when I grew up I would take over. As corny as that.'

'And did you?'

'No. She died.'

'Sob story.'

'Yes, I told you. Pure corn.'

She stirred the fruit with her straw, looking less mocking. 'You're afraid I'll laugh at you.'

'Sure of it,' I said.

'Try me, then.'

'Well . . . she was a rotten businesswoman, my Mum. My father got killed in a pointless sort of accident, and she was left having to bring me up alone. She was about thirty. I was nine.' I paused. Jossie was not actually laughing, so I struggled on. 'She rented a house just off the sea-front at Ryde and ran it as a holiday hotel, half a step up from a boarding house. Comfortable, but no drinks licence; that sort of thing. So she could be there when I got home from school, and in the holidays.'

'Brave of her,' Jossie said. 'Go on.'

'You can guess.'

She sucked down to the dregs of her glass and made a bubbling noise through the straw. 'Sure,' she said. 'She was good at cooking and welcoming people and lousy at working out how much to charge.'

'She was also paying tax on money she should have claimed as expenses.'

'And that's bad?'

'Crazy.'

'Well, go on,' she said encouragingly. 'Digging a story out of you is worse than looking for mushrooms.'

'I found her crying sometimes, mostly in the winter when there weren't any guests. It's pretty upsetting for a kid of ten or so to find his mother crying, so you can say I was upset. Protective also, probably. Anyway, at first

I thought it was still because of losing Dad. Then I realized she always cried when she'd been seeing Mr Jones, who was her accountant. I tried to get her to open up on her troubles, but she said I was too young.'

I stopped again. Jossie sighed with exasperation and said, 'Do get *on* with it.'

'I told her to ditch Mr Jones and get someone else. She said I didn't understand, I was too young. I promised her that when I got older I would be an accountant, and I'd put her affairs to rights.' I smiled lopsidedly. 'When I was thirteen she went down to Boots one morning and bought two hundred aspirins. She stirred them into a glass of water, and drank them. I found her lying on her bed when I came home from school. She left me a note.'

'What did it say?'

'It said "Dear Ro, Sorry, Love, Mum." '

'Poor girl.' Jossie blinked. Not laughing.

'She'd made a will,' I said. 'One of those simple things on a form from the stationers. She left me everything, which was actually nothing much except her own personal things. I kept all the account books and bank statements. I got shuttled around uncles and aunts for a few years, but I kept those account books safe, and then I got another accountant to look at them. He told me Mr Jones seemed to have thought he was working for the Inland Revenue, not his client. I told him I wanted to be an accountant, and I got him to show me exactly what Mr Jones had done wrong. So there you are. That's all.'

'Are you still killing Mr Jones to dry your mother's tears?' The teasing note was back, but gentler.

I smiled, 'I enjoy accountancy. I might never have thought of it if it hadn't been for Mr Jones.'

'So God bless villains.'

'He was ultra-righteous. A smug pompous ass. There are still a lot of Mr Joneses around, not pointing out to their clients all the legitimate ways of avoiding tax.'

'Huh?'

'It's silly to pay tax when you don't have to.'

'That's obvious.'

'A lot of people do, though, from ignorance or bad advice.'

I ordered refill drinks and told Jossie it was her turn to unbutton with the family skeletons.

'My Ma?' she said in surprise. 'I thought the whole world knew about my Ma. She canoes up and down the Amazon like a yo-yo, digging up ancient tribes. Sends back dispatches in the shape of earnest papers to obscure magazines. Dad and I haven't seen her for years. We get telegrams in January saying Happy Christmas.'

Revelation dawned. 'Christabel Saffray Finch! Intrepid female explorer, storming about in rain forests?'

'Ma,' Jossie nodded.

'Good heavens.'

'Good grief, more like.'

'Trevor never told me,' I said. 'But then he wouldn't, I suppose.'

Jossie grinned. 'Trevor disapproves. Trevor also

146

always disapproves of Dad's little consolations. Aunts, I used to call them. Now I call them Lida and Sandy.'

'He's very discreet.' Even on the racecourse, where gossip was a second occupation, I hadn't heard of Lida and Sandy. Or that Christabel Saffray Finch, darling of anthropological documentaries, was William's wife.

'Sandy is his ever-sick secretary,' Jossie said, 'perpetually shuttling between bronchitis, backache and abortion.'

I laughed. 'And Lida?'

Jossie made a face, suddenly vulnerable under all the bright froth.

'Lida's got her hooks into him like a tapeworm. I can't stand her. Let's talk about food; I'm starving.'

We read the menu and ordered, and finished our drinks, and went in to dinner in the centuries-old dining-room: stone walls, uncovered oak beams, red velvet and soft lights.

Jossie ate as if waistlines never expanded, which was refreshing after the finicky picker I'd taken out last.

'Luck of the draw,' she said complacently, smothering a baked-in-the-skin potato with a butter mountain. I reflected that she'd drawn lucky in more ways than metabolism. A quick mind, fascinating face, tall, slender body: there was nothing egalitarian about nature.

Most of the tables around us were filled with softly chattering groups of twos and fours, but over by a far wall a larger party were making the lion's share of the noise.

'They keep looking over here,' Jossie said. 'Do you know them?'

'It looks like Sticks Elroy with his back to us.'

'Is it? Celebrating his winner?'

Sticks Elroy, named for the extreme thinness of his legs, had studiously avoided me in the Towcester changing room, and must have been thoroughly disconcerted to find me having dinner in his local pub. He was one of my jockey clients, but for how much longer was problematical. I was not currently his favourite person.

The noise, however, was coming not from him but from the host of the party, a stubborn-looking man with a naturally loud voice.

'Avert your gaze,' I said to Jossie.

The large eyes regarded me over salad and steak.

'An ostrich act?' she said.

I nodded. 'If we bury our heads, maybe the storm won't notice us.'

The storm, however, seemed to be gathering force. Words like 'bastard' rose easily above the prevailing clatter and the uninvolved majority began to look interested.

'Trouble,' Josie said without visible regret, 'is on its feet and heading this way.'

'Damn.'

She grinned. 'Faint heart.'

Trouble arrived with the deliberate movements of the slightly drunk. Late forties, I judged. About five feet eight, short dark hair, flushed cheeks and aggressive eyes. He stood four-square and ignored Jossie altogether.

'My son tells me you're that bastard Roland Britten.' His voice, apart from fortissimo, was faintly slurred.

To ignore him was to invite a punch-up. I laid down my knife and fork. Leaned back in my chair. Behaved as if the enquiry was polite.

'Is Sticks Elroy your son?'

'Too right, he bloody is,' he said.

'He had a nice winner today,' I said. 'Well done.'

It stopped him for barely two seconds.

'He doesn't need your bloody "well done".'

I waited mildly, without answering. Elroy senior bent down, breathed alcohol heavily, and pointed an accusing finger under my nose.

'You leave my son alone, see? He isn't doing anyone any harm. He doesn't want any bastard like you snitching on him to the bloody tax man. Judas, that's what you are. Going behind his back. Bloody informer, that's what you are.'

'I haven't informed on him.'

'What's that?' He wagged the finger to and fro, belligerently. 'Costing him hundreds, aren't you, with the bloody tax man. Bastard like you ought to be locked up. Serve you bloody well right.'

The head waiter arrived smoothly at Elroy's shoulder.

'Excuse me, sir,' he began.

Elroy turned on him like a bull. 'You trot off. You majordomo, or whatever you are. You trot off. I'll have my say, and when I've had my say I'll sit down, see? Not before.'

The head waiter cravenly retired, and Elroy returned to his prime target. Jossie's eyes stared at him with disfavour, which deflected him not at all.

'I hear someone locked you up for ten days or so just now, and you got out. Bloody shame. You deserve to be locked up, you do. Bastard like you. Whoever it was locked you up had the right idea.'

I said nothing. Elroy half turned away, but he had by no means finished. Merely addressing a wider audience.

'You know what this bastard did to my son?' The audience removed its eyes in thoroughly British embarrassment, but they got told the answer whether they liked it or not.

'This boot-licking, creeping bastard went crawling to the tax man and told him my son had some cash he hadn't paid taxes on.'

'I didn't,' I said to Jossie.

He swung round to me again and poked the finger rigidly under my nose. 'Bloody liar. Locking up's too bloody good for bastards like you.'

The manager arrived, with the head waiter hovering behind.

'Mr Elroy,' the manager said courteously. 'A bottle of wine for your party, compliments of the management.' He beckoned a finger to the head waiter, who deftly proffered a bottle of claret.

The manager was young and well-dressed, and

reminded me of Vivian Iverson. His unexpected oil worked marvels on the storm, which abated amid a few extra 'bastards' and went back to its table muttering under its breath.

The people at the other tables watched from the cover of animated conversation, while the head waiter drew the cork for Elroy and poured the free wine. The manager drifted casually back to Jossie and me.

'There will be no charge for your dinner, sir.' He paused delicately. 'Mr Elroy is a valued customer.' He bowed very slightly and drifted on without waiting for an answer.

'How cool of him,' Josie said, near explosion.

'How professional.'

She stared at me. 'Do you often sit still and let people call you a bastard?'

'Once a week and twice on Sundays.'

'Spineless.'

'If I'd stood up and slogged him, our steaks would have gone cold.'

'Mine has, anyway.'

'Have another,' I said. I started to eat again where I had left off, and so, after a moment or two, did Jossie.

'Go on,' she said. 'I'm all agog. Just what was that all about?' She looked round the restaurant. 'You are now the target of whispers, and the consensus looks unfavourable.'

'In general,' I said, spearing lettuce, 'people shouldn't expect their accountants to help them break the law.'

'Sticks?'

'And accountants unfortunately cannot discuss their clients.'

'Are you being serious?'

I sighed. 'A client who wants his accountant to connive at a massive piece of tax-dodging is not going to be madly pleased when the accountant refuses to do it.'

'Mm.' She chewed cheerfully. 'I do see that.'

'And,' I went on, 'an accountant who advises such a client to declare the loot and pay the tax, because otherwise the nasty Revenue men will undoubtedly find out, and the client will have to pay fines on top of tax and will end up very poorly all round, because not only will he get it in the neck for that one offence, but every tax return he makes in the future will be inspected with magnifying glasses and he'll be hounded for evermore over every penny and have inspectors ransacking every cranny of his house at two in the morning . . .' I took a breath ' . . . such an accountant may be unpopular.'

'Unreasonable.'

'And an accountant who refuses to break the law, and says that if his client insists on doing so he will have to take his custom somewhere else, such an accountant may possibly be called a bastard.'

She finished her steak and laid down her knife and fork. 'Does this hypothetical accountant snitch to the tax man?'

I smiled. 'If the client is no longer his client, he doesn't know whether his ex-client is tax-dodging or not. So no, he doesn't snitch.'

'Elroy had it all wrong, then.'

'Er,' I said, 'it was he who set up the scheme from which Sticks drew the cash. That's why he is so furious. And I shouldn't be telling you that.'

'You'll be struck off, or strung up, or whatever.'

'Sky high.' I drank some wine. 'It's quite extraordinary how many people try to get their accountants to help them with tax fiddles. I reckon if someone wants to fiddle, the last person he should tell should be his accountant.'

'Just get on with it, and keep quiet?'

'If they want to take the risk.'

She half laughed. 'What risk? Tax-dodging is a national sport.'

People never understood about taxation, I thought. The ruthlessness with which tax could be collected put Victorian landlords in the shade, and the Revenue people now had frightening extra powers of entry and search.

'It's much safer to steal from your employer than the tax man,' I said.

'You must be joking.'

'Have some profiteroles,' I said.

Jossie eyed the approaching trolley of super-puds and agreed on four small cream-filled buns smothered in chocolate sauce.

'Aren't you having any?' she demanded.

'Think of Tapestry on Wednesday.'

'No wonder jockeys get fat when they finally let themselves eat.' She spooned up the dark brown goo with satisfaction. 'Why is it safer to steal from your employer?'

'He can't sell your belongings to get his money back.'

The big eyes widened.

'Golly!' she said.

'If you run up debts, the courts can send bailiffs to take your furniture. If you steal instead, they can't.'

She paused blankly in mid-mouthful, then went on chewing, and swallowed. 'Carry right on,' she said. 'I'm riveted.'

'Well ... it's theft which is the national sport, not tax-dodging. Petty theft. Knocking off. Nicking. Most shop-lifting is done by the staff, not the customers. No one really blames a girl who sells tights all day if she tucks a pair into her handbag when she goes home. Pinching from employers is almost regarded as a rightful perk, and if ever a manufacturing firm puts an efficient checker on the staff exits there's practically a riot until he's removed.'

'Because he stops the outward march of spanners and fork-lift trucks?'

I grinned. 'You could feed an army on what disappears from the fridges of hotels.'

'Accountants,' she said, 'shouldn't find it amusing.'

'Especially as they spend their lives looking for fraud.'

'Do you?' she said, surprised. 'Do you really? I thought accountants just did sums.'

'The main purpose of an audit is to turn up fiddles.'

'I thought it was . . . well . . . to add up the profit or loss.'

'Not really.'

She thought. 'But when Trevor comes to count the hay and saddles and stuff, that's stocktaking.'

I shook my head. 'More like checking on behalf of your father that he hasn't got a stable lad selling the odd bale or bridle on the quiet.'

'Good heavens.' She was truly astounded. 'I'll have to stop thinking of auditors as fuddy-duddies. Change their image to fraud squad policemen.'

'Not that, either.'

'Why not?'

'If an auditor finds that a firm is being swindled by its cashier, for instance, he simply tells the firm. He doesn't arrest the cashier. He leaves it to the firm to decide whether to call in the handcuffs.'

'But surely they always do.'

'Absolutely not. Firms get red faces and tend to lose business if everyone knows their cashier took them for a ride. They sack the cashier and keep quiet, mostly.'

'Are you bored with telling me all this?'

'No,' I said truthfully.

'Then tell me a good fraud.'

I laughed. 'Heard any good frauds lately?'

'Get on with it.'

'Um . . .' I thought. 'A lot of the best frauds are complicated juggling with figures. It's the paperwork which deceives the eye, like a three card trick. I paused, then smiled. 'I know a good one, though they weren't my clients, thank God. There was a manager of a broiler-chicken factory farm which sold thousands of chickens every week to a freezing firm. The manager was also quietly selling a hundred a week to a butcher who didn't know the chickens had fallen off the back of a lorry, so to speak. No one could ever tell how many chickens there actually were on the farm, because the turnover was so huge and fast, and baby chicks tend to die. The manager pocketed a neat little untaxed regular income, and like most good frauds it was discovered by accident.'

'What accident?'

'The butcher used to pay the manager by cheque, made out in the manager's name. One day he happened to meet one of the directors of the firm which owned the chicken farm, and to save postage he got out his chequebook, wrote a cheque in the manager's name, and asked the director to give it to him, to pay for that month's delivery of chickens.'

'And the lid blew off.'

'With a bang. They sacked the manager.'

'No prosecution?'

'No. The last I heard, he was selling rose bushes by mail order.'

'And you wondered for whose nursery he was working?'

I grinned and nodded. She was quick and funny, and it seemed incredible that I'd met her only the day before.

We drank coffee and talked about horses. She said she had been trying her hand at three-day-eventing, but would be giving it up soon.

'Why?' I asked.

'Lack of talent.'

'What will you do instead?'

'Marry.'

'Oh.' I felt obscurely disappointed. 'Who?'

'I've no idea. Someone will turn up.'

'Just like that?'

'Of course just like that. One finds husbands in the oddest places.'

'What are you doing tomorrow?' I said.

Her eyes gleamed with light and life. 'Visiting a girl friend. What will you do instead?'

'Sums, I expect.'

'But tomorrow's Sunday.'

'And I can have the office to myself all day, without any interruption. I often work on Sundays. Nearly always.'

'Good grief.'

We went out to where the Midget and the Dolomite stood side by side in the car park.

'Thanks for the grub,' Jossie said.

'And for your company.'

'Do you feel all right?'

'Yes,' I said, surprised. 'Why?'

'Just checking,' she said. 'Dad'll ask. It looked such a crunching fall.'

I shook my head. 'A bruise or two.'

'Good. Well, goodnight.'

'Goodnight.' I kissed her cheek.

Her eyes glinted in the dim light from the pub's windows. I kissed her mouth, rather briefly, with closed lips. She gave me the same sort of kiss in return.

'Hm,' she said, standing back. 'That wasn't bad. I do hate wet slobbers.'

She slid expertly into the Midget and started the engine.

'See you in the hay,' she said. 'Counting it.'

She was smiling as she drove away, probably with a mirror expression of my own. I unlocked my car door, and, feeling slightly silly, I looked into the dark area behind the front seats.

No one there.

I sat in the car and started it, debating whether or not to risk going home to the cottage. Friday and Saturday had passed safely enough; but maybe the cats were still watching the mousehole. I decided that another night away would be prudent, and from the pub drove northwards around Oxford again, to the anonymity of the large motel and service station built beside a busy route-connecting roundabout.

The place as usual was bright with lights and bustle: flags flying on tall poles and petrol pumps rattling. I booked in at the reception office, took the key, and drove round to the slightly quieter wing of bedrooms at the rear.

Sleep would be no problem, I thought. The constant rumble of traffic would be soporific. A lullaby.

I yawned, took out my suitcase, locked the car, and fitted the key into the bedroom door.

Something hit me very hard between the shoulders. I fell against the still closed door, and something immediately hit me very hard on the head.

This time, it was brutal. This time, no ether.

I slid in a daze down the door and saw only dark unrecognizable figures bending over to punch and kick. The thuds shuddered through my bones, and another bang on the head slid me deep into peaceful release.

CHAPTER ELEVEN

I awoke in the dark. Black, total darkness.

I couldn't make out why I should be lying on a hard surface in total darkness, aching all over.

A fall, I thought. I had a fall at Towcester. Why couldn't I remember?

I felt cold. Chilled through and through. When I moved, the aches were worse.

I suddenly remembered having dinner with Jossie. Remembered it all clearly, down to kissing her goodnight in the car park.

So then what?

I tried to sit up, but raising my head was as far as I got. The result was whirling nausea and a pile-driving headache. I inched my fingers tentatively through my hair and found a wince-making area of swelling. I let my head down again, gingerly.

There was no sound except the rustle of my clothes. No engine. No creakings or rushings or water noises. I was not lying on a bunk, but on a larger surface, hard and flat.

I might not be in a sail locker, but I was certainly still in the dark. In the dark in every sense. Weak frustrated anger mocked me that in four days of freedom I hadn't found out enough to save me from the gloomy present.

Every movement told me what I still couldn't remember. I knew only that the fall off Notebook could not be the source of the soreness all over my body. There would have been a few bruises which would have stiffened up overnight, but nothing like the overall feeling of having been kneaded like dough. I rolled with a grunt on to my stomach and put my head on my folded arms. The only good thing that I could think of was that they hadn't tied my hands.

They. Who were *they?*

When my head stopped hammering, I thought, I would have enough energy to find out where I was and try to get out. Meanwhile it was enough just to lie still and wait for things to get better.

Another thing to be grateful for, I thought. The hard flat surface I was lying on was not swaying about. With luck, I was not on a boat. I wasn't going to be sick. A bruised body was absolutely nothing compared with the agonies of seasickness.

I had no shoes on, just socks. When I squinted at my wrist there was no luminous dial there: no watch. I couldn't be bothered to check all my pockets. I was certain they'd be empty.

After a while I remembered deciding to go to the

motel, and after that, bit by bit, I remembered booking in, and the affray on the doorstep.

They must have followed me all the way from Towcester, I thought. Waited through dinner with Jossie. Followed me to the motel. I hadn't spotted them once. I hadn't even heard their footsteps behind me, against the constant noise of traffic.

My instinctive feeling of being safe with Jossie had been dead right.

Ages passed.

The racket inside my skull gradually subsided. Nothing else happened.

I had a feeling that it was nearly dawn, and time to wake up. It had been ten-thirty when I'd been knocked out. There was no telling how long I'd been unconscious, or lain feebly in my present state, but the body had its own clock, and mine was saying six in the morning.

The dawn feeling stirred me to some sort of action, though if there was dawn outside it was not making its way through to me. Perhaps, I thought uneasily, I was wrong about the time. It was still night outside. I prayed for it to be still night outside.

I had another go at sitting up. One couldn't say that I felt superbly healthy. Concussion took a while to go away, and cold was notoriously bad for bruised muscles. The combination made every movement a nuisance. A familiar sort of pain, because of racing falls in the past. Just worse.

The surface beneath me was dirty: I could feel the gritty dust. It smelled faintly of oil. It was flat and smooth and not wood.

I felt around me in all directions, and on my left connected with a wall. Slithering on one hip, I inched that way and cautiously explored with my fingers.

Another smooth flat surface, at right angles to the floor. I banged it gently with my fist, and got back the noise and vibration of metal.

I thought that if I sat for a while with my back against the wall it would soon get light, and it would be easy then to see where I was. It had to get light, I thought forlornly. It simply had to.

It didn't, of course.

When they'd given me light on the boat, I'd escaped. A mistake to be avoided.

It had to be faced. The darkness was deliberate, and would go on. It was no good, I told myself severely, sitting in a miserable huddle feeling sorry for myself.

I made a further exploration into unmapped territory, and found that my world was a good deal smaller than Columbus's. It seemed prudent to move while still sitting down, on the flat-earth theory that one might fall over the edge; but two feet of shuffling to the right brought me to a corner.

The adjacent wall was also flat, smooth, and metal. I

shifted my spine round on to it, and set off again to the right.

The traverse was short. I came almost at once to another corner. I found that if I sat in the centre of the wall I could reach both side walls at once quite easily with my fingertips. Five feet, approximately, from side to side.

I shuffled round the second corner and pressed on. Three feet down that side, I knew where I was. The flatness of the metal wall was broken there by a big rounded bulge, whose meaning was as clear to my touch as if I'd been seeing it.

It was the semi-circular casing over a wheel; and I was inside a van.

I had a powerful, immediate picture of the fake ambulance I'd climbed into at Cheltenham. A white van, of a standard pattern, with the doors opening outwards at the rear. If I continued past the wheel, I would come to the rear doors.

And I would feel a proper fool, I thought, if all I had to do was open the doors and step out.

I wouldn't have minded feeling a proper fool. The doors were firmly shut, and likely to remain so. There was no handle on the inside.

In the fourth corner I came across what I had this time been given in the way of life support systems, and if my spirits had already been at zero, at that point they went way below.

There was a five-gallon plastic jerrycan full of liquid, and a large carrier bag.

I unscrewed the cap of the jerrycan and sniffed at the contents. No smell. Sloshed some of the liquid out on to my hand, and tasted it.

Water.

I screwed the cap on again, fumbling in the dark.

Five gallons of water.

Oh no, I thought numbly. Oh dear God.

The carrier was packed to the top with flat plastic packets, each about four inches square. There was again no smell. I pulled one of the packets open, and found the contents were thin four-inch squares of sliced processed cheese.

I counted the packets with a sinking heart, taking them one by one from the carrier and stacking them on the floor. There were sixty of them. All, as far as I could tell, exactly the same.

Wretchedly I counted them from the floor back into the carrier, one by one, and there were still sixty. They had given me enough food and water to last for at least four weeks. There were going to be no twice a day visits: no one to talk to at all.

Sod them, I thought violently. If this was revenge, it was worse than anything I'd ever brought on any crook.

Spurred by anger, I stood without caution to explore the top part of the van, and banged my sore head on the roof. It was very nearly altogether too much. I found myself back on my knees, cursing and holding my head, and trying not to weep. A battered feeble figure, sniffing in the dark.

It wouldn't do, I thought. It was necessary to be sternly unemotional. To ignore the aches and pains. To take a good cold grip of things, and make a plan and routine for survival.

When the fresh waves of headache passed, I got on with it.

The presence of food and drink meant, I thought, that survival was expected. That one day, if I didn't manage a second escape, I would be released. Death, again, was not apparently on the agenda. Well, then, why was I getting into such a fuss?

I had read once of a man who had spent weeks down a pothole in silence and darkness to see how a total lack of external reference would affect the human body. He had survived with his mind intact and his body none the worse for wear, and his sense of time had gone remarkably little astray. What he could do, so could I. It was irrelevant, I thought sternly, that the scientist had volunteered for his incarceration, and had had his heartbeat and other vital signs monitored on the surface, and could have got out again any time he felt he'd had enough.

Feeling a good deal steadier for the one-man pep-talk, I got more slowly to my feet, sliding my spine up the side wall, and feeling for the roof with my hands. It was too low for me to stand upright, by four or six inches. With head and knees bent, I felt my way again right round the van.

Both sides were completely blank. The front wall was broken by the shape of a small panel which must have opened through to the driving cab. It seemed to be intended to slide, but was fastened shut as firmly as if it had been welded. There was no handle or bolt on the inside; only smoothed metal.

The rear doors at first seemed to be promising, as I discovered they were not entirely solid, but had windows. One each side, about twelve inches across, the distance from my wrist to my elbow, and half as high.

There was no glass in the windows. I stretched my hand cautiously through the one on the right, and immediately came to a halt. Something hard was jammed against the doors on the outside, holding them shut.

I was concentrating so much on the message from my fingers that I realized that I was crouching there with my eyes shut. Funny, really. I opened them. No light. What good were eyes without light?

Outside each window there was an area of coarse cloth, which felt like heavy canvas. At the outer sides of the window it was possible to push the canvas, to move it three or four inches away from the van. On the inner halves it was held tight against the van by whatever was jamming the doors shut.

I put an arm out of each outer section of window in turn, and felt as much of the outside of the van as I could reach. It was very little, and of no use. The whole of the back of the van was sheeted in canvas.

I slid down again to the floor and tried to visualize

167

what I'd felt. A van covered in canvas with its rear doors
jammed shut. Where could one park such a thing so that
it wouldn't be immediately discovered? In a garage? A
barn? If I banged on the sides, would anyone hear me?

I banged on the sides of the van, but my fists made
little noise, and there was nothing else to bang with. I
shouted 'Help' a good many times through the windows,
but no one came.

There was air perceptibly leaking in through the
missing windows: I could feel it when I pushed the canvas
outwards. No fear of asphyxiation.

It irritated me that I could do nothing useful with
those windows. They were too small to crawl through,
even without the canvas and whatever was holding it
against the van. I couldn't get my head through the
spaces, let alone my shoulders.

I decided to eat some cheese and think things over.
The cheese wasn't bad. The thoughts produced the
unwelcome reflection that this time I had no mattress, no
blanket, no pillow, and no loo. Also no paperback novel,
spare socks, or soap. The sail locker had been a Hilton
compared with the van.

On the other hand, in an odd sort of way the time in
the sail locker had prepared me better for this dourer
cell. Instead of feeling more frightened, more hysterical,
more despairing, I felt less. I had already been through
all the horrors. Also, during the four days of freedom, I
had not gone to the South Pole to avoid capture. I'd

feared it and done my best to dodge it, but in returning to my usual life, I'd known it might come.

The reason for the first abduction presumably still existed. I had escaped before the intended time, and in someone's eyes this had been a very bad thing. Bad enough to send the squad to retake me, from the cottage, within a day of my return to England. Bad enough to risk carting me off again when this time there would, I hoped, be a police search.

I was pretty sure I must still be in England. I certainly had no memory of being transported from the motel to wherever I was now, but the impression that I'd been unconscious for only an hour or two was convincingly strong.

Sunday morning. No one would miss me. It would be Monday before Debbie and Peter began to wonder. Tuesday, perhaps, before the police took it seriously, if indeed they did, in spite of their assurance. A day or two more before anyone really started looking: and I had no wife or parents to keep the search alive, if I wasn't to be found soon after that.

Jossie might have done, I thought regretfully, if I'd known her for longer. Jossie with her bright eyes and forthright tongue.

At the very least, at the most hopeful assessment, the future still looked a long, hard, weary grind.

Shortening the perspective dramatically, it was becoming imperative to solve immediately the question of liquid waste disposal. I might be having to live in a tin box, but not, if I could help it, in a filthy stinking tin box.

Necessity concentrated the mind wonderfully, as others before me had observed. I took the cheese slices out of one of the thick plastic packets, and used that, and emptied it in relays out of the rear window, pushing the canvas away from the van as far as I could. Not the most sanitary of arrangements, but better than nothing.

After that little excitement, I sat down again. I was still cold, though not now with the through-and-through chill of injury-shock. I could perhaps have done some warming-up arm-swinging exercises, if it hadn't been for protesting bruises. As things were, with every muscle movement a reminder, I simply sat.

Exploration had kept me busy up to that point, but the next few hours revealed the true extent of my isolation.

There was absolutely no external sound. If I suppressed the faint noise of my own breathing, I could hear literally nothing. No traffic, no hum of aircraft, no wind, no creak, no rustle. Nothing.

There was absolutely no light. Air came steadily in from between the outside of the van and its canvas shroud, but no light came with it. Eyes wide open, or firmly shut, it was all the same.

There was no perceptible change in temperature. It remained just too low for comfort, defying my body's efforts to acclimatize. I had been left trousers, underpants, shirt, sports jacket and socks, though no tie, no belt, no loose belongings of any sort. It was Sunday, April 3rd. It might have been a sunny spring day outside, but wherever I was, it was simply too cold.

People would be reading about the Grand National in their Sunday newspapers, I thought. Lying in bed, warm and comfortable. Getting up and strolling to the pub. Eating hot meals, playing with the kids, deciding not to mow the lawn for another week. Millions of people, living their Sunday.

I served myself a Sunday lunch of cheese slices, and with great care drank some water from the can. It was heavy, being full, and I couldn't afford to tip it over. Enough water went down my neck to make me think of the uses of cheese packets as drinking cups.

After lunch, a snooze, I thought. I made a fairly reasonable pillow by rearranging the cheese packets inside the carrier, and resolutely tried to sleep, but the sum of discomfort kept me awake.

Well, then, I thought, lying on my back and staring at the invisible ceiling, I could sort out what I'd learned during my four free days.

The first of them could be discounted, as I'd spent it in Minorca, organizing my return home. That left two days in the office and one at the races. One night hiding in the cottage, one sleeping soundly in the Gloucester hotel. For all of that period I'd been looking for reasons, which made this present dose of imprisonment a great deal different from the first. Then, I'd been completely bewildered. This time I had at least one or two ideas.

Hours passed.

Nothing got any better.

I sat up for a while, and lay down again, and everything hurt, just the same. I cheered myself up with the thought that the stiff ache of bruises always finally got better, never worse. Suppose, for instance, it had been appendicitis. I'd heard that people going off to Everest or other Backs of Beyond had their perfectly healthy appendix removed, just in case. I wished on the whole that I hadn't thought of appendicitis.

Or toothache.

I had a feeling that it was evening, and then that it was night.

There was no change, except in me. I grew slowly even colder, but as if from the inside out. My eyelids stayed heavily shut. I drifted gradually in and out of sleep, a long drowsy twilight punctuated by short groaning awakenings every time I moved. When I woke with a clear mind, it felt like dawn.

If the cycle held, I thought, I could keep a calendar. One empty cheese packet for every day, stacked in the right-hand front corner of the van. If I put one there at every dawn, I would know the days. One for Sunday: a second for Monday. I extracted two wads of cheese slices and shuffled carefully a couple of feet forward to leave the empties.

I ate and drank what I thought of as breakfast: and I had become, I realized, much more at home in the dark. Physically, I was less clumsy. I found it easier to manage the water can, for instance, and no longer tended to put the cap on the floor and feel frustrated when I couldn't at once find it after I'd drunk. I now put my hand back automatically to where I'd parked the cap in the first place.

Mentally, too, it was less of a burden. On the boat I'd loathed it, and of all the rotten prospects of a second term of imprisonment, it had been being thrown back into the dark which I had shrunk from most. I still hated it, but its former heavy oppression was passing. I found that I no longer feared that the darkness on its own would set me climbing the walls.

I spent the morning thinking about reasons for abduction, and in the afternoon made an abacus out of pieces of cheese arranged in rows, and did a string of mathematical computations. I knew that other solitary captives had kept their minds occupied by repeating verses, but I'd always found it easier to think in numbers and symbols, and I'd not learned enough words by heart for them to be of any present use. Goosey goosey gander had its limitations.

*

173

Monday night came and went. When I woke I planted another cheese packet in the front right-hand corner, and flexed arms and legs which were no longer too sore to be worth it.

Tuesday morning I spent doing exercises and thinking about reasons for abduction, and Tuesday afternoon I felt my way delicately round the abacus, enlarging its scope as a calculator. Tuesday evening I sat and hugged my knees, and thought disconsolately that it was all very well telling myself to be staunch and resolute, but that staunch and resolute was not really how I felt.

Three days since I'd had dinner with Jossie. Well . . . at least I had her to think about, which I hadn't had on the boat.

The dozing period came round again. I lay down and let it wash over me for hours, and counted it Tuesday night.

Wednesday, for the twentieth time, I felt round the van inch by inch, looking for a possible way out. For the twentieth time, I didn't find one.

There were no bolts to undo. No levers. There was nothing. No way out. I knew it, but I couldn't stop searching.

Wednesday was the day I was supposed to be riding Tapestry at Ascot. Whether because of that, or simply because my body was back approximately to normal, the time passed more slowly than ever.

I whistled and sang, and felt restless, and wished passionately that there was room to stand up straight. The only way to straighten my spine was to lie down flat. I could feel my hard-won calm slipping away round the edges, and it was a considerable effort to give myself something to do with the pieces-of-cheese slide rule.

Wednesday I lost track of whether it was noon or evening, and the idea of days and days more of that existence was demoralizing. Dammit, I thought mordantly. Shut up, shut up with the gloomsville. One day at a time. One day, one hour, one minute at a time.

I ate some cheese and felt sleepy, and that at long last was Wednesday done.

Thursday midday, I heard a noise.

I couldn't believe it.

Some distant clicks, and a grinding noise. I was lying on my back doing bicycling exercises with my legs in the air, and I practically disconnected myself getting to my knees and scrambling over to the rear doors.

I pushed the canvas away from one of the windows, and shouted at the top of my lungs.

'Hey . . . hey . . . Come here.'

There were footsteps; more than one set. Soft footsteps, but in that huge dead silence, quite clear.

I swallowed. Whoever it was, there was no point in keeping quiet.

'Hey,' I shouted again. 'Come here.'

The footsteps stopped.

A man's voice, close to the van, spoke very loudly.

'Are you Roland Britten?'

I said weakly, 'Yes . . . who are you?'

'Police, sir,' he said.

CHAPTER TWELVE

They took a good long while getting me out, because, as the disembodied voice explained, they would have to take photographs and notes for use in any future prosecution. Also there was the matter of fingerprints, which would mean further delay.

'And we can't get you out without moving the van, you see, sir,' said the voice. 'On account of it's backed hard up against a brick pillar, and we can't open the rear doors. On top of that the driving cab doors are both locked, and the brake's hard on, and there's no key in the ignition. So if you'll be patient, sir, we'll have you out as soon as we can.'

He sounded as if he were reassuring a small child who might scream the place down at any minute, but I found it easy to be patient, if only he knew.

There were several voices outside after a while, and from time to time they asked me if I was all right, and I said yes; and in the end they started the van's engine and drove it forward a few feet, and pulled off the canvas cover.

The return of sight was extraordinary. The two small windows appeared as oblongs of grey, and I had difficulty in focusing. A face looked in, roundly healthy, enquiring and concerned, topped by a uniform cap.

'Have you out in a jiffy now, sir,' he said. 'We're having a bit of difficulty with these doors, see, as the handle's been sabotaged.'

'Fine,' I said vaguely. The light was still pretty dim, but to me a luxury like no other on earth. A half-forgotten joy, newly discovered. Like meeting a dead friend. Familiar, lost, precious, and restored.

I sat on the floor and looked around my prison. It was smaller than I'd imagined: cramped and claustrophobic, now that I could see the grey enclosing walls.

The jerrycan of water was of white plastic, with a red cap. The carrier was brown, as I'd imagined it. The little calendar stack of five empty packets lay in its corner, and the hardening pieces of cheese from my counting machine, in another. There was nothing else, except me and dust.

They opened the doors eventually and helped me out, and then took notes and photographs of where I'd been. I stood a pace or two away and looked curiously at my surroundings.

The van was indeed the white one from Cheltenham, or one exactly like it. An old Ford. No tax disc, and no number-plates. The canvas which had covered it was a huge, dirty dark grey tarpaulin, the sort used for sheeting loads on lorries. The van had been wrapped in it like a parcel, and tied with ropes threaded through eyelets in the tarpaulin's edges.

The van, the police and I were all inside a building of about a hundred feet square. All round the walls rose huge lumpy heaps of dust-covered unidentifiable bundles, grey shapes of boxes and things that looked like sandbags. Some of the piles reached the low flat ceiling, which was supported at strategic points by four sturdy brick pillars.

It was against one of these, in the small clear area in the centre, that the van had been jammed.

'What is this place?' I said to the policeman beside me.

'Are you all right, sir?' he said. He shivered slightly. 'It's cold in here.'

'Yes,' I said. 'Where exactly are we?'

'It used to be one of those army surplus stores, selling stuff to the public. Went bust a while back, though, and no one's ever shifted all the muck.'

'Oh. Well . . . whereabouts is it?'

'Down one of those tracks that used to be the railway branch line, before they closed it.'

'Yes,' I said apologetically. 'But what town?'

'Eh?' He looked at me in surprise. 'Newbury, of course, sir.'

The town clocks pointed to five o'clock when the police drove me down to the station. My body's own time had proved remarkably constant, I thought. Much better than

179

on the boat, where noise and tossing and sickness had upset things.

I was given a chair in the office of one of the same policemen as before, who showed no regrets at having earlier thought I was exaggerating.

'How did you find me?' I said.

He tapped his teeth with a pencil, a hard-working Detective Inspector with an air of suspecting the innocent until they were found guilty.

'Scotland Yard had a call,' he said grudgingly. 'We'll want a statement from you, sir, if you don't mind.'

'A cup of tea first,' I suggested.

His gaze wandered over my face and clothes. I must have looked a wreck. He came somewhere near a smile, and sent a young constable on the errand.

The tea tasted marvellous, though I daresay it wasn't. I drank it slowly and told him fairly briefly what had happened.

'So you didn't see their faces at all, this time?'

'No,' I said.

'Pity.'

'Do you think,' I said tentatively, 'that some one could drive me back to the motel, so I can collect my car?'

'No need, sir,' he said. 'It's parked beside your cottage.'

'What?'

He nodded. 'With a lot of your possessions in it. Suitcase. Wallet. Shoes. Keys. All in the boot. Your assistants notified us on Monday that you were missing again. We sent a man along to your cottage. He reported your car was there, but you weren't. We did what you asked, sir. We did look for you. The whole country's been looking for you, come to that. The motel rang us yesterday to say you'd booked in there last Saturday but hadn't used the room, but apart from that there was nothing to go on. No trace at all. We thought you might have been taken off on another boat, to be frank.'

I finished the tea, and thanked him for it.

'Will you run me back to the cottage, then?'

He thought it could be arranged. He came with me out to the entrance hall, to fix it.

A large man with an over-anxious expression came bustling in from the street, swinging the door wide and assessing rapidly the direction from which he would get most satisfaction. My partner at his most bombastic, his deep voice echoing round the hall as he demanded information.

'Hello, Trevor,' I said. 'Take it easy.'

He stopped in mid-commotion, and stared at me as if I were an intrusive stranger. Then he recognized me, and took in my general appearance, and his face went stiff with shock.

'Ro!' He seemed to have trouble with his voice. 'Ro, my dear fellow. My dear fellow. I've just heard . . . My God, Ro . . .'

I sighed. 'Calm down, Trevor. All I need is a razor.'

'But you're so *thin*.' His eyes were appalled. I reflected

that I was probably a good deal thinner than when he'd seen me last, some time in the dim, distant, and safe past.

'Mr King has been bombarding us all day,' said the Detective Inspector with a touch of impatience.

'My dear Ro, you must come back with me. We'll look after you. My *God*, Ro . . .'

I shook my head. 'I'm fine, Trevor. I'm grateful to you, but I'd really rather go home.'

'Alone?' he said anxiously. 'Suppose . . . I mean . . . do you think it's safe?'

'Oh yes,' I nodded. 'Whoever put me in, let me out. It's all over, I think.'

'What's all over?'

'That,' I said soberly, 'is a whole new ball game.'

The cottage embraced me like a balm.

I had a bath, and shaved, and a grey face of gaunt shadows looked at me out of the mirror. No wonder Trevor had been shocked. Just as well, I thought, that he hadn't seen the black and yellow blotches of fading bruises which covered me from head to foot.

I shrugged, and thought the same as before: nothing that a few days' freedom wouldn't fix. I put on jeans and a jersey and went downstairs in search of a large Scotch, and that was the last peaceful moment of the evening.

The telephone rang non-stop. Reporters, to my amazement, arrived at the doorstep. A television camera appeared. When they saw I was astounded, they said hadn't I read the papers.

'What papers?'

They produced them, and spread them out.

The Sporting Life: headline on Tuesday: 'Where is Roland Britten?' followed by an article about my sea trip, as told by me to friends. I had not been seen since Towcester. Friends were worried.

On Wednesday, paragraphs in all the dailies: 'Tapestry's rider again missing' in one of the staider, and 'Fun Jock Twice Removed?' from a tits-and-bums.

Thursday – that day – many front pages carried a broadly smiling picture of me, taken five minutes after the Gold Cup. 'Find Roland Britten' ordered one, and 'Fears for Jockey's Life' gloomed another. I glanced over them in amazement, remembering ironically that I'd been afraid no one would really look for me at all.

The telephone rang beside my hand. I picked up the receiver and said hello.

'Ro? Is that you?' The voice was fresh and unmistakable.

'Jossie!'

'Where the hell have you been?'

'Have dinner with me tomorrow, and I'll tell you.'

'Pick me up at eight,' she said. 'What's all that noise?'

'I'm pressed by Press,' I said. 'Journalists.'

'Good grief.' She laughed. 'Are you all right?'

'Yes, fine.'

'It was on the news, that you'd been found.'

'I don't believe it.'

'Big stuff, buddy boy.' The mockery was loud and clear.

'Did you start it . . . all this publicity?' I said.

'Not me, no. Moira Longerman. Mrs Tapestry. She tried to get you Sunday, and she tried your office on Monday, and they told her you were missing, and they thought you might have been kidnapped again, so she rang up the editor of *The Sporting Life*, who's a friend of hers, to ask him to help.'

'A determined lady,' I said gratefully.

'She didn't run Tapestry yesterday, you know. There's a sob-stuff bit in *The Sporting Life*. "How can I run my horse while Roland is missing" and all that guff. Fair turns your stomach.'

'Fair turned Binny Tomkins's, I'll bet.'

She laughed. 'I can hear the wolves howling for you. See you tomorrow. Don't vanish before eight.'

I put the telephone down, but the wolves had to wait a little longer, as the bell immediately rang again.

Moira Longerman, excited and twittering, coming down the wire like an electric current.

'Thank heavens you're free. Isn't it marvellous? Are you all right? Can you ride Tapestry on Saturday? Do tell me all about the horrible place where they found you . . . and Roland, dear, I don't want you listening to a word Binny Tomkins says about you not being fit to ride after all you've been through.'

'Moira,' I said, vainly trying to stop the flow. 'Thank you very much.'

'My dear,' she said, 'it was rather *fun*, getting everyone mobilized. Of course I was truly dreadfully worried that something awful had happened to you, and it was quite clear that somebody had to do *something*, otherwise you might stay kidnapped for *weeks*, and it seemed to me that a jolly good fuss was what was wanted. I thought that if the whole country was looking for you, whoever had taken you might get cold feet and turn you loose, and that's precisely what happened, so I was right and the silly police were all wrong.'

'What silly police?' I said.

'Telling me I might have put you in danger by getting *The Sporting Life* to say you'd vanished again. I ask you! They said if kidnappers get panicky they could kill their victim. Anyway, they were wrong, weren't they?'

'Fortunately,' I agreed.

'So do tell me all about it,' she said. 'Is it true you were shut up in a van? What was it like?'

'Boring,' I said.

'Roland, *really*. Is that all you've got to say?'

'I thought about you all day on Wednesday, imagining you'd be furious when I didn't turn up at Ascot.'

'That's better.' She laughed her tinkly laugh. 'You can make up for it on Saturday. Tapestry's in the Oasthouse Cup at Kempton, though of course he's got top weight there, which was why we wanted to run at Ascot instead. But now we're going to Kempton.'

'I'm afraid . . .' I said, 'that Binny's right. This time, I'm really not fit enough. I'd love to ride him, but . . . well . . . at the moment I couldn't go two rounds with a kitten.'

There was a short silence at the other end.

'Do you mean it?' she demanded doubtfully.

'I hate to say so, but I do.'

The doubt in her voice subsided. 'I'm sure you'll be a hundred per cent after a good night's sleep. After all, you'll have nearly two days to recover, and even Binny admits you're pretty tough as amateurs go . . . so *please*, Roland, *please* ride on Saturday, because the horse is jumping out of his skin, and the opposition is not so strong as it will be in the Whitbread Gold Cup in two weeks' time, and I feel in my bones that he'll win this race but not the other. And I don't want Binny putting up any other jockey, as to be frank I only trust you, which you know. So *please* say you will. I was so *thrilled* when I heard you were free, so that you could ride on Saturday.'

I rubbed my hand across my eyes. I knew I shouldn't agree, and that I was highly unlikely to be fit enough even to walk the course on my feet, let alone control half a ton of thoroughbred muscle on the rampage. Yet to her, if I refused, it would seem like gross ingratitude after her lively campaign to free me, and I too suspected that if Tapestry started favourite with a different jockey of Binny's choice, he wouldn't win. There was also the insidious old desire to race which raised its head in defiance of common sense. Reason told me I'd fall off from weakness at the first fence, and the irresistible temptation of a go at another of the season's top 'chases kidded me not to believe it.

'Well . . .' I said, hesitating.

'Oh, you *will*,' she said delightedly. 'Oh Roland, I'm so *glad*.'

'I shouldn't.'

'If you don't win,' she said gaily, 'I promise I won't blame you.'

I'd blame myself, I thought, and I'd deserve it.

I went to the office at nine the next morning, and Trevor fussed about a great deal too much.

'You need rest, Ro. You should be in bed.'

'I need people and life and things to do.'

He sat in the clients' armchair in my office and looked worried. The sun-tan of his holiday suited him, increasing his air of distinction. His silvery hair was fluffier than usual, and his comfortable stomach looked rounder.

'Did you have a good time,' I said, 'in Spain?'

'What? Oh yes, splendid. Splendid. Until the car broke down, of course. And all the time, while we were enjoying ourselves, you . . .' He stopped and shook his head.

'I'm afraid,' I said wryly, 'that I'm dreadfully behind with the work.'

'For heaven's sake . . .'

'I'll try to catch up,' I said.

'I wish you'd take it easy for a few days.' He looked as

if he meant it, his eyes full of troubled concern. 'It won't do either of us any good if you crack up.'

My lips twitched. That was more like the authentic Trevor.

'I'm made of plasticine,' I said; and despite his protests I stayed where I was and once again tried to sort out the trail of broken appointments.

Mr Wells was in a worse mess than ever, having sent a cheque which had promptly bounced. A prosecution for that was in the offing.

'But you knew the bank wouldn't pay it,' I protested when he telephoned with this latest trouble.

'Yes . . . but I thought they *might*.'

His naïvety was frightening: the same stupid hopefulness which had got him enmeshed in the first place. He blanked out reality and believed in fantasies. I'd known others like him, and I'd never known them change.

'Come on Monday afternoon,' I said resignedly.

'Supposing someone kidnaps you again.'

'They won't,' I said. 'Two-thirty, Monday.'

I went through the week's letters with Debbie and sorted out the most urgent. Their complexity made me wilt.

'We'll answer them on Monday morning,' I said.

Debbie fetched some coffee and said at her most pious that I wasn't fit to be at work.

'Did we get those postponements from the Commissioners for Axwood Stables and Coley Young?' I said.

'Yes, they came on Wednesday.'

188

'And what about Denby Crest's certificate?'

'Mr King said he'd see about that this morning.'

I rubbed a hand over my face. No use kidding myself. However much I disliked it, I did feel pathetically weak. Agreeing to ride Tapestry had been a selfish folly. The only sensible course was to ring Moira Longerman at once, and cry off: but when it came to race-riding, I'd never been sensible.

'Debbie,' I said, 'please would you go down to the store in the basement, and bring up all the old files on Connaught Powys, and on Glitberg and Ownslow.'

'Who?'

I wrote the names down for her. She glanced at them, nodded, and went away.

Sticks Elroy telephoned, words tumbling out in a rush, incoherent and thick with Oxfordshire accent. A lot more talkative than he'd been at dinner in the pub, when overshadowed by his bull-like dad.

'Stop,' I said. 'I didn't hear a word. Say it slowly.'

'I said I was ever so sorry you got shut up in that van.'

'Well . . . thanks.'

'My old man couldn't have done it, you know.' He sounded anxious, more seeking to convince than convinced.

'Don't you think so?'

'I know he said . . . Look, well, he went on cursing all evening, and I know he's got a van, and all, which is off somewhere getting the gearbox fixed, or something, and I know he was that furious, and he said you should be locked up, but I don't reckon he could have done it, not for real.'

'Did you ask him?' I said curiously.

'Yeah.' He hesitated. 'See . . . we had a bloody big row, him and me.' Another pause. 'He always knocked us about when we were kids. Straps, boots, anything.' A pause. 'I asked him about you . . . he punched me in the face.'

'Mm,' I said. 'What did you decide to do about that cash?'

'Yeah, well, that's what the row was about, see. I reckoned you were right and I didn't want any trouble with the law, and Dad blew his top and said I'd never been grateful for everything he'd done for me. He says if I declare that cash and pay tax on it he'll be in trouble himself, see, and I reckon he was mad enough to do anything.'

I reflected a bit. 'What colour is his van?'

'White, sort of. An old Ford.'

'Um. When did you decide to go to that pub for dinner?'

'Dad drove there straight from the races, for a drink, like, and then he phoned and said they could fit us all in for dinner, and we might as well celebrate my win.'

'Would he be likely,' I said, 'to be able to lay his hands on sixty packets of cheese slices?'

'Whatever are you on about?'

I sighed. 'They were in the van with me.'

'Well, I don't know, do I? I don't live with him any

more. I wouldn't reckon on him going to a supermarket, though. Women's work, see?'

'Yes. If you've decided to declare that cash, there are some legitimate expenses to set off against the profit.'

'Bloody tax,' he said. 'Sucks you dry. I'm not going to bother sweating my guts out on any more schemes. Not bloody worth it.'

He made an appointment for the following week and grumbled his way off the phone.

I sat and stared into space, thinking of Sticks Elroy and his violent father. Heavy taxation was always self-defeating, with the country losing progressively more for every tightening of the screw. Overtime and enterprise weren't worth it. Emigration was. The higher the tax rates, the less there was to tax. It was crazy. If I'd been Chancellor, I'd have made Britain a tax haven, and welcomed back all the rich who had taken their money and left. A fifty per cent tax on millions would be better for the country than a ninety-eight per cent on nothing. As it was, I had to interpret and advise in accordance with what I thought of as bad economics; uphold laws which I thought irrational. If the fury the Elroys felt against the system took the form of abuse of the accountant who forced them to face nasty facts, it wasn't unduly surprising. I did doubt though that even Elroy senior would make his abuse physical. Calling me a bastard was a long way from imprisonment.

Debbie came in with her arms full of files and her face full of fluster.

DICK FRANCIS

'There's a lady outside who insists on seeing you. She hasn't got an appointment and Mr King said you were definitely not to be worried today, but she won't go away. Oh!'

The lady in question was walking into the office in Debbie's wake. Tall, thin, assured, and middle-aged.

I stood up, smiling, and shook hands with Hilary Margaret Pinlock.

'It's all right, Debbie,' I said.

'Oh, very well.' She shrugged, put down the files, and went out.

'How are you?' I said. 'Sit down.'

Hilary Margaret Pinlock sat in the clients' chair and crossed her thin legs.

'You,' she said, 'look half-dead.'

'A half-empty bottle is also half-full.'

'And you're an optimist?'

'Usually,' I said.

She was wearing a brownish-grey flecked tweed coat, to which the sunless April day added nothing in the way of life. Behind the spectacles the eyes looked small and bright, and coral-pink lipstick lent warmth to her mouth.

'I've come to tell you something,' she said. 'Quite a lot of things, I suppose.'

'Good or bad?'

'Facts.'

'You're not pregnant?'

She was amused. 'I don't know yet.'

'Would you like some sherry?'

'Yes, please.'

I stood up and produced a bottle and two glasses from a filing cupboard. Poured. Handed her a generous slug of Harvey's Luncheon Dry.

'I came home yesterday,' she said. 'I read about you being kidnapped again, on the aeroplane coming back. They had newspapers. Then I heard on the news that you were found, and safe. I thought I would come and see you myself, instead of taking my information to the police.'

'What information?' I said. 'And I thought you were due back home last Saturday.'

She sipped her sherry sedately.

'Yes, I was. I stayed on, though. Because of you. It cost me a fortune.' She looked at me over her glass. 'I was sorry to read you had been recaptured after all. I had seen . . . your fear of it.'

'Mm,' I said ruefully.

'I found out about that boat for you,' she said.

I almost spilled the sherry.

She smiled. 'About the man, to be more exact. The man in the dinghy, who was chasing you.'

'How?' I said.

'After you'd gone, I hired a car and drove to all the places on Minorca where they said yachts could be moored. The nearest good harbour to Cala St Galdana was Ciudadela, and I should think that's where the boat went after they lost you, but it had gone by the time I started looking.' She drank some sherry. 'I asked some

193

English people on a yacht there, and they said there had been an English crew on a sixty-footer there the night before, and they'd overheard them talking about wind for a passage to Palma. I asked them to describe the captain, and they said there didn't seem to be a proper captain, only a tall young man who looked furious.' She stopped and considered, and explained further. 'All the yachts at Ciudadela were moored at right angles to the quayside, you see. Stern on. So that they were all close together, side by side, and you walked straight off the back of them on to dry land.'

'Yes,' I said. 'I see.'

'So I just walked along the whole row, asking. There were Spaniards, Germans, French, Swedes . . . all sorts. The English people had noticed the other English crew just because they *were* English, if you see what I mean.'

'I do,' I said.

'And also because it had been the biggest yacht that night in the harbour.' She paused. 'So instead of flying home on Saturday, I went to Palma.'

'It's a big place,' I said.

She nodded. 'It took me three days. But I found out that young man's name, and quite a lot about him.'

'Would you like some lunch?' I said.

CHAPTER THIRTEEN

We walked along to La Riviera at the end of the High Street and ordered moussaka. The place was full as usual, and Hilary leaned forward across the table to make herself privately heard. Her strong plain face was full of the interest and vigour she had put into her search on my behalf, and it was typical of her self-confidence that she was concentrating only on the subject in hand and not the impression she was making as a woman. A headmistress, I thought: not a lover.

'His name,' she said, 'is Alastair Yardley. He is one of a whole host of young men who seem to wander around the Mediterranean looking after boats while the owners are home in England, Italy, France, and wherever. They live in the sun, on the water's edge, picking up jobs where they can, and leading an odd sort of drop-out existence which supplies a useful service to boat owners.'

'Sounds attractive.'

'It's bumming around,' she said succinctly.

'I wouldn't mind dropping out, right now,' I said.

'You're made of sterner stuff.'

Plasticine, I thought.

'Go on about Alastair Yardley,' I said.

'I asked around for two days without any success. My description of him seemed to fit half the population, and although I'd seen the boat, of course, I wasn't sure I would know it again, as I haven't an educated eye for that sort of thing. There are two big marinas at Palma, both of them packed with boats. Some boats are moored stern-on, like at Ciudadela, but dozens more were anchored away from the quays. I hired a boatman to take me round the whole harbour in his motorboat, but with no results. I'm sure he thought I was potty. I was pretty discouraged, actually, and was admitting defeat, when he – the boatman, that is – said there was another small harbour less than a day's sail away, and why didn't I look there. So on Wednesday I took a taxi to the port of Andraitx.'

She stopped to eat some moussaka, which had arrived and smelled magnificent.

'Eat,' she said, scooping up a third generous forkful and waving at my still full plate.

'Yes,' I said. It was the first proper meal I'd approached since the dinner with Jossie, and I should have been ravenous. Instead, the diet of processed cheese seemed to have played havoc with my appetite, and I found difficulty in eating much at all. I hadn't been able to face any supper, the evening before, when the journalists had finally gone, and not much breakfast either.

'Tell me about Andraitx,' I said.

'In a minute,' she said. 'I'm not letting this delicious food get cold.' She ate with enjoyment and disapproved of my unsuccessful efforts to do the same. I had to wait for the next instalment until she had finished the last morsel and lain down her fork.

'That was *good*,' she said. 'A great treat.'

'Andraitx,' I said.

She half laughed. 'All right, then. Andraitx. Small by Palma's standards, but bigger than Ciudadela. The small ports and harbours are the old parts of the islands. The buildings are old . . . there are no new ritzy hotels there, because there are no beaches. Deep water, rocky cliffs, and so on. I found out so much more about the islands this week than if I'd stopped in Cala St Galdana for my week and come home last Saturday. They have such a bloody history of battles and sieges and invasions. A horrible violent history. One may sneer now at the way they've been turned into a tourist paradise, but the brassy modern civilization must be better than the murderous past.'

'Dearest Hilary,' I said. 'Cut the lecture and come to the grit.'

'It was the biggest yacht in Andraitx,' she said. 'I was sure almost at once, and then I saw the young man on the quayside, not far from where I paid off the taxi. He came out of a shop and walked across the big open space that there is there, between the buildings and the water. He was carrying a heavy box of provisions. He dumped it on the edge of the quay, beside that black rubber dinghy which he brought ashore at Cala St Galdana. Then he went off again, up a street leading away from the quay. I didn't exactly follow him, I just watched. He went into a doorway a little way up the street, and soon came out again carrying a bundle wrapped in plastic. He went back to the dinghy, and loaded the box and the bundle and himself, and motored out to the yacht.'

The waiter came to take our plates and ask about puddings and coffee.

'Cheese,' Hilary decided.

'Just coffee,' I said. 'And do go on.'

'Well . . . I went into the shop he'd come out of, and asked about him, but they spoke only Spanish, and I don't. So then I walked up the street to the doorway I'd seen him go into, and that was where I hit the jackpot.'

She stopped to cut cheese from a selection on a board. I wondered how long it would be before I liked the stuff again.

'It was a laundry,' she said. 'All white and airy. And run by an English couple who'd gone to Majorca originally for a holiday and fallen in love with the place. A nice couple. Friendly, happy, busy, and very, very helpful. They knew the young man fairly well, they said, because he always took his washing in when he was in Andraitx. They do the boat people's laundry all the time. They reckon to have a bag of dirty clothes washed and ironed in half a day.'

She ate a biscuit and some cheese, and I waited.

'Alastair Yardley,' she said. 'The laundry people said he is a good sailor. Better than most of his kind. He often takes yachts from one place to another, so that they'll be wherever the owner wants. He can handle big boats, and is known for it. He sails into Andraitx four or five times a year, but three years ago he had a flat there, and used it as his base. The laundry people said they don't really know much about him, except that his father worked in a boat-building yard. He told them once that he'd learned to sail as soon as walk, and his first job was as a paid deck-hand in sea-trials for ocean-racing yachts. Apart from that, he hasn't said much about himself or who he's working for now, and the laundry people don't know because they aren't the prying sort, just chatty.'

'You're marvellous,' I said.

'Hm. I took some photographs of the boat, and I've had them processed at an overnight developers.' She opened her handbag, and drew out a yellow packet, which contained, among holiday scenes, three clear colour photographs of my first prison. Three different views, taken as the boat swung round with the tide.

'You can have them, if you like,' she said.

'I could kiss you.'

Her face lit with amusement. 'If you shuffle through that pack, you'll find a rather bad picture of Alastair Yardley. I didn't get the focus right. I was in a bit of a hurry, and he was walking towards me with his laundry, and I didn't want him to think I was taking a picture of him personally. I had to pretend to be taking a general view of the port, you see, and so I'm afraid it isn't very good.'

She had caught him from the waist up, and, as she said, slightly out of focus, but still recognizable to anyone who knew him. Looking ahead, not at the camera, with a white-wrapped bundle under his arm. Even in fuzzy outline, the uncompromising bones gave his face a powerful toughness, a look of aggressive determination. I thought that I might have liked him, if we'd met another way.

'Will you take the photos to the police?' Hilary asked.

'I don't know.' I considered it. 'Could you lend me the negatives, to have more prints made?'

'Sort them out and take them,' she said.

I did that, and we lingered over our coffee.

'I suppose,' she said, 'that you have thought once or twice about . . . the time we spent together?'

'Yes.'

She looked at me with a smile in the spectacled eyes. 'Do you regret it?'

'Of course not. Do you?'

She shook her head. 'It may be too soon to say, but I think it will have changed my entire life.'

'How could it?' I said.

'I think you have released in me an enormous amount of mental energy. I was being held back by feelings of ignorance and even inferiority. These feelings have entirely gone. I feel full of rocket fuel, ready for blast off.'

'Where to?' I said. 'What's higher than a head-mistress?'

'Nothing measurable. But my school will be better, and there are such things as power and influence, and the ear of policy makers.'

'Miss Pinlock will be a force in the land?'

'We'll have to see,' she said.

I thought back to the time I'd first slept with a girl, when I was eighteen. It had been a relief to find out what everyone had been going on about, but I couldn't remember any accompanying upsurge of power. Perhaps, for me, the knowledge had come too easily, and too young. More likely that I'd never had the Pinlock potential in the first place.

I paid the bill and went out into the street. The April air was cold, as it had been for the past entire week, and Hilary shivered slightly inside her coat.

'The trouble with warm rooms . . . life blasts you when you leave.'

'Speaking allegorically?' I said.

'Of course.'

We began to walk back towards the office, up the High Street, beside the shops. People scurried in and out of the doorways like bees at a hive mouth. The familiar street scene, after the last three weeks, seemed superficial and unreal.

We drew level with a bank: not, as it happened, the one where I kept my own money, nor that which we used as a firm, but one which dealt with the affairs of many of our clients.

'Would you wait a sec?' I said. 'I've had a thought or two this week . . . just want to check something.'

Hilary smiled and nodded cheerfully, and waited without comment while I went on my short errand.

'OK?' I said, rejoining her.

'Fine,' she said. 'Where did they keep you, in that van?'

'In a warehouse.' I looked at my watch. 'Do you want to see it? I want to go back for another look.'

'All right.'

'My car's behind the office.'

We walked on, past a small, pleasant-looking dress shop. I glanced idly into the window, and walked two strides past, and then stopped.

'Hilary . . .'

'Yes?'

'I want to give you a present.'

'Don't be ridiculous,' she said.

She protested her way into the shop and was reduced to silence only by the sight of what I wanted her to wear: the garment I'd seen in the window; a long bold scarlet cloak.

'Try it,' I said.

Shaking her head, she removed the dull tweed coat and let the girl assistant lower the bright swirling cape on to her shoulders. She stood immobile while the girl fastened the buttons and arranged the neat collar. Looked at herself in the glass.

Duck into swan, I thought. She looked imposing and magnificent, a plain woman transfigured, her height making dramatic folds in the drop of clear red wool.

'Rockets,' I said, 'are powered by flame.'

'You can't buy me this.'

'Why not?'

I wrote the girl a cheque, and Hilary for once seemed to be speechless.

'Keep it on,' I said. 'It looks marvellous.'

The girl packed the old coat into a carrier, and we continued our walk to the office. People looked at Miss Pinlock as they passed, as they had not done before.

'It takes courage,' she said, raising her chin.

'First flights always do.'

She thought instantly of the night in Cala St Galdana: I saw it in the movement of her eyes. She smiled to herself, and straightened a fraction to her full height. Nothing wrong with the Pinlock nerve, then or ever.

From the front the warehouse looked small and dilapidated, its paint peeling off like white scabs to leave uneven grey scars underneath. A weatherboard screwed to the wall offered 10,500 square feet to let, but judging from the aged dimness of the sign, the customers had hardly queued.

The building stood on its own at the end of a side road

which now had no destination, owing to the close-down of the branch railway and the subsequent massive re-organization of the landscape into motorways and roundabouts.

There was a small door let into a large one on rollers at the entrance, neither of them locked. The locks, in fact, appeared to have been smashed, but in time gone by. The splintered wood around them had weathered grey with age.

I pushed open the small door for Hilary, and we stepped in. The gloom as the door swung behind us was as blinding as too much light; I propped the door open with a stone, but even then there were enfolding shadows at every turn. It was clear why vandals had stopped at breaking down the doors. Everything inside was so thick with dust that to kick anything was to start a choking cloud.

Sounds were immediately deadened, as if the high, mouldering piles of junk were soaking up every echo before it could go a yard.

I shouted 'Hey' into the small central space, and it seemed to reach no further than my own throat.

'It's cold in here,' Hilary said. 'Colder than outside.'

'Something to do with ventilation bricks, I expect,' I said. 'A draught, bringing in dust and lowering the temperature.'

Our voices had no resonance. We walked the short distance to where the white van stood, with the dark tarpaulin sprawling in a huge heap beside it.

With eyes adjusting to the dim light, we looked inside. The police had taken the water carrier and the bag of cheese, and the van was empty.

It was a small space. Dirty, and hard.

'You spent nearly a week in there,' Hilary said, disbelievingly.

'Five nights and four and a half days,' I said. 'Let's not exaggerate.'

'Let's not,' she said dryly.

We stood looking at the van for a minute or two, and the deadness and chill of the place began to soak into our brains. I shuddered slightly and walked away, out through the door into the living air.

Hilary followed me, and kicked away the door-stop. The peeling door swung shut.

'Did you sleep well, last night?' she said bleakly.

'No.'

'Nightmares?'

I looked up to the grey sky, and breathed deep luxurious breaths.

'Well . . . dreams,' I said.

She swallowed. 'Why did you want to come back here?'

'To see the name of the estate agent who has this place on his books. It's on the board, on the wall. I wasn't noticing things much when the police took me out of here yesterday.'

She gave a small explosive laugh of escaping tension. 'So practical!'

205

'Whoever put the van in there knew the place existed,' I said. 'I didn't, and I've lived in Newbury for six years.'

'Leave it to the police,' she said seriously. 'After all, they did find you.'

I shook my head. 'Someone rang Scotland Yard to tell them where I was.'

'Leave it to them,' she urged. 'You're out of it now.'

'I don't know. To coin a cliché, there's a great big iceberg blundering around here, and that van's only the tip.'

We got into my car, and I drove her back to the park in town where she'd left her own. She stood beside it, tall in her scarlet cloak, and fished in her handbag for a pen and notebook.

'Here,' she said, writing. 'This is my address and telephone number. You can come at any time. You might need . . .' She paused an instant, ' . . . a safe place.'

'Can I come for advice?' I said.

'For anything.'

I smiled.

'No,' she said. 'Not for that. I want a memory, not a habit.'

'Take your glasses off,' I said.

'To see you better?' She took them off, humouring me quizzically.

'Why don't you wear contact lenses?' I said. 'Without glasses, your eyes are great.'

*

On the way back to the office I stopped to buy food, on the premise that if I didn't stock up with things I liked, I wouldn't get back to normal eating. I also left Hilary's negatives for a rush reprint, so that it was nearly five before I went through the door.

Debbie and Peter had both done their usual Friday afternoon bolt, for which dentists and classes were only sample reasons. The variety they had come up with over the years would have been valuable if applied to their work: but I knew from experience that if I forced them both to stay until five I got nothing productive done after a quarter past four. Bess, infected by them, had already covered her typewriter, and was busy applying thick new make-up on top of the old. Bess, eighteen and curvy, thought of work as a boring interruption of her sex life. She gave me a bright smile, ran her tongue round the fresh glistening lipstick, and swung her hips provocatively on her way to the weekend's sport.

There were voices in Trevor's room. Trevor's loud voice in short sentences, and a client's softer tones in long paragraphs.

I tidied my own desk, and carried the Glitberg, Ownslow and Connaught Powys files into the outer office on my way to the car.

The door to Trevor's room opened suddenly, and Trevor and his client were revealed there, warmly shaking hands.

The client was Denby Crest, solicitor, a short plump man with a stiff moustache and a mouth permanently twisted in irritation. Even when he smiled at you personally, he gave an impression of annoyance at the state of things in general. Many of his own clients saw that as sympathy for their troubles, which was their mistake.

'I'll make it worth your while, Trevor,' he was saying. 'I'm eternally grateful.'

Trevor suddenly saw me standing there and stared at me blankly.

'I thought you'd gone, Ro,' he said.

'Came back for some files,' I said, glancing down at them in my arms. 'Good afternoon, Denby.'

'Good afternoon, Roland.'

He gave me a brief nod and made a brisk dive for the outer door; a brusque departure, even by his standards. I watched his fast disappearing back and said to Trevor, 'Did you sign his certificate? He said he would wait until you got back.'

'Yes, I did,' Trevor said. He too showed no inclination for leisurely chat, and turned away from me towards his own desk.

'What was I doing wrong?' I said. 'I kept making him fifty thousand pounds short.'

'Decimal point in the wrong place,' he said shortly.

'Show me,' I said.

'Not now, Ro. It's time to go home.'

I put the files down on Bess's desk and walked into Trevor's office. It was larger than mine, and much tidier, with no wall of waiting cardboard boxes. There were three armchairs for clients, some Stubbs prints on the walls, and a bowl of flowering daffodils on his desk.

'Trevor . . .'

He was busy putting together what I recognized as Denby Crest's papers, and didn't look up. I stood in his room, waiting, until in the end he had to take notice. His face was bland, calm, uninformative, and if there had been any tension there a minute ago, it had now evaporated.

'Trevor,' I said. 'Please show me where I went wrong.'

'Leave it, Ro,' he said pleasantly. 'There's a good chap.'

'If you did sign his certificate, and he really is fifty thousand pounds short, then it concerns me too.'

'You're dead tired, Ro, and you look ill, and this is not a good time to discuss it.' He came round his desk and put his hand gently on my arm. 'My dear chap, you know how horrified and worried I am about what has been happening to you. I am most concerned that you should take things easy and recover your strength.'

It was a long speech for him, and confusing. When he saw me hesitate, he added. 'There's nothing wrong with Denby's affairs. We'll go through them, if you like, on Monday.'

'It had better be now,' I said.

'No.' He was stubbornly positive. 'We have friends coming for the evening, and I promised to be home early. Monday, Ro. It will keep perfectly well until Monday.'

I gave in, partly because I simply didn't want to face

what I guessed to be true, that Trevor had signed the certificate knowing the figures were false. I'd done the sums over and over on my cheese abacus, and the answer came monotonously the same, whichever method I used to work them out.

He shepherded me like an uncle to his door, and watched while I picked up the heap of files from Bess's desk.

'What are those?' he said. 'You really mustn't work this weekend.'

'They're not exactly work. They're back files. I just thought I'd take a look.'

He walked over and peered down at the labels, moving the top file to see what was underneath.

'Why these, for heaven's sake?' he said, frowning, coming across Connaught Powys.

'I don't know . . .' I sighed. 'I just thought they might possibly have some connection with my being abducted.'

He looked at me with compassion. 'My dear Ro, why don't you leave it all to the police?'

'I'm not hindering them.' I picked up the armful of files and smiled. 'I don't think I'm high on their urgency list, though. I wasn't robbed, ransomed, or held hostage, and a spot of unlawful imprisonment on its own probably ranks lower than parking on double yellow lines.'

'But,' he said doubtfully, 'don't you think they will ever discover who, or why?'

'It depends on where they look, I should think.' I shrugged a shoulder, walked to the door, and stopped to look back. He was standing by Bess's desk, clearly troubled. 'Trevor,' I said, 'I don't mind one way or the other whether the police come up with answers. I don't madly want public revenge, and I've had my fill of court-case publicity, as a witness. I certainly don't relish it as a victim. But for my own peace of mind, I would like to know. If I find out, I won't necessarily act on the knowledge. The police would have to. So there's the difference. It might be better – you never know – if it's I who did the digging, not the police.'

He shook his head, perturbed and unconvinced.

'See you Monday,' I said.

CHAPTER FOURTEEN

Jossie met me on the doorstep, fizzing with life.

'Dad says please come in for a drink.' She held the door open for me and looked uncertainly at my face. 'Are you all right? I mean . . . I suppose I didn't realize . . .'

I kissed her mouth. Soft and sweet. It made me hungry.

'A drink would be fine,' I said.

William Finch was already pouring Scotch as we walked into his office-sitting-room. He greeted me with a smile and held out the glass.

'You look as if you could do with it,' he said. 'You've been having a rough time, by all accounts.'

'I've a fellow feeling for footballs.' I took the glass, lifted it in a token toast, and sipped the pale fine spirit.

Jossie said, 'Kicked around?'

I nodded, smiling. 'Somebody,' I said, 'is playing a strategic game.'

Finch looked at me curiously. 'Do you know who?'

'Not exactly. Not yet.'

Jossie stood beside her father, pouring grapefruit juice

out of a small bottle. One could see heredity clearly at work: they both had the same tall, well-proportioned frame, the same high carriage of head on long neck, the same air of bending the world to their ways, instead of being themselves bent. He looked at her fondly, a hint of civilized amusement in his fatherly pride. Even her habitual mockery, it seemed, stemmed from him.

He turned his greying head to me again, and said he expected the police would sort out all the troubles, in time.

'I expect so,' I said neutrally.

'And I hope the villains get shut up in small spaces for years and years,' Jossie said.

'Well,' I said, 'they may.'

Finch buried his nose in a large gin and tonic and surfaced with a return to the subject which interested him most. Kidnappings came a poor second to racing.

'My next ride?' I echoed. 'Tomorrow, as a matter of fact. Tapestry runs in the Oasthouse Cup.'

His astonishment scarcely boosted my non-existent confidence. 'Good heavens,' he said. 'I mean, to be frank, Ro, is it wise?'

'Totally not.'

'Then why?'

'I have awful difficulty in saying no.'

Jossie laughed. 'Spineless,' she said.

The door opened and a dark-haired woman came in, walking beautifully in a long black dress. She seemed to

213

move in a glow of her own; and the joy died out of Jossie like an extinguished fire.

Finch went towards the newcomer with a welcoming smile, took her elbow proprietorially, and steered her in my direction. 'Lida, my dear, this is Roland Britten. Ro, Lida Swann.'

A tapeworm with hooks, Jossie had said. The tapeworm had a broad expanse of unlined forehead, dark blue eyes, and raven hair combed smoothly back. As we shook hands, she pressed my fingers warmly. Her heavy, sweet scent broadcast the same message as full breasts, tiny waist, narrow hips, and challenging smile: the sexual woman in full bloom. Diametrically opposite, I reflected, to my own preference for astringency and humour. Jossie watched our polite social exchanges with a scowl, and I wanted to walk over and hug her.

Why not, I thought. I disengaged myself from the sultry aura of Lida, took the necessary steps, and slid my arm firmly round Jossie's waist.

'We'll be off, then,' I said. 'To feed the starving.'

Jossie's scowl persisted across the hall, into the car, and five miles down the road.

'I hate her,' she said. 'That sexy throaty voice . . . it's all put on.'

'It's gin,' I said.

'What?'

'Too much gin alters the vocal chords.'

'You're having me on.'

'I think I love you,' I said.

'That's a damn silly thing to say.'

'Why?'

'You can't love someone just because she hates her father's girlfriend.'

'A better reason than many.'

She turned her big eyes searchingly my way. I kept my own looking straight ahead, dealing with night on the country road.

'Strong men fall for her like ninepins,' she said.

'But I'm weak.'

'Spineless.' She cheered up a good deal, and finally managed a smile. 'Do you want me to come to Kempton tomorrow and cheer you on?'

'Come and give Moira Longerman a double brandy when I fall off.'

Over dinner she said with some seriousness, 'I suppose it's occurred to you that the last twice you've raced, you've been whipped off into black holes straight after?'

'It has,' I said.

'So are you – uh – at all scared, about tomorrow?'

'I'd be surprised if it happened again.'

'Surprise wouldn't help you much.'

'True.'

'You're absolutely infuriating,' she said explosively. 'If you know why you were abducted, why not tell me?'

'I might be wrong, and I want to ask some questions first.'

'What questions?'

215

'What are you doing on Sunday?'

'That's not a question.'

'Yes, it is,' I said. 'Would you care for a day on the Isle of Wight?'

With guilty misgivings about riding Tapestry I did my best to eat, and later, after leaving Jossie on her doorstep, to go home and sleep. As my system seemed to be stubbornly resisting my intention that it should return to normal, both enterprises met with only partial success. The Saturday morning face in the shaving mirror would have inspired faith in no one, not even Moira herself.

'You're a bloody fool,' I said aloud, and my reflection agreed.

Coffee, boiled egg and toast to the good, I went down into the town to seek out owners of destitute warehouses. The estate agents, busy with hand-holding couples, told me impatiently that they had already given the information to the police.

'Give it to me, too, then,' I said. 'It's hardly a secret, is it?'

The bearded pale-faced man I'd asked looked harried and went off to consult. He came back with a slip of paper which he handed over as if contact with it had sullied his soul.

'We have ceased to act for these people,' he said earnestly. 'Our board should no longer be affixed to the wall.'

I'd never known anyone actually say the word 'affixed'

before. It wasn't all he could say, either. 'We wish to be considered as disassociated from the whole situation.'

I read the words written on the paper. 'I'm sure you do,' I said. 'Could you tell me when you last heard from these people? And has anyone been enquiring recently about hiring or using the warehouse?'

'Those people,' he said disapprovingly, 'appear to have let the warehouse several years ago to some army surplus suppliers, without informing us or paying fees due to us. We have received no instructions from them, then or since, regarding any further letting or sub-letting.'

'Ta ever so,' I said, and went grinning out to the street.

The words on the paper, which had so fussed the agents in retrospect, were 'National Construction (Wessex) Ltd', or in other words the mythical builders invented by Ownslow and Glitberg.

I picked up the rush reprint enlargements of Hilary's photographs, and walked along to the office. All quiet there, as usual on Saturdays, with undone work still sitting reproachfully in heaps.

Averting my eyes, I telephoned the police.

'Any news?' I said; and they said no there wasn't.

'Did you trace the owner of the van?' I asked. No, they hadn't.

'Did it have an engine number?' I said. Yes, they said, but it was not the original number for that particular vehicle, said vehicle having probably passed through many hands and rebuilding processes on its way to the warehouse.

217

'And have you asked Mr Glitberg and Mr Ownslow what I was doing in a van inside their warehouse?'

There was silence at the other end.

'Have you?' I repeated.

They wanted to know why I should ask.

'Oh come off it,' I said. 'I've been to the estate agents, same as you.'

Mr Glitberg and Mr Ownslow, it appeared, had been totally mystified as to why their warehouse should have been used in such a way. As far as they were concerned, it was let to an army surplus supply company, and the police should direct their enquiries to them.

'Can you find these army surplus people?' I asked. Not so far, they said. They cleared the police throat and cautiously added that Mr Glitberg and Mr Ownslow had categorically denied that they had imprisoned Mr Britten in a van in their warehouse, or anywhere else, for that matter, as revenge for the said Mr Britten having been instrumental in their custodial sentences for fraud.

'Their actual words?' I asked with interest. Not exactly. I had been given the gist.

I thanked them for the information, and disconnected. I thought they had probably not passed on everything they knew, but then neither had I, which made us quits.

The door of Trevor's private office was locked, as mine had been, but we both had keys for each other's rooms. I knew all the same that he wouldn't have been pleased to see me searching uninvited through the papers in his filing cupboard, but I reckoned that as I'd had access to them anyway while he was on holiday, another peep would be no real invasion. I spent a concentrated hour reading cash books and ledgers; and then with a mind functioning more or less as normal I checked through the Denby Crest figures yet again. I had made no mistake with them, even in a daze. Fifty thousand pounds of clients' trust funds were missing. I stared unseeingly at 'Lady and Gentleman in a Carriage' and thought bleakly about consequences.

There was a photocopier in the outer office, busily operated every weekday by Debbie and Peter. I spent another hour of that quiet Saturday morning methodically printing private copies for my own use. Then I put all the books and papers back where I'd found them, locked Trevor's office, and went down to the store in the basement.

The files I was looking for there were easy to find but were slim and uninformative, containing only copies of audits and not all the invoices, cash books and paying-in books from which the accounts had been drawn.

There was nothing odd in that. Under the Companies Act 1976, and also under the value added tax system, all such papers had to be kept available for three years and could legally be thrown away only after that, but most accountants returned the books to their clients for keeping, as like us they simply didn't have enough storage space for everyone.

I left the files where they were, locked all the office doors, sealed my folder of photocopies into a large

envelope, and took it with me in some depression to
Kempton Park.

The sight of Jossie in her swirly brown skirt brought the
sun out considerably, and we despatched grapefruit juice
in amicable understanding.

'Dad's brought the detestable Lida,' she said, 'so I
came on my own.'

'Does she live with you?' I asked.

'No, thank God.' The idea alarmed her. 'Five miles
away, and that's five thousand miles too close.'

'What does the ever-sick secretary have to say about
her?'

'Sandy? It makes her even sicker.' She drank the
remains of her juice, smiling over the glass. 'Actually
Sandy wouldn't be so bad, if she weren't so wet. And you
can cast out any slick theories about daughters being
possessive of their footloose fathers, because actually I
would have liked it rather a lot if he'd fallen for a peach.'

'Does he know you don't like Lida?'

'Oh sure,' she sighed. 'I told him she was a flesh-eating
orchid and he said I didn't understand. End of conversation. The funny thing is,' she added, 'that it's only when
I'm with you that I can think of her without spitting.'

'Appendicitis diverts the mind from toothache,' I said.

'What?'

'Thoughts from inside little white vans.'

'Half the time,' she said, 'I think you're crazy.'

She met some friends and went off with them, and I repaired to the weighing room to change into breeches, boots, and Moira Longerman's red and white colours. When I came out, with my jacket on over the bright shirt, Binny Tomkins was waiting. On his countenance, the reverse of warmth and light.

'I want to talk to you,' he said.

'Fine. Why not?'

He scowled. 'Not here. Too many people. Walk down this way.' He pointed to the path taken by the horses on their way from parade ring to track: a broad stretch of grass mostly unpopulated by racegoing crowds.

'What is it?' I said, as we emerged from the throng round the weighing room door, and started in the direction he wanted. 'Is there something wrong with Tapestry?'

He shook his head impatiently, as if the idea were silly. 'I want you to give the horse an easy race.'

I stopped walking. An easy race, in those terms, meant trying not to win.

'No,' I said.

'Come on, there's more . . .' He went on a pace or two, looking back and waiting for me to follow. 'I must talk to you. You must listen.'

There was more than usual scowling bad temper in his manner. Something like plain fear. Shaking my head, I went on with him, across the grass.

'How much would you want?' he said.

I stopped again. 'I'm not doing it,' I said.

'I know, but . . . How about two hundred, tax free?'

221

'You're stupid, Binny.'

'It's all right for you,' he said furiously. 'But if Tapestry wins today I'll lose everything. My yard, my livelihood – everything.'

'Why?'

He was trembling with tension. 'I owe a lot of money.'

'To bookmakers?' I said.

'Of course to bookmakers.'

'You're a fool,' I said flatly.

'Smug bastard,' he said furiously. 'I'd give anything to have you back inside that van, and not here today.'

I looked at him thoughtfully. 'Tapestry may not win anyway,' I said. 'Nothing's a certainty.'

'I've got to know in advance,' he said incautiously.

'And if you assure your bookmaker Tapestry won't win, he'll let you off the hook?'

'He'll let me off a bit,' he said. 'He won't press for the rest.'

'Until next time,' I said. 'Until you're in deeper still.'

Binny's eyes stared inwards to the hopeless future, and I guessed he would never take the first step back to firm ground, which was in his case to stop gambling altogether.

'There are easier ways for trainers to lose races,' I pointed out, 'than trying to bribe the jockey.'

His scowl reached Neanderthal proportions. 'She pays the lad who does her horse to watch him like a hawk and give her a report on everything that happens. I can't sack him or change him to another horse, because she says if I do she'll send Tapestry to another trainer.'

'I'm amazed she hasn't already,' I said: and she would have done, I thought, if she'd been able to hear that conversation.

'You've only got to ride a bad race,' he said. 'Get boxed in down the far side and swing wide coming into the straight.'

'No,' I said. 'Not on purpose.'

I seemed to be remarkably good at inspiring fury. Binny would happily have seen me fall dead at his feet.

'Look,' I said, 'I'm sorry about the fix you're in. I really am, whether you believe it or not. But I'm not going to try to get you out of it by cheating Moira or the horse or the punters or myself, and that's that.'

'You *bastard*,' he said.

Five minutes later, when I was back in the hub of the racecourse outside the weighing room, a hand touched me on the arm and a drawly voice spoke behind my ear.

'My dear Ro, what are your chances?'

I turned, smiling, to the intelligent face of Vivian Iverson. In the daylight on a racecourse, where I'd first met him, he wore his clothes with the same elegance and flair that he had extended to his Vivat Club. Dark green blazer over grey checked trousers; hair shining black in the April sun. Quiet amusement in the observant eyes.

'In love, war, or the three-thirty?' I said.

'Of remaining at liberty, my dear chap.'

I blinked. 'Um,' I said. 'What would you offer?'

'Five to four against?'

'I hope you're wrong,' I said.

Underneath the banter, he was detectably serious. 'It just so happens that last night in the club I heard our friend Connaught Powys talking on the telephone. To be frank, my dear Ro, after I'd heard your name mentioned, I more or less deliberately *listened*.'

'On an extension?'

'Tut tut,' he said reprovingly. 'Unfortunately not. I don't know who he was talking to. But he said – his exact words – "As far as Britten is concerned you must agree that precaution is better than cure," and a bit later he said "If dogs start sniffing around, the best thing to do is chain them up." '

'Charming,' I said blankly.

'Do you need a bodyguard?'

'Are you offering yourself?'

He shook his head, smiling. 'I could hire you one. Karate. Bulletproof glass. All the mod cons.'

'I think,' I said thoughtfully, 'that I'll just increase the insurance policies.'

'Against kidnapping? No one will take you on.'

'Checks and balances,' I said. 'No one'll push me off a spring-board if it means a rock falling on their own head.'

'Be sure to let them know the rock exists.'

'Your advice,' I said, smiling, 'is worth its weight in ocean-going sailing boats.'

*

224

Moira Longerman twinkled with her bright bird-eyes in the parade ring before Tapestry's race and stroked my arm repeatedly, her small thin hand sliding delicately over the shiny scarlet sleeve.

'Now, Roland, you'll do your best, I know you'll do your best.'

'Yes,' I said guiltily, flexing several flabby muscles and watching Tapestry's highly tuned ones ripple under his coat as he walked round the ring with his lad.

'I saw you talking to Binny just now, Roland.'

'Did you, Moira?' I switched my gaze to her face.

'Yes, I did.' She nodded brightly. 'I was up in the stands, up there in the bar, looking down to the paddock. I saw Binny take you away for a talk.'

She looked at me steadily, shrewdly, asking the vital question in total silence. Her hand went on stroking. She waited intently, expecting an answer.

'I promise you,' I said plainly, 'that if I make a hash of it, it'll be against my will.'

She stopped stroking, patted my arm instead, and smiled. 'That will do nicely, Roland.'

Binny stood ten feet away, unable to make even a show of the civility due from trainer to owner. His face was rigid, his eyes expressionless, and even the usual scowl had frozen into a more general and powerful gloom. I thought I had probably been wrong to think of Binny as a stupid fool. There was something about him at that moment which raised prickles on the skin and images of murder.

225

The bell rang for jockeys to mount, and it was the lad, not Binny, who gave me a leg-up into the saddle.

'I'm not going to take much more of this,' Moira said pleasantly to the world in general.

Binny ignored her as if he hadn't heard; and maybe he hadn't. He'd also given me no riding instructions, which I didn't mind in the least. He seemed wholly withdrawn and unresponsive, and when Moira waved briefly as I walked away on Tapestry, he did not accompany her across to the stands. Even for him, his behaviour was incredible.

Tapestry himself was in a great mood, tossing his head with excitement and bouncing along in tiny cantering strides as if he had April spring fever in all his veins. I remembered his plunging start in the Gold Cup and realized that this time I'd be lucky if he didn't bolt with me from the post. Far from being last from indecision, this time, in my weakened state, I could be forty lengths in front by the second fence, throwing away all chance of staying power at the end.

Tapestry bounced gently on his toes in the parade past the stands, while the other runners walked. Bounced playfully back at a canter to the start, which in three mile 'chases at Kempton Park was to the left of the stands and in full view of most of the crowd.

There were eleven other jockeys walking around there, making final adjustments to girths and goggles and answering to the starter's roll call. The starter's assistant, tightening the girths of the horse beside me, looked over his shoulder and asked me if mine were all right, or should he tighten those too.

If I hadn't recently been through so many wringers, I would simply have said yes, and he would have pulled the buckles up a notch or two, and I wouldn't have given it another thought. As it was, in my over-cautious state, I had a sudden sharp vision of Binny's dangerous detachment, and remembered the desperation behind his appeal to me to lose. The prickles returned in force.

I slid off Tapestry's back and looped his reins over my arm.

'Just want to check . . .' I said vaguely to the starter's assistant.

He nodded briefly, glancing at his watch. One minute to racetime, his face said, so hurry up.

It was my own saddle. I intimately knew its every flap, buckle, scratch and stain. I checked it thoroughly inch by inch with fingers and eyes, and could see nothing wrong. Girths, stirrups, leathers, buckles; everything as it should be. I pulled the girths tighter myself, and the starter told me to get mounted.

Looking over my shoulder, I thought, for the rest of my life. Seeing demons in shadows. But the feeling of danger wouldn't go away.

'Hurry up, Britten.'

'Yes, sir.'

I stood on the ground, looking at Tapestry tossing his head.

'*Britten!*'

Reins, I thought. Bridle. Bit Reins. If the bridle broke, I couldn't control the horse and he wouldn't win the race. Many races had been lost, from broken bridles.

It was not too difficult to see, if one looked really closely. The leather reins were stitched on to the rings at each side of the bit, and the stitches on the off-side rein had nearly all been severed.

Three miles and twenty fences at bucketing speed with just two strands of thread holding my right-hand rein.

'*Britten!*'

I gave a jerking tug, and the remaining stitches came apart in my hand. I pulled the rein off the ring and waved the free end in the air.

'Sorry, sir,' I said. 'I need another bridle.'

'What? Oh very well . . .' He used his telephone to call the weighing room to send a replacement out quickly. Tapestry's lad appeared, looking worried, to help change the headpiece, and I pointed out to him, as I gave him Binny's bridle, the parted stitching.

'I don't know how it could have got like that,' he said anxiously. 'I didn't know it was like that, honest. I cleaned it yesterday, and all.'

'Don't worry,' I said. 'It's not your fault.'

'Yes, but . . .'

'Give me a leg-up,' I said, 'and don't worry.'

He continued all the same to look upset. Good lads took it grievously to heart if anything was proved lacking in the way they turned out their horses, and Tapestry's lad was as good as the horse deserved. Binny, I thought

not for the first time, was an all-out, one-man disaster
area, a blight to himself and everyone around.

'Line up,' shouted the starter, with his hand on the
lever. 'We're five minutes late.'

Tapestry did his best to put that right two seconds
later with another arm-wrenching departure, but owing
to one or two equally impetuous opponents I thankfully
got him anchored in mid-field; and there we stayed for all
of the first circuit. The pace, once we'd settled down, was
nothing like as fast as the Gold Cup, and I had time to
worry about the more usual things, like meeting the
fences right, and not running out altogether, which was
an added hazard at Kempton where the wings leading to
the fences were smaller and lower than on other courses,
and tended to give tricky horses bad ideas.

During the second circuit my state of unfitness raised
its ugly head in no uncertain way, and it would be fair to
say that for the last mile Tapestry's jockey did little
except cling on. Tapestry truly was, however, a great per-
former, and in consequence of the cheers and acclaim in
the unsaddling enclosure after the Gold Cup, he seemed,
like many much-fêted horses, to have become conscious
of his own star status. It was the extra dimension of his
new pride which took us in a straight faultless run over
the last three fences in the straight, and his own will to
win which extended his neck and his stride on the run-in.
Tapestry won the Oasthouse Cup by four lengths, and it
was all the horse's doing, not mine.

Moira kissed her horse with tears running down her

cheeks, and kissed me as well, and everyone else within mouth-shot, indiscriminately. There was nothing uptight or inhibited about the Longerman joy, and the most notable person not there to share it was the horse's trainer. Binny Tomkins was nowhere to be seen.

'Drink,' Moira shrieked at me. 'Owners and trainers bar.'

I nodded, speechless from exertion and back-slapping, and struggled through the throng with my saddle to be weighed in. It was fabulous, I thought dazedly; fantastic, winning another big race. More than I'd ever reckoned possible. A bursting delight like no other on earth. Even knowing how little I'd contributed couldn't dampen the wild inner rejoicing. I'd never be able to give it up, I thought. I'd still be struggling round in the mud and the rain at fifty, chasing the marvellous dream. Addiction wasn't only a matter of needles in the arm.

Moira in the bar was dispensing champagne and bright laughs in copious quantities, and had taken Jossie closely in tow.

'Ro, darling Ro,' Moira said, 'have you seen Binny anywhere?'

'No, I haven't.'

'Wasn't it odd, the bridle breaking like that?' Her innocent-seeming eyes stared up into my own. 'I talked to the lad, you see.'

'These things do happen,' I said.

'You mean, no one can prove anything?'

'Roughly that.'

'But aren't you the teeniest bit angry?'

I smiled from the glowing inner pleasure. 'We won the race. What else matters?'

She shook her head. 'It was a wicked thing to do.'

Desperation, I thought, could spawn deeds the doers wouldn't sanely contemplate. Like cutting loose a rein. Like kidnapping the enemy. Like whatever else lay ahead before we were done. I shut out the shadowy devils and drank to life and the Oasthouse Cup.

Jossie, too, had a go at me when we wandered later out to the car park.

'Is Moira right?' she demanded. 'Did Binny rig it for you to come to grief?'

'I should think so.'

'She says you ought to report it.'

'There's no need.'

'Why not?'

'He's programmed to self-destruct before the end of the season.'

'Do you mean *suicide*?' she said.

'You're too literal. I mean he'll go bust to the bookies with a reverberating bang.'

'You're drunk.'

I shook my head, grinning. 'High. Quite different. Care to join me on my cloud?'

'A puff of wind,' she said, 'and you'd evaporate.'

231

CHAPTER FIFTEEN

Jossie drove off to some party or other in London, and I, mindful of earlier unscheduled destinations after racing, took myself circumspectly down the road to the nearest public telephone box. No one followed, that I could see.

Hilary Margaret Pinlock answered at the twentieth ring, when I had all but given up, and said breathlessly that she had only that second reached home; she'd been out playing tennis.

'Are you busy this evening?' I said.

'Nothing special.'

'Can I come and see you?'

'Yes.' She hesitated a fraction. 'What do you want? Food? A bed?'

'An ear,' I said. 'And baked beans, perhaps. But no bed.'

'Right,' she said calmly. 'Where are you? Do you need directions?'

She told me clearly how to find her, and I drew up forty minutes later outside a large Edwardian house in a leafy road on the outskirts of a sprawling Surrey town.

Hilary, it transpired, owned the ground floor, a matter of two large, high-ceilinged rooms, modern kitchen, functional bathroom, and a pleasant old-fashioned conservatory with plants, cane armchairs, and steps down to an unkempt garden.

Inside, everything was orderly and organized, and comfortable in an uninspired sort of way. Well-built easy chairs in dim covers, heavy curtains in good velvet but of a deadening colour somewhere between brown and green, patterned carpet in olive and fawn. The home of a vigorous academic mind with no inborn response to refracted light. I wondered just how much she would wear the alien scarlet cloak.

The evening sun still shone into the conservatory, and there we sat, in the cane armchairs, drinking sherry, greenly surrounded by palms and rubber plants and *Monstera deliciosa*.

'I don't mind *watering*,' Hilary said. 'But I detest *gardening*. The people upstairs are supposed to do the garden, but they don't.' She waved disgustedly towards the view of straggly bushes, unpruned roses, weedy paths, and dried coffee-coloured stalks of last year's unmown grass.

'It's better than concrete,' I said.

'I'll use you as a parable for the children,' she said, smiling.

'Hm?'

'When things are bad, you endure what you must, and thank God it's not worse.'

I made a protesting sound in my throat, much taken aback. 'Well,' I said helplessly, 'what else is there to do?'

'Go screaming off to the Social Services.'

'For a gardener?'

'You know darned well what I mean.'

'Endurance is like tax,' I said. 'You're silly to pay more than you have to, but you can't always escape it.'

'And you can whine,' she said, nodding, 'or suffer with good grace.'

She drank her sherry collectedly and invited me to say why I'd come.

'To ask you to keep a parcel safe for me,' I said.

'But of course.'

'And to listen to a fairly long tale, so that . . .' I paused. 'I mean, I want someone to know . . .' I stopped once more.

'In case you disappear again?' she said matter-of-factly.

I was grateful for her calmness.

'Yes,' I said. I told her about meeting Vivian Iverson at the races, and our thoughts on insurance, springboards, and rocks. 'So you see,' I ended, 'you'll be the rock, if you will.'

'You can expect,' she said, 'rock-like behaviour.'

'Well,' I said, 'I've brought a sealed package of photocopied documents. It's in the car.'

'Fetch it,' she said.

I went out to the street and collected the thick envelope from the boot. Habit induced me to look into the back seat floor space, and to scan the harmless street. No one hiding, no one watching, that I could see. No one had followed me from the racecourse, I was sure.

Looking over my shoulder for the rest of my life.

I took the parcel indoors and gave it to Hilary, and also the negatives of her photographs, explaining that I already had the extra prints. She put everything on the table beside her and told me to sit down and get on with the tale.

'I'll tell you a bit about my job,' I said. 'And then you'll understand better.' I stretched out with luxurious weariness in the cane chair and looked at the intent interest on her strong plain face. A pity, I thought, about the glasses.

'An accountant working for a long time in one area, particularly in an area like a country town, tends to get an overall picture of the local life.'

'I follow you,' she said. 'Go on.'

'The transactions of one client tend to turn up in the accounts of others. For instance, a racehorse trainer buys horse food from the forage merchants. I check the invoice through the trainer's accounts, and then, because the forage merchant is also my client, I later check it again through his. I see that the forage merchant has paid a builder for an extension to his house, and later, in the builder's accounts, I see what *he* paid for the bricks and cement. I see that a jockey had paid *x* pounds on an air-taxi, and later, because the air-taxi firm is also my client, I see the receipt of *x* pounds from the jockey. I see the movement of money around the neighbourhood ... the interlocking of interests ... the pattern of commerce. I learn the names of suppliers, the size of businesses, and the kinds of services people use. My knowledge increases until I have a sort of mental map like a wide landscape, in which all the names are familiar and occur in the proper places.'

'Fascinating,' Hilary said.

'Well,' I said, 'if a totally strange name crops up, and you can't cross-reference it with anything else, you begin to ask questions. At first of yourself, and then of others. Discreetly. And that was how I ran into trouble in the shape of two master criminals called Glitberg and Ownslow.'

'They sound like a music-hall turn.'

'They're as funny as the Black Death.' I drank some sherry ruefully. 'They worked for the council, and the council's accounts and audits were done by a large firm in London, who naturally didn't have any intimate local knowledge. Ownslow and Glitberg had invented a construction firm called National Construction (Wessex) Limited, through which they had syphoned off more than a million pounds each of taxpayers' money. And I had a client, a builders' merchant, who had received several cheques from National Construction (Wessex). I'd never heard of National Construction (Wessex) in any other context, and I asked my client some searching questions, to which his reply was unmistakable panic. Glitberg and

Ownslow were prosecuted and went to jail swearing to be revenged.'

'On you?'

'On me.'

'Nasty.'

'A few weeks later,' I said, 'much the same thing happened. I turned up some odd payments made by a director of an electronics firm through the company's computer. His name was Connaught Powys. He'd taken his firm for over a quarter of a million, and he too went to jail swearing to get even. He's out again now, and so are Glitberg and Ownslow. Since then I've been the basic cause of the downfall of two more big-time embezzlers, both of whom descended to the cells swearing severally to tear my guts out and cut my throat.' I sighed. 'Luckily, they're both still inside.'

'And I thought accountants led dull lives!'

'Maybe some do.' I drained my sherry. 'There's another thing that those five embezzlers have in common besides me, and that is that not a penny of what they stole has been recovered.'

'Really?' She seemed not to find it greatly significant. 'I expect it's all sitting around in bank deposits, under different names.'

I shook my head. 'Not unless it is in literally thousands of tiny weeny deposits, which doesn't seem likely.'

'Why thousands?'

'Banks nowadays have to inform the Tax Inspectors of the existence of any deposit account for which the annual interest is £15 or more. That means the Inspectors know of all deposits of over three or four hundred quid.'

'I had no idea,' she said blankly.

'Anyway,' I said, 'I wanted to know if it could be Powys or Glitberg or Ownslow who had kidnapped me for revenge, so I asked them.'

'Good heavens.'

'Yeah. It wasn't a good idea. They wouldn't say yes or no.' I looked back to the night at the Vivat Club. 'They did tell me something else, though . . .' I said, and told Hilary what it was. Her eyes widened behind the glasses and she nodded once or twice.

'I see. Yes,' she said.

'So now,' I said. 'Here we are a few years later, and now I have not only my local area mental map but a broad view of most of the racing world, with uncountable interconnections. I do the accounts for so many racing people, their lives spread out like a carpet, touching, overlapping, each small transaction adding to my under- standing of the whole. I'm part of it myself, as a jockey. I feel the fabric around me. I know how much saddles cost, and which saddler does most business, and which owners don't pay their bills, and who bets and who drinks, who saves, who gives to charity, who keeps a mistress. I know how much the woman whose horse I rode today paid to have him photographed for the Christmas cards she sent last year, and how much a bookmaker gave for his Rolls, and thousands and thousands of similar facts. All fitting, all harmless. It's when they don't fit . . . like a jockey

238

suddenly spending more than he's earned, and I find he's running a whole new business and not declaring a penny of it . . . it's when the bits don't fit that I see the monster in the waves. Glimpsed, hidden . . . But definitely there.'

'Like now?' she said, frowning. 'Your iceberg?'

'Mm.' I hesitated. 'Another embezzler.'

'And this one – will he too go to jail swearing to cut your throat?'

I didn't answer at once, and she added dryly, 'Or is he likely to cut your throat before you get him there?'

I gave her half a grin. 'Not with a rock like you, he won't.'

'You be careful, Roland,' she said seriously. 'This doesn't feel to me like a joke.'

She stood up restlessly, towering among the palm fronds, as thin in her way as their stems.

'Come into the kitchen. What do you want to eat? I can do a Spanish omelette, if you like.'

I sat with my elbows on the kitchen table, and while she chopped onions and potatoes and green peppers I told her a good deal more, most of it highly unethical, as an accountant should never disclose the affairs of a client. She listened with increasing dismay, her cooking actions growing slower. Finally she laid down the knife and simply stood.

'Your partner,' she said.

'I don't know how much he's condoned,' I said, 'but on Monday . . . I have to find out.'

'Tell the police,' she said. 'Let them find out.'

'No. I've worked with Trevor for six years. We've always got on well together, and he seems fond of me, in his distant way. I can't shop him, just like that.'

'You'll warn him.'

'Yes,' I said. 'And I'll tell him of the existence of . . . the rock.'

She started cooking again, automatically, her thoughts busy behind her eyes.

'Do you think,' she said, 'that your partner knew about the other embezzlers, and tried to hush them up?'

I shook my head. 'Not Glitberg and Ownslow. Positively not. Not the last two, either. The firms they worked for were both my clients, and Trevor had no contact with them. But Connaught Powys . . .' I sighed. 'I really don't know. Trevor always used to spend about a week at that firm, doing the audit on the spot, as one nearly always does for big concerns, and I went one year only because he had an ulcer. It was Connaught Powys's bad luck that I cottoned on to what he was doing. Trevor might genuinely have missed the warning signs, because he doesn't always work the way I do.'

'How do you mean?'

'Well, a lot of an accountant's work is fairly mechanical. Vouching, for instance. That's checking that cheques written down in the cash book really were issued for the amount stated or, in other words, if the cashier writes down that cheque number 1234 was issued to Joe Bloggs in the sum of eighty pounds to pay for a load of sand, the auditor checks that the bank actually paid eighty pounds to Joe Bloggs on cheque no. 1234. It's routine work and takes a fairly long time on a big account, and it's often, or even usually, done, not by the accountant or auditor himself, but by an assistant. Assistants in our firm tend to come and go, and don't necessarily develop a sense of probability. The present ones wouldn't be likely to query, for instance, whether Joe Bloggs really existed, or sold sand, or sold eighty quid's worth, or delivered only fifty quid's worth, with Joe Bloggs and the cashier conspiring to pocket the thirty pounds profit.'

'Roland!'

I grinned. 'Small fiddles abound. It's the first violins that threaten to cut your throat.'

She broke four eggs into a bowl. 'Do you do all your own ... er ... vouching, then?'

'No, not all. It would take too long. But I do all of it for some accounts, and some of it for all accounts. To get the feel of things. To know where I am.'

'To fit into the landscape,' she said.

'Yes.'

'And Trevor doesn't?'

'He does a few himself, but on the whole not. Don't get me wrong. More accountants do as Trevor does, it's absolutely normal practice.'

'You want my advice?' she said.

'Yes, please.'

'Go straight to the police.'

'Thank you. Get on with the omelette.'

She sizzled it in the pan and divided it, succulent and

soft in the centre, onto the plates. It tasted like a testimonial to her own efficiency, the best I'd ever had. Over coffee, afterwards, I told her a great deal about Jossie.

She looked into her cup. 'Do you love her?' she said.

'I don't know. It's too soon to say.'

'You sound,' she said dryly, 'bewitched.'

'There have been other girls. But not the same.' I looked at her downturned face. My mouth twitched. 'In case you're wondering about Jossie,' I said, 'no, I haven't.'

She looked up, the spectacles flashing, her eyes suddenly laughing, and a blush starting on her neck. She uttered an unheadmistressly opinion.

'You're a sod,' she said.

It was an hour's drive home from Hilary's house. No one followed me, or took the slightest interest, that I could see.

I rolled quietly down the lane towards the cottage with the car lights switched off, and made a silent reconnoitre on foot for the last hundred yards.

Everything about my home was dark and peaceful. The lights of Mrs Morris's sitting-room, next door, shone dimly through the pattern of her curtains. The night sky was powdered with stars, and the air was cool.

I waited for a while, listening, and was slowly reassured. No horrors in the shadows. No shattering black prisons yawning like mantraps before my feet. No cut-throats with ready steel.

To be afraid, I thought, was no way to live; yet I couldn't help it.

I unlocked the cottage and switched on all the lights; and it was empty, welcoming and sane. I fetched the car from the lane, locked myself into the cottage, pulled shut the curtains, switched on the heaters, and hugged round myself the comforting illusion of being safe in the burrow.

After that I made a pot of coffee, fished out some brandy, and sprawled into an armchair with the ancient records of the misdeeds of Powys, Glitberg and Ownslow.

At one time I'd known every detail in those files with blinding clarity, but the years had blurred my memory. I found notes in my own handwriting about inferences I couldn't remember drawing, and conclusions as startling as acid. I was amazed, actually, at the quality of work I'd done, and it was weird to see it from an objective distance, as with a totally fresh eye. I supposed I could understand the comment there had been then, though at the time what I was doing had seemed a perfectly natural piece of work, done merely as best I could. I smiled to myself in pleased surprise. In that far-off time, I must have been hell to embezzlers. Not like nowadays, when it took me six shots to see Denby Crest.

I came across pages of notes about the workings of computers, details of which I had forgotten as fast as I'd learned them on a crash course in an electronics firm much like Powys's. It had pleased me at the time to be able to dissect and explain just what he'd done, and nothing had made him more furious. It had been vanity on my part, I thought: and I was still vain. Admiring your own work was one of the deadlier intellectual sins.

I sighed. I was never going to be perfect, so why worry.

There was no record anywhere in the Glitberg/ Ownslow file of the buying of the warehouse, but it did seem possible, as I dug deeper in the search for clues, that it actually had been built by Glitberg and Ownslow, and was the sole concrete fabrication of National Construction (Wessex). Anyone who could invent whole streets of dwellings could put up a real warehouse without much trouble.

I wondered why they'd needed it, when everything else had been achieved on paper.

A tangible asset, uncashed, gone to seed, in which I had been dumped. The police had been told I was there, and the estate agent trail had led without difficulty straight to Ownslow and Glitberg.

Why?

I sat and thought about it for a good long time, and then I finished the coffee and brandy and went to bed.

I picked Jossie up at ten in the grey morning, and drove to Portsmouth for the hovercraft ferry to the Isle of Wight.

'The nostalgia kick?' Jossie said. 'Back to the boarding house?'

I nodded. 'The sunny isle of childhood.'

'Oh yeah?' She took me literally and looked up meaningfully at the cloudy sky.

'It heads the British sunshine league,' I said.

'Tell that to Torquay.'

A ten-minute zip in the hovercraft took us across the sea at Spithead, and when we stepped ashore at Ryde, the clouds were behind us, hovering like a grey sheet over the mainland.

'It's unfair,' Jossie said, smiling.

'It's often like that.'

The town was bright with new spring paint, the Regency buildings clean and graceful in the sun. Every year, before the holiday-makers came, there was the big brush-up and every winter, when they'd gone, the comfortable relapse into carpet slippers and salt-caked windows.

'Ryde pier,' I said, 'is two thousand, three hundred and five feet long, and was opened in 1814.'

'I don't want to know that.'

'There are approximately six hundred hotels, motels and boarding houses on this sunny island.'

'Nor that.'

'Nine towns, two castles, a lot of flamingoes and Parkhurst Prison.'

'Nor that, for God's sake.'

'My Uncle Rufus,' I said, 'was chief mucker-out at the local riding school.'

'Good grief.'

'As his assistant mucker-out,' I said, 'I scrambled under horses' bellies from the age of six.'

'That figures.'

'I used to exercise the horses and ponies all winter when the holiday people had gone home. And break in new ones. I can't really remember not being able to ride, but there's no racing here, of course. The first race I ever rode in was the Isle of Wight Foxhounds point-to-point over on the mainland, and I fell off.'

We walked along the Esplanade with the breeze blowing Jossie's long green scarf out like streamers. She waved an arm at the sparkling water and said, 'Why horses? Why not boats, for heaven's sake, when you had them on your doorstep.'

'They made me seasick.'

She laughed. 'Like going to heaven and being allergic to harps.'

I took her to a hotel I knew, where there was a sunny terrace sheltered from the breeze, with a stunning view of the Solent and the shipping tramping by to South-ampton. We drank hot chocolate and read the lunch menu, and talked of this and that and nothing much, and the time slid away like a mill-stream.

After roast beef for both of us, and apple pie, ice-cream and cheese for Jossie, we whistled up a taxi. There weren't many operating on a Sunday afternoon in April, but there was no point in being a native if one didn't know where to find the pearls.

The driver knew me, and didn't approve of my having deserted to become a 'mainlander', but as he also knew I knew the roads backwards, we got a straight run over Blackgang Chine to the wild cliffs on the south-west coast, and no roundabout guff to add mileage. We dawdled along there for about an hour, stopping often to stand out of the car, on the windswept grass. Jossie took in great lungfuls of the soul-filling landscape and said whyever did I live in Newbury.

'Racing,' I said.

'So simple.'

'Do you mind if we call on a friend on the way back?' I said. 'Ten minutes or so?'

'Of course not.'

'Wootton Bridge, then,' I said to the driver. 'Frederick's boatyard.'

'They'll be shut. It's Sunday.'

'We'll try, anyway.'

He shrugged heavily, leaving me to the consequences of my own stupidity, and drove back across the island, through Newport and out on the Ryde road to the deep inlet which formed a natural harbour for hundreds of small yachts.

The white-painted façade of the boatyard showed closed doors and no sign of life.

'There you are,' said the driver. 'I told you so.'

I got out of the car and walked over to the door

marked 'Office', and knocked on it. Within a few moments it opened, and I grinned back to Jossie and jerked my head for her to join me.

'I got your message,' Johnny Frederick said. 'And Sunday afternoon, I sleep.'

'At your age?'

His age was the same as mine, almost to the day: we'd shared a desk at school and many a snigger in the lavatories. The round-faced, impish boy had grown into a muscular, salt-tanned man with craftsman's hands and a respectable hatred of paperwork. He occasionally telephoned me to find out if his own local accountant was doing things right, and bombarded the poor man with my advice.

'How's your father?' I said.

'Much the same.'

A balk of timber had fallen on Johnny's father's head in days gone by. There had been a lot of unkind jokes about thick as two planks before, three planks after, but the net result had been that an ailing family business had woken up in the hands of a bright new mind. With Johnny's designs and feeling for materials, Frederick Boats were a growing name.

I introduced Jossie, who got a shrewd once-over for aerodynamic lines and a shake from a hand like a piece of calloused teak.

'Pleased to meet you,' he said, which was about the nearest he ever got to social small-talk. He switched his gaze to me. 'You've been in the wars a bit, according to the papers.'

'You might say so.' I grinned. 'What are you building, these days?'

'Come and see.'

He walked across the functional little office and opened the far door, which led straight into the boatyard itself. We went through, and Jossie exclaimed aloud at the unexpected size of the huge shed which sloped away down to the water.

There were several smallish fibreglass hulls supported in building frames, and two large ones, side by side in the centre, with five-foot keels.

'What size are those?' Jossie said.

'Thirty-seven feet overall.'

'They look bigger.'

'They won't on the water. It's the largest size we do, at present.' Johnny walked us round one of them, pointing out subtleties of hull design with pride. 'It handles well in heavy seas. It's stable, and not too difficult to sail, which is what most people want.'

'Not a racer?' I said.

He shook his head. 'Those dinghies are. But the big ocean-racers are specialist jobs. This yard isn't large enough; not geared to that class. And anyway, I like cruisers. A bit of carpet in the saloon and lockers that slide like silk.'

Jossie wandered off down the concrete slope, peering into the half-fitted dinghies and looking contentedly interested. I pulled the envelope of enlarged photographs from my inner pocket and showed them to Johnny. Three views of a sailing boat, one of an out-of-focus man.

'That's the boat I was abducted on. Can you tell anything about it from these photos?'

He peered at them, his head on one side. 'If you leave them with me, maybe. I'll look through the catalogues, and ask the boys over at Cowes. Was there anything special about it, that you remember?'

I explained that I hadn't seen much except the sail locker. 'The boat was pretty new, I think. Or at any rate well maintained. And it sailed from England on Thursday, March 17th, some time in the evening.'

He shuffled the prints to look at the man.

'His name is Alastair Yardley,' I said. 'I've written it on the back. He came from Bristol, and worked from there as a deck-hand on sea-trials for ocean-going yachts. He skippered the boat. He's about our age.'

'Are you in a hurry for all this info?'

'Quicker the better.'

'OK. I'll ring a few guys. Let you know tomorrow, if I come up with anything.'

'That's great.'

He tucked the prints into their envelope and let his gaze wander to Jossie.

'A racing filly,' he said. 'Good lines.'

'Eyes off.'

'I like earthier ones, mate. Big boobs and not too bright.'

'Boring.'

'When I get home, I want a hot tea, and a cuddle when I feel like it, and no backchat about women's lib.'

When I got home, I thought, I wouldn't mind Jossie.

She walked up the concrete with big strides of her long legs, and came to a stop at our side. 'I had a friend whose boyfriend insisted on taking her sailing,' she said. 'She said she didn't terribly mind being wet, or cold, or hungry, or seasick, or frightened. She just didn't like them all at once.'

Johnny's eyes slid my way. 'With this boyfriend she'd be all right. He gets sick in harbour.'

Jossie nodded. 'Feeble.'

'Thanks,' I said.

'Be my guest.'

We went back through the office and into the taxi, and Johnny waved us goodbye.

'Any more chums?' Jossie said.

'Not this trip. If I start on the aunts, we'll be here for ever. Visit one, visit all, or there's a dust-up.'

We drove, however, at Jossie's request, past the guest house where I'd lived with my mother. There was a new glass sun lounge across the whole of the front, and a car park where there had been garden. Tubs of flowers, bright sun-awnings, and a swinging sign saying 'Vacancies'.

'Brave,' Jossie said, clearly moved. 'Don't you think?'

251

I paid off the taxi there and we walked down to the
sea, with seagulls squawking overhead and the white
little town sleeping to tea-time on its sunny hillside.

'It's pretty,' Jossie said. 'And I see why you left.'

She seemed as content as I to dawdle away the rest of
the day. We crossed again in the hovercraft, and made
our way slowly northwards, stopping at a pub at dusk for
a drink and rubbery pork pie, and arriving finally outside
the sprawling pile of Axwood House more than twelve
hours after we'd left.

'That car,' Jossie said, pointing with disfavour at an
inoffensive Volvo parked ahead, 'belongs to the detestable Lida.'

The light over the front door shone on her disgruntled
face. I smiled, and she transferred the disfavour to me.

'It's all right for you. You aren't threatened with her
moving into your home.'

'You could move out,' I said mildly.

'Just like that?'

'To my cottage, perhaps.'

'Good grief!'

'You could inspect it,' I said, 'for cleanliness, dry rot
and spiders.'

She gave me her most intolerant stare. 'Butler, cook,
and housemaids?'

'Six footmen and a lady's maid.'

'I'll come to tea and cucumber sandwiches. I suppose
you do have cucumber sandwiches?'

'Of course.'

'Thin, and without crusts?'

'Naturally.'

I had really surprised her, I saw. She didn't know what to answer. It was quite clear, though, that she was not going to fall swooning into my arms. There was a good deal I would have liked to say, but I didn't know how to. Things about caring, and reassurance, and looking ahead.

'Next Sunday,' she said. 'At half past three. For tea.'

'I'll line up the staff.'

She decided to get out of the car, and I went round to open the door for her. Her eyes looked huge.

'Are you serious?' she said.

'Oh yes. It'll be up to you . . . to decide.'

'After tea?'

I shook my head. 'At any time.'

Her expression slowly softened to unaccustomed gentleness. I kissed her, and then kissed her again with conviction.

'I think I'll go in,' she said waveringly, turning away.

'Jossie . . .'

'What?'

I swallowed. Shook my head. 'Come to tea,' I said helplessly. 'Come to tea.'

CHAPTER SIXTEEN

Monday morning, after another night free of alarms and excursions, I went back to the office with good intentions of actually doing some work. Peter was sulking with Monday morning glooms, Bess had menstrual pains, and Debbie was tearful from a row with the screw-selling fiancé: par for office life as I knew it.

Trevor came into my room looking fatherly and anxious, and seemed reassured to find my appearance less deathly than on Friday.

'You did rest, then, Ro,' he said relievedly.

'I rode in a race and took a girl to the seaside.'

'Good heavens. At any rate, it seems to have done you good. Better than spending your time working.'

'Yes . . .' I said. 'Trevor, I did come into the office on Saturday morning, for a couple of hours.'

His air of worry crept subtly back. He waited for me to go on with the manner of a patient expecting bad news from his doctor: and I felt the most tremendous regret in having to give it to him.

'Denby Crest,' I said.

'Ro . . .' He spread out his hands, palms downwards, in a gesture that spoke of paternal distress at a rebellious son who wouldn't take his senior's word for things.

'I can't help it,' I said. 'I know he's a client, and a friend of yours, but if he's misappropriated fifty thousand pounds and you've condoned it, it concerns us both. It concerns this office, this partnership, and our future. You must see that. We can't just ignore the whole thing and pretend it hasn't happened.'

'Ro, believe me, everything will be all right.'

I shook my head. 'Trevor, you telephone Denby Crest and tell him to come over here today, to discuss what we're going to do.'

'No.'

'Yes,' I said positively. 'I'm not having it, Trevor. I'm half of this firm, and it's not going to do anything illegal.'

'You're uncompromising.' The mixture of sorrow and irritation had intensified. The two emotions, I thought fleetingly, that gave you regrets while you shot the rabbit.

'Get him here at four o'clock,' I said.

'You can't bully him like that.'

'There are worse consequences,' I said. I spoke without emphasis, but he knew quite well that it was a threat.

Irritation won hands down over sorrow. 'Very well, Ro,' he said sourly. 'Very well.'

He went out of my room with none of the sympathetic concern for me with which he had come in, and I felt a lonely sense of loss. I could forgive him anything myself,

I thought in depression, but the law wouldn't. I lived by the law, both by inclination and choice. If my friend broke the law, should I abandon it for his sake: or should I abandon my friend for the sake of the law? In the abstract, there was no difficulty in my mind. In the flesh, I shrank. There was nothing frightfully jolly in being the instrument of distress, ruin, and prosecution. How much easier if the miscreant would confess of his own free will, instead of compelling his friend to denounce him: a sentimental solution, I thought sardonically, which happened only in weepy films. I was afraid that for myself there would be no such easy way out.

Those pessimistic musings were interrupted by a telephone call from Hilary, whose voice, when I answered, sounded full of relief.

'What's the matter?' I said.

'Nothing. I just . . .' She stopped.

'Just what?'

'Just wanted to know you were there, as a matter of fact.'

'Hilary!'

'Sounds stupid, I suppose, now that we both know you *are* there. But I just wanted to be sure. After all, you wouldn't have cast me in the role of rock if you thought you were in no danger at all.'

'Um,' I said, smiling down the telephone. 'Sermons in stones.'

She laughed. 'You just take care of yourself, Ro.'

'Yes, ma'am.'

I put down the receiver, marvelling at her kindness; and almost immediately the bell rang again.

'Roland?'

'Yes, Moira?'

Her sigh came audibly down the wire. 'Thank goodness! I tried all day yesterday to reach you, and there was no reply.'

'I was out all day.'

'Yes, but I didn't know that. I mean, I was imagining all sorts of things, like you being kidnapped again, and all because of me.'

'I'm so sorry.'

'Oh, I don't mind, now that I know you're safe. I've had this terrible picture of you shut up again, and needing someone to rescue you. I've been so worried, because of Binny.'

'What about Binny?'

'I think he's gone really *mad*,' she said. 'Insane. I went over to his stables yesterday morning to see if Tapestry was all right after his race, and he wouldn't let me into the yard. Binny, I mean. All the gates were shut and locked with padlocks and chains. It's insane. He came and stood on the inside of the gate to the yard where Tapestry is, and waved his arms about, and told me to go away. I mean, it's *insane*.'

'It certainly is.'

'I told him he could have caused a terrible accident, tampering with that rein, and he screamed that he hadn't done it, and I couldn't prove it, and anything that

257

happened to you was my fault for insisting that you rode the horse.' She paused for breath. 'He looked so . . . well, so *dangerous*. And I'd never thought of him being dangerous, but just a fool. You'll think I'm silly, but I was quite frightened.'

'I don't think you were silly,' I said truthfully.

'And then it came to me, like a revelation,' she said, 'that it had been Binny who had kidnapped you before, both times, and that he'd done it again, or something even worse . . .'

'Moira . . .'

'Yes, but you didn't *see* him. And then there was no answer to your telephone. I know you'll think I'm silly, but I was so worried.'

'I'm very grateful . . .' I started to say.

'You see, Binny never thought you'd win the Gold Cup,' she said, rushing on. 'And the very second you had, I told him you'd ride Tapestry always from then on, and he was *furious*, absolutely furious. You wouldn't believe. So of course he had you kidnapped at once, so that you'd be out of the way, and I'd *have* to have someone else, and then you escaped, and you were going to ride at Ascot, so he kidnapped you *again*, and he went absolutely berserk when I wouldn't let Tapestry go at Ascot with another jockey. And I made such a fuss in the press that he had to let you out, and so he had to try something else, like cutting the rein, and now I think he's so insane that he doesn't really know what he's doing. I mean, I think he thinks that if he kidnaps you, or kills you even, that I'll *have* to get another jockey for the Whitbread Gold Cup a week next Saturday, and honestly I think he's out of his *senses*, and really awfully dangerous because of that *obsession*, and so you see I really was terribly worried.'

'I do see,' I said. 'And I'm incredibly grateful for your concern.'

'But what are you going to *do*?' she wailed.

'About Binny? Listen, Moira, please listen.'

'Yes,' she said, her voice calming down. 'I'm listening.'

'Do absolutely nothing.'

'But *Roland*,' she protested.

'Listen. I'm sure you are quite right that Binny is in a dangerous mental state, but anything you or I could do would make him worse. Let him cool down. Give him several days. Then send a horsebox with if possible a police escort – and you can get policemen for private jobs like that, you just apply to the local nick, and offer to pay for their time – collect Tapestry, and send him to another trainer.'

'Roland!'

'You can carry loyalty too far,' I said. 'Binny's done marvels with training the horse, I agree, but you owe him nothing. If it weren't for your own strength of mind he'd have manipulated the horse to make money only for himself, as well you know, and your enjoyment would have come nowhere.'

'But about kidnapping you . . .' she began.

'No, Moira,' I said. 'He didn't; it wasn't Binny. I don't doubt he was delighted it was done, but he didn't do it.'

She was astonished. 'He must have.'

'No.'

'But why not?'

'Lots of complicated reasons. But for one thing, he wouldn't have kidnapped me straight after the Gold Cup. He wouldn't have had any need to. If he'd wanted to abduct me to stop me riding Tapestry, he wouldn't have done it until just before the horse's next race, nearly three weeks later.'

'Oh,' she said doubtfully.

'The first abduction was quite elaborate,' I said. 'Binny couldn't possibly have had time to organize it between the Gold Cup and the time I was taken, which was only an hour or so later.'

'Are you sure?'

'Yes, Moira, quite sure. And when he really did try to stop me winning, he did very direct and simple things, not difficult like kidnapping. He offered me a bribe, and cut the rein. Much more in character. He always was a fool, and now he's a dangerous fool, but he isn't a kidnapper.'

'Oh dear,' she said, sounding disappointed. 'And I was so *sure*.'

She cheered up a bit and asked me to ride Tapestry in the Whitbread. I said I'd be delighted, and she deflated my ego by passing on the opinion of a press friend of hers to the effect that Tapestry was one of those horses who liked to be in charge, and an amateur who just sat there doing nothing very much was exactly what suited him best.

Grinning to myself I put down the receiver. The press friend was right; but who cared.

For the rest of the morning I tried to make inroads into the backlog of correspondence, but found it impossible to concentrate. The final fruit of two hours of reading letters and shuffling them around was three heaps marked 'overdue', 'urgent', and 'if you don't get these off today there will be trouble'.

Debbie looked down her pious nose at my inability to apply myself, and primly remarked that I was under-utilizing her capability. Under-utilizing ... Ye Gods! Where did the gobbledegook jargon come from?

'You mean I'm not giving you enough to do.'

'That's what I said.'

At luncheon I stayed alone in the office and stared into space: and my telephone rang again.

Johnny Frederick, full of news.

'Do you mind if I send you a bill for 'phone calls?' he said. 'I must have spent thirty quid. I've been talking all morning.'

'I'll send you a cheque.'

'OK. Well, mate, pin back your lugholes. That boat you were on was built at Lymington, and she sailed from there after dark on March 17th. She was brand spanking new, and she hadn't completed her trials, and she wasn't registered or named. She was built by a top-notch shipyard called Goldenwave Marine, for a client called Arthur Robinson.'

'Who?'

261

'Arthur Robinson. That's what he said his name was, anyway. And there was only one slightly unusual thing about Mr Robinson, and that was that he paid for the boat in cash.'

He waited expectantly.

'How much cash?' I said.

'Two hundred thousand pounds.'

'Crikey.'

'Mind you,' Johnny said, 'that's bargain basement stuff for Goldenwave. They do a nice job in mini-liners at upwards of a million, with gold taps, for Arabs.'

'In cash?'

'Near enough, I dare say. Anyway, Arthur Robinson always paid on the nail, in instalments as they came due during the boat-building, but always in your actual folding. Goldenwave Marine wouldn't be interested in knowing whether the cash had had tax paid on it. None of their business.'

'Quite,' I said. 'Go on.'

'That Thursday – March 17th – in the morning, some time, Arthur Robinson rang Goldenwave and said he wanted to take some friends aboard for a party that evening, and would they please see that the water and fuel tanks were topped up, and everything shipshape. Which Goldenwave did.'

'Without question.'

'Of course. You don't argue with two hundred thousand quid. Anyway, the boat was out on a mooring in the deep water passage, so they left her fit for the owner's visit and brought her tender ashore, for him to use when he got there.'

'A black rubber dinghy?'

'I didn't ask. The nightwatchman had been told to expect the party, so he let them in, and helped generally, and saw them off. I got him out of bed this morning to talk to him, and he was none too pleased, but he remembers the evening quite well, because of course the boat sailed off that night and never came back.'

'What did he say?'

'There were two lots of people, he said. One lot came in an old white van, which he didn't think much of for an owner of such a boat. You'd expect a Rolls, he said.' Johnny chuckled. 'The first arrivals, three people, were the crew. They unloaded stores from an estate car and made two trips out to the boat. Then the white van arrived with several more men, and one of those was lying down. They told the nightwatchman he was dead drunk, and that was you, I reckon. Then the first three men and the drunk man went out to the boat, and the other men drove away in the old van and the estate car, and that was that. The nightwatchman thought it a very boring sort of party, and noted the embarkation in his log, and paid no more attention. Next morning, no boat.'

'And no report to the police?'

'The owner had taken his own property, which he'd fully paid for. Goldenwave had expected him to take command of her a week later, anyway, so they made no fuss.'

'You've done absolute marvels,' I said.

'Do you want to hear about Alastair Yardley?'

'There's more?'

'There sure is. He seems to be quite well-known. Several of the bigger shipyards have recommended him to people who want their boats sailed from England, say, to Bermuda, or the Caribbean, and so on, and don't have a regular crew, and also don't want to cross oceans themselves. He signs on his own crew, and pays them himself. He's no crook. Got a good reputation. Tough, though. And he's not cheap. If he agreed to help shanghai you, you can bet Mr Arthur Robinson paid through the nose for the service. But you can ask him yourself, if you like.'

'What do you mean?'

Johnny was justifiably triumphant. 'I struck dead lucky, mate. Mind you, I chased him round six shipyards, but he's in England now to fetch another yacht, and he'll talk to you if you ring him more or less at once.'

'I don't believe it!'

'Here's the number.' He read out the numbers, and I wrote them down. 'Ring him before two o'clock. You can also talk to the chap in charge of Goldenwave, if you like. This is his number. He said he'd help in any way he could.'

'You're fantastic,' I said, stunned to breathlessness by his success.

'We got a real lucky break, mate, because when I took those photographs to Cowes first thing this morning, I asked around everybody, and there was a feller in the third yard I tried who'd worked at Goldenwave last year, and he said it looked like their Golden Sixty Five, so I rang them, and it was the departure date that clinched it.'

'I can't begin to thank you.'

'To tell you the truth, mate, it's been a bit of excitement, and there isn't all that much about, these days. I've enjoyed this morning, and that's a fact.'

'I'll give you a ring. Tell you how things turn out.'

'Great. Can't wait. And see you.'

He disconnected, and with an odd sinking feeling in my stomach I rang the first of the numbers he'd given me. A shipyard. Could I speak to Alastair Yardley? Hang on, said the switchboard. I hung.

'Hullo?'

The familiar voice. Bold, self-assertive, challenging the world.

'It's Roland Britten,' I said.

There was a silence, then he said, 'Yeah,' slowly.

'You said you'd talk to me.'

'Yeah.' He paused. 'Your friend this morning, John Frederick, the boat-builder, he tells me I was sold a pup about you.'

'How do you mean?'

'I was told you were a blackmailer.'

'A *what*?'

'Yeah.' He sighed. 'Well, this guy Arthur Robinson, he said you'd set up his wife in some compromising photographs and were trying to blackmail her, and he wanted you taught a lesson.'

'Oh,' I said blankly. It explained a great deal, I thought.

'Your friend Frederick told me that was all crap. He said I'd been conned. I reckon I was. All the other guys in the yard here know all about you winning that race and going missing. They just told me. Seems it was in all the papers. But I didn't see them, of course.'

'How long,' I said, 'were you supposed to keep me on board?'

'He said to ring him Monday evening, April 4th, and he'd tell me when and where and how to set you loose. But of course, you jumped ship the Tuesday before, and how you got that lever off is a bloody mystery ... I rang him that night, and he was so bloody angry he couldn't get the words out. So then he said he wouldn't pay me for the job on you, and I said if he didn't he could whistle for his boat, I'd just sail it into some port somewhere and walk away, and he'd have God's own job finding it. So I said he could send me the money to Palma, where I bank, and when I got it I'd do what he wanted, which was to take his boat to Antibes and deliver it to the ship brokers there.'

'Brokers?'

'Yeah. Funny, that. He'd only just bought it. What did he want to sell it for?'

'Well ...' I said. 'Do you remember his telephone number?'

'No. Threw it away, didn't I, as soon as I was shot of his boat.'

'At Antibes?'

'That's right.'

'Did you meet him?' I asked.

'Yeah. That night at Lymington. He told me not to talk to you, and not to listen, because you'd tell me lies, and not to let you know where we were, and not to leave a mark on you, and to watch out because you were as slippery as an eel.' He paused a second. 'He was right about that, come to think.'

'Do you remember what he looked like?'

'Yeah,' he said, 'what I saw of him; but it was mostly in the dark, out on the quay.' He described Arthur Robinson as I'd expected, and well enough to be conclusive.

'I wasn't intending to go for another week,' he said. 'The weather forecasts were all bad for Biscay, and I'd only been out in her once, in light air, not enough to know how she'd handle in a gale, but he rang Golden-wave that morning and spoke to me, and told me about you, and said gale or no gale he'd make it worth my while if I'd go that evening and take you with me.'

'I hope it was worth it,' I said.

'Yeah,' he said frankly. 'I got paid double.'

I laughed in my throat. 'Er . . .' I said, 'is it possible for a boat just to sail off from England and wander round Mediterranean ports, when it hasn't even got a name? I mean, do you have to pass Customs, and things like that?'

'You can pass Customs if you want to waste a bloody lot of time. Otherwise, unless you tell them, a port doesn't know whether you've come from two miles down the coast, or two thousand. The big ports collect mooring fees, that's all they're interested in. If you drop anchor at somewhere like Formentor, which we did one night with you, no one takes a blind bit of notice. Easy come, easy go, that's what it's like on the sea. Best way to live, I reckon.'

'It sounds marvellous,' I sighed enviously.

'Yeah. Look . . .' he paused a second, 'are you going to set the police on me, or anything? Because I'm off today, on the afternoon tide, and I'm not telling where.'

'No,' I said. 'No police.'

He let his breath out audibly in relief. 'I reckon . . .' He paused. 'Thanks, then. And well, sorry, like.'

I remembered the paperback, and the socks, and the soap and I had no quarrel with him.

From Goldenwave Marine, ten minutes later, I learned a good many background facts about big boats in general and Arthur Robinson in particular.

Goldenwave had four more Golden Sixty Fives on the stocks at the moment, all commissioned by private customers, and Arthur Robinson had been one of a stream. Their Golden Sixty Five had been a successful design, they were pleased and proud to say, and their standard of ship-building was respected the world over.

End of commercial.

I replaced the receiver gratefully. Sat, thinking, chewing bits off my fingernails. Decided, without joy, to take a slightly imprudent course.

Debbie, Peter, Bess and Trevor came back, and the place filled up with tap-tap and bustle. Mr Wells arrived for his appointment twenty minutes before the due time, reminding me of the psychiatrists'-eye-view of patients: if they're early, they're anxious, if they're late, they're aggressive, and if they're on time, they're pathological. I often thought the psychiatrists didn't understand about trains, buses and traffic flow, but in this case there wasn't much doubt about the anxiety. Mr Wells' hair, manner and eyes were all out of control.

'I rang the people you sent the rubber cheque to,' I said. 'They were a bit sticky, but they've agreed not to prosecute if you take care of them after the inevitable Receiving Order.'

'I what?'

'Pay them later,' I said. Jargon . . . I did it myself.

'Oh.'

'The order of paying,' I said, 'will be first the Inland Revenue, who will collect tax in full, and will also charge interest for every day overdue.'

'But I haven't anything to pay them with.'

'Did you sell your car, as we agreed you should?'

He nodded, but wouldn't meet my eyes.

'What have you done with the money?' I said.

'Nothing.'

'Pay it to the Revenue, then, on account.'

He looked away evasively, and I sighed at his folly. 'What have you done with the money?' I repeated.

He wouldn't tell me, and I concluded that he had been following the illegal path of many an imminent bankrupt, selling off his goods and banking the proceeds distantly under a false name, so that when the bailiffs came there wouldn't be much left. I gave him some good advice which I knew he wouldn't take. The suicidal hysterics of his earlier visit had settled into resentment against everyone pressing him, including me. He listened with a mulish stubbornness which I'd seen often enough before, and all he would positively agree to was not to write any more cheques.

By three-thirty I'd had enough of Mr Wells, and he of me.

'You need a good solicitor,' I said. 'He'll tell you the same as me, but maybe you'll listen.'

'It was a solicitor who gave me your name,' he said glumly.

'Who's your solicitor?'

'Fellow called Denby Crest.'

It was a small community, I thought. Touching, overlapping, a patchwork fabric. When the familiar names kept turning up, things were normal.

As it happened, Trevor was in the outer office when I showed Mr Wells to the door. I introduced them, explaining that Denby had sent him to see us. Trevor cast a benign eye, which would have been jaundiced had he known the Wells state of dickiness, and made affable small talk. Mr Wells took in Trevor's substantial air, seniority, and general impression of worldliness, and I practically saw the thought cross his mind that perhaps he had consulted the wrong partner.

And perhaps, I thought cynically, he had.

When he'd gone, Trevor looked at me sombrely.

'Come into my office,' he sighed.

CHAPTER SEVENTEEN

I sat in one of the clients' chairs, with Trevor magisterially behind his desk. His manner was somewhere between unease and cajoling, as if he were not quite sure of his ground.

'Denby said he'd be here by four.'

'Good.'

'But Ro . . . he'll explain. He'll satisfy you, I'm sure. I think I'll leave it to him to explain, and then you'll see . . . that there's nothing for us to worry about.'

He raised an unconvincing smile and rippled his fingertips on his blotter. I looked at the familiar, friendly figure, and wished with all my heart that things were not as they were.

Denby came ten minutes early, which would have gratified the psychiatrists, and he was wound up like a tight spring, as well he might be. His backbone was ramrod stiff inside the short plump frame, the moustache bristling on the forward jutting mouth, the irritated air plainer than ever.

He didn't shake hands with me: merely nodded.

Trevor came round his desk to offer a chair, a politeness I thought excessive.

'Well, Ro,' Denby said crossly. 'I hear you have reservations about my certificate.'

'That's so.'

'What, exactly?'

'Well,' I said. 'To be exact . . . fifty thousand pounds missing from the clients' deposit account.'

'Rubbish.'

I sighed. 'You transferred money belonging to three separate clients from the clients' deposit to the clients' current account,' I said. 'You then drew five cheques from the current account, made out to yourself, in varying sums, over a period of six weeks, three to four months ago. Those cheques add up to fifty thousand pounds exactly.'

'But I've repaid the money. If you'd've looked more carefully you'd have seen the counter credits on the bank statement.' He was irritated. Impatient.

'I couldn't make out where those credits had come from,' I said, 'so I asked the bank to send a duplicate statement. It came this morning.'

Denby sat as if turned to stone.

'The duplicate statement,' I said regretfully, 'shows no record of the money having been repaid. The bank statement you gave us was . . . well . . . a forgery.'

Time ticked by.

Trevor looked unhappy. Denby revised his position.

'I've only *borrowed* the money,' he said. There was

still no regret, and no real fear. 'It's perfectly safe. It will be repaid very shortly. You have my word for it.'

'Um . . .' I said. 'Your word isn't enough.'

'Really, Ro, this is ridiculous. If I say it will be repaid, it will be repaid. Surely you know me well enough for that?'

'If you mean,' I said, 'would I have thought you a thief, then no, I wouldn't.'

'I'm not a thief,' he said angrily. 'I told you, I borrowed the money. A temporary expediency. It's unfortunate that . . . as things turned out . . . I was not able to repay it before the certificate became due. But as I explained to Trevor, it is only a matter of a few weeks, at the most.'

'The clients' money,' I said reasonably, 'is not entrusted to you so that you can use it for a private loan to yourself.'

'We all know that,' Denby said snappily, in a teaching-grandmother-to-suck-eggs manner. My grandmother, I reflected fleetingly, had never sucked an egg in her life.

'You're fifty thousand short,' I said, 'and Trevor's condoned it, and neither of you seems to realize you'll be out of business if it comes to light.'

They both looked at me as if I were a child.

'But there's no need for it to come to light, Ro,' Trevor said. 'Denby will repay the money soon, and all will be well. Like I told you.'

'It isn't ethical,' I said.

'Don't be so pompous, Ro,' Trevor said, at his most fatherly, shaking his head with sorrow.

'Why did you take the money?' I asked Denby. 'What for?'

Denby looked across enquiringly at Trevor, who nodded.

'You'll have to tell him everything, Denby. He's very persistent. Better tell him, then he'll understand, and we can clear the whole thing up.'

Denby complied with bad grace. 'I had a chance,' he said, 'of buying a small block of flats. Brand new. Not finished. Builder in difficulties, wanted a quick sale, that sort of thing. Flats were going cheap, of course. So I bought them. Too good to miss. Done that sort of deal before, of course. Not a fool, you know. Knew what I was doing, and all that.'

'Your own conveyancer?' I said.

'What? Oh yes.' He nodded. 'Well, then, I needed a bit more extra capital to finance the deal. Perfectly safe. Good flats. Nothing wrong with them.'

'But they haven't sold?' I said.

'Takes time. Market's sluggish in the winter. But they're all sold now, subject to contracts. Formalities, mortgages, all that. Takes time.'

'Mm.' I said. 'How many flats in the block, and where is it?'

'Eight flats, small, of course. At Newquay, Cornwall.'

'Have you seen them?' I said.

'Of course.'

'Do you mind if I do?' I said. 'And will you give me the

addresses of all the people who are buying the flats, and tell me how much each is paying?'

Denby bristled. 'Are you saying you don't believe me?'

'I'm an auditor,' I said. 'I don't believe. I check.'

'You can take my word for it.'

I shook my head. 'You sent us a forged bank statement. I can't take your word for anything.'

There was a silence.

'If those flats exist, and if you repay that money this week, I'll keep quiet,' I said. 'I'll want confirmation by letter from the bank. The money must be there by Friday, and the letter here by Saturday. Otherwise, no deal.'

'I can't get the money this week,' Denby said peevishly.

'Borrow it from a loan shark.'

'But that's ridiculous. The interest I would have to pay would wipe out all my profit.'

Serve you right, I thought unfeelingly. I said, 'Unless the clients' money is back in the bank by Friday, the Law Society will have to be told.'

'Ro!' Trevor protested.

'However much you try to wrap it up as "unfortunate" and "expedient",' I said, 'the fact remains that all three of us know that what Denby has done is a criminal offence. I'm not putting my name to it as a partner of this firm. If the money is not repaid by Friday, I'll write a letter explaining that in the light of fresh knowledge we wish to cancel the certificate just issued.'

'But Denby would be struck off!' Trevor said.

They both looked as if the stark realities of life were something that only happened to other people.

'Unfriendly,' Denby said angrily. 'Unnecessarily aggressive, that's what you are, Ro. Righteous. Unbending.'

'All those, I dare say,' I said.

'It's no good, I suppose, suggesting I . . . er . . . cut you in?'

Trevor made a quick horrified gesture, trying to stop him.

'Denby, Denby,' he said, distressed. 'You'll never bribe him. For God's sake have some sense. If you really want to antagonize Ro, you offer him a bribe.'

Denby scowled at me and got explosively to his feet.

'All right,' he said bitterly. 'I'll get the money by Friday. And don't ever expect any favours from me for the rest of your life.'

He strode furiously out of the office leaving eddies of disturbed air and longer trails of disturbed friendship. Turbulent wake, I thought. Churning and destructive, overturning everything it touched.

'Are you satisfied, Ro?' Trevor said gently, in sorrow.

I sat without answering.

I felt like a man on a high diving board, awaiting the moment of strength. Ahead, the plunge. Behind, the quiet way down. The choice, within me.

I could walk away, I thought. Pretend I didn't know what I knew. Settle for silence, friendship and peace.

Refrain from bringing distress and disgrace and dreary unhappiness.

My friend or the law. To which did I belong? To the law or my own pleasure . . .

O great God almighty.

I swallowed with a dry mouth.

'Trevor,' I said, 'do you know Arthur Robinson?'

There was no fun, no fun at all, in looking into the face of ultimate disaster.

The blood slowly drained from Trevor's skin, leaving his eyes like great dark smudges.

'I'll get you some brandy,' I said.

'Ro . . .'

'Wait.'

I fetched him a tumbler, from his entertaining cupboard, heavy with alcohol, light on soda.

'Drink it,' I said with compassion. 'I'm afraid I've given you a shock.'

'How . . .' His mouth quivered suddenly, and he put the glass to his lips to hide it. He drank slowly, and took the glass a few inches away: a present help in trouble. 'How much . . . do you know?' he said.

'Why I was abducted. Who did it. Who owns the boat. Who sailed her. Where she is now. How much she cost. And where the money comes from.'

'My God . . . My God . . .' His hands shook.

'I want to talk to him,' I said. 'To Arthur Robinson.'

A faint flash of something like hope shone in his eyes.

'Do you know . . . his other name?'

I told him what it was. The spark of light died to a pebble-like dullness. He clattered the glass against his teeth.

'I want you to telephone,' I said. 'Tell him I know. Tell him I want to talk. Tell him, if he has any ideas of doing anything but what I ask, I'll go straight from this office to the police. I want to talk to him tonight.'

'But Ro, knowing you . . .' He sounded despairing. 'You'll go to the police anyway.'

'Tomorrow morning,' I said.

He stared at me for a long, long time. Then with a heavy half-groaning sigh, he stretched out his hand to the telephone.

We went to Trevor's house. Better for talking, he suggested, than the office.

'Your wife?' I said.

'She's staying with her sister, tonight. She often does.'

We drove in two cars, and judging by the daze of his expression Trevor saw nothing consciously of the road for the whole four miles.

His big house sat opulently in the late afternoon sunshine, nineteen-twenties respectability in every brick. Acres of diamond-shaped leaded window panes, black paint, a wide portico with corkscrew pillars, wisteria

279

creeping here and there, lots of gables with beams stuck
on for effect.

Trevor unlocked the front door and led the way into
dead inside air which smelled of old coffee and furniture
polish. Parquet flooring in the roomy hall, and rugs.

'Come into the snug,' he said, walking ahead.

The snug was a longish room which lay between the
more formal sitting and dining rooms, looking outwards
to the pillared loggia, with the lawn beyond it. To Trevor
the snug was psychologically as well as geographically the
heart of the house, the place where he most felt a host to
his businessmen friends.

There was the bar, built in, where he liked to stand,
genially pouring drinks. Several dark red leather armchairs. A small, sturdy dining table, with four leather-
seated dining chairs. A large television. Bookshelves. An
open brick fireplace, with a leather screen. A palm in a
brass pot. More Stubbs prints. Several small chair-side
tables. A leaf-patterned carpet. Heavy red velvet curtains. Red lampshades. On winter evenings, with the fire
lit, curtains drawn, and lights glowing warmly, snug, in
spite of its size, described it.

Trevor switched on the lights, and although it was full
daylight, drew the curtains. Then he made straight for the
bar.

'Do you want a drink?' he said.

I shook my head. He fixed himself a brandy of twice
the size I'd given him in the office.

'I can't believe any of this is happening,' he said.

He took his filled glass and slumped down in one of the red leather armchairs, staring into space. I hitched a hip on to the table, which like so much in that house was protected by a sheet of plate glass. We both waited, neither of us enjoying our thoughts. We waited nearly an hour.

Nothing violent, I told myself numbly, would happen in that genteel house. Violence occurred in back alleys and dark corners. Not in a well-to-do sitting-room on a Monday evening. I felt the flutter of apprehension in every nerve and thought about eyes black with the lust for revenge.

A car drew up outside. A door slammed. There were footsteps outside on the gravel. Footsteps crossing the threshold, coming through the open front door, treading across the parquet, coming to the door of the snug. Stopping there.

'Trevor?' he said.

Trevor looked up dully. He waved a hand towards me, where I sat to one side, masked by the open door.

He pushed the door wider. Stepped into the room.

He held a shotgun; balanced over his forearm, butt under the armpit, twin barrels pointing to the floor.

I took a deep steadying breath, and looked into his firm, familiar face.

Jossie's father. William Finch.

*

281

'Shooting me,' I said, 'won't solve anything. I've left photostats and all facts with a friend.'

'If I shoot your foot off, you'll ride no more races.'

His voice already vibrated with the smashing hate: and this time I saw it not from across a courtroom thick with policemen, but from ten feet at the wrong end of a gun.

Trevor made jerky calming gestures with his hands.

'William . . . surely you see. Shooting Ro would be disastrous. Irretrievably disastrous.'

'The situation is already irretrievable.' His voice was thick, roughened and deepened by the tension in throat and neck. 'This little creep has seen to that.'

'Well,' I said, and heard the tension in my own voice, 'I didn't make you steal.'

It wasn't the best of remarks. Did nothing to reduce the critical mass: and William Finch was like a nuclear reactor with the rods too far out already. The barrels of the gun swung up into his hands and pointed at my loins.

'William, for God's sake,' Trevor said urgently, climbing ponderously out of his armchair. 'Use your reason. If he says killing him would do no good, you must believe him. He'd never have risked coming here if it wasn't true.'

Finch vibrated with fury through all his elegant height. The conflict between hatred and common sense was plain in the bunching muscles along his jaw and the claw-like curve of his fingers. There was a fearful moment when I was certain that the blood-lust urge to avenge himself would blot out all fear of consequences, and I thought disconnectedly that I wouldn't feel it . . . you never felt the worst of wounds in the first few seconds. It was only after, if you lived, that the tide came in. I wouldn't know . . . I wouldn't feel it, and I might not even know . . .

He swung violently away from me and thrust the shotgun into Trevor's arms.

'Take it. Take it,' he said through his teeth. 'I don't trust myself.'

I could feel the tremors down my legs, and the prickling of sweat over half my body. He hadn't killed me at the very start, when it would have been effective, and it was all very well risking he wouldn't do it now when he'd nothing to gain. It had come a good deal too close.

I leaned my behind weakly against the table, and worked some saliva into my mouth. Tried to set things out in a dry-as-dust manner, as if we were discussing a small point of policy.

'Look . . .' It came out half-strangled. I cleared my throat and tried again. 'Tomorrow I will have to telephone to New York, to talk to the Nantucket family. Specifically, to talk to one of the directors on the board of their family empire; the director to whom Trevor sends the annual Axwood audited accounts.'

Trevor took the shotgun and stowed it away out of sight behind the ornate bar. William Finch stood in the centre of the room with unreleased energy quivering through all his frame. I watched his hands clench and unclench, and his legs move inside his trousers, as if wanting to stride about.

'What will you tell them, then?' he said fiercely. 'What?'

'That you've been ... er ... defrauding the Nantucket family business during the past financial year.'

For the first time some of the heat went out of him.

'During the past ...' He stopped.

'I can't tell,' I said, 'about earlier years. I didn't do the audits. I've never seen the books, and they are not in our office. They have to be kept for three years, of course, so I expect you have them.'

There was a lengthy silence.

'I'm afraid,' I said, 'that the Nantucket director will tell me to go at once to the police. If it was old Naylor Nantucket who was involved, it might be different. He might just have hushed everything up, for your sake. But this new generation, they don't know you. They're hard-nosed businessmen who disapprove of the stable anyway. They never come near the place. They do look upon it as a business proposition, though, and they pay you a good salary to manage it, and they undoubtedly regard any profits as being theirs. However mildly I put it, and I'm not looking forward to it at all, they are going to have to know that for this financial year their profits have gone to you.'

My deadpan approach began to have its results. Trevor poured two drinks and thrust one into William

Finch's hand. He looked at it unseeingly and after a few moments put it down on the bar.

'And Trevor?' he said.

'I'll have to tell the Nantucket director,' I said regretfully, 'that the auditor they appointed has helped to rip them off.'

'Ro,' Trevor said, protesting, I gathered, at the slang expression more than the truth of it.

'Those Axwood books are a work of fiction,' I said to him. 'Cash books, ledgers, invoices . . . all ingenious lies. William would never have got away with such a wholesale fraud without your help. Without, anyway . . .' I said, modifying it slightly, 'without you knowing, and turning a blind eye.'

'And raking off a bloody big cut,' Finch said violently, making sure he took his friend down with him.

Trevor made a gesture of distaste, but it had to be right. Trevor had a hearty appetite for money, and would never have taken such a risk without the gain.

'These books look all right at first sight,' I said. 'They would have satisfied an outside auditor, if the Nantuckets had wanted a check from a London firm, or one in New York. But as for Trevor, and as for me, living here . . .' I shook my head. 'Axwood Stables have paid thousands to forage merchants who didn't receive the money, to saddlers who don't exist, to maintenance men, electricians and plumbers who did no work. The invoices are there, all nicely printed, but the transactions they refer to are thin air. The cash went straight to William Finch.'

Some of the slowly evaporating heat returned fast to Finch's manner, and I thought it wiser not to catalogue aloud all the rest of the list of frauds.

He'd charged the Nantuckets wages for several more lads than he'd employed: a dodge hard to pin down, as the stable-lad population floated from yard to yard.

He'd charged the Nantucket company more than nine thousand pounds for the rent of extra loose boxes and keep for horses by a local farmer, when I knew he had paid only a fraction of that, as the farmer was one of my clients.

He'd charged much more for shares in jockeys' retainers than the jockeys had received; and had invented travelling expenses to the races for horses which according to the form books had never left the yard.

He had pocketed staggering sums from a bloodstock agent in the form of commission on the sales of Nantucket horses to outside owners: fifty thousand or so in the past year, the agent had confirmed casually on the telephone, not knowing that Finch had no right to it.

I imagined Finch had also been sending enlarged bills to all the non-Nantucket owners, getting them to make out their cheques to him personally rather than to the company, and then diverting a slice to himself before paying a reasonable sum into the business.

The Nantuckets were far away, and uninterested. All I guessed they'd wanted had been a profit on the bottom line, and he'd given them just enough to keep them quiet.

As a final irony, he'd charged the Nantuckets six thousand pounds for auditors' fees, and nowhere in our books was there a trace of six thousand pounds from Axwood Stables. Trevor might have had his half, though, on the quiet: it was enough to make you laugh.

A long list of varied frauds. Much harder to detect than one large one. Adding up, though, to an average rake-off for Finch of over two thousand pounds a week. Untaxed.

Year in, year out.

Assisted by his auditor.

Assisted also, it was certain, by the ever-sick secretary, Sandy, though with or without her knowledge I didn't know. If she was ill as often as all that, and away from her post, maybe she didn't know. Or maybe the knowledge made her ill. But as in most big frauds, the paperwork had to be done well, and in the Axwood Stables case, there had been a great deal of it done well.

Ninety to a hundred horses. Well trained, well raced. A big stable with a huge weekly turnover. A top trainer. A trainer, I thought, who didn't own his own stable, who was paid only a salary, and a highly taxed one at that, and who faced having no capital to live on in old age, in a time of inflation. A man in his fifties, an employee, seeing into a future without enough money. An enforced retirement. No house of his own. No power. A man with money at present passing daily through his hands like a river in flood.

All racehorse trainers were entrepreneurs, with

organizing minds. Most were in business on their own account, and had no absent company to defraud. If William Finch had been his own master, I doubted that he would ever have thought of embezzlement. With his abilities, in the normal course of things, he would have had no need.

Need. Ability. Opportunity. I wondered how big a step it had been to dishonesty. To crime.

Probably not very big. A pay-packet for a non-existent stable lad, for a little extra regular cash. The cost of an unordered ton of hay.

Small steps, ingenious swindles, multiplying and swelling, leading to a huge swathing highway.

'Trevor,' I said mildly, 'how long ago did you spot William's . . . irregularities?'

Trevor looked at me sorrowfully, and I half-smiled.

'You saw them . . . some of the first ones . . . in the books,' I said, 'and you told him it wouldn't do.'

'Of course.'

'You suggested,' I said, 'that if he really put his mind to it you would both be a great deal better off.'

Finch reacted strongly with a violent gesture of his whole arm, but Trevor's air of sorrow merely intensified.

'Just like Connaught Powys,' I said. 'I tried hard to believe that you genuinely hadn't seen how he was rigging that computer, but I reckon . . . I have to face it that you were doing it together.'

'Ro . . .' he said sadly.

'Anyway,' I said to Finch, 'you sent the books in for

the annual audit, and after all this time neither you nor Trevor are particularly nervous. Trevor and I have been chronically behind with our work for ages, so I guess he just locked them in his cupboard, to see to as soon as he could. He would know I wouldn't look at your books. I never had, in six years; and I had too many clients of my own. And then, when Trevor was away on his holidays, the unforeseen happened. On Gold Cup day, through your letterbox, and mine, came the summons for you to appear before the Tax Commissioners a fortnight later.'

He stared at me with furious dark eyes, his strong, elegant figure tall and straight like a great stag at bay against an impudent hound. Round the edges of the curtains the daylight was fading to dark. Inside, electric lights shone smoothly on civilized man.

I smiled twistedly. 'I sent you a message. Don't worry, I said, Trevor's on holiday, but I'll apply for a postponement, and make a start on the books myself. I went straight off to ride in the Gold Cup and never gave it another thought. But you, to you, that message meant ruin. Degradation, prosecution, probably prison.'

A quiver ran through him. Muscles moved along his jaw.

'I imagine,' I said, 'that you thought the simplest thing would be to get the books back; but they were locked in Trevor's cupboard, and only he and I have keys. And in any case I would have thought it very suspicious, if, with the Commissioners breathing down our necks, you refused to let me see the books. Especially suspicious if the office had been broken into and those papers stolen. Anything along those lines would have led to investigation, and disaster. So as you couldn't keep the books from *me*, you decided to keep *me* from the books. You had the means to hand. A new boat, nearly ready to sail. You simply arranged for it to go early, and take me with it. If you could keep me away from the office until Trevor returned, all would be well.'

'This is all nonsense,' he said stiffly.

'Don't be silly. It's past denying. Trevor was due back in the office on Monday, April 4th, which would give him three days to apply for a postponement to the Commissioners. A perfectly safe margin. Trevor would then do the Axwood books as usual, and I would be set free, never knowing why I'd been abducted.'

Trevor buried his face in his brandy, which made me thirsty.

'If you've any mineral water, or tonic, Trevor, I'd like some,' I said.

'Give him nothing,' Finch said, the pent-up violence still thick in his voice.

Trevor made fluttery motions with his hands, but after a moment, with apologetic glances at Finch's tightened mouth, he fetched a tumbler and poured into it a bottle of tonic water.

'Ro . . .' he said, giving me the glass. 'My dear chap . . .'

'My dear *shit*,' Finch said.

I drank the fizzy quinine water gratefully.

'I bust things up by getting home a few days early,' I

said. 'I suppose you were frantic. Enough, anyway, to send the kidnapping squads to my cottage to pick me up again. And when they didn't manage it, you sent someone else.' I drank bubbles and tasted gall. 'Next day, you sent your daughter Jossie.'

'She knows nothing, Ro,' Trevor said.

'Shut up,' Finch said. 'She strung him along by the nose.'

'Maybe she did,' I said. 'It was supposed to be only for a day or two. Trevor was due back that Sunday. But I told you, while you were busy filling my time by showing me round your yard, that Trevor's car had broken down in France, and he wouldn't be back until Wednesday or Thursday. And I assured you again that you didn't have to worry, I had already applied for the postponement, and I would start the audit myself. The whole situation was back to square one, and the outlook was as deadly as ever.'

Finch glared, denying nothing.

'You offered me a day at the races with Jossie,' I said. 'And a ride in the novice hurdle. I'm a fool about accepting rides. Never know when to say no. You must have known that Notebook was unable to jump properly. You must have hoped when you flew off to the Grand National, that I'd fall with him and break a leg.'

'Your neck,' he said vindictively, with no vestige of a joke.

Trevor glanced at his face and away again, as if embarrassed by so much raw emotion.

'Your men must have been standing by in case I survived undamaged, which of course I did,' I said. 'They followed us to the pub where I had dinner with Jossie, and then to the motel where I planned to stay. Your second attempt at abduction was more successful, in that I couldn't get out. And when Trevor was safely back, you rang Scotland Yard, and the police set me free. From one point of view all your efforts had produced precisely the desired result, because I had not in fact by then seen one page or one entry of the Axwood books.'

I thought back, and amended that statement. 'I hadn't seen any except the petty cash book, which you gave me yourself. And that, I imagine, was your own private accurate record, and not the one re-written and padded for the sake of the audit. It was left in my car with all my other belongings, and I took it to the office when I went back last Friday. It was still there on Saturday. It was Saturday morning that I got out the Axwood books and studied them, and made the photocopies.'

'But why, Ro?' Trevor asked frustratedly. 'What made you think . . . Why did you think of William?'

'The urgency,' I said. 'The ruthless haste, and the time factors. I believed, you see, when I was on the boat, that I'd been kidnapped for revenge. Any auditor who's been the downfall of embezzlers would think that, if he'd found himself in such a position. Especially if he's been directly threatened, face to face, as I had, by Connaught Powys, and earlier by Ownslow and Glitberg, and later also by others. But when I escaped and came home, there was hardly any interval before I was in danger again. Hunted, really. And caught. So the second time, last week, in the van, I began to think . . . that perhaps it wasn't revenge, but *prevention*, and after that, it was a matter of deduction, elimination, boring things, on the whole. But I had hours . . .' I swallowed involuntarily, remembering. 'I had hours in which to think of all the possible people, and work it out. So then, on Saturday morning, I went to the office, when I had the place to myself, and checked.'

Finch turned on Trevor, looking for a whipping boy. 'Why the hell did you keep those books where he could see them? Why didn't you lock them in the bloody safe?'

'I've a key to the safe,' I said dryly.

'Christ!' He raised his hands in a violent, exploding, useless gesture. 'Why didn't you take them home?'

'I never take books home,' Trevor said. 'And you told me that Ro was going to the races Saturday, and out with Jossie Sunday, so we'd nothing to worry about. And anyway, neither of us dreamt that he knew . . . or guessed.'

Finch swung his desperate face in my direction.

'What's your price?' he said. 'How much?'

I didn't answer. Trevor said protestingly, 'William . . .'

'He must want something,' Finch said. 'Why is he telling us all this instead of going straight to the police? Because he wants a deal, that's why.'

'Not money,' I said.

Finch continued to look like a bolt of lightning

trapped in bones and flesh, but he didn't pursue the subject. He knew, as he'd always known, that it wasn't a question of money.

'Where did you get the men who abducted me?' I said.

'You know so much. You can bloody well find out.'

Rent-a-thug, I thought cynically. Someone, somewhere, knew how to hire some bully boys. The police could find out, I thought, if they wanted to. I wouldn't bother.

'The second time,' I said. 'Did you tell them not to leave a mark on me?'

'So what?'

'Did you?' I said.

'I didn't want the police taking any serious interest,' he said. 'No marks. No stealing. Made you a minor case.'

So the fists and boots, I thought, had been a spot of private enterprise. Payment for the general run-around I'd given the troops. Not orders from above. I supposed I was glad, in a sour sort of way.

He'd chosen the warehouse, I guessed, because it couldn't have been easy to find a safer place in a hurry: and because he thought it would divert my attention even more strongly towards Ownslow and Glitberg, and away from any thought of himself.

Trevor said, 'Well . . . What . . . what are we going to do now?' but no one answered, because there were wheels outside on the gravel. Car doors slammed.

'Did you leave the front door open?' Trevor said.

Finch didn't need to answer. He had. Several feet

tramped straight in, crossed the hall, and made unerringly for the snug.

'Here we are then,' said a powerful voice. 'Let's get on with it.'

The light of triumph shone in Finch's face, and he smiled with grateful welcome at the newcomers crowding into the room.

Glitberg. Ownslow. Connaught Powys.

'Got the rat cornered, then?' Powys said.

CHAPTER EIGHTEEN

I had an everlasting picture of the five of them, in that freezing moment. I straightened to my feet, and my heart thumped, and I looked at them one by one.

Connaught Powys in his city suit, as Establishment as a pillar of the government. Coffee-coloured tan on his fleshy face. Smooth hair; pale hands. A large man aiming to throw his weight about, and enjoying it.

Glitberg with his mean eyes and the repulsive four-inch frill of white whiskers, which stood out sideways from his cheeks like a ruff. Little pink lips, and a smirk.

Ownslow the bull, with his bald crown and long straggling blond hair. He'd shut the door of the snug and leaned against it, and folded his arms with massive satisfaction.

William Finch, tall and distinguished, vibrating in the centre of the room in a tangle of fear, and anger, and unpleasant pleasure.

Trevor, silver-haired, worldly, come to dust. Sitting apprehensively in his armchair, facing his future with more sorrow than horror. The only one of them who showed the slightest sign of realizing that it was they who had got themselves into trouble, not I.

Embezzlers were not normally men of violence. They robbed on paper, not with their fists. They might hate and threaten, but actual physical assault wasn't natural to them. I looked bleakly at the five faces and thought again of the nuclear effect of critical mass. Small separate amounts of radio-active matter could release harnessable energy. If small amounts got together into a larger mass, they exploded.

'Why did you come?' Trevor said.

'Finchy rang and told us he'd be here,' Powys said, jerking his head in my direction. 'Never get another opportunity like it, will we? Seeing as you and Finchy will be out of circulation, for a bit.'

Finch shook his head fiercely: but I reckoned there were different sorts of circulation, and it would be a very long time before he was back on a racetrack. I wouldn't have wanted to face the ruin before him: the crash from such a height.

Glitberg said, 'Four years locked in a cell. Four sodding years, because of him.'

'Don't bellyache,' I said. 'Four years in jail for a million pounds is a damned good bargain. You offer it around, you'd get a lot of takers.'

'Prison is dehumanizing,' Powys said. 'They treat you worse than animals.'

'Don't make me cry,' I said. 'You chose the way that led there. And all of you have got what you wanted.

Money, money, money. So run away and play with it.'
Maybe I spoke with too much heat, but nothing was
going to defuse the developing bomb.

Anger that I'd let myself in for such a mess was a stab
in the mind. I simply hadn't thought of Finch summoning
reinforcements. He'd had no need of it: it had been
merely spite. I'd believed I could manage Finch and
Trevor with reasonable safety, and here all of a sudden
was a whole new battle.

'Trevor,' I said, flatly, 'don't forget the photostats I left
with a friend.'

'What friend?' Finch said, gaining belligerence from
his supporters.

'Barclays Bank,' I said.

Finch was furious, but he couldn't prove it wasn't true,
and even he must have seen that any serious attempt at
wringing out a different answer might cost them more
time in the clink.

I had hoped originally to make a bargain with Finch,
but it was no longer possible. I thought merely, at that
point, of getting through whatever was going to happen
with some semblance of grace. A doubtful proposition, it
seemed to me.

'How much does he know?' Ownslow demanded of
Trevor.

'Enough . . .' Trevor said. 'Everything.'

'Bloody hell.'

'How did he find out?' Glitberg demanded.

'Because William took him on his boat,' Trevor said.

'A mistake,' Powys said. 'That was a mistake, Finchy. He came sniffing round us in London, asking about boats. Like I told you.'

'You chain dogs up,' Finch said.

'But not in a floating kennel, Finchy. Not this bastard here with his bloody quick eyes. You should have kept him away from your boat.'

'I don't see that it matters,' Trevor said. 'Like he said, we've all got our money.'

'And what if he tells?' Ownslow demanded.

'Oh, he'll tell,' Trevor said with certainty. 'And of course there will be trouble. Questions and enquiries and a lot of fuss. But in the end, if we're careful, we should keep the cash.'

'Should isn't enough,' Powys said fiercely.

'Nothing's certain,' Trevor said.

'One thing's certain,' Ownslow said. 'This creep's going to get his come-uppance.'

All five of the faces turned my way together, and in each one, even in Trevor's, I read the same intent.

'That's what we came for,' Powys said.

'Four bloody years,' Ownslow said. 'And the sneers my kids suffered.' He pushed off the door and uncrossed his arms.

Glitberg said, 'Judges looking down their bloody noses.'

They all, quite slowly, came nearer.

It was uncanny, and frightening. The forming of a pack.

299

Behind me there was the table, and behind that, solid wall. They were between me and the windows, and between me and the door.

'Don't leave any marks,' Powys said. 'If he goes to the police it'll be his word against ours, and if he's nothing to show that can't do much.' To me, directly, he said, 'We'll have a bloody good alibi, I'll tell you that.'

The odds looked appalling. I made a sudden thrusting jump to one side, to dodge the menacing advance, out-flank the cohorts, scramble for the door.

I got precisely nowhere. Two strides, no more. Their hands clutched me from every direction, dragging me back, their bodies pushing against me with their collective weight. It was as if my attempt to escape had triggered them off. They were determined, heavy, and grunting. I struggled with flooding fury to disentangle myself, and I might as well have wrestled with an octopus.

They lifted me up bodily and sat me on the end of the table. Three of them held me there with hands like clamps.

Finch pulled open a drawer in the side of the table, and threw out a checked red and white table cloth, which floated across the room and fell on a chair. Under the cloth, several big square napkins. Red and white checks. Tapestry's racing colours. Ridiculous thought at such a moment.

Finch and Connaught Powys each rolled a napkin into a shape like a bandage and knotted it round one of my ankles. They tied my ankles to the legs of the table. They pulled my jacket off. They rolled and tied a red and white napkin round each of my wrists, pulling the knots tight and leaving cheerful bright loose ends like streamers.

They did it fast.

All of the faces were flushed, and the eyes fuzzy, in the fulfilment of lust. Glitberg and Ownslow, one on each side, pushed me down flat on my back. Finch and Connaught Powys pulled my arms over my head and tied the napkins on my wrists to the other two legs of the table. My resistance made them rougher.

The table was, I supposed, about two feet by four. Long enough to reach from my knees to the top of my head. Hard, covered with glass, uncomfortable.

They stood back to admire their handiwork. All breathing heavily from my useless fight. All overweight, out of condition, ripe to drop dead from coronaries at any moment. They went on living.

'Now what?' said Ownslow, considering. He went down on his knees and took off my shoes.

'Nothing,' Trevor said. 'That's enough.'

The pack instinct had died out of him fastest. He turned away, refusing to meet my eyes.

'Enough!' Glitberg said. 'We've done nothing yet.'

Powys eyed me assessingly from head to foot, and maybe he saw just what they had done.

'Yes,' he said slowly. 'That's enough.'

Ownslow said 'Here!' furiously, and Glitberg said,

'Not on your life.' Powys ignored them and turned to Finch.

'He's yours,' he said. 'But if I were you I'd just leave him here.'

'*Leave* him?'

'You've got better things to do than fool around with him. You don't want to leave marks on him, and I'm telling you, the way we've tied him will be enough.'

William Finch thought about it, and nodded, and came half way back to cold sense. He stepped closer until he stood near my ribs. He stared down, eyes full of the familiar hate.

'I hope you're satisfied,' he said.

He spat in my face.

Powys, Glitberg and Ownslow thought it a marvellous idea. They did it in turn, as disgustingly as they could.

Not Trevor. He looked on uncomfortably and made small useless gestures of protest with his hands.

I could hardly see for slime. It felt horrible, and I couldn't get it off.

'All right,' Powys said. 'That's it, then. You push off now, Finchy, and you get packed, Trevor, and then we'll all leave.'

'Here!' Ownslow said again, protestingly.

'Do you want an alibi, or don't you?' Powys said. 'You got to make some effort. Be seen by a few squares. Help the lies along.'

Ownslow gave in with a bad grace, and contented

302

himself with making sure that none of the table napkins had worked loose. Which they hadn't.

Finch had gone from my diminished sight and also, it appeared, from my life. A car started in the drive, crunched on the gravel, and faded away.

Trevor went out of the room and presently returned carrying a suitcase. In the interval Ownslow sniggered, Glitberg jeered, and Powys tested the amount that I could move my arms. Half an inch, at the most.

'You won't get out of that,' he said. He shook my elbow and watched the results. 'I reckon this'll make us even.' He turned as Trevor came back. 'Are all doors locked?'

'All except the front one,' Trevor said.

'Right. Then let's be off.'

'But what about *him?*' Trevor said. 'We can't just leave him like that.'

'Can't we? Why not?'

'But . . .' Trevor said: and fell silent.

'Someone will find him tomorrow,' Powys said. 'A cleaner, or something. Do you have a cleaner?'

'Yes,' Trevor said doubtfully. 'But she doesn't come in on Tuesdays. My wife will be back though.'

'There you are, then.'

'All right.' He hesitated. 'My wife keeps some money in the kitchen. I'll just fetch it.'

'Right.'

Trevor went on his errand and came back. He stood near me, looking worried.

'Ro . . .'

'Come on,' said Powys impatiently. 'He's ruined you, like he ruined us. You owe him bloody nothing.'

He shepherded them out of the door; Trevor unhappy, Glitberg sneering, Ownslow unassuaged. Powys looked back from the doorway, his own face, what I could see of it, full of smug satisfaction.

'I'll think of you,' he said. 'All night.'

He pulled the door towards him, to shut it, and switched off the light.

Human bodies were not designed to remain for hours in one position. Even in sleep, they regularly shifted. Joints bent and unbent, muscles contracted and relaxed.

No human body was designed to lie as I was lying, with constant strain already running up through legs, stomach, chest, shoulders and arms. Within five minutes, while they were still there, it had become in any normal way intolerable. One would not have stayed in that attitude from choice.

When they had gone, I simply could not visualize the time ahead. My imagination short-circuited. Blanked out. What did one do if one couldn't bear something, and had to?

The worst of the spit slid slowly off my face, but the rest remained, sticky and itching. I blinked my eyes wide open in the dark and thought of being at home in my own quiet bed, as I'd hoped to be that night.

I realized that I was having a surprising amount of difficulty in breathing. One took breathing so much for granted; but the mechanics weren't all that simple. The muscles between the ribs pulled the ribcage out and upwards, allowing air to rush down to the lungs. It wasn't, so to speak, the air going in which expanded the chest, but the expansion of the chest which drew in the air. With the ribcage pulled continuously up, the normal amount of muscle movement was much curtailed.

I still wore a collar and tie. I would choke, I thought.

The other bit that breathed for you was the diaphragm, a nice hefty floor of muscle between the heart-lung cavity and the lower lot of guts. Thank God for diaphragms, I thought. Long may they reign. Mine chugged away, doing its best.

If I passed the night in delirium, I thought, it would be a good idea. If I'd studied Yoga . . . mind out of body. Too late for that. I was always too late. Never prepared.

Stabs of strain afflicted both my shoulders. Needles. Swords.

Think of something else.

Boats. Think of boats. Big expensive boats, built to high standards in top British boat yards, sailing away out of Britain to ship-brokers in Antibes and Antigua.

Huge floating assets in negotiable form. None of the usual bureaucratic trouble about transferring money abroad in huge amounts. No dollar premiums to worry about, or other such hurdles set up by grasping governments. Just put your money in fibreglass and ropes and sails, and float away on it on the tide.

The man at Goldenwave had told me they never lacked for orders. Boats, he said, didn't deteriorate like aeroplanes or cars. Put a quarter of a million into a boat, and it would most likely increase in value, as years went by. Sell the boat, bank the money, and hey presto, all nicely, tidily, and legally done.

There were frightful protests from my arms and legs. I couldn't move them in any way more than an inch: could give them no respite. It really was, I thought, an absolutely bloody revenge.

No use reflecting that it was I who had stirred up Powys and Ownslow and Glitberg. Poke a rattlesnake with a stick, don't be surprised if he bites you. I'd gone to find out if it was they who'd abducted me, and found out instead what they'd done with all the missing money.

Paid for boats. The mention of boats had produced the menace, not the mention of abduction. Boats paid for by the taxpayers, the electronics firm, and the Nantuckets of New York. Gone with the four winds. Exchanged for a pile of nice strong currency, lying somewhere in a foreign bank, waiting for the owners to stroll along and collect.

Trevor linked them all. Maybe the boats had originally been his idea. I hadn't thought of William Finch knowing Connaught Powys: certainly not as well as he clearly did. But through Trevor, along the track from embezzlement to ship building . . . along the way, they had met.

The pains in my arms and legs intensified, and there was a great shaft of soreness up my chest.

I thought: I don't know how to face this. I don't know how. It isn't possible.

Trevor, I thought. Surely Trevor wouldn't have left me like this . . . not like this . . . if he had realized. Trevor, who had been so distressed at my dishevelled appearance in the police station, who as far as I could see had really cared about my health.

Ye Gods, I thought, I'd go gladly back to the sail locker . . . to the van . . . to almost anywhere one could think of.

Some of my muscles were trembling. Would the fibres simply collapse? I wondered. Would the muscles just tear apart; the ligaments disconnect from the bones? Oh for God's sake, I told myself, you've got enough to worry about, without that. Think of something cheerful.

I couldn't, off-hand. Even cheerful subjects like Tapestry were no good. I couldn't see me being able to ride in the Whitbread Gold Cup.

Minutes dragged and telescoped, stretching to hours. The various separate pains gradually coalesced into an all pervading fire. Thought became fragmentary, and then, I reckon, more or less stopped.

The unbearable was there, inside, savage and consuming. Unbearable . . . there was no such word.

By morning I'd gone a long way into an extreme land I hadn't known existed. A different dimension, where the memory of ordinary pain was a laugh.

307

An internal place; a heavy core. The external world had retreated. I no longer felt as if I were any particular shape: had no picture of hands or feet, or where they were. Everything was crimson and dark.

I existed as a mass. Unified. A single lump of matter, of a weight and fire like the centre of the earth.

There was nothing else. No thought. Just feeling, and eternity.

A noise dragged me back.

People talking. Voices in the house.

I saw that daylight had returned and was trickling in round the edge of the curtains. I tried to call out, and could not.

Footsteps crossed and recrossed the hall, and at last, at last, someone opened the door, and switched on the light.

Two women came in. I stared at them, and they stared at me: on both sides with disbelief.

They were Hilary Pinlock, and Jossie.

Hilary cut through the red checked table napkins with a small pair of scissors from her handbag.

I tried to sit up and behave with sangfroid, but my stretched muscles wouldn't respond to directions. I ended somehow with my face against her chest and my throat heaving with unstoppable half-stifled groans.

'It's all right, Ro. It's all right, my dear, my dear.'

Her thin arms held me close and tight, rocking me

gently, taking into herself the impossible pain, suffering for me like a mother. Mother, sister, lover, child . . . a woman who crossed the categories and left them blurred.

I had a mouthful of blouse button and was comforted to my soul.

She put an arm round my waist and more or less carried me to the nearest chair. Jossie stood looking on, her face filled with a greater shock than finding me there.

'Do you realize,' she said, 'that Dad's gone?'

I didn't feel like saying much.

'Did you hear?' Jossie said. Her voice was tight, unfriendly. 'Dad's gone. Walked out. Left all the horses. Do you hear? He's cleared half the papers out of the office and burned them in the incinerator, and this lady says it is because my father is an embezzler, and you . . . you are going to give him away to the Nantuckets, and the police.'

The big eyes were hard. 'And Trevor, too. Trevor. I've known him all my life. How could you? And you *knew* . . . you knew on Sunday . . . all day . . . what you were going to do. You took me out, and you knew you were going to ruin all our lives. I think you're hateful.'

Hilary took two strides, gripped her by the shoulders, and positively shook her.

'Stop it, you silly girl. Open your silly eyes. He did all this for you.'

Jossie tore herself free. 'What do you mean?' she demanded.

'He didn't want your father to go to prison. Because he's your father. He's sent others there, but he didn't want it to happen to your father, or to Trevor King. So he warned them, and gave them time to destroy things. Evidence. Paper and records.' She glanced back at me. 'He told me on Saturday what he planned . . . to tell your father how much he knew, and to offer him a bargain. Time, enough time, if he would destroy his tracks and go, in a way which would cause you least pain. Time to go before the police arrived to confiscate his passport. Time to arrange his life as best he could. And they made him pay for the time he gave them. He paid for every second of it . . .' She gestured in frustrated disgust towards the table and the cut pieces of cloth, ' . . . in *agony*.'

'Hilary,' I protested.

There never had been any stopping Hilary Pinlock in full flight. She said fiercely to Jossie, 'He can put up with a lot, but I reckon it's too much to have you reviling him for what he's suffered for your sake. So you just get some sense into your little bird-brain, and beg his pardon.'

I helplessly shook my head. Jossie stood with her mouth open in shattered shock, and then she looked at the table, and discarded the thought.

'Dad would never have done that,' she said.

'There were five of them,' I said wearily. 'People do

things in gangs which they would never have done on their own.'

She looked at me with shadowed eyes. Then she turned abruptly on her heel and walked out of the room.

'She's terribly upset,' Hilary said, making allowances.

'Yes.'

'Are you all right?'

'No.'

She made a face. 'I'll get you something. They must at least have aspirins in this house.'

'Tell me first,' I said, 'how you got here.'

'Oh. I was worried. I rang your cottage all evening. Late into the night. And again this morning, early. I had a feeling . . . I didn't think it would hurt if I came over to check, so I drove to your cottage . . . but of course you weren't there. I saw your neighbour, Mrs Morris, and she said you hadn't been home all night. So then I went to your office. They were in a tizzy because some time between last night and this morning your partner had taken away a great many papers, and neither of you had turned up for work.'

'What time . . .' I said.

'About half past nine, when I went to the office.' She looked at her watch. 'It's a quarter to eleven, now.'

Fourteen hours, I thought numbly. It must have been at least fourteen hours, that I'd been lying there.

'Well, I drove to Finch's house,' she said. 'I had a bit of

311

trouble finding the way, and when I got there, everything was in a shambles. There was a girl secretary weeping all over the place. People asking what was going on . . . and your girl Jossie in a dumbstruck state. I asked her if she'd seen you. I said I thought you could be in real trouble. I asked her where Trevor King lived. I made her come with me, to show me the way. I tried to tell her what her father had been doing, and how he'd abducted you, but she didn't want to believe it.'

'No.'

'So then we arrived here, and found you.'

'How did you get in?'

'The back door was wide open.'

'Wide . . .?'

I had a sudden picture of Trevor going out to the kitchen, saying it was to fetch some money. To open the door. To give me a tiny chance. Poor Trevor.

'That package I gave you,' I said. 'With all the photostats. When you get home, will you burn it?'

'If that's what you want.'

'Mm.'

Jossie came back and sprawled in a red armchair, all angular legs.

'Sorry,' she said abruptly.

'So am I.'

'You did help him,' she said.

Hilary said, 'Do good to those who despitefully use you.'

I slid my eyes her way. 'That's enough of that.'

312

'What are you talking about?' Jossie demanded.

Hilary shook her head with a smile and went on an aspirin hunt. Butazolidin, I imagined, would do more good. Things were better now I was sitting in a chair, but a long old way from right.

'He left me a letter,' Jossie said. 'More or less the same as yours.'

'How do you mean?'

'Dear Jossie, Sorry, Love, Dad.'

'Oh.'

'He said he was going to France . . .' She broke off, and stared ahead of her, her face full of misery. 'Life's going to be unutterably bloody, isn't it,' she said, 'for a long time to come?'

'Mm.'

'What am I going to do?' The question was a rhetorical wail, but I answered it.

'I did want to warn you,' I said. 'But I couldn't . . . before I'd talked to your father. I meant it, though, about you coming to live in the cottage. If you thought . . . that you could.'

'Ro . . .' Her voice was little more than a breath.

I sat and ached, and thought in depression about telephoning the Nantuckets, and the chaos I'd have to deal with in the office.

Jossie turned her head towards me and gave me a long inspection.

'You look spineless,' she said. Her voice was halfway back in spirit to the old healthy mockery; shaky, but doing its best. 'And I'll tell you something else.' She paused and swallowed.

'When Dad went, he left *me* behind, but he took the detestable Lida with him.'

There was enough, in that, for the future.